Agnes Short was born in Yorkshire of Scots-English parents and studied English Literature at Exeter University. She has worked as a teacher, a secretary, a research assistant and in the editorial offices of a Sunday newspaper, and has lived in London, Oxford, Wiltshire and Malaya before settling in Old Aberdeen.

Also by Agnes Short

The First Fair Wind

The Flowing Tide

Agnes Short

HEADLINE

First published in Great Britain in 1986
by Constable and Company Limited
under the title THE RUNNING TIDE

First published in paperback in 1989
by HEADLINE BOOK PUBLISHING PLC

ISBN 0 7472 3180 X

Printed and bound in Great Britain by
Collins, Glasgow

HEADLINE BOOK PUBLISHING PLC
Headline House
79 Great Titchfield Street
London W1P 7FN

For Lucy

1819

'But Louise, dear,' protested Mrs Forbes, 'I do think you might consider a new gown, at the least. After all, it is a wedding, if only a penny one.'

'My grey is perfectly suitable, Mamma,' said her daughter calmly, turning a page of the book she was reading. A tall, angular girl with pale hair drawn back from a high forehead, she bore no resemblance to her plumply pretty mother whose taste favoured ribbons and lace.

'Other girls,' twittered her mother with an edge of petulance to her voice, 'would welcome the opportunity to buy cloak and bonnet, petticoats, everything, and it is not as if your Papa cannot afford it. I saw the *sweetest* little boots in the Broadgait only yesterday.'

Louise made no answer except to dip pen into inkwell and scratch a quick note on the paper before her.

Mrs Forbes bit her lip in exasperation, laid aside her embroidery, and stood up. 'Really, Louise, you are too tiresome, reading those unsuitable books and scribbling like . . . like an office clerk!' She made the words sound like a disease, or a particularly unpleasant insect. 'You might at least *try* to do yourself justice.'

She began to move aimlessly round the room, as she always did when agitated, straightening a cushion here, aligning one chair with another there. The upstairs sitting-room in the house in Correction Wynd was old and small, panelled in unadorned wood as warm-hued and smoothly velvet as the floor. There were one or two oil paintings in

1

the same brown-gold colours, a settle and high-backed chairs, family heirlooms and much prized – as Mrs Forbes prized everything in her narrow, elegant little house, built two centuries before and redolent of time and loving care.

The fire burnt bright and cheerful, the brass and crystal gleamed. Why then did she feel unhappy? It was, of course, Louise. Mrs Forbes stood with her back to the room, pretending to trim the wick of a candle with her silver embroidery scissors. There were two window seats, each with a recess that was the full depth of the three-feet-thick stone wall, each with wooden jointed shutters, folded back now to reveal the green expanse of St Nicholas's churchyard with, somewhere under that February turf, her children . . . Strange that Louise, such a scrawny, fretful child, should have survived the scarlet fever when the others had not. She suppressed a sigh. After all, it had been long ago. Too long.

'You are not getting any younger, Louise. You cannot afford to throw away your chances.'

Still Louise made no reply. Baffled and increasingly nervous as she often was when closeted alone with her 'cuckoo' child (as she had once daringly described Louise to her friend, Mrs Abercrombie) Mrs Forbes stared out of the window, wondering how to proceed. For proceed she must. The wedding was not exactly in their social class, of course – the penny wedding of Andrew Noble's half-sister. But Andrew Noble was making a name for himself in Aberdeen medical circles, and his half-sister was no ordinary fisher-girl, by all accounts. The man she was marrying had his own shipyard, of sorts. Louise was doing them a favour by attending at all, but, because of that, she must dress with a style befitting her superior social position. Mrs Forbes could not allow Louise to disgrace herself and her family by her unorthodox ways, not in front of half the town. For George Abercrombie

2

and his wife were going to the wedding, and what Kirsty Abercrombie heard of a morning was certain sure to be common knowledge by sundown. She might as well publish the news herself in the *Aberdeen Journal*: 'Louise Forbes, unmarried daughter of the eminent lawyer Ewan Forbes of Correction Wynd, wore the same grey merino gown she has worn for the last four seasons, by now threadbare at the elbows and much frayed at the hem. Her outfit was completed by scuffed brown boots that would do better service on the feet of a scaffy, and was topped by her only known hat, the dubious ornithological adornments of which have seen better days, in the *far* distant past.' Mentally seeing the offending passage in glaring newsprint, Mrs Forbes regarded her daughter with something bordering on dislike before turning her back and seeking comfort from the prospect beyond the window. At least the view did not contradict her.

To her right, just out of sight, was the church whose bells reassured and regulated her life: to the left, that hateful engineering triumph of the new street which ran on a huge bridge above the old town, so that her own house and the rest of Correction Wynd crouched in its shadow. Not long ago her friends had envied her her 'jewel' of a town house. No longer. All eyes were on the new street now and the new houses being built on either side, houses for the up-and-coming people of the city, gracious houses with gracious porticoes and driveways, ostentatious houses with proportions twice the size of her own dear rooms. Her house was in a backwater now, with yesterday's people. She could not prevent a sniff at the melancholy thought.

'What *is* the matter, Mamma?' demanded Louise with a mixture of tolerance and irritation. 'Surely you are not upset because I do not want a dress?'

'No, dear,' said her mother hastily. With an effort she

3

turned back to what she could not help thinking of as the 'fray'. 'But I do wish you would allow me to guide you,' she continued more firmly, her resolution strengthened by the sight of Louise's bony grey-clad frame, and those half-moon glasses she insisted on wearing. 'It is not fair to the bride,' she continued, on a different tack. 'You owe it to her to look your best.'

'Rachel will not mind what I wear,' said Louise cheerfully, 'as long as I am there.'

'But it is the custom, Louise,' wailed her mother. 'And if you will not think of yourself, you might at least consider your father and me. What will people think if you appear yet again in the same gown? If you wish to make any sort of impression in society you must . . .'

'But I *don't*, Mamma. I care not a fig for your "impression". It is people who matter to me, not clothes. Why cannot you see that?'

Louise's patience was almost spent. Her mother was shrewd enough to see it, but she could not resist one last attempt.

'I know, dear,' she said placatingly, 'and that is why I thought you would want to look nice for Andrew.'

'Nice? For Andrew?' Louise threw back her head and laughed with a heartiness that made her mother flinch. 'But Andrew and I are friends, Mamma. I have no need to resort to such artificial enticements with him. He would only laugh at me if I did.'

Mrs Forbes was not so sure. 'All men like a girl to look her best,' she said. 'And if you mean to catch him,' she continued under her breath, for she was sufficiently in awe of her daughter not to speak the thought aloud, 'you had best try something soon, before someone prettier and less averse to fashion snatches him from under your bespectacled nose.'

* * *

4

Two years ago, thought Isla, with the familiar pain. Two years ago come April. 'Hush, hush,' she murmured automatically as the child whinged and grumbled from the depths of its woollen cocoon. 'It wasna' your doing, ye poor wee mite.' She stopped a moment to draw breath and lean against the dyke, the frosted stone striking cold through layers of homespun petticoat and woollen cloth. The wind needled her cheeks with sand from the shore, the grey sky raced with scudding cloud, while from somewhere over the cliff to her right came the smack and sucking roar of surf on rock. Stonehaven lay six miles to the south behind her, the Girdleness, Footdee and the future over the hillock ahead. But the baby's wail had changed to a pitiful and anguished keening, while the small fists struggled to fight free from the swathing folds of cloth.

'Wisht now,' soothed Isla, 'my poor wee bairnie. I'll find a place out o' the wind where ye can feed in peace.'

She huddled into the lee of the dyke, chose a suitable stone on which to sit and another against which to lean her back, and unfastened her bodice while her baby nuzzled impatiently, small mouth searching for the familiar nipple. When she found it, her lips clamped tight, her tiny hands clutched at cloth or softer flesh as she tugged and sucked, stopping only to gulp air and, once, to cough.

Isla's eyes misted over as the sweet sensations tingled. But only for a moment. The wind was cold, the day short, and there were several miles still to go. Though she knew the road well enough – years of carrying loaded creels to the market had seen to that – she had no wish to be overtaken by darkness, alone. Especially as she must seek out somewhere to sleep for the night.

'Git where ye belong, ye feckless hussy,' her stepmother had shrieked at her, 'and tak' yon whingeing quinie wi' ye. I'll have nae screeching bastard bairnie i' my hoose, to tak' the bread from my ain bairns' mouthies and the clothes from their wee backs.'

'Ye wouldna' say that if Da were alive,' she had answered, standing straight and proud. She was neat and fair, her blue eyes and blonde hair in defiant contrast to her stepmother's mediocre colouring. She was half a head taller, too, but since Davy's death had lost her vigour. The sad, lost look still haunted her face as she confronted her stepmother, but, with her father dead, Isla knew she had no protector.

'Well he's nae alive and I am saying it,' her tormentor continued. 'Ye're nae wanted here, and yer babby neither. So the pair o' ye can foot it to yon grand folk in Aberdeen ye're aye boastin' of. To yer wee bastard's *father*.'

'He is dead,' Isla had said, in the toneless anguish with which she always spoke of Davy. Davy Christie would have helped her, married her, shared the burden of their baby. Davy would have loved her. Since his death she had known only loneliness. He had died without her, coughed his life away in blood from diseased lungs after a fire on the Christie ship. He had died without knowing she was carrying his child and when that child was born, under the disapproving frown of a gaggle of Duthie relatives and the opprobrium of the kirk, Isla's spirit had finally broken. Pearl was a lusty, demanding child, and though Isla loved her, it was with an anxious, burdened love, at the same time helpless and acquiescent. Increasingly the infant's small needs and vehement demands left her drained and spiritless. The fisherman's cottage in Stonehaven was comfortable enough, but overcrowded – as Isla's stepmother lost no chance to remind her.

'And since yon babby came ye havena' even earned yer keep,' she would screech. 'I've nae time for ye. Get oot from under my feet.'

Isla would gather up her burden and wander to the seashore, dandling the child aimlessly in her arms and watching the sea-gulls wheel and dip over the foam-flecked water, or ride, plump breasted, on the silken surface of an evening sea when the horseshoe of the bay lay calm and gleaming in the pink-shadowed evening. Davy had come that way, slipping into the bay from the north on a turbulent afternoon to ride out the storm in the safety of Stonehaven harbour. He had stepped ashore, and into her life.

Remembering, she would grow misty-eyed, forgetful of the mussel-pails yet to fill, of the haddock to be split and strung in pairs to be smoked in the smokesheds behind the cottage or packed into creels to sell in Aberdeen. Forgetful even of little Pearl, warm against her breast, or looped in a fold of plaid at her back.

Pearl. The Duthie tribe had scorned her choice of name as yet another instance of her overweening pride. 'She's nae content wi' boastin' of what her husband's family would hae been, had she had a husband, but she mun choose a daft, highfalootin' name that's nae name at a'. What's amiss wi' Kirsty or Elspeth or Anne?' But Isla remembered Davy talking of pearls and promising one day to buy her a ring with a single, perfect pearl, '*Beautiful as you are, my own heart's darlin'*,' and she closed her ears against their taunts and named her baby as her heart dictated, in memory of Davy.

But on that last morning, this very morning of this very day, 'He is dead,' she had said, and her stepmother had shrieked, 'Dead he may be, but his family are nae dead. Let *them* pay for their bastard. If they'll believe ye. 'Tis safe enough to claim a man's the father when he's dead and canna' deny it. Who's to say it wasna' one of a dozen drunken loons i' the tavern of a Saturday? And when his family say the same and send ye packing, ye'd best get

7

back to the tavern and seek 'em out. But see ye charge good money, for ye'll have twa mouths to feed, till the quine's of an age to help ye.'

Isla had not waited to hear any more of the filth which spewed from her stepmother's mouth. Instead, she had picked up wee Pearl from her bed in the wooden cradle which had rocked countless Duthie children over the years, and had walked out of the house.

In her agitation she had brought nothing with her except her plaid. Not even her creel and gutting knife, with which she might perhaps have earned herself a shilling or two; not even her purse. But one thing she had, the most important of all. Remembering, her fingers strayed to the neck of her dress, fumbled with the woollen plaid where it shrouded her head and her baby tight against the wind and found the outline of the collar. Tracing the familiar shape, she drew fresh comfort. She would do as her stepmother had said and go to Aberdeen, to the north square at Footdee. The Christies were a close family, Davy had said, caring for and helping one another. She would not ask for anything for herself, but surely they would help Davy's child? When they knew he had a child? And though she had no possessions, she had her hands and her health. She could work. She could bait the lines, gut the fish, clean or bake or scrub. Drawing her plaid tighter about her shoulders, she adjusted the weight of little Pearl, asleep now on her breast, turned her face towards the north, and set out once more for Aberdeen.

'Are you sure it is what you want, Rachel?' Andrew Noble looked searchingly into the serious grey eyes which he had known since they were children together at his mother's house in Cove. Though 'hovel' would be a more appropriate word, he thought, as he looked briefly round

8

his own small parlour. The house the hospital had provided for him was simple enough – a but-and-ben of two rooms, a kitchen and an outside privy – but it was luxury compared to that fish-reeking, overcrowded, one-roomed cottage where he and Rachel had grown up, with the sound of the sea at their backs and the sound of his mother's tongue ever clacking in rebuke or complaint.

'Yes,' Rachel answered with simple conviction, sweeping aside all argument. A trim, straight figure in a simple blue dress, Rachel had a presence which Andrew had long recognized and which stopped the protests on his tongue.

He contented himself with a gentle reminder. 'And the many mansions?' *'In my father's house are many mansions'* had been a favourite quotation in Rachel's childhood when together they had woven dreams over a guttering candle.

'But the many mansions were to be yours, Andrew, not mine,' smiled Rachel. 'I wanted only . . .' She stopped, too late.

'I know,' he said quietly. 'You wanted only to escape my mother's beatings and one day to have a home of your own. A loving home.'

The word hung between them, nebulous, ephemeral as breath on a frosty morning, or spume on the sea.

'Do you . . . love . . . him, Rachel?' Andrew's pale, ascetic face was earnest and intense. 'It is not just propinquity?'

Again Rachel smiled, this time with teasing affection. 'Are you being coy, Andrew? Are you asking if we have kept the bedboard safe between us – or snapped it to splinters and burnt the pieces to heat the porridge pot?'

Unexpectedly, Dr Andrew Noble, MRCS, blushed scarlet and spluttered, 'I meant only that you have lived together for . . . I mean, that you kept house . . . that you . . .'

'That I have been James's bidey-in, as some folks say?' Rachel's eyes were sparkling now with mischief.

'*No!* Ye ken fine I dinna', ye daft quine!' Andrew lapsed in exasperation into dialect and, laughing, Rachel relented.

'You mean that I have lived in the same house as James since I was a child of nine? If that is your "propinquity", then surely it must be good? At least James is no stranger.'

'No, but . . .' Andrew paused, torn between the wish to throw no shadow over his adopted sister's wedding day and the need, as her only 'relative' to guard her interests and her happiness as best he could. 'He is . . . he has . . . well, to put it bluntly, Rachel,' he finished in a rush which left his cheeks hot with embarrassment, an embarrassment he never felt in the consulting room, even when asking the most intimate questions, 'he is not unacquainted with the female sex.'

'Not unacquainted?' Rachel was deliberately flippant, though his innocent reminder had hurt her more than she acknowledged. 'Are double negatives the latest style in that medical society of yours, or are you growing pompous in your old age?'

'Old age?' It was Andrew's turn to protest. 'And me a mere twenty-five? I meant only . . .'

'You meant only to play the big brother and warn me for my own good,' interrupted Rachel, 'and I am glad you care enough for me to bother, but there is no need. I know James.' Her face was shadowed with brief memory, before she continued, 'And I have made my choice – though it was none of my choice to have a penny wedding with the whole Square asked to bring their offerings, nor my choice to come and live with you these last two weeks

10

neither. I would have been content to be contracted by the minister with none but Maitland, Alex and the twins to see. But James wanted everything to be done right, for his mother's sake.' And perhaps also for his own conscience's sake?

'Aye. Had Bonnie Annie been alive, she'd have insisted right enough,' agreed Andrew, adjusting his neck-cloth before the glass which hung over the plain oak dresser. There was a heavy Bible on the polished surface and a candle in a brass candlestick, but nothing else. Andrew had no time for anything that did not serve a purpose, and as the house had already been furnished with the barest necessities when he moved in, he saw no need to add to them. Besides, his job at the hospital took up all his time. The Infirmary was small and cramped, built eighty years before and designed for no more than twenty patients too sick in body or mind to be cared for at home. The town of Aberdeen had grown since then, with the influx of business and expanding trade, and the little Infirmary had long been straining at its old-fashioned seams. Especially this last winter, with the fever epidemic at its height. Had it not been for the loan of the town barracks they could not have coped. The Bedlam cells were no more than straw-layered boxes and, though since the opening of the asylum at Clerkseat they were rarely used for their original purpose, in times of epidemic they too were utilized to house as many as there was space for, one way or another.

With such conditions commonplace, was it any wonder that Andrew found the sparsely furnished chill of his own house more than adequate for his simple needs? A woman came in daily to cook for him and do his washing – the latter the greater part of her job, for though Andrew's linen was threadbare, it was scrupulously clean. 'Dirt is the great enemy, Rachel, and I teach by example as well as precept – with clean linen, light to study by, quietude, and a fire to warm the feet, what more could a man want?'

'Companionship?' she had ventured on that first evening, when she had seen how bare and hermit-like was his existence, but Andrew had only taken both her hands in his and shaken his head, smiling. 'My work is all the companionship I need, Rachy, and the chance to talk with friends once in a while, and to see you.'

Now, however, satisfied that his appearance was as neat as it would ever be, he turned away from the mirror and said, seriously, 'I will miss you, Rachy. I have grown used to your company. We could live very happily together, you and I. But not for long,' he went on, suddenly brisk. 'You need a husband and a family. I can see it in your sparkling eyes, and the sooner I deliver you safely to your wee house in the Square, the happier you will be. Am I not right?'

It was Rachel's turn to blush, but only for a moment. 'First there must be the plenishing, Andrew. I must take my belongings to the Square, then wait again till Saturday. But I wish . . .' She stopped, before continuing demurely, 'We may not go till we are sent for. Alex and Maitland and the twins are to come for my kist. James said.'

'I know,' interrupted Andrew, laughing. 'Bonnie Annie would have wished it. She was aye a stickler for correct behaviour. She wouldna' want the Square to say a Christie didna' know how to conduct things. Besides, she was awful fond of you.'

'And I of her. She treated me like a daughter.' But the memory brought others which Rachel had thought forgotten, and her face saddened.

'Nay, lass, there's no cause to grieve,' said Andrew, misunderstanding. 'She's been dead a year past come May, and lies in peace.'

A rattle of wooden wheels on iron earth broke the momentary silence which followed his words; there was a hearty bang on the door, the stamp and shuffle of impatient feet, and an eruption of male laughter at some whispered joke.

'Open up, Andrew, ye canny wee devil, we've come to tak' her awa' and gie ye peace.'

Andrew stepped into the tiny hall and lifted the latch. In the narrow lane which led up from the town, past Woolmanhill Hospital and the Denburn, stood a group of men and several lassies bundled up against the cold. In their midst was a wooden handcart and at their head four tall and lusty fellows, clapping cold hands across jerseyed chests and stamping thigh-booted feet.

'Well, let us in, man,' said the youngest, cheerfully. 'Here's Jamie's brothers come to fetch his bride's kist, wi' the Baxter lads and the Brands to help wi' the barrow and a lassie or two to sing us on our way. But first, canna' ye see we're fair nippit wi' the cold and in need of a warming dram to ward off the frostbite?'

'Come in, Alex – all of you.' Andrew stood aside to let them pass as one by one they stooped heads and shoulders to negotiate the low doorway, with Baxter's Davy, Red Willie, the oldest unmarried Brand girls and Kirsty Guyan. When the Christie men stood upright their heads barely cleared the ceiling and Rachel said anxiously, 'Ye'd best sit down, all of you, quick, before someone bruises his head on a beam.'

'Rachel's right,' called Andrew from the back regions where he had gone in search of the whisky jar. 'I am not on duty today, and anyone who splits his head stitches it up himself.'

'A cod to a kipper it'll be Maitland,' said the twin with the front teeth missing.

'Na, na, Willy. He's nae handy wi' a needle,' said

13

George, the twin with the broken nose. 'It'd best be Wee Alex.'

'Aye, then Kirsty can stitch it for him.'

Kirsty Guyan, a fresh-faced lass of fifteen, squealed in mock horror. 'I'd faint. Truly I would. Wi' Alex all helpless and bleeding.'

'Who says I'd be helpless?' growled Alex with an expressive roll of the eyes. 'I'd lie back till ye were bending over me, all tender and loving, then I'd . . .'

'Leave the lass alone,' interrupted Rachel firmly. 'Sit still and mind your manners. Ye're not in your own house now.'

'Rachy's right,' said William with a wink at George. 'We're in *Dr Noble*'s wee hoosie and if we dinna treat him right . . .'

'He'll dig us up when we're dead, right enough,' finished George with a grin. 'He'll chop us into wee pieces . . .'

'And he'll nay put us together again,' finished William.

'But every wee piece of us will haunt yon doctor-mannies at the Medico society,' went on George, warming to his theme, 'till they canna sleep easy i' their beds, but . . .'

'Ye'll not sleep easy in yours neither,' interrupted Rachel, 'for I'll take my besom and skelp the backsides o' the pair o' ye if ye dinna' behave and remember your manners. I can see ye've got into bad habits while I've been away,' she went on more gently as they meekly accepted their whisky glasses from Andrew and winked at each other in silence.

'Aye,' said Wee Alex cheerfully. 'The hale hoose's gone to pot. Jamie's like a tethered bull, aye pawing the ground and snortin' wi' frustrated passion, and as for Maitland, he's aye keenin' to the moon and weepin' into his kerchief on account o' he's lost ye to Anither.'

'Idiot!' said Maitland and Rachel in one breath, then everyone laughed, raised their brimming glasses and shouted '*Slange!*' The next toast was 'Rachel', then 'Rachel and James', then 'James and Rachel', then 'the Christies', and after that, people lost count. Rachel fetched bread and cheese from the kitchen and the mutton pies she had baked that morning. There were bannocks and good barley broth, so that it was late in the day and the sun low behind the hill before they loaded Rachel's chest on to the handcart and set out along the road, past the bleach green at the Denburn, with the grand new houses in Union Terrace above.

'Yon's our Jessie's hoose,' said one of the Brand girls, pointing. 'Let's call on her and annoy her.'

'Na,' said the other. 'She'll send us awa' wi' a flea i' the ear for showing her up. Ye ken fine she thinks she's gentry now, and too high and mighty to speak wi' the likes o' her ain sisters.'

'Is she coming to yer weddin', Rachy? Wi' you and she being friends once?'

But they were passing under the cornermost house of Union Terrace now and Alex, seeing Rachel's flushed face, said quickly, 'Yon's the Lumsdens' house, wi' all the lamps lit. They've a house i' the country, too, and send their daughters all the way to England, to school. They sail on Farquharson's *Dora* to London, but when our new ship's launched, I reckon we'll persuade the Lumsdens and all their friends to ship wi' us instead. Eh, Rachy?'

Rachel looked up at him gratefully and agreed. With Andrew on one side and Maitland on the other, each linking her arm with his, she felt happy and protected, even from the memories the Brand girls had unwittingly revived. 'Of course we will, Alex,' she said, 'and why not, when our ship will be the best on the high seas for comfort and convenience?'

15

'*And* speed,' said Maitland seriously. 'I reckon we'll cut two hours off the London run at the least. Maybe as much as six with a following wind. Five days is the best Farquharson's *Dora* can do and that only rarely. It's more often six or seven. But we'll maybe not put the new ship on the London run after all. There's the Baltic trade . . .'

But they had left the high ground of the new street with its scattering of stately new buildings and its vacant, waiting feus, out of sight behind them to follow the ancient, narrow road which twisted down under the new sweep of the Union Bridge. Wooden wheels echoed on cobbles and echoed again from the arches of the bridge above them as the procession wound its noisy way towards the Green, Alex and the twins trundling the wooden barrow with Rachel's kist jolting askew at every rut in the road, the others strung out behind. Kirsty bore an earthenware coggie and milk jug, while the Brand girls carried Rachel's creel and skull and gutting knife.

'Not that she'll need to follow the fishing,' said one girl, with envy in her voice. 'Nae if yon ship o' Jamie's sails.'

'Wee Alex says 'tis a fine wee ship,' put in Kirsty Guyan, heaving the weight of the coggie from one arm to the other. 'He's going to tak' me wi' him to London, to see the Queen. Isna' that right, laddie?'

Alex's answer was lost in the echoing laughter under the bridge as they moved through the darkness towards the lamp-lit cheer of the Green. Rachel shivered and drew closer to Andrew. As if the others felt her apprehension they chattered suddenly louder and one of them broke into tuneless song. But it was not the sudden darkness that had made Rachel shiver. It was the echoing memory that darkness had brought, of a time long past. 'Do you remember, Andrew?' she murmured.

'Aye.' He had no need to ask what she meant. 'You and I were young then, both of us nervous and afraid,

16

both setting out to a new life, you in the Square with Bonnie Annie, me in the University.'

It had been years ago, in her childhood, but Rachel felt something of the same fear now, as they left the shadow of the bridge and erupted into the cheerful evening bustle of the Green. In two days' time she was going to marry James and she loved him – but as on that evening so many years ago, she felt a shiver of apprehension. As he had done then, Andrew understood.

'Dinna' worry,' he said, low in her ear. 'You have nought to fear. He is a good man. He'll treat ye right.'

'He'll treat ye right.' The words echoed in Rachel's head without comfort. She had no doubt of their truth, for James Christie was fair-minded and honest, but suddenly and with unbearable yearning she wanted more than that.

'Cheer up, Rachy,' urged Maitland as the singing swelled around them. 'Dinna' look so solemn. It's your wedding ye're preparing for, nae a wake!'

'So I am,' Rachel laughed, and when the chorus rose loud around her, her own clear voice topped them all.

Isla Duthie saw the untidy procession from across the Green where she stood huddled in a darkened doorway, as near to the open brazier of the dulse-seller as she dared. The blackened pan of seaweed sizzled and spat over the embers with a particularly pungent aroma which set her taste buds working feverishly and clamped the cold hand of hunger over her vitals. But she had no money and no means of earning any. The bundle in her arms stirred with increasing agitation and a thin wail escaped the constriction of binding plaid. At the same time a warm dampness spread over Isla's hands, accompanied by the faint odour of urine. 'Davy,' she whispered inside her head. 'Davy, help me. Tell me what I must do.

17

Our Pearl has nae clean clothes and she'll stink if I dinna find her any. Her wee bum's already red and splittin' wi' the soreness. What'll I do, Davy?'

As always, the words inside her head found only echoes – or a great empty silence worse than echoes, empty as the sea when the boats were over the horizon, empty as the sky on a clouded night.

'Here lass, draw closer to the fire,' said a gruff voice at her elbow. 'Warm yer wee bairnie.'

The dulse-seller's face was pleated with years, like the sand when the tide is out, his small old eyes bright as pebbles, but his grin was kindly enough, in spite of the tobacco-stained, broken teeth.

'Have ye come far?' he added, giving the embers a poke with a blackened stick.

Isla did not answer. Painfully torn between politeness and fear, she could think of nothing to say. Suppose he were evil? Luring her into some trap? Isla had heard of women who sold themselves to men and made a living by it – her stepmother had told her often enough – but there were also other men who owned the women, stole them sometimes and sold them to other men to ship abroad. White slaves. Davy, Davy help me.

'Nay lass, dinna' look sae feart. I'll not harm ye. But sure as my name's Dulse Willy, the snow and the haar atween them will finish ye off if ye dinna' tak' care – and yer babby wi' ye. So draw up closer, and here – tak' this.' He thrust a stick into the steaming seaweed, twisted it deftly, and held out the blackened offering. 'Nay,' he said, as she drew back in protest, 'I'm telling ye for yer ain good. Tak' it lass, and eat it. I dinna' want ye droppin' dead at my feet wi' hunger and me wi' more dulse than I can sell the nicht.'

Hesitantly, Isla took the offering and ate, at first gingerly, then with gusto, for it was the first food she had

18

taken that day and wouldn't her milk dry up if she starved herself? 'Hush,' she murmured automatically, as Pearl whimpered again and squirmed with discomfort.

'My, but yon babby stinks,' said Dulse Willy, without censure. 'Ye'd best awa' home and see to the poor wee mite, wi' hot water and a clean cloutie.' A thought struck him. 'Ye're nae up frae Stonehaven, or one o' they far places, are ye? Ye've a fisher lass's look about ye, but I see ye've nae creel.'

'I . . .' gulped Isla, then went on quickly, to stall further questions, 'I am visiting my husband's folk, in Footdee.' As everyone did, she pronounced it 'Fittie'.

'Then ye've nae far to go and ye'll be fine and welcome for ye've picked a rare time to come and no mistake. 'Tis the Christie wedding on Saturday. Yon hullabaloo across the Green is the plenishing party. They'll be right glad to see ye, lass. Hey! Wee Alex!' The dulse-seller raised a surprisingly loud and penetrating voice. 'There's a lassie here says she's kith and kin o' yours.' But his words were lost in the singing and general hubbub of the Green and he shrugged.

'Nae matter. Awa' wi' ye after them, lassie, quick, and ye'll be in time for a dram, gin ye hurry.'

'Thank you.' Carefully Isla laid down the dulse stick, pulled her plaid about her and, Pearl clasped against her breast, followed the procession out of the Green along the Shiprow.

But once the dulse-man was safely out of sight, her steps slowed. How could she follow them? How could she put herself forward, in the middle of a plenishing and she with no gift to bring? How could she say, 'Here I am, Davy's mistress, with Davy's child'? Davy had been dead nearly two years and none of them knew her. She had met the girl Rachel once, after Davy's death, but no one

19

else and Rachel would have forgotten her. Her stepmother's words echoed cruelly in her head: '*They'll nae believe ye.*'

By the time the procession had reached the softer turf of the Fittiegait, Isla's courage had fled. She would find a corner somewhere, out of the wind, to sleep. The morning would be soon enough to introduce herself to the Christies. Bleak-eyed and shivering, she unfastened her bodice and pressed the little, downy-haired scrap against her breast. But though the searching, sucking mouth clamped and tugged, there was little there to satisfy and after five minutes the baby had not the strength to continue such unrewarding work and fell, whimpering and hungry, into fitful sleep.

'Davy,' mourned Isla as she rocked the infant gently to and fro with the soothing rhythm of the sea not ten feet away beyond the breakwater. 'Help me, Davy. Tell me what I should do.'

'Finest French rennet in barrels,' dictated George Abercrombie, looking round the crowded shelves and counters of his expanding business. 'French grapes. Bilbao chestnuts. Lisbon oranges.'

He remembered the beginnings in that dark, underground cavern in the Netherkirkgate, with a mixture of satisfaction and sentimental regret. They had had only two rooms over the shop to house himself, Kirsty and the children. But they had prospered, taken better rooms in the Broadgait, with a bit more style about them and, finally, a house in the Guestrow. Their new house was both stylish and commodious, with plenty of room for his wife's pretensions as well as for the shop. As for their family, Fenton and Clementina were both married now, with homes of their own. Kirsty spent all her time with her women friends, or dressing herself up in ridiculous taffeta stuff and traipsing off to charity concerts and suchlike, for all the world as if she'd been born a duchess instead of plain Kirsty Bain, a fisherman's daughter in Torry. She was aye nagging him to put up for the Country Club, too. What did he want wi' Clubs when he'd enough work to do in the shop — and enough company, when he'd the mind for it, in the Lemon Tree Tavern, practically on his own doorstep? For often the new house seemed over-large and over-lonely. Besides, Kirsty had filled it with flimsy modern furniture – mahogany card tables, inlaid chairs as delicate as matchwood so a man daren't sit on them, brocaded sofas and such. Abercrombie was a big man, grown larger with age and prosperity, and he liked his food. But he preferred the porridge and stovies Kirsty used to give him in the old days to the invalid slops she put on his table now. In retrospect, the cramped quarters of the Netherkirkgate acquired a halo of warm, domestic happiness, redolent of aromatic cooking . . . Abruptly, he remembered his shop.

'Soft-shell almonds, Bitter, Valencia and Jordan ditto,' he went on, savouring each item with undiminished pride. It was not every tradesman in Aberdeen who could offer the variety and quality of Abercrombie and Son, and he had the Christie lads to thank for that. No more hanging about for overdue consignments, no more shipments left to moulder on a distant quay. The Christies delivered what they promised – a fast, efficient and reliable service. One in the eye for Atholl Farquharson.

Remembering his rival's discomfiture, Abercrombie chuckled aloud. Startled, Fenton looked up from the desk where he was writing out the advertisement for the *Aberdeen Journal* with copperplate precision. 'Is anything the matter, Father?'

'Not wi' me, lad, though I liked it fine when ye called me Da. Till ye caught a whiff of your Ma's ideas. No, I

21

was thinking o' Farquharson's face when the new ship's launched.'

Fenton did not answer, but his face took on the troubled, almost wary look it often wore when Atholl Farquharson's name was mentioned, as if he were afraid he might hear something he would prefer not to hear.

'Well, lad?' prompted Abercrombie. 'Nothing to say, eh? Has not that wife o' yours brought ye any gossip frae the Farquharson camp lately? I thought she was aye flittin' in and oot o' yon palace o' theirs i' the West End.'

Jessie had been a disappointment to Abercrombie. When Fenton married a fisher lass from Footdee, against his mother's and sister's expressed disapproval and prejudice, Abercrombie had had high hopes of the match. A fine, strong lass, he had said, healthy and hard-working. A help to the business, and a good breeder.

But it was Fenton who wrote out the announcement for the *Journal*, Fenton who drew up the accounts and kept the books in order, Fenton who served in the shop when there were too many customers for Archie, the assistant, and the new lad, Willie, to cope with. The only interest Jess took in the family business was to walk about the premises like visiting royalty, sampling the pineapple syrup or the French plums and irritating Kirsty. A pity there was not a closer friendship between them, coming as they did from near enough the same stock.

Still, at least Jessie had produced a healthy grandchild for him, even if it was a quinie. Not like poor Clemmy who had nothing but miscarriages – not surprising when you looked at her husband, but a pity all the same.

The reminder of little Augusta cheered him. She was a fine, healthy lass like her Ma and already promised to be a beauty. Perhaps the next would be a boy, to carry on the family business? At least Fenton was doing his duty there.

'Well, lad,' he prompted again. 'No gossip?'

'What about tobacco, Father?' reminded Fenton, ignoring the question. Fenton had developed a real taste in tobacco and in snuff, so that Abercrombie could safely leave all that side of the ordering to him.

'Aye. I was coming to that. Let's see. We'll put "Just landed. Another parcel of the famous Segars. Also Prince's, Dr Ruddiman's and the real Macouba snuff." You'd best put in a repeat order, fast, for more o' that, Fenton.' There had been a most gratifying surge in sales of snuff, since word got about that it prevented the typhus. 'Then you'd best finish the notice with the usual list o' spices and so on and when ye get to the spirits, see ye dinna' forget the new Rum and Orange Shrub. Let me see a fair copy before ye send the lad round wi' it – and dinna' forget the wedding. Ye'll need to leave time to fetch Jess.'

'Yes, Father.' Fenton kept his eyes on the page and tried, unsuccessfully, to keep all expression from his voice. But Abercrombie had gone back into the front of the shop and noticed nothing. Besides, it was too late now to tell his father that Fenton and Jess had not been invited to the Christie wedding. James Christie, bridegroom, was Abercrombie's partner in their shipping venture so it was only natural that Abercrombie should be invited. Jess, Fenton's wife, had once been the bride's friend – why they were no longer friends Fenton did not know, but there had certainly been no invitation.

'She doesna' need to ask,' said Jess airily. 'She ken's fine I'll go anyway. The whole Square's askit, wi' my ain Ma and Da. That means me too – and you,' she added with too much of an afterthought to escape Fenton's notice.

Fenton, however, was not convinced. 'My father had a

written invitation,' he said. 'We did not. We cannot throw our company upon them uninvited.'

'Why not?' Jess tossed her fine head in defiance. 'Ye dinna' ken how it is wi' us fisherfolk.' For once Jessie allowed her background to be an ally instead of something to be hidden at all costs. 'We call at folks' houses to bid them to a weddin' and ye'd nae expect Rachel and James to come a' the way to Union Terrace, not wi' the shipyard and a'thing to see to. But they'll be expectin' us. You'll see. And I'd not miss the dancing for a' the world.'

'Are you sure it is wise, Jessica?' Fenton knew from experience that when Jessie wanted something, she usually got it: by a show of temper, or by obduracy, or a campaign of private torment which inevitably ended in Fenton's capitulation. But where their unborn child was concerned, he was on stronger ground. 'You would not want to miscarry.'

A strange gleam came into Jessie's eyes as she said, 'Dinna' worry, Fenton. It'll tak' more than a jig or two to shift *this* child. And I wouldna' miss the wedding for a' the tea in your Ma's wee shoppie.'

Fenton winced at this reminder of the enmity between his mother and his wife, but he made no comment. As he had made none on his father's reference to Jess's friendship with the Farquharsons. There had been occasions in the autumn when he had suspected Jess of calling on Atholl Farquharson alone, though on the one occasion when he had dared to mention it she had said airily, 'Who? Oh, *him*,' and added dismissively, 'Shipping business, that's all.' Since the turn of the year, however, there had been little social contact with the Farquharson camp. At least . . . Fenton had the uncomfortable suspicion that he did not know the half of what his wife got up to when he was out of the house and though Aberdeen was no doubt full of people ready and willing to tell him, he preferred not to give them the chance.

'I still think it would be wiser not to go,' he said. 'We might lay ourselves open to rebuff.'

'Rebuff?' Jess laughed delightedly, though there was a hard edge to her laughter which made Fenton uneasy. 'James wouldna' rebuff *me*, I promise ye, and as for Rachy . . . she wouldna' dare.'

'I would not want there to be any unpleasantness,' said Fenton weakly, but he knew already that he had lost.

'Unpleasantness? At a wedding? What are ye thinking of, Fenton?' She turned away from him, but not before he had seen that odd gleam in her eyes again, and a hint of a smile which held no mirth. 'I think I will wear my scarlet silk. Or shall it be the eau-de-nil wi' the ostrich plumes?'

'Whatever you like,' sighed Fenton. He could see no way out of what was sure to be at best an embarrassing and at worst a humiliating experience. He only hoped their coming would not spoil the day for Rachel, for whom he felt admiration and a real affection.

'See and behave yourself,' hissed Wee Alex, his face dark with fury, 'or I swear to God I'll throw ye out mysel'.'

'Oh yes?' Jessie Abercrombie, née Brand, dusted an imaginary speck from the shoulder of her red silk gown, tweaked the lace drapery to reveal more of her plump-swelling bosom, and looked at him challengingly. 'And what about our share o' the boatie?'

'It's nae your share,' mouthed Alex, his young face almost purple with the effort of keeping his voice down and his expression unrevealingly bland. He would not have Rachel upset, not on her wedding day, not by this . . . this . . . 'It is Mr Abercrombie's share,' he managed

25

through clenched teeth, 'and *he* is welcome. But *you were not invited.*'

'And why not, and me an old friend?' Jess's face was cheerfully defiant now that she saw the way the wind lay. Wee Alex would not cause a scene. None of them would, not on Rachel's wedding day. 'I was hurt,' she went on, pouting provocatively. 'I dinna' mind telling ye so. Just on account of I live i' Union Terrace now, wi' the gentry o' the town, doesna' mean I'm too grand to remember my ain folk. And my ain friends. And if there have been little differences i' the past – well, a wedding's for making up and being friends again, surely?'

Her eyes had sought out and found James Christie in the crowds which packed the hall. James, the eldest of the Christie boys, was dark-haired, dark-bearded, tall as all the Christie boys were, and strong. His strange eyes, one brown, one crystal blue, held a disconcerting sparkle which at the same time tantalized and baffled, in an otherwise flawless face. Since his father's death from drowning six years ago he had assumed the responsibility for his mother, now dead, for his five brothers – four since Davy died – and for Rachel, the orphan lassie who had come to live with them years ago and who was now to be his bride. Since childhood James had fascinated Jessie Brand, as she had then been. Jess had had the pick of the Square's lads – except James – and it was as much his mocking unattainability as anything else which had intrigued her and, in spite of everything, still did.

Yet Rachel had managed to hook him. When the Cove lass had first arrived in the Square Rachel had been a fleshless, ill-kempt scrap of a thing, with a haunted look about her. Now, Jess had to admit, she was, well, striking anyway, if you liked that pale, self-contained look. Haughty, some folks called it, though what Rachel had to be superior about the devil alone knew. But then Annie

Christie, James's ma, had been like that, till she went 'fou'.

Remembering the witlessness of the woman's last years, Jessie's confidence flowed back and she gave Alex her most practised smile.

'I am sure Rachel will be delighted to see me,' she said in her best imitation of a drawing-room manner.

'I'm nae,' growled Alex, uncomfortably aware of the animal scent of the woman and the warm, bare flesh practically under his nose. Wee Alex, the youngest and tallest of the Christie boys, was fiercely loyal to his brothers and to Rachel, but he was also, in the unpredictable vigour of newly gained manhood, almost comically susceptible to a provocative woman, wherever or whatever she might be. 'But now ye're here, ye might as well come in.'

'Thank you.' Jess laughed the tinkling, social laugh which made her husband cringe and stepped down into the room. The Christies had hired the school hall for the festivities, as the planning loft of the little shipyard was too crowded with the paraphernalia of their latest building enterprise and the cottage too small to house the dozens of guests expected. And there were dozens: no one in the Square was going to miss a wedding and though the Christies seemed set on abandoning the fishing which had been the livelihood of their father and grandfather before them, they were still fisherfolk, and still part of North Square. Not like yon Jessie Brand, thought Kirsty Guyan, pushing through the crowd towards Wee Alex. She was a small, slight girl, but a firebrand of a lassie when her temper was up, as it was now, seeing that woman leering and simpering at her Alex. Jessie had been born no better than the rest o' them, but she gave herself such airs since she wed a townie there was no putting up wi' her, wi' yon carriage and dressmaker and maid she was aye rammin'

27

down folks' throats. I know what I'd like to ram down *her* throat, thought Kirsty. A haddy, tail first!

Jess, standing on the slight eminence of the doorway, was fully aware of the hostile looks she attracted from the womenfolk, and exulted in them. She knew they stemmed from envy – envy of her looks, her position, and, most of all, her money. Fenton's money, a voice at the back of her mind prompted, but as the voice had unpleasant echoes of her father-in-law who had not been as susceptible lately as he used to be, she ignored it.

Instead, her foot tapping in rhythm, she watched the swirling vigour of the dancing and particularly that leaping dark head and bobbing, lighter one that marked where bride and bridegroom were taking their part in the reel. At the far end of the hall, on a makeshift platform of trestles, a trio of fiddlers joined to produce a frenzied, joyous skirling which lost none of its rhythm as first one then another briefly laid bow aside to drink from the proffered glass, only to resume playing with added vigour. All around the room were tables, benches and stools, crowded with those who preferred food and drink to exercise, or who were resting their feet in preparation for the next affray. Old, young, middle-aged, even babies were there, cradled by toothless grannies or humped by siblings scarcely larger than themselves, while their parents danced and squealed and laughed with the rest.

Unexpectedly, Jess felt a stab of envy. Her own wedding had been respectable and refined, as she had wanted, with none of this sweaty leaping and yelling. But there was an infectious gaiety in the air here which had not been present in the Abercrombie drawing-room and suddenly Jess wanted to be part of it. She saw her mother, conspicuously and merrily drunk, huger than ever in her party finery, but jigging and squealing with the best of them. At the same moment, her mother saw her.

'Come awa' in, Jessie lass,' Mrs Brand yelled, 'if ye're nae too snotty-nosed to kick a heel wi' us,' and Jessie, tossing aside gentility, looped up her skirts, grabbed the nearest lad, one of the Baxters, and plunged into the mêlée.

Rachel Christie heard Ma Brand's cry, caught a fleeting glimpse of Jessie's flamboyant finery through the press, and felt the first cloud on her day's happiness.

'What is it, Rachel?' panted James, red-faced and laughing as he linked arms and swung her in the woven pattern of an eightsome reel.

'Nothing,' she managed, smiling up at him.

'Tired?' he asked, the next time the elaborate movements of the dance brought them together. His eyes were teasing, gentle and full of promise.

'Perhaps.'

With a low laugh, he kissed her lightly on the forehead before the dance pattern took him one way, and her another.

She can't hurt us, Rachel told herself over and over inside her head as she danced and laughed and answered her well-wishers, sometimes with James at her side, sometimes not, for there were many guests to thank and to make welcome. She is a silly woman, that is all, vain and greedy and perhaps a little jealous. But surely no more than that?

Rachel found herself watching Jess, and James too, with a new anxiety, though her face remained serene above the creamy folds of her lace-tucked bodice and rustling taffeta skirts, as she danced with each of her brothers in-law in turn, Maitland, William, George and Wee Alex; then with the Baxters and the Brands, with Fenton and finally his father, James's business partner and friend.

'Ye look lovely, lass,' gasped George Abercrombie,

29

'and if she leads ye half as merry a dance as she's led me this last five minutes, James lad, ye'll need all yer strength to keep up wi' her.'

James slipped an arm round Rachel's waist and said, grinning, 'Dinna' worry, Mr Abercrombie. I'll not let her escape, not now I've caught her.'

But the fiddlers were reviving their flagging energies at the whisky jar and the rest of the company took the opportunity to do the same, or to sample the beer, whisky punch, and bread and cheese, of which there was a seemingly endless supply.

George Abercrombie liked Rachel. Since he had bought himself a share in the Christie ship-building enterprise he had noted how hard the lot of them worked in their different ways, but particularly Rachel, with her meticulous book-keeping, her flair for attracting the right kind of freight for their ship, the *Steadfast*, and her plans for the second one, almost ready now for launching.

'I reckon we'll name a ship for you one day, Rachel,' said Abercrombie when refreshment and rest had revived him. He heaved himself reluctantly to his feet and added, 'But there's Kirsty glaring at me. I reckon it's time we made a move for home.'

Kirsty Abercrombie had spent most of the evening at the best table, sipping daintily from a glass of whisky punch and nibbling, 'for a' the world like a sick mousie' as one of the Brand kids said, at a perfectly edible scone. Louise Forbes had joined her on occasions and a succession of reluctant Christies, sent by Rachel to 'be polite', had come, talked awkwardly, asked dutifully for a dance, been refused, and gone again, much relieved. Once her husband had persuaded her to dance and Kirsty had almost enjoyed herself – until the constriction of her newest corset grew too uncomfortable to bear and she resumed her stiff-backed vigil on the sidelines. Now, however, it was plain from her unsmiling face that social duty had been done.

'I'll say goodbye then, James lad. I am honoured that ye asked me – and ye're a lucky man. Mind if I kiss the bride?' Without waiting for James's consent, he did so, then, catching sight of his son Fenton who had been remarkably unsociable all evening considering the occasion, he called, 'Come on, Fenton, you're awfu' forward i' hanging back. Come and give the bride her wedding kiss.'

Blushing with embarrassment, for the fact that he and Jess were there without invitation had blighted the whole evening for him, he kissed Rachel hesitantly on the cheek, saying 'I wish you both health and happiness.'

'Thank you.' Rachel had a soft spot for Fenton, the gentle, honest-eyed lad whom Jess had cold-bloodedly chosen as her prey. 'And do not worry,' she murmured. 'I know it is not your fault – and I'm glad you came.'

Her unwitting emphasis on the 'you' did not escape Fenton's notice and instead of reassuring him, as had been Rachel's design, her words left him more troubled than before. He sought out his wife in a group of which Ma Brand seemed to be the lusty centre and drew her aside. 'Come home, Jessie,' he urged. 'We have stayed long enough.'

'Home?' Jess laughed in his face. 'You go home if ye've a mind to, but the night's nae half done yet and I'm enjoying myself.'

Fenton bit his lip in frustration, but it would not do to make a scene, not at Rachel's wedding, whatever the circumstances. Baffled, he retreated to a quiet corner to brood on his wife's frivolity, to watch and worry and wait. Later, Andrew Noble joined him – they were old college friends – and Louise Forbes, but though they talked

31

interestingly enough of the new public rooms, the progress of the new medical hall and its library, and of Baillie Galen's new house which was to occupy a prime site in the Castlegate and set the style for the whole area, Fenton could give no more than half his attention. The rest was on his wife. She ought not to be dancing and drinking and behaving as she had been behaving, not when she was expecting, even though it was still early days. But worse than that, he knew, with the intuition born of their two-year marriage, that she was up to something. Why else had she insisted, against all argument, on coming? He did not believe the 'family ties' bit or the 'old times' sake'. She had been anxious enough to get out of the Square and only returned, he suspected, to show off her carriage and her clothes.

Perhaps that was it? Perhaps she thought to outshine the bride? But the dancing had resumed and for a moment he lost sight of both Rachel and Jess. Then the crowd parted for a moment and with a sinking of the heart he saw them – together.

'I'm sitting this one out,' said Jessie cheerfully, coming up behind Rachel who was surveying the nearest tables to make sure the jugs were full and the platters replenished. 'It's early days yet, but I'd best not addle the wee one's pate over much.'

Rachel stood very still. Then, remembering her own happiness and those childhood years of friendship, said politely and without looking at Jess, 'Are you expecting again so soon?'

Jess leant forward conspiratorially and said, close to Rachel's ear, 'I reckon so. But dinna' tell Fenton, will ye? When I was expecting Augusta he was aye fussing over me till I could ha' screamed. No, he doesna' know about *this* one.' In spite of herself Rachel turned to look at Jess's face. 'Ye see,' went on Jess slowly, and her eyes were suddenly very bright, 'I wanted *you* to be the first to know.'

'Rachel.' James was at her side, at once protective and in charge. 'Dance with me.'

Jessie looked up into his face and said boldly, 'What about me, James Christie? I thought the bridegroom had to tak' turns wi' all the lassies?'

'Lassies maybe,' said James coolly, 'but the matrons have their own menfolk to stand up wi' them. What was she saying to you?' he asked Rachel as he led her firmly into the dancing, one arm tight around her waist.

'Nothing,' she lied. Not for the world would she tell him what Jessie had said, whether it was true or not.

'I do not believe you,' said James, his eyes serious. 'She is a mischief-maker. I will not have her upsetting you, so ye'd best tell me.'

'It is not important, James, really,' and as the joyful rhythm of the fiddles caught them up and tossed them, laughing and breathless, into the swirling merriment of the dance, Rachel realized that it was true. Nothing was important except that she and James were together at last and would be so now for the rest of their lives.

'They look happy, don't they?' said Louise.

'Aye.' Andrew sounded relieved and Louise raised an eyebrow in enquiry, but he went on to say only, 'It has been fine having her to stay this last two weeks, but I have not paid the attention I should have to my own work.'

'How is the hall progressing?' The Aberdeen Medico-Chirurgical Society of which Andrew was a devoted member had commissioned the architect, Archibald Simpson, to design a building for them in which, among other uses, they could house their expanding library.

'Fine, I believe. It should be ready to receive our

33

possessions and, in particular, our books by the end of the year. It will be a splendid sight, with its huge Ionic portico, but I only hope it will not look out of proportion. Those four pillars will be gigantic.'

'I heard the rest of the block is to be developed in complementary style,' said Louise, 'so I would not worry too much about it. Besides,' she added, teasing, 'how long has the architecture of the building been your prime concern? I thought it was what happened inside that mattered to you.'

'It is, Louise. You know the new building will be invaluable for our work. It is difficult enough to find a suitable meeting place where we can collect, undisturbed, for our lectures, and public opinion is still so prejudiced and ill-informed.'

'They do not like the idea of being cut up, that is all,' said Louise cheerfully. 'One can see their point of view. It is only scientists like you who see beyond the personal to the universal. How is your study of the motor mechanism of the arm progressing?'

Andrew looked swiftly to left and right before saying, in low tones, 'I need another "subject" to confirm my findings. As soon as one becomes available I think I shall be able to complete my thesis. As you know, it is not easy.' Louise knew he was referring to the obtaining of suitable bodies for dissection, not to the thesis itself. 'Meanwhile, I have enough to do with the fever epidemic, though I am glad to say the worst seems to be over now. Yesterday there was only one new case . . .'

Louise listened with complete understanding as he expounded his theories of the cause and best treatment of such fevers. For three years now she had studied all the medical books she could borrow, usually from Andrew or his friends, and taken all her queries to him for patient explanation. Together they had broken new medical ground, new to Louise anyway, but sometimes new to both of them. Louise had attended also all the public lectures available. Usually she enjoyed their scientific conversations, but tonight she found herself unaccountably restless after the first few minutes until, acknowledging the incongruity of their solemn conversation in the midst of the wedding celebrations, she said suddenly, 'Andrew, shall we join in the dancing?'

'Dancing?' Andrew's pale, ascetic face looked startled. 'Oh . . .' He studied the moving knot of revellers for a moment, then shook his head. 'I think not. I should be at the hospital as it is. In fact, if you do not mind, Louise, I think we should seek out Rachel and say goodbye. I know she will understand and forgive us.'

With a small sigh, Louise collected her gloves and shawl, knowing, with sudden intensity, that she had wanted to dance, had wanted Andrew to ask her, had wanted them for once to be an ordinary couple, doing ordinary things. For once she glimpsed something of her mother's outlook on life; for a brief, shaming moment even wondered whether she should have taken her mother's advice and worn a new dress. She did not want to go home. She wanted to be part of the wedding party and stay till it was time to escort Rachel and James to their house and see them safely inside. Instead she followed Andrew out of the doorway and into the cold night street.

Isla Duthie, from the shadow of a nearby doorway, saw them leave and took a step forward, only to withdraw again into the concealing darkness as the couple turned towards her and approached along the empty street. Yet again she told herself, 'Next time'. She had come all those hours ago with the intention of joining the crowd, of using the wedding celebrations as a means of introducing herself, but yet again her courage had failed her. She told herself she was not dressed for a wedding. With her hair uncombed, her dress dishevelled, her baby a sodden, malodorous scrap of misery, how could she hope to find any welcome? Least of all from Davy's unsuspecting kin. What would they think of him, choosing such as she? What would they think of *her*?

And yet she knew she must do something and soon, before she or her child grew ill. But she could not accost this couple with the glow of the wedding party still about them. Nor could she slip inside that lamplit hall, briefly and enticingly revealed as the door had opened to release them. She *couldn't*. Pride would not allow. 'Tomorrow, Pearl,' she breathed. 'I promise.'

But the pair were drawing closer. The man was talking earnestly to his companion who had taken his arm and neither noticed the pale and shivering girl with her pathetic little bundle. A snatch of conversation floated towards her as they passed: '. . . most encouraging number of cures this week. Ten more discharged from the House of Recovery, but we are still in need of more bedding . . .' and 'The Barrack gates are open daily from 11.0 till noon. I will do my best . . .' Then they were gone and with them all the warmth and health and comfort which had travelled with them, like a miasma clinging to the man's greatcoat and to the woman's hooded cloak. Isla heard their footsteps echo fainter and fainter in the empty street till the sounds merged with the rasping of her own breath and the distant sighing of the sea.

The child whimpered and nuzzled at her breast with pathetic hope. Tears stung Isla's eyes as she murmured hoarsely, 'Hush . . . hush. I will go tomorrow, Pearl, I promise. Tomorrow.'

She had been saying that for the past two days, ever since the evening of her arrival when she had seen the plenishing procession and followed at a careful distance, drinking in the friendliness and vitality of the Christies, picking out faces and naming them in her head, according to Davy's long ago descriptions: those two must be William and George, identical but for one's broken nose and the other's missing teeth; that tall young one must be Alex, though Davy had always called him Wee Alex, and that other, serious-faced, older one must be Maitland – or James. The dulse-seller had said it was the Christie wedding, but not which Christie. She had followed the procession along the Fittiegait to the edge of the North Square, had watched its arrival at the cottage on the far, most north-easterly corner, had seen the door open and heard the laughter – and suddenly had felt a wave of exclusion as solid as a wall, and the bitter aftertaste of envy. If only Davy had not died. Remembering, tears blurred her eyes again, though there was self-pity as well as envy now, and longing and loneliness and need.

The baby stirred, struggled, whimpered and coughed. With a thud of fear, Isla's eyes at the same time cleared and widened. Suppose Pearl were ill? The croup? The measles? Or, remembering that scrap of overheard conversation, the *fever*? Surely the child's skin was hot? Guilt flooded through her. She had put her own pride before her baby's need, and now her baby was ill. Suppose Pearl were to die? Isla was shaking now with fear. If Pearl died, the last of Davy would die with her. Wildly Isla cast about her for help – but the street was empty of light or hope, only from the hall came the dull thud of dancing feet and the faint skirl of laughter and fiddle music. Resolutely, Isla turned her face towards the building. She would go up the steps, through the door and to the first person she saw. She would ask for food and drink so that her milk might flow again. She would not give her name to anyone, nor the reason she was there, but keep in the background so the sight of her misery would not blight the Christies'

37

day. She would find some sheltered corner in which to sleep and then, when morning came, she knew exactly what she must do.

'Well, Rachel?' murmured James in the firelit warmth of the cottage. 'How does it feel to be Mrs James Christie?'

'I'm not sure,' confessed Rachel. 'Yet.' She looked slowly around the room which was so familiar to her – the earthen floor, newly sanded with clean sand from the shore, the fire with its iron sway from which hung a huge black kettle and another, smaller, pot for the morning's porridge. There was the fireside chair in which James's mother had sat to do her endless knitting of vests and jumpers and fisherman's stockings, and her own little creepie stool by the hearth. Dividing the long room in half was a sailcloth partition, looped back now to show the bunk beds of the Christie brothers on one of which James himself had slept until tonight. There was a clothes kist and the dresser on which, in pride of place, lay a fiddle, beautifully polished, and beside it a mouth organ and penny whistle, and a pearl-lipped conch shell.

Seeing it, Rachel smiled. 'Do you remember when you gave me that shell, James? It was the first present I had ever had.'

'And you looked at me as if I had given you the moon and all the stars together. You were a strange wee creature. Sometimes I think you still are.'

'Would ye like anything else before . . .' Rachel stopped, unaccountably confused.

'Before we go to bed, did ye mean? No, I dinna' think so. I've had my fill o' food and drink, Rachy. It's something else I'm needing now.'

'Then I'll just make up the fire.' She reached for the fire-irons and stopped suddenly, her hand in mid-air.

'What is it, Rachel?'

'Nothing. Only that I do not feel any different, James, than I did the last time I was here, making up the fire before I went to bed. My hand knows its way to the poker without me,' she finished, smiling up at her husband.

'Aye, there'll be no difference for ye in the house, right enough, for ye've lived here more than half your life,' said James, frowning. 'But one day, I promise ye, we'll have a fine house on the Quay, with our children and my brothers and their children, too. But in case ye're worrying, I tellt the boys to leave us in peace for this night anyway, and I've barred the door. I'm sorry, Rachel, if it isna' more exciting for ye, but I've tried to . . .'

'Exciting?' interrupted Rachel. 'I want nothing more than I have now, James. *Nothing.* So take that unbecoming frown from your face and let us go to bed.'

Later, as they lay in the warm darkness of the box bed, its doors firmly closed – for neither of them trusted James's brothers not to burst in upon them somehow, in spite of barred outer door and solemn warnings, to perpetrate some mischievous wedding-night trick – Rachel knew that what she had said was not entirely true. There was one thing which no one could give her, not even James with his tender, passionate and overwhelming love. Least of all James. Remembering Jess's innuendoes, the slow, cold shadow of unwelcome memory crept over her heart and she shivered.

'Are you cold, my love? Then come closer and I'll warm ye.' James was in a state of drowsy contentment, on the brink between waking and slumber, but as he slid his arm round her bare shoulders and she turned towards him, her mouth seeking his, they moved together into a different waking, and afterwards into a deep, contented sleep from which Rachel started suddenly and frighteningly awake as the first dawn light touched the sea. James was still sleeping. She bit her lip to stop the trembling, for in spite of all logic she heard inside her head the old, old adage – the first to fall asleep would be the first to die – but which of them had slept first? She could not remember. Pray God they had fallen asleep together . . . Quietly, she unhooked the wooden panels and eased them back. Quietly she slipped out of the warmth of the blanketed bed and stood a moment, naked, looking down at her sleeping husband. At least she had wakened first and saved him from the pangs of childbed which he might otherwise have felt. Gently she kissed his brow and closed the doors again, washed quickly in the basin in the corner, towelled the goose-pimples from her skin and dressed in shift and petticoats and thick woollen gown. She tied an apron over her skirts, opened up the fire and blew it into life, swung the porridge pot nearer to the flames and checked the kettle was full. Then, singing softly to herself, she set two wooden bowls, two spoons and two plates upon the new chequered table cloth which had been a present, with other table linen, from Louise Forbes. By evening the others would be back again, pushed out of whatever temporary nests they had found for the night, but for the moment James and the little cottage were hers alone to enjoy. She cast a housewifely eye over the fire and table, rafters and floor, then tied a plaid over her shoulders and eased back the bolt of the cottage door.

The Square lay quiet under the Sunday silence, induced as much today by the hospitality of the Christie wedding as by any Sunday observance. The tide was half way between high and low, the sand ridged in rivulets of shadow, and beyond the pierhead to the south the hump of the Girdleness was black against the dawn sky. It was there, beyond that dark mass, in the bay of Nigg, that James's father had been drowned in a futile attempt to aid a shipwrecked seaman. But today no ships would put to sea. On a weekday at this time the little fishing fleet would already be making for the horizon on a dawn-dark sea, while the womenfolk moved about the mussel beds, collecting the day's bait. In the harbour, the ships were sleeping at their moorings, the shipyards on the quayside silent and still. In spite of the tranquillity of the scene, and her own inner contentment, the old anxiety began to niggle at the back of her mind and instead of returning to the cottage, Rachel walked round the headland by the lifeboat station and back towards the town, seeking the familiar outline.

But the little *Steadfast* lay meekly at her moorings, all apparently as it should be and, further along the Quay, behind Dixon's patch, the double doors which barred entry to the Christie yard and their newest shipping venture were firmly secured. As Rachel drew level with the *Steadfast* a head appeared briefly at the gunwales, nodded and disappeared again. Good. The new deck-hand was as conscientious as Rachel had hoped. She made a mental note to tell Maitland so. With one last searching look along the Quay towards the Shiprow and the offices of the rival Farquharson Shipping Company, Rachel turned back towards the Square and James.

Rachel Christie was not the only one to be up betimes on that Sunday morning. In the office on the Shiprow, Atholl Farquharson was studying plans and accounts, while downstairs in the close his man was awaiting him, a stout cudgel in one hand and a spy-glass in the other, with instructions to train the latter on the Quay and particularly the Christie yard, and to report any movement immediately. Seeing the outline of a figure near the *Steadfast*, this he duly did.

'What?' Farquharson snatched up his own spy-glass and stared through the window eastwards. The sun had risen over the headland now, sending shafts of gold and pink

41

and aquamarine across the still waters of the harbour and touching the mastheads with rainbow hues. Gulls glided lazily in and out of the shallows, or rode the wavelets at the harbour mouth and the chimneys of the town were still. It was a scene of tranquillity quite at odds with the schemes and machinations of Farquharson's devious brain, and the small figure which his glass at last located was equally irrelevant.

'Fool!' he snarled. 'It's only a woman. Get back to your post.' But after the fellow had gone, scrambling over-hastily down the wooden stairway so that he lost his footing and fell the last few steps, Atholl turned the glass again on that small, grey figure. It was not a woman, but a girl: a slim, well-turned out girl with a certain dignity of bearing. It was the Christie girl, of course, the orphan Rachel who had married James. Farquharson's lip curled in hatred. Jessie Abercrombie had told him of the wedding as she told him everything, the dangerous bitch. But he knew how to keep her in order and it was to both their advantages that she should hold her tongue about certain events in the Christie shipyard. They were doing well, curse them. Jess had told him of the Christies' newest ship, the *Bonnie Annie*, due to be launched any day now and destined for the Baltic trade, though he had known that already. Again he took up the hated letter. '. . . inform you, in accordance with permission graciously granted to us by you, of our intention to cross that piece of land known as Dixon's patch for the purpose of launching . . .'

His eyes filmed over with fury. '*Graciously granted!*' He remembered that misty November night when the Christie twins had caught him, humiliated him, and finally marched him to the deserted Christie yard and the office where more Christies, including the girl Rachel, had been waiting. Jess Abercrombie had been there too, for her own devious reasons, and had been forced to act as witness to his shame. But he would have his revenge, in time. The Christies would live to regret the day they had extorted his signature to that pernicious document. As for the Baltic trade . . . Farquharson selected a second ledger and opened it at 'Riga'. He had ships trading to most parts of the world. He had contacts in all the major ports and many of the minor. If James Christie wanted to pit his puny ship against Farquharson's own, let him try. Christie might have got the better of him once, but he would not do so again. Next time it would be Farquharson who triumphed. Next time there would be no mistake.

A bell sounded from somewhere in the city and was answered by another. Swiftly, Farquharson pulled out the watch from his waistcoat pocket, then dropped it back into place. Ten minutes to go. Euphemia would be in the pew and waiting. He had best lock up and leave at once if he was to reach St Nicholas's church in time for the service.

Andrew heard the church bell from his room at the barracks hospital. Since the fever epidemic, which had reached its height in December, the hospital resources had been sorely strained. Had not the Marquis of Huntly obtained the use of the Barrack Hospital for fever patients who could not be accommodated in the already overflowing Infirmary, the situation would have been impossible. As it was, all hospital staff took turns to man the Infirmary, the Barrack Hospital and the Houses of Recovery as well as run the Public Dispensary and treat a constant stream of patients with all manner of complaints. Since December they had treated more than 400 fever victims of which, praise be to God, almost 300 had been cured. It had been hard though rewarding work, and Andrew Noble's thin, clever face showed the strain.

This morning, however, was a quiet one, with no new admissions and no deaths. There were still some 130 patients in the Houses of Recovery but, unless there were unforeseen complications, those patients could safely be left to the domestic staff to care for. And as for the hospital itself, the few fever patients remaining were making good progress. There might be time, thought Andrew, to put his notes together and see what conclusions could be drawn from them. There had been one or two cases of the worst kind of *typhus gravior* exhibiting most interesting symptoms of *petechiae* and suppuration of the parotid glands. There might well be enough material in his observations for a paper to be read at one of the Medico-Chirurgical Society meetings.

His thoughts were interrupted by a knock on the door.

'Dr Noble. There's a woman at the gate seekin' treatment. I telt her it's the Sabbath and to come back tomorrow, but she is an obstinate wee bitch and she willna' budge.'

'Was she sent by the Dispensary?' asked Andrew, without looking up. The Dispensary steered all fever patients quickly towards the isolation hospitals.

'No. Dispensary's closed.'

'Has she signs of fever?'

The orderly shrugged. 'Canna' tell. She's dirty, unkempt, snivelling and hysterical. Oh and she has a wee bairn wi' her, as dirty as hersel'.'

'Why did you not say so?' Andrew was on his feet in a moment. 'A child's life is at risk and ye stand blethering. Do ye not know, man, that a child hasna' the strength of a grown woman? Where are they?' Without waiting for an answer, Andrew pushed past the orderly and strode along the echoing passages towards the barracks gate and the officers' guardroom. It was a square, bare room, with one small window and a smaller fire before which stood a

44

bedraggled creature with a tear-streaked face and a pathetic, mewing scrap clasped to her chest. As always at the sight of poverty, illness and distress, Andrew's heart swelled with compassion and anger. 'I am Dr Noble,' he said quietly. 'What is your name?'

'Duthie,' faltered the girl. 'Isla Duthie.'

'And your child's name?'

'Pearl.'

'And what has brought you here, Mrs Duthie?'

Isla accepted the title without correction. 'My baby is coughing and hot and I am sure she's caught the fever. She willna' die, will she, Doctor?'

But Andrew Noble had seen too many deaths to offer false hopes. 'Follow me,' he said briskly as the orderly, breathless from the need to combine dignity with haste, appeared in the doorway behind them. 'Not you, Sergeant. I will see to the lady myself. Come, Mrs Duthie,' he said, more gently, and laid a hand on her elbow. 'It is not far.'

But the kindness in his voice was the last straw and Isla's fragile composure shattered into silent tears. Blindly she moved where he steered her, seeing nothing of the bleak stone corridor, the cold, high walls and narrow windows. Then they were in a brighter room, with a fire and a lamp to lighten the gloom, for although it was past midday there was little light left in the thin February sky. There was a table, a couch, steel instruments on a steel tray. Along one wall were bottles and stoppered jars with strange coloured substances named Belladonna, Gentian, Ipecac . . . Seeing a pair of forceps and scalpel flashing silver in the lamplight, Isla flinched and would have fled had not a woman in a large apron appeared in answer to Andrew's summons.

'The child first, I think,' said Andrew in a low voice

and the woman took the sodden scrap from Isla's arms and laid it on the table in the full glare of the lamp.

'Has the child coughed? Vomited? Any signs of convulsions or diarrhoea?' As Dr Noble's large, gentle hands moved over the tiny body, probing, testing, Isla's fear drained away. Here, she recognized, was someone who would carry her burden for her. This thin, kind man would care for Pearl and for herself. He would tell her what to do. He would take charge. With a long sigh of relief and trust, Isla's tears dried and suddenly all she wanted was to sleep.

'A slight cough, nothing worse. No fever, anyway, and no sign of any putrid infection in the throat. I would say,' went on Dr Noble, looking solemnly at Isla, 'that what your little Pearl needs more than anything else is dry raiment and a full belly. Where is your home?'

But Isla's relief was so great she could not speak. Pearl had no fever. She was not going to die after all. She was only hungry. Isla could have laughed aloud, except that she was afraid that if she did so, she would also cry.

'No matter,' said Dr Noble briskly. 'Such things can wait. First let me examine the mother. The bodice, Mrs McInnes.'

Isla blushed as the nurse bared Isla's breasts to the stethoscope, blushed again as Dr Noble's fingers felt their roundness for the presence of milk. But she breathed as she was told, long-drawn breaths in and out, opened her mouth to the spoon which held down her tongue, submitted her ears and eyes to the closest inspection. Finally Dr Noble turned away. 'Thank you, Mrs McInnes.' He stood discreetly looking out of the window while Isla put her clothes to rights, then turned back with a brisk 'No fever. A slight cold, that is all. And a slight attack of hunger perhaps? You cannot hope to feed your child, Mrs Duthie, if you do not feed yourself. Where do you live?'

'I . . .' She stopped, confused. 'I do not know,' she finished in a voice as pitiful as a lost child's. Again Andrew's heart twisted with sadness. How could such children ever hope to cope with ordinary life, let alone with children of their own, or with sickness, adversity and trouble?

'Wait.' Andrew made a rare decision. 'Mrs McInnes, would you be so good as to ask that surly sergeant to bring us food? A dish of barley broth and bread will serve, and ask him for a bottle of porter or good stout. After that, will you take the child and clean her – gently, mind – and see the water is no more than blood heat. Then warm a little milk and sugar and feed her with a spoon. It will be much the best, I assure you,' he went on when Mrs McInnes had left them and Isla opened her mouth to make some vague protest. 'Pearl is big enough now to learn to fend for herself. How old is she?'

'Fourteen months,' confessed Isla, hanging her head.

'And not yet weaned? Shame on you, Mrs Duthie. No wonder you are drained of energy. You must wean her on to slops and broze at once. Now, you were telling me where you live. Or rather, you were not.' His eyes twinkled, though his face remained solemn and suddenly Isla gave up all pretence. Dr Noble was clever and kind and too shrewd to believe any lies she might invent and, to be truthful, she was too weak to make up anything at all, let alone a convincing story.

'I have no home,' she said, looking down at her hands which were twisted together awkwardly in her lap. 'I left . . .' Haltingly she told him of her quarrel with her stepmother and of her journey to Aberdeen, though she did not mention the Christies for, having seen the wedding party, the closeness of the family and their joy together, how could she intrude? Besides, at the back of her mind,

47

her stepmother's words pricked and burned like a festering splinter. Suppose they did not believe her? No, she would wait till Pearl was well again, till she and her child were established, then she could meet them on equal terms. 'I thought Aberdeen a better place to look for work than Stonehaven,' she said and added only, 'My husband died.'

When she finished, Andrew made no comment. Instead he seemed absorbed in some private thought, broken abruptly by the arrival of the sergeant with a steaming tray which he dumped on to the table with 'That'll be 1s 8d, Doctor.' He stood, exuding disapproval and outrage, while Andrew rummaged in his pockets for the money, then slammed, without a thank-you, out of the room.

'Good,' said Andrew, lifting the lid of the covered dish. 'There's marrow bone broth today. That'll warm you.'

'But I thought . . .'

'No,' said Andrew firmly, dismissing protest. 'It is for you. You may not have the fever, but hunger needs treatment too. You cannot stay here,' he went on after a few moments' silence during which Isla tasted the broth, first delicately and with hesitation, then as her taste buds burst into joyful life, with greedy gusto. 'This place is for fever patients only. It would be harmful for you to stay any longer than necessary. Nor in the Houses of Recovery. But you must go somewhere else, you and the child.'

Isla made no answer but looked trustingly back at him, waiting for whatever decision he might make. The broth was finished. She had supped up every last drop of it with the hunk of bread and now, when Dr Noble offered her the mug of porter, she took that too and drank, feeling its goodness flowing through her veins with comforting strength. She was content to let Dr Noble, like the victuals, take over the work of maintaining health and strength, for herself and for Pearl, until she felt strong enough to resume control. At the moment she had strength only to drink and wait submissively for his decision.

Andrew Noble was in a quandary. He did not normally become emotionally involved with his patients. As a rule he directed them to the hospital or to the street with brisk efficiency, knowing who needed care and who could find sufficient in their family. When he came across the homeless he directed them to the town soup kitchen, or to one of the organizations run by townswomen, such as Euphemia Farquharson, for Fallen Women, Homeless Destitutes, or Widows and Orphans. There was the Whitefishers' Benevolent Society in Footdee, and had Isla Duthie been a Footdee lass instead of from Stonehaven there would have been no problem. But Mrs Duthie was no ordinary widow, no ordinary mother without a man. He could not have said on what evidence he based that knowledge. He had only to look at her pale hair, her trusting blue eyes and clear skin, already regaining some of its rose-pink lustre as the heat of broth and fire set her circulation moving, to know that she was not tough enough or insensitive enough to survive destitution – and he suspected she would prove too proud for charity, at least of Mrs Farquharson's kind.

Yet she was patently not fit to spend another night under the stars, nor her little child Pearl. Pearl was a strange name for a fisherlass's baby, and yet not so strange when you thought about it. Andrew studied the girl's face with a new interest. Isla was an unusual name, too. Yet it suited her. There was something of the Viking about her, in her blonde hair and blue eyes, something of the stranger in her bearing. Abruptly, Andrew made up his mind.

'If you continue as you have been doing, Mrs Duthie, taking food and shelter when you can find it and, when you cannot, doing without them, that poor child of yours will have more than a mild cough. As for yourself, you look weak enough as it is and the weather at this time of year can turn treacherous. Today, you will come home with me. I have a woman, Mrs Mutch, who sees to my simple needs. She will make you up a pallet bed in the kitchen where you will at least be warm and dry until such time as you can find lodgings in the town. You will be looking for work?' It was as much a statement as a question and required no answer. 'Then you will do so the more easily from a fixed dwelling place. Would you like me to inquire among my acquaintances for a position for you?'

Dr Noble seemed to assume that she sought domestic work rather than work among the fish and, accepting his decision, Isla nodded and added, in a low voice whose sweetness did not escape Andrew's ears, 'Thank you, Doctor.'

'Good,' said Andrew, suddenly brisk. 'Then we will go in search of Mrs McInnes and your child. I am sure she will find some small jobs to occupy you until such time as I am free to take you home.'

It was only when he had left her in the worthy Mrs McInnes's charge that the import of his words occurred to him.

'But, after all, what else could I do?' he argued inside his head. 'I could not turn her and the child out into the street again, could I? She is not fit. Besides, my house is far too big for me now that Rachel is gone.' The thought of Rachel stilled his doubts. Rachel would surely approve of his charity and the fact that the house, before Rachel's brief visit, had been no less in size than it was now did not occur to him, nor that he had never before felt the urge to extend such personal charity to the homeless, of whom he had treated plenty in his time.

No, he decided firmly, no one could possibly dispute my decision. And it is, after all, the Sabbath day.

'Andrew is late,' said Mrs Forbes with an edge of petulance to her voice. Even a member of the Royal College of Surgeons should have the grace not to keep her fricassee waiting.

'I expect he is changing his linen, Mamma,' said Louise calmly. 'You know how scrupulous he is about such matters and after a day in the Fever Hospital he will be doubly careful, knowing how nervous you are,' she added, with a touch of mischief. Her mother's attitude to Andrew Noble amused her, combining as it did a patent wish to encourage and flatter him as the nearest thing to a suitor Louise had ever had, and an equally patent nervousness of all things medical and infectious.

'Your father will be angry,' continued Mrs Forbes, tapping with her carefully buffed fingernails on the gleaming surface of the occasional table where she had laid down her embroidery, as the clock on St Nicholas's church struck five.

Louise did not trouble to answer. They both knew the remark was a mere ritual. Mr Forbes, as like as not, had not even noticed the hour and would, as usual, have to be prised from his books and his study before the soup grew cold in the dish. Equally likely, he would arrive with his oval pince-nez still in place and not remove them till they were so steamed up he could not see his plate. All the past week Mr Ewan Forbes had been absorbed by the intricate question facing the creditors of the Treasury of Aberdeen of whom he, in company with several prominent citizens including Atholl Farquharson, was one. But Farquharson was also a client and had asked Forbes to investigate this new proposal with the utmost thoroughness. The proposal was that the town should sell various pieces of unproductive land along the new streets with the option to redeem the feu at twenty years' purchase, by cash or bonds and bills of the Treasurer. It was this last which warranted closest investigation, for both Farquharson and Forbes himself held several of those bills. The question was, was such a purchase a good investment or should they stick out for full cash payment of the moneys owed? The new streets were undoubtedly expanding. Land bought in Union Street or King Street or Union Terrace would surely gain in value? Depending, of course, on size and quality of feu. Forbes had covered pages with meticulous copperplate reckoning, balancing outlay, building costs, and estimated returns both for Farquharson's proposed investment and for his own more modest one, and on this particular Sunday had come to the conclusion that although a house in the West End did not figure in his own list of desirable attainments, it could provide a comfortable income for Louise, if not a home. If she remained unmarried, she would need it. If she married that doctor fellow he could start up a practice there, like Cadenhead and Cockerill had done in St Nicholas Street, with his own Apothecary's room for compounding medicines. Yes, the proposition seemed on the whole a good one. He would recommend the creditors to give it their consideration and make a few pertinent inquiries on his own account. He extracted the list of proposed feus from the pile of papers and, oblivious of all else, began to examine them once more, one by one.

'It is almost half past the hour,' said Mrs Forbes at last, unable to contain her annoyance a moment longer. She stabbed the needle into a harmless blue butterfly's wing and tossed aside her petit-point with an expressive 'Where *can* the wretched man be?'

'I expect he has been detained at the hospital, Mamma!' Louise herself was beginning to be anxious. It was not like Andrew to be so late without sending a word of explanation. Five or ten minutes perhaps, for they both knew people cannot be expected only to be ill at set hours, but not half an hour late. Not without sending word.

'Oh dear. You do not suppose he is *ill* do you?' Mrs Forbes had gone pale. 'The fever has been so very bad this winter and he will go in among them when really he has no need. If they are going to die they will do so without Andrew's help and if they are going to recover, the same applies. I have told him that he should keep away from infections for who is to heal the healer if *he* falls sick?'

'Yes, Mamma, but how can he be a healer, as you call him, if you will not let him near his patients?'

'Really, Louise, you always were a tiresome, argumentative child, and you know exactly what I mean.'

'I am not a child, Mamma, and I do not know what you mean at all when you deliberately contradict yourself. But I do know,' she hurried on hastily, 'that you are hungry and a little worried, and so am I.'

'Do you suppose he has forgotten? You *did* invite him, did you not?'

'Of course I did, Mamma. You know Andrew *always* comes to dine on a Sunday if he is free. I must have misunderstood the hours he is working today. I had thought it was till three, but it must have been till five.'

'Well I hope the sole is not dried to a frazzle or the capon burnt. It is difficult enough getting a bird with any flesh upon it at this time of year without having it overcooked and diminished by thoughtless . . .' her complaint trailed into silence as a bell rang loudly through the lower regions, followed by hurried steps on the stairs and the opening of the door.

'I am so sorry, Mrs Forbes. Louise, do forgive me. I am afraid I have kept you waiting.'

'We were just beginning to worry about you, dear,' said Mrs Forbes sweetly, animosity instantly forgotten. 'I do hope nothing terrible has happened at your hospital?'

'No, nothing terrible,' smiled Andrew. 'Merely time-consuming. A young mother worried about her child, that is all.'

'Then I will ring for dinner at once, if you will excuse me. Louise, bring Andrew to the dining-room while I fetch your father.' In the general bustle that followed as the four took their places at table, Louise had no time to ask about the unfortunate mother and child, and Andrew did not mention them again.

'Well, dear,' said Mrs Forbes when Andrew had taken his leave of them – a little earlier than usual, but then he had had a hard working day. 'I think it went off very well. Very well indeed. The apple pie was particularly good today. Remind me to compliment Cook. She put in exactly the right amount of cloves. I declare she added a fistful on the last occasion, purely out of spite because I had reminded her of the receipt.'

During this speech her husband rose, collected spectacles and brandy glass and disappeared into his study leaving Louise to bear the brunt of the social post-mortem. 'Well, Louise? Do you not agree? Was it not a delightful evening?'

'Yes, Mamma.' Louise was vaguely troubled, though she could not detect the cause. Had there been something said in the course of the evening, or perhaps *not* said? She puzzled over the question while her mother twittered on.

'. . . such a charming young man, though not all that young after all, but then you are getting on yourself, Louise, like it or not. Practically on the shelf in fact, by ordinary standards, and not many men will even consider a girl as old as you are, dear, as I have told you many times . . . though I suppose an elderly widower might just . . . but then we do not know any widowers, elderly or otherwise. No, I am afraid Andrew Noble is your best chance and though his work is not entirely desirable – those dreadful epidemics are so dangerous – yet he is honest and hardworking. I do declare he has a certain regard for you, Louise. I thought there was a particular sparkle in his eye this evening. Ooooh . . .' Mrs Forbes gave a high-pitched, girlish giggle of pure glee. 'Would not a spring wedding be *lovely*?' As Louise made no reply, for what could she possibly say to such inanity, her mother continued, in sterner tones, 'You had best take him while you can, Louise, before some pert young lass with an eye for an up-and-coming fellow whisks him away. Do not say I did not warn you, Louise. I declare you are not listening to me.'

'Yes I am, Mamma, though you talk ridiculous nonsense sometimes.'

'Is it ridiculous to hope that you will marry?'

'No, of course not, but . . .'

'Do you not *like* Andrew?'

'I like him very much. We are good friends with many interests in common. But that does not mean that we must marry.'

'It would for any normal couple. Why can you not be like other girls, Louise?'

'Because . . . I am sorry, Mamma. If it makes you feel any happier I admit that if I were to marry anyone, though I am not at all convinced that marriage is the only life for a woman, then it would be Andrew. Except for the small point,' she finished wryly, 'that he has not actually asked me.'

'Then we must see to it that he does,' said her mother, popping another sugar plum into her mouth. 'Now come along, dear, and get your beauty sleep.' She did not need to add, 'You will need it.'

'Sleep well,' said Andrew, closing the kitchen door. He had taken his leave early from the Forbes, claiming exhaustion and a hard day ahead on the morrow. In reality, he had been anxious to see how Mrs Duthie and her child had settled in. It was not until he had looked in on them in the darkened kitchen, insisted that Mrs Duthie take a glass of hot milk with whisky and brown sugar, and checked for her comfort that baby Pearl's temperature was still normal, that he realized he had not mentioned their presence to Louise. 'Why did I not mention it?' he asked himself as he closed the door for the night. 'After all, it is a perfectly innocent arrangement, made purely out of charity.' But he had to admit Louise might not see it as that. Mrs Forbes certainly would not. At the thought of what that woman would say Andrew blushed, in spite of the knowledge of his own rectitude, and when he carried his solitary candle from the study across the hallway to his bedroom and the simple, truckle bed, for the first time in his life he shot the bolt on the door.

The day of the launch could not have been more perfect, with a fresh-washed sky and little, scudding, puff-ball clouds, pink-tinged at the edges. The harbour water danced in the crisp March sunlight and the gulls' cries had a cheerful note to them as they congregated, greedy and hopeful, on the edges of the crowd.

The Christie shipyard had no direct access to the quayside – a fault long niggling at the back of their minds – and this time the lane which ran from yard to quay was too narrow to take the splendid, gleaming curves of the new ship. Laboriously over the past week the carpenters had worked at fashioning a rolling platform under the

56

ship's hull so that now, at a signal from Maitland whose design it was, the *Bonnie Annie* could move majestically forward, drawn by ropes and steadied by more ropes at the rear.

Rachel, in her best blue dress, cast a last look over the trestle tables which had been cleared of plans and drawing boards to make way for the bread and cheese, the side of cold beef and the flagons of ale which were to mark the new ship's launch. Abercrombie had given the beef, as he had for the launching of their first ship, the *Steadfast*, and a firkin of whisky in which to toast the new ship's future. Rachel had spread bleached sailcloth over the trestles and, to mark the happiness of the occasion, had sent the youngest Brand children in search of snowdrops or wild daffodils. The daffodils they brought her and which they assured her solemnly had come from the woods above the Don, looked too sleek and plump for wild ones, their golden trumpets rich as butter and their scent as delicate as French perfume. But Rachel would not spoil the day by ferreting out which of the gardens of Ferryhill or Union Terrace had been plundered for her benefit. Instead, she gave the children a penny each, put the flowers in what jars she could find, and admired yet again the effect of their massed yellow heads and slender swords of leaves against the white cloth and the rich golds and creamy browns of her home-baked scones and loaves and bannocks, and the solid blocks of cheese. It was a good spread, wholesome and generous, a feast for the stomach as well as for the eye.

'Lovely,' murmured a voice in her ear, 'as you are.' James kissed her lightly on the cheek, but his voice and his touch, brief though they were, contained all the reassurance she needed. She smiled briefly up at her husband and nodded in agreement. 'The table looks fine. Is everything ready for the launch?'

'Aye. We're just waiting for George Abercrombie. We canna' start without him.'

'Of course not.' Abercrombie was a shareholder in the new ship, as he was in the *Steadfast*. Through the window of the building she could see the gleaming hull of the *Bonnie Annie*, curving up above the heads of what looked like the whole of North and South Squares together, come to cheer and help and give advice. Small boys were already heaving ineffectually at the ropes of the platform while Maitland, in clean shirt, formal jacket and high black hat kept a wary eye lest any of them heave too hard, and the twins, William and George, moved among them good-naturedly cuffing the more playful. Wee Alex was nowhere to be seen. Rachel was just opening her mouth to ask James where his youngest brother had got to when a movement from the timber yard beyond the *Bonnie Annie* caught her eye. She saw Wee Alex emerge, with Kirsty Guyan in her best yellow petticoats, tugging at his hand and laughing. Alex was learning fast, she thought, with a stir of unease. James followed the direction of her eyes and frowned in mock disapproval.

'We'll have to watch young Alex,' he said. 'We don't want him wearing down his health before he's even sixteen.' But there was no real censure in his voice and Rachel realized James saw Alex as a child still, harmless and innocent. Rachel herself was not so sure. Since her marriage to James, she had noticed a change in Wee Alex. Whereas before he had been her self-appointed guardian and slave, following her devotedly and almost pathetically anxious to help, since her wedding he seemed to have abdicated completely. Like a dog let off the chain, he ranged and roamed with his own kind so that half the time they did not know where he was.

But when Rachel mentioned it to James, he only

laughed. 'The lad's growing up. Besides, he is being discreet, leaving us alone together.'

Rachel thought it was more than that, but could not have explained why. It had something to do with James who had always been Wee Alex's idol, and with the life James had led before his marriage. Remembering certain incidents in that past life, Rachel thought it best not to pursue the subject, but watched Wee Alex all the same with the anxiety of an inexperienced mother.

Now, however, there was no time for anxiety of any sort except for the new ship, as a great shout went up from outside. 'Abercrombie's arrived,' said James. 'Come on.' They hurried out of the shed and into the crowd, James thrusting a way for them through the press till they were at the forefront, with the gilded figurehead of the mermaid above them and the curved splendour of the gleaming hull.

Maitland and James each took a rope at the front with Alex, while William, George and a gaggle of miniature helpers wound the staying ropes round shoulder and waist to act as brakes in the rear. Slowly the platform creaked into motion and the vessel eased forward on her first, stately journey towards the quayside and her natural element. Afterwards the company adjourned to celebrate.

'A splendid launch,' cried Abercrombie, slapping James on the back. 'Never saw a better, nor a better ship, eh, Maitland?'

Maitland Christie, the second of the Christie brothers, was the most serious and thoughtful. Fair-haired where James was dark, his clear grey eyes were sometimes tinged with green from the sea which he studded with dream ships of unbelievable speed and grace, or with blue from the faded shirt he habitually wore in the planning shed and shipyard. James might be head of the family and master of the family fleet, but Maitland was undisputed head of the planning loft.

'The *Bonnie Annie* is beautiful,' he said now, with honest pride. 'She sits the water exactly as I had expected and should handle well. But . . .' He stopped, an abstracted look in his eye.

'But ye've already thought of a better, eh lad?' supplied Abercrombie.

'No, it is not that, though I do have plans.'

'Maitland always has,' put in James, his arm round Rachel's waist.

'Then what is it, Maitland?' asked Rachel gently. She loved Maitland with the protective love of a mother or elder sister, and had a high respect for his abilities, both as craftsman and original thinker.

'Have you heard, sir, of Mr Bain's experiment in the Basin of the Caledonian canal?'

'Yon mechanical frigate?' said Abercrombie. He drank reflectively from the whisky glass in his hand. 'Aye, I've heard something. But ye'll not need to let yon iron contraptions worry ye, lad. Not wi' a ship like the *Bonnie Annie*.'

'Perhaps not,' said Maitland. 'Yet they say the model was impelled against wind and tide merely by the power of the screw. Taken to logical conclusions that would mean a ship could guarantee a passage time, given fair wind or no.'

'You mean there would be no need of sail at all?' asked Rachel.

'Apparently not. It is to be iron ships and steam,' said Maitland. 'Noisy, cumbersome and sluggish vessels, but chugging through all weathers undeterred. Or so their champions say.'

'And I say,' said James cheerfully, 'that no ships on the high seas will better ours for speed and grace, so fill your glasses everyone and let us drink a toast to the *Bonnie Annie* and the Christie fleet.'

'The Christie fleet.' The words echoed in Rachel's mind with the thrill of promise and were echoing still when the guests had gone, the table had been cleared and the debris swept away. At the quayside the *Bonnie Annie* rode at her moorings, awaiting the final fittings necessary before her maiden voyage, while at the adjoining mooring her sister ship, the *Steadfast*, waited only for her captain and crew to resume her usual London run. But William and George had thrown themselves wholeheartedly into the family celebration and it would be the morrow before James gave them clearance to put to sea.

Meanwhile, there was work to be done. While Maitland laid out his plans once more upon the tables which only an hour before had carried the launching feast, James prised Wee Alex, protesting, from his companions and repaired to the *Bonnie Annie*, with the company carpenter, to arrange the final fittings to cabin and superstructure. Rachel took up pen and paper to bring her receipts up to date. There were the carpenter's wages to enter up, the cost of the rolling platform and hausers, as well as the victuals for the launching. That done, she turned to the composition of the advertisement which would launch the *Bonnie Annie* finally on her voyage to success.

'The fine brig *Bonnie Annie*, 300 tons, newly launched from the shipyard of Christie Brothers, will be ready to take in goods by 15 April for Riga and the Baltic ports. The *Bonnie Annie* has excellent accommodation for three or four cabin passengers. Freight unusually moderate. For freight and passage apply . . .'

'No.' James's hand came down over the writing and covered the page. Startled, Rachel looked up at him, but

61

before she could speak, he had taken the pen from her hand and drawn a thick, black line across the page.

'But why?' she protested. 'What have I done wrong? It is the correct form of advertisement surely, and . . .'

'No,' he repeated firmly, but his mismatched eyes were sparkling now with private mirth. 'And take that solemn expression off your face, Mrs Christie. You are not a shipping clerk today, but my wife. Besides, the *Bonnie Annie* will not sail to Riga.'

'Not sail?' Rachel was aghast. 'But I thought you said she was for the Baltic trade. Why, I have already secured orders for best Rhine hemp and . . .'

'Next time, Rachel, when the ice has melted. Ye wouldna' want us frozen, now, would ye? The ice of the Neva's not yet broken up. The Commander of the Fort sends a glass o' its melted water to the Imperial Palace, Rachy, to announce when navigation is open. That'll be a month yet and Riga's mighty cold.'

'But the *Flora* is daily expected from Riga. I read it in . . .' James stopped her with a finger on her lips.

'I might have known that I couldna' fool you, Rachy. Ye'll be telling me next that Riga isna' St Petersburg and the Dvina isna' the Neva. But ye can put off your orders for hemp and flax till next time. After London.'

'But the *Steadfast* is for the London run.'

'Rachel, will ye forget the business for five minutes and listen to me, you exasperating wee woman? Have you forgotten I promised you that when the *Bonnie Annie* was launched, I would take you with me? I know I said to Mandalay or Rio, but will London do to begin with?'

'London? You mean I am to sail with you? But . . .'

'No buts, Rachel. It will be our honeymoon – a little late, perhaps, but none the worse for that. And if it makes you feel any better about it, you can regard it as a test. After all, you would not want to advertise "excellent accommodation" unless you had sampled it yourself, would you?'

'But are you sure, James? Really sure? You are not superstitious about having women aboard?'

'Who mentioned women? The captain's wife is a different matter. No, Rachel, you need not worry,' he reassured her. 'The men will be glad to have you aboard, at least the victuals might improve, and as for Alex, you can help me keep an eye on him, the wee devil.'

'And Maitland?' asked Rachel anxiously. 'Will he be all right alone?'

'If by "all right" you mean will he eat regular meals and put on clean linen, probably not. On the other hand, if "all right" means contented, he will be in his element with no one to interrupt his work and tell him it is time to stop.'

'And what of the shipyard and the bookings for freight?' Rachel handled all that side of the enterprise as well as running the household of menfolk and looking after their linen, knitting their jerseys and stockings and any other garments they might need. In the past, before the *Steadfast* was built, she had also collected mussels from the shore, baited the lines for the small line fishing, helped unload the catch and taken creels of fish to market every day, as well as looking after James's dottled mother and the house. She had never known idleness in the whole span of her nineteen years and could not imagine it now. But James would not be moved. 'Maitland will take care of everything till our return.'

This London voyage was important to him, not only as a trial run of the new Christie ship, and a business visit to suppliers in the capital, but as a token of his commitment to Rachel and to marriage – and as an atonement for the past. Besides, he was looking forward to it. During the weeks since their wedding he had grown to depend on their intimacy and, though he loved the sea with a true sailor's devotion, the company of his wife to admire his seamanship, to supervise the galley, to bring her fine, practical mind to bear on the small details necessary to turn an ordinary cabin into an excellent one, and, most of all, to warm his bed, was something that would make the *Bonnie Annie*'s maiden voyage perfect. Besides, it was only appropriate. They had named the new ship for his mother, and it had been his mother's dying wish that he and Rachel should marry.

'Dinna' ask another question,' he said now as Rachel still looked anxious. 'Or I declare I will take Mrs Abercrombie instead. She at least would be glad of the chance to see London, if only to boast about it to her fine friends.'

'I am sorry, James. I did not mean to question your decision. I meant only that it is such a . . . such a huge undertaking for me. After all, I have never been in a ship, not even our little fishing boat, and the farthest I have travelled in my life is from Cove to Aberdeen. I cannot begin to imagine London. It must be vast and frightening and full of strange sights.'

'It is,' teased James. 'But soon you will see for yourself. We will be five days at sea. I hope for less than five if the *Bonnie Annie* is as speedy as Maitland promises she will be; then a week or more in London while we make various trading arrangements. I want to introduce you to our London representative and I thought we might visit Vauxhall if you would like to.'

Rachel's eyes were shining now with excitement and wonder. 'Oh James, I should like it more than anything in the world.' Into her memory had come stories of her childhood, fables of far places which she and Andrew had read together in the candlelight of their cottage in Cove, with other tales, told round the Fittee fireside by James's father – and a memory of her arrival on the quayside all those years ago, amid bales and packets which had exuded to her child's mind all the tantalizing scents and splendours of the East. London, to be sure, was not the East, but it was far enough distant to be strange and full of promise. Forgetting in her eagerness, she looked up at her husband with grey eyes full of trust and excitement. 'James, are you really sure?'

'I said, no questions,' said James sternly, 'except for one which I will answer for you. We sail within the month.'

They passed the *Steadfast* in the roads off Cromer and the cheer of greeting came sweetly over the dividing waters. On both ships the azure and emerald pennant of the Christie line with its silver 'C' dipped and rose again in salute as the two mermaid figureheads ploughed onwards, the smaller, painted one northwards and the newer, gold-leafed one south towards the Thames.

'She's made good time,' said James with approval, his eyes following the neat lines of the *Steadfast* as her sails filled on the eastern tack. He and Rachel stood on the foredeck. 'William is a good Master, I think, though with George at his side the greater part of the day it would be hard to say which of the two is Master and which Mate.'

'Have you ever thought, James,' said Rachel idly, 'what would happen if circumstances required that one or other sail alone?'

'George without William?' James looked at her in astonishment. 'William without George? Impossible.' But her question had disquieted him. Suppose one or other of the twins were injured or ill, would the other sail alone? And if he did, would he be competent? James's eye sought out the figure of his youngest brother Alex, who was taking his turn at the wheel, and regarded him with new seriousness. He was a good sailor, but young and inexperienced, flighty too of late, and a mite heedless. James turned towards Rachel who was leaning on the guard rail beside him, her face to the wind and her cheeks pink with health and happiness. After the first two days of uncertainty when tipping deck and rocking sea seemed to affect head and lungs and stomach alike, and had left her white-faced and anxious, one eye continually on the guard rail or the nearest bucket, she had found what James called her 'sea legs' and had sprung to life again, with all of her old vigour, darting here and there, inspecting every inch of the ship from bilges to crow's nest and from prow to stern. She had noted the position of every item of equipment in the tiny galley and moved what needed moving for convenience or safety. She had tested every fitment of the cabin she shared with James and which was, in future trips, to be the State cabin, had summoned the ship's carpenter to add a ledge here, to prevent her hairbrush and other toilet articles sliding to the floor, or to put up hooks there for this and that. But with the panelled bed she could find no fault, especially when she and James were safe inside it and the beautifully wrought folding doors were firmly shut on their privacy.

Remembering her love, her competence and her sweet, unfailing loyalty, James said softly, 'Rachel, I hope we have many sons.'

'And I.' Rachel did not need to look at him to see the tenderness in his eyes or the remembrance of shared love. It flowed over her in his voice, to fill her with the familiar glow. His arm circled her shoulder, so small under his muscular strength, and he drew her closer. 'Do you remember my father, Rachel? I promised him to look after you all when he died. He thought no further than the fishing, but I thought even then of wider horizons. Ships of our own, trading the high seas, and more ships, made to order, for sale and profit. I still see it, Rachel. I mean to have a ship for every Christie man one day, for I'll have only Christies as Masters in my fleet and when we have sons, they must have ships too.'

Together they gazed at the green, foam-flecked billows, the darker, swirling troughs of trailing spume, flashing where sunlight caught bubble, or gleaming like curved and polished steel and, in the distance, where sea met sky, the glorious grandeur of massed clouds. But the clouds were not threatening – Rachel, too, was beginning to learn sea lore – and the wind was clean and strong. In their minds' eyes both saw that empty sea peopled with ships, at each masthead the Christie pennant and at each helm a Christie son.

'What do you think of Alex?' asked James suddenly, breaking the reverie.

'Think of him?' Rachel was surprised. She turned to look behind her to the wheelhouse and the tall, lean figure of Alex, his blond hair tousled by the wind, his cheeks still beardless and pink now, as a girl's. But his eyes were on the sea ahead, his feet planted firm, and there was confidence in every line of his youthful body. 'Alex is a dear boy, affectionate and loyal, growing a little too fast for his strength perhaps, but he seems healthy enough and . . .'

'No. I meant as a seaman and a responsible one. Do you see him as a ship's captain?'

'But he is not yet sixteen,' protested Rachel, laughing. 'You would not expect a lad at his age to be responsible, surely?' And yet . . . She thought of his brothers and of Davy, now dead. He, at sixteen, would have shouldered any burden cheerfully and well. 'Perhaps it is because Alex is the youngest,' she faltered and added, teasing, 'He obviously feels he can leave responsibility to his big brother now.' And yet, she thought with a stir of unease, perhaps Alex is kicking his heels a little too high?

James seemed to read her thoughts. 'I expect him to be responsible enough to keep out of mischief,' he said and added, with the air of a burdened father, 'especially in port.'

But when they finally reached Tilbury exactly five days and two hours after leaving Aberdeen, there was too much to occupy all of them in the first twenty-four hours after their arrival for high spirits of any kind. When the routine business of harbour dues and pilotage had been disposed of, there was the unloading of the cargo they had brought from Aberdeen – mostly salt fish and stockings on the first trip – and the reloading of an order of dried fruit and tobacco for Abercrombie's shop. There were the inevitable teething troubles of the new ship's handling to be sorted out, and James and the ship's carpenter spent hours discussing to a fraction of an inch the positioning of a cleat or the exact length of a spar, while Alex supervised the unloading and reloading and the redistribution of ballast, and the crewmen not otherwise occupied touched up any paintwork still to be done or holystoned the deck. Rachel busied herself with her own and James's linen, hanging the clean clothes from a line on deck and re-stocking the galley with fresh food. When no immediate job required her attention, she watched the fascinating panorama of the river traffic and the great, crouching mass of London city.

They were moored below London Bridge, near Billingsgate where they had unloaded a cargo of salt herring for the market, with constant noise and movement all around them. The river traffic included ships such as Rachel had never seen before: river barges, tug boats, every kind of schooner and, as they had sailed past the East India docks, East Indiamen of 500 tons and more, their masts and yards like a winter forest, their canvas together enough to cover at least a hundred bleaching greens. There were figureheads of every kind and colour, and more incomprehensible tongues than Rachel dreamed existed – Lascars and Portuguese with earrings and gaudy neck-cloths, Madagascans, Philippinos, Chinese, and one day she saw a negro. She had heard talk of negros at home in Aberdeen. Someone knew someone who had a negro servant somewhere in the country, and someone in South Square had been to Jamaica where everyone, he said, was black. The foreigners were strange enough to her naive, untravelled eyes, but the Londoners were more so – little, quick-silver people of laughter and ready wit, with a patois incomprehensible as Hindustani. The costumes were fascinating, too, especially on the womenfolk. Rachel had not known such styles existed. Though, in spite of the different styles and materials, she recognized the gaudy finery of the dockland ladies instantly for what it was.

But at last all the varied business transactions were completed and James announced a holiday for all but two of the crew who must stay aboard to keep watch. To Rachel he said only, 'Put on your best gown, Rachy, and look out my wedding shirt, the one you stitched for me.' Both garments had been carefully folded and packed into one of the panelled chests in their cabin, with James's tall hat and Rachel's best plaid. 'We might have important clients to impress,' James had said, teasing, when Rachel had protested that sea water and salt air could be harmful. Now she shook the garments carefully from their folds, smoothed any creases and dusted imaginary specks from the black hat which all self-respecting ship's masters wore, certainly in the port of Aberdeen.

James took an unusually long time dressing. Normally he regarded clothes merely as necessary adjuncts to work, to be donned and removed with little ceremony and all speed. Now, he insisted that Rachel wear her cameo brooch and her best lace collar.

'But James, it is not the King we are visiting, surely?'

'My wife and I,' said James solemnly, 'are to take a glass coach and see the sights of London town. Then we will visit Vauxhall gardens and finally a theatre.'

'But are you sure we can afford it?' Rachel laid a gentle hand on his arm. 'You know the trip itself is adventure enough for me, and just to be with you. I need no more.'

'Do as you are told, woman,' said James with mock severity, 'and put on your finery. Not because ye need it – ye've adornment enough in your fine eyes and shining hair – but because we'll nae give these Londoners any cause to say we dinna' ken what's what.' With a final, approving glance he ushered her up the companionway and out on deck into the crisp April sunlight and a sea-laced breeze.

'Mind and behave yourself, Alex,' warned James. 'There's sharks in every water, and mostly female ones.'

'I'm well acquaint wi' London, Jamie,' swaggered Alex, thumbs in the waist-band of his trousers and feet spread in an attitude of confident masculinity. 'Have ye forgotten I've been here a dozen times and more wi' the *Steadfast*? Ye dinna' need to worry about me.'

'Mind and watch the company ye keep,' warned James and added, behind Rachel's back, 'and keep away from the whorehouses.'

The day passed for Rachel in a dream. The Tower of London was a wonder beyond imagining, especially as James insisted they pay the entrance money and walk about inside, to see the Tower Green where Anne Boleyn's head had rolled, and the ravens strutting. They saw the haunted terrace and the little cell where Sir Walter Raleigh was imprisoned, and they looked over the solid stone battlements of Traitor's Gate on to the sluggish, murky waters of the Thames.

'Is it not dirty?' said Rachel, with distaste, 'compared to the Dee at home?' James laughed and lapsed into dialect.

'Ye sound like a wee country quinie,' he teased, 'who's nivver been oot o' her ain kailyard.'

'Well, I am sae and I havena',' she retorted, 'and I'm nae ashamed neither, to say as much. But I find it all very strange and wondrous,' she went on, tucking her hand under James's arm. 'You have travelled to London a score of times, but it is all new to me. I never dreamed of so many buildings and people. But the river is as big a marvel as anything,' she went on, when James paid for two tickets for a trip on a penny steamer to Greenwich and Blackwall.

'Aye. 'Tis the shipping I like to see. You see yon fine East Indiaman?' he went on as they reached Blackwall and the East India Docks. 'See the line o' the bows and the stern. I reckon our Maitland can fine that down one day to something faster, more elegant and still wi' room enough for the tea chests and the spices.'

'I like the river barges,' confessed Rachel, 'like wee houses on the water.'

'That's the homemaker in you. But if you would like to cast your eye over this one for any feature we could adapt for our own ships, tell me, love. We must work together now, even more than before, if we are to make Christie Brothers into a shipping company of any size.'

That was the theme of all their sightseeing, realized Rachel, as they strolled through Vauxhall Gardens, noting the elaborate fashions and exotic refreshments of the '*beau monde*'.

'There's Indian silks, Rachy, and jewels from Ceylon, China tea and sherbet, chocolate from the West Indies, coffee from Kenya, and Turkish delight. Think, Rachel, here in London our own porridge and herring and good roast beef are all fine enough, but they are nothing to the commerce of the Port of London. With a fast ship and a capacious hold, we can play our part. We can introduce variety and luxury to the burghers of Aberdeen, with the town expanding and the businessmen building grand houses for themselves, they will need grand clothes for the ladies and grander food for their guests. We will bring our stockings and granite, our salt fish and whisky and our fine linen cloth and barter them for all the exotic spices and sweetmeats Abercrombie ever dreamed of, with brandy and claret and fine silks.'

'But for that, James, ye'll need to sail to the Indian Ocean, surely, and the China Seas? Do you mean to sail the *Bonnie Annie* so far away?' Rachel's happiness trembled at the idea of such a long and dangerous journey.

'No, my love, not the *Bonnie Annie*. She's a fine wee ship, but she's for Riga and the Baltic trade. No, I mean the next one. But this is supposed to be a holiday,' he said, grinning. 'What would you say to a cup of chocolate? In a real London chocolate house?'

'Yes, please,' said Rachel, catching his mood, and when James hailed a passing horse-drawn cab and asked the cabby to take them to the best, she did not ask 'Can we afford it?' or even think the words. James was right. A honeymoon was a unique occasion and she might never visit London again. It was past midnight when they took the last cab to the wharf and, arm in arm, walked the last stretch of quay to the *Bonnie Annie* in the echoing silence of the sleeping river. There was a riding light on the *Bonnie Annie*'s stern and a glow from the cabin window.

'All's well,' said the watchman as they stepped aboard.

'Good,' said James with a relief which did not escape Rachel's notice as they made their way below decks.

'It was a lovely day,' said Rachel when they were in their own cabin, the oil lamp burning and the shutters closed across the port holes. The night was shut out and with it the glint of moonlight on water, the gleam and shadow of the wharf, and here and there a glow of light from some late-burning candle, or a watchman's lantern. In the cabin, lamplight was reflected from polished panelling in a warm, dark glow. Rachel reached up to unpin her hair which tumbled thick about her shoulders to reach almost to her waist.

'Here, let me,' said James softly and took the brush from her hand, drawing it slowly through the thick hair with long, lingering strokes. 'Such a lovely sheen, like polished elm,' he murmured, 'or that new batch o' larch wood we bought for Maitland's new venture.'

'Do you ever forget the shipyard?' teased Rachel, looking into his eyes in the mahogany framed mirror on the chest.

'No. And nor do you,' retorted James. 'Who was it pricing everything in sight today? Who was it asking which ports shipped madeira or Brussels lace or sugared almonds? Why, even the orange I bought you wasn't sacred, and as for the chocolate . . .'

Rachel laughed. 'Well, you said yourself we might send a ship to the West Indies one day.'

'Aye, but first we must sail for Aberdeen, so come to bed, wife, before it's time to rise again.' But as he reached to unbutton his shirt, a thought struck him. 'I reckon I'll just check . . .' The *Bonnie Annie* was a new vessel, still with the bloom of novelty upon her. It would add the final pleasure to his day to see her safe to bed. 'I'll not be long, my love.'

So James made the round of his ship once more in the sleeping darkness, laying a loving hand on the polished wood of bulkhead and beam, feeling the crisp strength of furled canvas on yardarm, scenting the fresh oakum and the sharp tang of new rope. The river smelt dank and laced with seaweed from the glimmering mudflats of low tide, and from a neighbouring ship came the gentle creak of timbers stirring with the movement of the water.

'All is well,' he breathed and turned for a last word with the watchman. Then, as an idle afterthought, asked what time Alex had come aboard. The watchman did not know. 'Weren't my watch,' he said. 'Must ha' been before.'

But when James opened the door of the rear bulkhead where Alex had his bunk, it was to see that the only occupant was the youngest member of the crew, a boy from the Square, fast asleep. James frowned and when a quick poll count had ascertained that young Alex had indeed not returned, the pleasure of the day evaporated in anxiety and anger. It would not be the first time a young man, let ashore for the evening, had not returned. What with press gangs, loose women, and the dangers of gangplanks to unsteady feet, the hazards were many. For a seaman to fall drunk into the harbour and drown was commonplace.

'Where is the young fool?' muttered James, but to Rachel he said only, 'No matter. He will be here shortly and as long as he is aboard in good time for the tide, there's no harm done.'

But the harm was done. For neither James nor Rachel could sleep in spite of their tiredness, until the sound of distant singing, hastily shushed, the noise of someone climbing clumsily aboard and almost immediately falling, of smothered laughter and female jeers from the shore, and of muttered oaths from close at hand, assured them that Alex was indeed home. They had just slipped wearily into sleep when the sound of distant snoring rose to a reverberating crescendo which seemed to shake every

74

plank in the ship. They lay awake for five minutes, hoping it would stop, till James could stand it no longer. 'I will strangle him,' he growled, 'the young fool.' Pulling his shirt over his head, he went out of the cabin, through saloon and galley to the aft quarters. There he found Alex blissfully inert, mouth open, shirt awry, blond hair dishevelled, the sound of his breathing rasping with splendid resonance from the curved sounding board of the hull at his head. James leaned close and straightened again in disgust. 'Rum,' he told Rachel, when he had pushed the boy, none too gently, on to his side to still the snoring and had returned to his cabin. 'And more than one man's ration.'

'Never mind, James,' said Rachel softly, drawing him close. 'At least he is aboard and not . . .' She did not need to finish the sentence.

'Aye,' agreed James grimly. 'But he'll have a head in the morning, I'll warrant, as'll make him wish he'd never set foot ashore. And so, I fear, will we if we do not sleep Remember we sail tomorrow for home.'

Rachel was glad to be going home, fascinating though London had been. She was anxious to see Maitland and the twins, to hear how the business had fared while they were away, to check on the *Steadfast*'s profits and to see their own wee cottage again.

Yet when the *Bonnie Annie* slipped her hawsers and put out into midstream, she could not resist one backward glance. 'Sorry to leave?' asked James at her side. He stood, feet firmly planted, hands steady on the wheel and his eyes on the sea ahead.

'No,' said Rachel truthfully. 'Not at all sorry. I leave regrets to Wee Alex!'

'They'll be on their way home by now,' said Abercrombie, rubbing his hands with satisfaction. He was in the back room of the house in Guestrow, the room he called his office and where he kept the big, leather-bound account books of his expanding trade. 'Aye,' he went on as Fenton made no answer, 'We'll know soon enough what speed the new vessel's capable of and how she handles, but I reckon Maitland was right. She'll be as good as the *Steadfast* and better. He was telling me only this morning he's got more orders than he can cope with at yon wee yard o' his and that when James is back, they mean to look for a bigger. Good lads both.' When his son still did not speak, Abercrombie lost patience. 'Well, don't just sit there, fiddling wi' yon pen. Or has the cat stolen your tongue and your wits with it?'

'I was thinking,' said Fenton slowly. 'You know there is talk in Glasgow and Edinburgh of a vessel to be driven not by the power of the wind, but by a metal screw? Perhaps that is where the future lies and not with Maitland's sailing ships, however swift they be.'

'Nonsense, lad. The wind is *free*. Dinna' forget that. Yon new contraption needs to carry its own fuel wi' it and there goes your cargo space straight off. No, lad, a great, noisy, smelly device it sounds to me, power or no, and I'd back Maitland's designs against any o' yon West Coast inventions any day. But it's not that I want your advice on today, lad. It's this land the town's offering on advantageous terms. I'm wondering if we'll maybe buy ourselves a stance in Union Street after all, if we can find a piece to suit. There's a feu opposite Diamond Street at four shillings the foot of frontage, or a bigger, more expensive piece near Correction Wynd. We need something wi' a good frontage to catch the townsfolk's eye, but I reckon we need to cater not just for the West End gentry, but for the country folk on a visit to the city and for the ordinary townsfolk too – the honest tradesman wi' money to spend and a taste for something a bit better than tatties and salt herring. Though dinna' get me wrong, Fenton. Ye'd hae to gang far to beat a good salt herring. I mind well when I was a lad my Ma would . . .'

Fenton ceased to listen. He knew his father's reminiscing almost *verbatim*, for tales of the wholesome simplicity of life before Abercrombie had made money and prospered had been told often before, usually when Abercrombie's profits were less than expected, or he suspected someone had swindled him, or he was feeling dyspeptic from his wife's fancy cooking ideas, or just plain hungry. So Fenton followed his own train of thought as, with the surface of his mind, he continued to check one column of figures in the 'Tobacco' book against another.

As always the subject of his private worrying was his wife. Jessica was becoming impossibly awkward as her pregnancy advanced and this latest demand of hers – that his friend Andrew Noble attend her instead of the family doctor – was not new to him. She had demanded Andrew for her first pregnancy. That time Fenton had overruled her, but Jess had brought more powerful arguments to bear on the subject this time. McKinnon was past his best, whereas Andrew Noble was an up-and-coming doctor in touch with the newest medical developments – and when Augusta was born, had not Jessica been so weak and sore afterwards that she'd been ill for months? Fenton was not sure about the choice of words, for Jessica had recovered her health quickly enough. But if 'ill' meant not able to share her bed with her husband, then that was true. Perhaps, for everyone's peace of mind, it might be best if he spoke to Andrew?

'. . . the Baltic trade. Danzig Willy made a fortune and there's nae reason why we shouldna' do the same. What do you think, Fenton?'

With an effort, Fenton brought his mind back to the

77

business of shipping. 'What exactly had you in mind, Father?'

'What *exactly*? Why, I've just been telling ye, ye cloth-eared *gowk*!' Abercrombie thumped the table in exasperation before taking a long, slow breath of exaggerated patience. Then, slowly and clearly, as if speaking to an idiot, he said, 'We will invest in another ship. We will trade with the Baltic ports. We will sell them our goods and bring back theirs. We will make a profit. *Now* do you understand?'

'Yes, Father. But had you forgotten Atholl Farquharson? You know he has established links all the way from Rotterdam to St Petersburg. It is a profitable run, to be sure, but his ships already have the trade and he is not a man to brook competition.'

'No.' Unaccountably, Abercrombie giggled. 'But had ye forgotten when he tried to keep the Christie ship off the London run he didna' succeed? Nor when he tried to block the launch o' the *Bonnie Annie*? Though how they wangled permission to cross Dixon's patch against Farquharson's express orders I'll never know.'

'No,' agreed Fenton, though he had a niggling suspicion that his own wife Jessica had been mixed up in the business somehow. 'But Farquharson has not forgotten or forgiven, and he is a powerful man. Did you know he is thinking of ordering a steam-driven ship for the London run?'

'Let him throw his money away on machinery that breaks down every five minutes if he's a mind to, and boilers that tear their rivets apart and blow up. No one in their right mind would choose to travel in such a dangerous, stinking, noisy contraption when they can sail with speed and safety in a ship like the *Bonnie Annie*.'

'Maybe not, Father. Not yet anyway. But one day there may come a time when the mechanical problems have

78

been sorted, when folk want reliability, whatever the weather. Napier's steam packet boat is crossing regularly now between Greenock and Belfast.'

'Aye, wi' the ship so full o' coal for yon boilers that there's nae room for cargo and the smoke blowing such a load o' black soot over everybody that they disembark looking like a tribe o' blackamoors.'

'But it is steady and reliable, Father.'

'Aye, till it blows up. And it'll be a wee whilie yet afore yon steam-packets get as far as Riga, whereas the *Bonnie Annie*'ll fly swift as a bird, and back again, wi' not a single piece o' coal to pay for.' At that moment the door burst open and Maitland's excited face appeared in the gap.

'She's in! Sighted off the Girdleness a half-hour ago and at the harbour mouth now.'

'Come on, Fenton lad,' said Abercrombie, slamming the ledger closed. 'We'll away to the Quay to see her berth.' With a bellow of 'Mind the shop,' in the general direction of the two assistants, he followed Maitland out into the fresh breeze of the Guest Row, Fenton at his heels.

But in spite of the excitement and the hurry, Fenton's mind was still struggling with the question of his wife and as the three passed under the window of Atholl Farquharson's office in the Shiprow, on their way to the Quay, he was reminded again of the rivalry between Christies and Farquharsons and of his own unhappy position between the two. With his father a major shareholder in the Christie ships and his sister married to Farquharson's son, there was conflict enough, but add a rebellious and capricious wife with her finger in both pies and the situation became impossibly complicated and difficult.

But there was one positive thing he could do: speak to Andrew at the first opportunity and ask him to accept Jessica, with himself and little Augusta, as his patients.

At the thought of Augusta his brow cleared. At least his little daughter was happy, loving and uncomplicated.

The *Bonnie Annie* was not the only ship to berth in the port of Aberdeen that day. A large, handsome vessel, the *Dumbarton Castle*, steam-boat, commanded by Captain Robson from Glasgow, in seven days north about, arrived with passengers bound for Leith and caused a minor sensation in the shipbuilding world.

In spite of their averred loyalty to sail, Maitland and James studied the new vessel as avidly as Atholl Farquharson himself from the discretion of his leather-topped gig. Registering 108 tons, she had an engine of thirty-two horses' power, rumour had it, and consumed three-and-a-half tons of coal in twenty-four hours.

'Expensive,' commented Maitland. 'And dirty,' added James, looking at the sparkling paint and varnish of the *Bonnie Annie*. Yet both men were unusually preoccupied: it was common knowledge by sundown that the steam-boat was intended as a packet between Leith and Grangemouth and occasionally between Leith and Aberdeen. If the venture were to be successful, and spread to other routes, they would have to offer a faster and better service under sail – or turn to steam themselves. In the evening shadows, the planning loft was redolent of pine-wood, varnish and newly sawn timber. On the walls were the half-models of the *Steadfast* and the *Bonnie Annie*, with those of future ships the Christie yard planned to build, and the newest, Maitland knew, would be the best by far. As he ran a hand slowly over the elegant curves of his latest ship's model, Maitland had no doubt where his future lay. In the larger seclusion of his study in the West End of town, neither had Atholl Farquharson.

* * *

The *Bonnie Annie* herself was still not rigged entirely to James's satisfaction. After that first London trip, he and Maitland went to work on the set of the main topgallant and royal, for James had feared the strain on the spars was too great; then, when he was ready to test her new rigging in a firm wind, they struck a week of calm when heat shimmered up from the baking sand and not a blade stirred on the headland. New potatoes, green peas, cherries and strawberries appeared miraculously early in the Friday market. James spotted the latter from the doorway of the Athenaeum Reading Room where he had been checking the shipping notes and also, in passing, gleaned a report of the christening of the Duchess of Kent's little princess, Alexandrina Victoria. Impulsively, thinking of his own heir-to-be, he bought a punnet of the scarlet berries to give to Rachel and when she protested, said only, 'There's yon wee princess in London christened in a gold font wi' velvet coverings and a dinner "numerous and splendid" and ye grudge our ain wee bairn a dish o' strawberries? Fi, woman, where's your loyalty?' and Rachel had acquiesced. But the calm passed and a fair wind followed. James and Alex, with their hand-picked crew, took the *Bonnie Annie* to London in five and a half days and back again in an hour under five.

'Not good enough yet,' agreed James and Maitland, 'but we'll find no better set to the sails till she's tried her wings in the Baltic.'

It was agreed that the *Bonnie Annie* should sail for Riga in August.

'I'll investigate the timber market while I'm there,' said James, 'And maybe take a look at St Petersburg, for the future. But that will depend on the trade we get.'

Rachel set about advertising in the *Aberdeen Journal* for freight and lastage, though with a heavy heart. Riga seemed so far away. She had visited the Reading Room secretly, sought out an atlas and traced the route the *Bonnie Annie* would take, east across the North Sea to Skagerrak, round the north tip of Denmark and south to Kattegat and the Sound, then east again into the Baltic sea and north-eastwards to the Gulf of Riga – such a long, unknown and dangerous journey. Last month she had read of a ship for Riga totally lost on her way home: the mate and four crew were saved by a Norwegian vessel, but the master was drowned. The idea of that poor, drowned captain lodged in her mind and would not give her peace.

Since her pregnancy she had found herself waking in the night with sudden, paralysing fears so that she lay wide-eyed and trembling, heart painfully thudding and hands clenched till the grey shades of death and dreadful, un-named injury paled and parted. Then her hand would steal gently across the bed to find James and in the sleeping warmth beside her she found reassurance. But it was not only in sleep that such fears came. She had only to hear a snatch of conversation '. . . Farquharson's ships . . .' 'a record profit on the Riga run . . .', or 'found off Cairnbulg point without a soul aboard . . .' to fill out that scrap with horrifying detail of treachery or shipwreck, the pounding of seas against rock and the gurgling terrors of drowning. The debris of a ship was reported off Westray in the Orkneys and included in the wreckage at high water line was a piece of painted board bearing an ornamented 'A'. In a moment Rachel had supplied the name of *Bonnie Annie*, seen James's seaboots among the flotsam, and even a lifeless, sea-bloated body with 'J. C.' stitched inside the shirt. She told herself it was imagination, told herself it was the result of changes in her body as the baby grew, told herself over and over that such fears were manufactured inside her own head, not sent as warnings from beyond.

But her secret midnight fears were not her only worry. Farquharson's ships had been working the Baltic run for years and seemed to have practically a monopoly – or else Farquharson was deliberately working to block their venture on every side. She had to work harder than ever to secure orders and then to pare their profit margin down to the bone. The alternative was to fill the space themselves and trust to finding a market for whatever they chose to export and import. It would be a gamble and one that required an outlay they could ill afford, but to sail to the Baltic on ballast alone was out of the question. Rachel thought often of the simple, bygone days before the family fishing boat gave way to the little shipyard and the coastal trading. They had been poor then, true enough, but they needed only their own strength and skill to serve them, not the co-operation and support of a group of Aberdeen traders, all anxious to make the maximum profit for the minimum outlay. It took Rachel hours of patient persuasion to secure every square foot of freight and she grew increasingly tired. Yet in spite of these financial and emotional anxieties and her growing and irrational fear of the sea, when the eve of the day set for the *Bonnie Annie*'s voyage arrived, she begged once more, 'Take me with you, James? Please?' If the mission was to be a failure, then they would fail together, and she would rather drown with her husband, if she could not save him, than live on alone.

But James was adamant. 'Your job is here, Rachel, to keep hearth and home – and cradle – safe till my return. I shall think of you often, my love, in our wee cottage in the Square, but I want to remember you valiant and smiling, with no tears in those lovely eyes. No tears, remember?' With a huge effort of self-control, Rachel nodded, but James lifted her chin with a forefinger and looked into her blurred eyes with new concern.

'You are not ill, Rachel? Or in pain? Is there something you have not told me?' There was anxiety in his voice now. 'Something about the child?'

'No.' Seeing the trouble in James's face, Rachel was ashamed of her weakness. 'Nothing, James. It is just that . . . that I will miss you.' She buried her face in his breast and clung to him in a brief intensity of parting.

'Do not be troubled, Rachy, on my account. Promise me? I will be back again swift as the wind . . .' *Or may my boat be a bonnet to me*. Rachel heard the unspoken words clear as a warning bell in her brain and shuddered, but she lifted a bravely smiling face to receive her husband's farewell kiss. He, in company with Alex and the crew, was to sleep aboard tonight and sail with the early tide.

But, early though it was, Rachel was on the headland to see them sail. James, turning to look back, as he had done so often over the years, saw the straight, brave figure in the pale dress raise a hand in farewell. As always, the sight warmed his heart and lifted the corners of his mouth in a secret smile. It was a long and unknown passage to Riga but Rachel would wait for him. She would guard his house and hearth till he returned – and his little, unborn son.

August 1819

'Dr Noble! Andrew! Come *on* man, will ye?' William and George thundered on the door of the doctor's house till every rafter in the little building shook and from somewhere in the back region came the high-pitched wail of a child, woken suddenly from sleep. The door opened a crack to reveal a young woman in an apron, her hands and forearms white with flour.

'What is it ye want? The doctor's sleeping.'

'At this hour? But it's midday, woman.'

'He was up all night. He doesna' want to be disturbed.' She made to close the door, but William put his foot against it.

'They sent us here frae the hospital to find him.' George added a shoulder and the next moment both men were over the threshold, their height dwarfing both woman and room. 'Andrew!' called the two together, hammering on the wood of the bedroom door. 'Come away out, man. Rachel needs ye.'

There was the noise of a bolt being drawn, then the latch lifted and Andrew's head appeared in the gap between door jamb and door. Behind him the room was darkened by closed shutters and his face was confused with sleep, his hair awry. 'Rachel?' he repeated then, as the information sank in, '*Rachel?* What's amiss?'

'We dinna' ken.'

'She was in the Pocra yard wi' Maitland . . .'

'Then she came to the Quay . . .'

'Wi' the mannie wi' the salt herring . . .'

'And she was standing there like she aye does, supervising . . .'

'Then she put her hand to her head, wi' a little groan . . .'

'And fell . . .'

'Smack on to the cassies and naebody to catch her . . .'

'So we sent a lad for Maitland and we carried her home.'

'Maitland's wi' her now, but *hurry*, man.'

All the time the duet was in spate Andrew had been tossing on his clothes so that by the time the twins paused for breath, he was fastening the last button and running a smoothing hand through his hair. He took his hat from the chest, picked up his black leather bag and turned to the pale-faced girl who had been standing nervously in the doorway to the back kitchen.

'I am sorry, Doctor. I told them you were sleeping, but they . . .'

'I'll be in North Square if anyone needs me, Mrs Duthie,' he interrupted, then added kindly, 'You did quite right to let them in.'

It was only after the men had left that Isla realized who they were – the Christie twins of course, Davy's brothers, and the girl they were talking about was Rachel Christie, whose wedding she had seen not six months ago. She wished she had realized who they were, then perhaps she could have said something, done something to introduce herself. But as usual, she had left action till too late. Even Dr Noble did not know the whole truth about her. At first she had meant to tell him, then somehow it was too late, and he was so kind to her and to little Pearl.

Isla had been living in Dr Noble's house for months now, acting as his housekeeper until such time as she might find a job. He had promised to ask about for something suitable for her, but he was so busy, one way or another, that nothing had come of it and Isla herself made little attempt to find work. She was safe in Dr Noble's house. He was a good, kind man and if ever she was worried about Pearl he reassured her, and he made no personal demands on her. Sometimes, secretly, when the doctor was studying late by lamplight in the parlour and she lay supposedly asleep in the kitchen, with Pearl in a make-shift cradle beside her, she wished that he would. It was months now since Mrs Mutch had slept in the house and there was no impediment. She would have liked him to call her into the parlour, to ask her to sit beside him in the lamplight while he studied and she sewed, and the embers of the fire sank gently into sleep. He often came through to the kitchen to speak to her, even sat at her fireside with her, but just when they might have begun to grow intimate, he would push back his chair and hurry from the room on some pretext or other, and she would hear the parlour door close or the bolt ram home on his bedroom door. That bolt amused her. It was as if he expected . . . as if he was afraid that . . . Isla did not put words to the thought, but instead of barring her out, she saw that bolt as a hopeful and encouraging sign.

Rachel Christie was his half-sister, she remembered now. If Rachel were really ill, then Dr Noble would need comforting when he returned. Isla set about making a particularly flavoursome chicken broth, set it to simmer over the coals, then took out her best lace collar from the press, with the tortoiseshell comb and ribbons she had bought with the wages Dr Noble had insisted on paying her. She propped her scrap of looking glass against the flour crock near the window and began to rearrange her hair.

* * *

87

'Are ye sure she's nae hurt?' asked William, his kindly face troubled.

'We could send a message after the *Bonnie Annie*,' put in George, his brow creased with anxiety, 'to tell James to turn back. He's nae been gone more'n a day.'

'It is only a superficial bruise,' Andrew reassured them. 'She fainted, that is all. Common enough in women in her condition, especially in the heat. It is unfortunate she fell where she did, but the lump will soon subside and there is no damage done. Sponge her brow if she feels hot,' went on Andrew, drawing Maitland aside, 'and make her rest in bed for at least a day till we see if there are any ill effects.'

'A day?' protested Rachel, rising on one elbow in the box bed where Maitland had insisted she lie down. 'I canna' stay in bed. I've never spent a day in bed in my life and there's work to be done.'

'Listen to me,' said Andrew, sitting on the bed beside her and taking her hand in his. 'You have a baby growing inside you. Do you want to risk the loss o' the wee mite for the sake of a bale of Aberdeen stockings which these lads here are perfectly capable of loading into the hold without you?'

'No, but . . .'

'Then let them get on with it. They'll not go far amiss and Maitland will see to the paperwork for you, and the money.'

'But the customs and the harbour dues . . . There's the pilotage and . . .'

'They can see to all that, can't you, lads?' Andrew turned to the three brothers, who made an almost comical sight with their long faces and anxious eyes.

'Of course,' said Maitland, his eyes full of concern. 'We will see to everything, Rachel, till you are well again. So you do just as Andrew tells you and I'll ask Mrs Baxter to look in and see what she can do to help you out.'

'But really there is no need,' insisted Rachel. 'I feel quite well again, truly.'

'Do as you are told, woman,' said Andrew sternly. 'What do you think James would want you to do if he were here?'

At that, Rachel gave in. 'I am sorry, Andrew. I will do as you say.' She added mischievously, 'For today, anyway.'

'You will do as I say for longer than that, Mrs Christie,' retorted Andrew sternly and took his leave. 'I am worried about her,' he confided to Maitland, whom he had drawn over the threshold out of hearing. 'She is doing too much. She needs someone to help her.'

'There's the neighbours,' protested Maitland. 'They are aye ready to help out, and willingly, and I am always on hand if she needs me.'

'I meant another woman,' said Andrew. 'Is there no relative you could call on, for instance?' He deliberately shut out the idea of his own family in Cove. They had been glad enough to send Rachel to help out Annie Christie all those years ago, but they would certainly not feel the same way about helping her. 'Think about it,' he said, with a parting nod, and made his way back towards the hospital. He was wide awake now: there was no point in trying to go back to sleep. But perhaps he had better just call at the house to tell Isla Duthie where he was. There might have been other messages while he was out. Besides, he would not want her to worry.

'It is not right,' declared Mrs Forbes with unaccustomed vigour. 'That young woman in a young man's house. Mrs Abercrombie says when her son sent their maid round to fetch Dr Noble when Jess's pains started, the girl was sitting in the front parlour with him and he had her baby on his knee – just like a married couple, Mairi said. (Mairi was the maid and her exact words to describe Isla had been a 'bidey-in'.) It's disgraceful, when I think how good we have been to him, treating him like a son! The door has always been open to him, day or night, and the number of meals he has had at our table! And all the time he has been deceiving us with that *widow*.'

'Nonsense, Mamma,' said Louise with a cheerfulness she did not feel. 'Dr Noble is as entitled as anyone else to have a housekeeper.'

'Then why did he not mention her to us?' said Mrs Forbes triumphantly. 'There is guilt if ever I saw it. If it had not been for Jess Abercrombie's child – another daughter poor thing and Mr Abercrombie senior with his heart set on a grandson, though she had no need to name the wee mite Victoria as if she were royal family – we might not have found out for weeks. And *he is invited here this very Sunday*! I declare I do not know how he can look us in the face let alone dine with us with such a sin on his conscience.'

'Mamma, how can you talk of *sin* when you have no proof? You forget Andrew is a doctor. He is too honourable and high-principled to act in anything but the most correct and proper manner. Surely it is not yet a *sin* to hire a housekeeper!' Yet Louise felt an uncomfortable twist of doubt, and a pain that was new to her. It was not like Andrew to be secretive, yet he had made no mention of the departure of Mrs Mutch, the elderly woman who had seen to his simple needs, or of her replacement by any widow, with or without a child. It was strange that he had not spoken of the woman or of her infant. Usually he took a particular interest in children, especially with regard to the vaccination procedure in the city clinic, and he always told Louise of any new cases persuaded to seek protection from the smallpox.

'Oh dear,' her mother was saying now as the enormity of the situation grew upon her. 'I shall not be able to speak a civil word to him, I know it, and as for your dear father, why, I should not be surprised if he took down that fowling piece he keeps in his study and threatened the doctor with it!'

'I sincerely hope he does no such thing, Mamma. Andrew is blameless, I am certain of it, and when he comes on Sunday I forbid you to mention it.'

'Perhaps it would be better to put him off?' wavered Mrs Forbes. 'It would be so much easier. I will send and say I am indisposed.'

'Do not be ridiculous, Mamma! You cannot take to your bed for a mere malicious rumour. Andrew will come as invited and you will treat him as you always do, *do you understand*?'

At the vehemence in her daughter's voice, Mrs Forbes drew back, alarmed, and regarded Louise with wary eyes. 'Just as you say, dear,' she said nervously, then continued with returning righteousness, 'but I do think you had better inquire, for your own good, *exactly* what Dr Noble's domestic arrangements are.'

Though Louise countered with a loyal defence of Andrew and with repeated assertions of his innocence, her mother's words lingered at the back of her mind and would not give her rest. Two days later she fabricated an errand in order to call at his house, something she had rarely done, for she recognized Andrew's need for peace in which to study, or to recover from a night on duty. But all their recent meetings, she realized now, had taken place at the Forbes house, or at a pre-arranged venue such as the Dispensary or, lately, the Barrack Hospital where Louise had worked voluntarily and valiantly throughout the fever epidemic of the winter months, organizing the collection and distribution of blankets. Usually, Louise left such charitable duties to her mother's friends, but with the danger, imagined or otherwise, of infection, there had been too few volunteers and Louise herself had valued any opportunity given to her to share in Andrew's work. She had left the organization of charity concerts and the collection of money – the cost of the fever hospital alone was £40 a week – to Mrs Farquharson's circle of charitable ladies and had herself distributed and tucked in the more dangerous blankets.

Louise had visited Andrew at home no more than twice in the past six months, and both occasions had been long ago. Too long, she realized with a disturbing jolt to what had been complacency. It was not unusual for Andrew to behave like a recluse – he had always been that way inclined and recently, with the building of the new medical library nearing completion, Society business had taken up more of his time. As well as the Library there was to be a museum, great hall, committee room and housekeeper's room, all of which would need furnishing. The building itself, with its imposing portico of four Ionic pillars and its imaginative use of the local granite, had already caused a considerable stir in city circles and brought growing distinction to its architect. It also necessitated hard financial planning on the part of the Society and whereas Andrew was not personally involved in the endless search for funds, the stability of the Society was still his concern. He worked loyally and tirelessly on the planning of the new library, as well as producing essays to deliver at their meetings and continuing his own research.

Now, standing on the doorstep of the small, stone-built cottage above the Denburn, she wished she had called more often. Then she would have known whether the little piece of ground in front of the house had always

92

been so neatly tended; whether, with the south-facing wall of the house for shelter and reflected warmth, there had always been mint, verbena, lemon thyme and other herbs to perfume the afternoon air; whether the brass handle of the door had always shone so brightly, or the step been so well-swept and clean. Uneasiness grew as she noted more signs of what she dubbed 'female care'. Perhaps she should not have come? After all, Andrew's life was his own and she had no wish to be thought inquisitive or prying. He was probably out anyway. At the hospital or the Dispensary. She half turned to leave and a flash of gold and purple caught her eye. There in the small window to the left of the door was a jar of wildflowers, wood-anemones, forget-me-nots, king-cups, and violets. Surely Andrew had never had *flowers* in his study before?

That room was the parlour, to be sure, but one which he used only for his work. A bare room she remembered, a bare dresser with a Bible and candlestick, and a bare stone floor, but never flowers. The room to the right of the entrance was Andrew's bedroom. Ashamed of her own suspicions, Louise searched the sill of that room, too, and when she saw only plain wood was impatient with her own relief. Do not be ridiculous, Louise, she told herself. You are getting as bad as Mamma. She raised her gloved hand and knocked resolutely on the door.

After no more than an ordinary interval, the door was opened by a slim girl with pale hair and cornflower-blue eyes. With a shock, Louise noted how pretty she was. Somehow, listening to her Mamma's talk of widows and bidey-ins, Louise had expected someone older, plainer, coarser, even brazen.

'Who is it, Isla?' Andrew's voice sounded gentler than Louise remembered it and strangely relaxed. Louise bit her lip and before the girl could speak, stepped over the

93

threshold and into the open doorway of the tiny parlour. 'It is only I, Andrew,' she began, 'come to . . .' Then she stopped, her prepared speech forgotten.

For Andrew, in shirt sleeves, his collar undone, was sprawled in the leather armchair, a fair-haired child of perhaps eighteen months old astride his knees. Louise had obviously interrupted a game of some sort for, after one uninterested glance in Louise's direction, the child began to squeal 'More! More!' and bounce up and down in anticipated glee.

'You must excuse me for a moment,' smiled Andrew and resumed, 'This is the way the lady goes . . .' till the final toss in the air. Then, face flushed with exertion, he swung the child to the floor, with a firm, 'The game is over for today, Pearl. Now show the nice lady how well you can walk to your mother.'

The mother herself had remained standing in the doorway. Now she dropped to one knee, rearranging her skirts with a single, graceful movement, and held out her arms. Her dress was plain enough, of simple cotton, but the blue stripe exactly matched her eyes and the darker blue of her apron echoed and deepened them. The flesh of her arms was creamy and smooth and her outstretched hands, though large and capable-looking, were unroughened by salt or soap.

'Come to Ma, Pearl,' she urged and as the child took the first uncertain steps Louise felt a bond as strong as twine stretch between Andrew and the girl, as if it was a tightrope along which the baby was to walk and each was as anxious as the other that she should succeed. 'Like a married couple,' the maid Mairi had said, and a shadow slipped through Louise's mind, obscuring her faith. Then Pearl broke into a sudden, gurgling run to be snatched up safely into her mother's arms and the girl laughed with relief. But her eyes were on Andrew's and Louise followed their direction in time to see an answering smile on his face before he turned briskly away saying, 'Thank you, Mrs Duthie. Perhaps you will be good enough to bring us more tea and another cup?'

Louise saw there were two teacups on a small table which was new to her, and a simple china teapot with a blue pattern. 'Tea?' she echoed in disbelief. Andrew never drank tea. He had always been careful with money, never having had enough, as he said, 'to squander it on such luxuries', and tea was expensive.

Andrew blushed. 'I know what you are thinking,' he said, with an edge of bluster to his voice, 'But Isla . . . Mrs Duthie . . . likes it, and it is good for her. It builds up her strength.'

Since when was there strength in tea? retorted Louise, but only under her breath, for now that the girl had retired into the kitchen regions an awkward silence grew between them. Andrew obviously felt caught out in some way and for her part Louise was beginning to feel like a spy. Then she noted the new rag rug in front of the fire.

'I hear that . . .'

'How is the . . .' Both spoke together.

'I am sorry.'

'Do go on.' Again both spoke in unison, but this time Louise continued firmly, 'I hear that Mr Cadenhead and Mr Cockerill continue to prosper in their joint practice in St Nicholas Street. They compound and furnish their own medicines on the premises with great success, I believe. In the same manner, they say, as in London or Edinburgh. I wondered what your opinion was of the idea, as a general principle, especially as you have visited both cities?'

'Excellent,' said Andrew, obviously relieved to have the conversation steered into less personal channels. 'Of course such an establishment is of use only to those who can afford the fees – which may well be moderate enough, I cannot say. Dr Livingstone, who is a patron, I believe, of the two gentlemen in question, was extolling only the other evening at the Society meeting the benefits of co-operation which enable one or other doctor always to be available, and I wish their venture every success.' The door opened at that moment to admit Isla Duthie with a loaded tray. Andrew stood up to hold the door for her and while she set out the hot water and tea caddy and the paraphernalia of the tea-making, Louise noted his eyes followed the girl's every movement.

'Would you consider such an establishment yourself one day?' asked Louise brightly and with sharpened interest.

'What? Oh . . .' Andrew reassembled his thoughts. 'I think not. At least . . . As you know, Louise, surgery is my first interest, though I also practise medicine and am fully conversant with the latest diagnoses and treatments. But a surgeon needs a hospital for . . . for . . . thank you, Mrs Duthie.' He took the teacup from her and continued, 'Dissection. We have had requests from the magistrates and Council to restrain our students from body-raising, as they call it, but without such practices . . . no thank you, Mrs Duthie, we need nothing else . . . there would be no advancement of learning. What we need, and surely will have one day, is an Anatomy School where such scientific enquiry can be pursued in a spirit of open scholarship, free from furtive secrecy and deception.'

It was Andrew's favourite hobby horse and as she listened, Louise felt her fears recede. Yet what after all did she fear? She had found Andrew with little Pearl Duthie on his knee, that was all. The fact that Isla Duthie was in the parlour too and had been drinking tea with her employer was nothing. Andrew was notoriously generous to the weak and the Duthie girl was certainly that. A mouse of a thing, in spite of her looks, without a word to say for herself. The baby had more spirit. No, she was reading a volume into a single word, and ought to know better.

Yet Louise found she was not comforted. 'Could it be that I actually love Andrew?' she thought. It was a disturbing and humbling thought. Certainly over the years she had grown to depend upon him absolutely for companionship, for mutual trust and friendship, for shared ideas, for hours of absorbing discussion and lively conversation. She realized she had regarded him as hers and assumed he saw her in a similar light. Marriage had never been discussed between them, and whenever Mamma had mentioned it, Louise had turned on her with patronizing scorn. Mamma did not understand the friendship of mind and intellect. Yet, and the suspicion was both humiliating and painful, perhaps Mamma had been right after all? Otherwise why should Louise feel so mortified and wounded at the idea of Andrew with a – what was that picturesque expression? A bidey-in? The suspicion niggled in her mind throughout the conversation which had turned from the essay on sleep recently delivered to the Medical Society and which Andrew had been commenting upon, to his own study of the motor muscles of the arm. Fascinating though Louise found his account, when it was time to take her leave, she said impulsively, 'Andrew, why did you not tell me about Mrs Duthie and her child?'

Andrew stared, blushed, then said, with defensive bluster, 'Why ever should I tell you when there is nothing to tell? I came across a homeless mother of a young infant. I have room and to spare in my house since Rachel left – she is a little unwell, by the way, and would welcome a visit from you, I am sure – and am in need of a housekeeper. Where is the harm? Surely you do not

97

expect me to discuss anything as trivial as my domestic arrangements with you?'

'No,' agreed Louise and turned away. Yet Isla Duthie was not trivial and both Andrew and Louise knew it.

The Reading Room at the Athenaeum was crowded that afternoon and Rachel had to wait her turn to consult the pages of the *Aberdeen Journal*, not, as many others were, to read the accounts of the Greenland fisheries, though they were interesting enough: Rachel wanted only to find news of the *Bonnie Annie*. It was the first time James had made the crossing and whereas Rachel knew he was adept at charting course by both stars and sextant, she could not help but worry. There could be adverse winds, freak squalls, ships were often dismasted and driven helpless on to rocks, and since James's departure from Aberdeen there had been no word. Not even a message, sent by word of mouth, via another ship. Not a letter, not a sighting, nothing. Of course it took time for news to travel and time again for the newspaper to print it. She turned straight to the shipping columns, skimmed past 'Sailed' and 'Arrived' to that part of the column called 'Sound list'. There were ships' names, captains, vessels from London bound for Riga, from Liverpool for Riga, and one from Aberdeen! But it was Farquharson's *Flora*, not the name she sought. Then, right at the end of the column, she saw the entry she had longed to read: '*Bonnie Annie*, Christie, Aberdeen, Riga.'

James had reached the mouth of the Baltic sea! Relief flooded through her and with it the first real happiness she had felt since James had sailed. The ship was reliable, her husband experienced, the season fair, and with Wee Alex for company, James was not without friends. All was well. James would be enjoying the challenge of new waters and a new port. Meanwhile he would expect her to take good care of the old – and of herself.

Rachel laid a hand on the swelling firmness of her belly and felt the flutter of life under her fingers. Then, with a secret smile she waited for the familiar kick. Young James, as she thought of their unborn child, was growing restless. '*Dance to your Daddie, my little laddie,*' she crooned inside her head, then turned with new vigour to the columns of advertisements on the first two pages, to check first which ships were sailing where and with what passengers and cargo, then which wine or tobacco or cloth merchants were advertising what. She noted there had been an excellent harvest and good returns from the herring fishing too. That was worth considering. She saw that one Aberdeen ship was bound for Riga with a cargo of herring. Maybe James could do the same on the *Bonnie Annie*'s next trip? Cotton prices were rising as the crop in India had failed. It would be interesting to see what price the St Petersburg hemp fetched at next week's auctions in the Pocra warehouse. James should get a good return on the cargo of flax she had arranged for the return trip. The King was still gravely ill: when he died, there would be a demand for black crêpe. Was there a market for them there? She continued to read till she had absorbed all the information she thought relevant to the Christie interests. This reading, with the talk she gathered in the shipyard and on the Quay, kept her up to date with the movement of goods in the harbour and gave her new ideas for their own trading. Today, with the excitement of James's arrival in the Sound, she was full of plans for the future. It was only later, when she closed the doors of her bed on her loneliness at the end of the day, that she remembered that other entry in the Sound list: '*Flora*, Duncan, Aberdeen, Riga,' and the small worm of anxiety crept back into her thoughts.

* * *

99

'I hear Farquharson's sent another ship over to the West Coast, for the emigrants,' said Abercrombie, draining off a measure of cider into a metal cup. He sampled it, licked satisfied lips and added, 'This pipe o' Jersey cider was an excellent idea o' Rachel's. Wish I'd bought more when I had the chance. Two hundred and fifty passengers on his last ship, so they say.'

'*Two hundred and fifty?*' Fenton was appalled. 'But they must have been crammed like salt fish in a barrel! And it is at least thirty days to Nova Scotia.'

'Aye, but when yer belly's empty and ye've nae work, ye've nae much choice and they do say there's land and to spare in North America at most advantageous terms, though whether they'll have any money left by the time they've been through Farquharson's hands is another matter. Still there's aye hope. *Hope*'s one of the ships, and *Speculation*'s another, and right well named the pair o' them.'

'Talking of speculation, Father,' began Fenton hesitantly, 'Jessica was asking the other day whether we had any thoughts of putting our money into steam? Apparently Farquharson is talking seriously of buying a steam-packet for the London run one day.'

'Wi' the profits of his emigrant trade, no doubt,' said Abercrombie. 'The crafty devil. But I dinna' like yon steam contraptions and I'm thinking they eat up over much good coal. Besides, I tellt ye, lad, there's nae room for a cargo.'

'But with passengers, Father, would that matter? And designs are improving every day.'

'It's nae like you, Fenton, to stick up for steam,' said his father, eyeing him with new interest. 'Who's been getting at ye?'

'Nobody,' said Fenton, uncomfortably aware of his father's searching eyes. The truth was that Jessica was always getting at him, on one subject or another, and currently she had been nagging him unmercifully to persuade his father to 'put money into steam'.

'Look at Atholl,' she had said, ignoring his wince at her use of the Christian name. 'I reckon you Abercrombies could be rich as he is if ye'd only use yer heads. Why ye keep on pouring money into yon Christie business wi' their old-fashioned wee boaties, I dinna' ken. They'll get nowhere. It's steam they should be thinking of. Steam'll make the rich folk richer and folk like the Christies will be finished.'

Fenton suspected his wife's arguments came *verbatim* from another mouth – probably Atholl Farquharson's. It was not worth the aggravation to say so, but he wondered uneasily why she should have turned against the Christies with whom she had once been so friendly, and why Farquharson was so anxious to steer the Abercrombies into steam – if that really was his intention. Or did he just want them to stop supporting the Christies?

'Ye're nae listening, cloth-ears,' shouted his father suddenly. 'I've tellt ye twice yon last batch o' tobacco wasna' up to standard. Ye're slipping, laddie, and I'll not tolerate it. There's enough competition as it is, wi'out you handing our rivals custom on a plate.'

'I am sorry, Father.'

'Aye, so you should be. I'd ha' thought a married man wi' two wee daughters as well as a wife to support would ha' taken more interest in his work. Which reminds me. Have ye done as I said and got my grand-daughters protected? There's smallpox in the city again and ye'd best take care.'

'Yes, Father. Andrew's calling at the house himself to do it.'

'A good man, Andrew Noble,' said Abercrombie,

nodding approval. 'He'll see ye right. But mind yon flighty wife o' yours does as she's told.'

That, thought Fenton with an inner sigh, is easier said than done. But if anyone could make Jessica behave, it would be Dr Noble.

'What do you mean, *how* do I feel ill?' pouted Jessica. 'I just *do*, that's all.' She was in the drawing room of the apartment in Union Terrace, her new chintz skirts carefully chosen to show her at her well-covered best, especially against the brocade covering of the sofa. Although it was only September and the weather mild, firelight glimmered from polished floorboards and mahogany sofa-table, and Jessica had arranged her newest acquisition – a flower-bedecked fire-guard on an adjustable stand – so as to shield her cheeks from the heat, yet allow the glow from the flames to touch her thick, dark hair with light. She also held a fan over which she looked at Andrew now with feigned and touching suffering, the innocent young mother personified. 'My breasts are sore.'

'Only to be expected in a nursing mother,' said Dr Noble turning his back, apparently to re-arrange the contents of his medical bag, but really to collect his temper. Fenton's wife was becoming impossible. Had it not been for his long friendship with Fenton, dating back to their student years together, he would never have agreed to become the family doctor, and Jessica made it increasingly difficult with her flirtatious behaviour, bordering, he sometimes thought, on open invitation. Perhaps the rumours that he had heard in the town were true after all? But that was Fenton's affair, not his.

'Put your child to the breast more often, Mrs Abercrombie,' he said briskly, 'and in the interval try a soothing compress. It is early days yet, and in time Victoria and her food supply will adjust to each other.'

'Huh!' said Jessica, with spectacular scorn, tossing aside the helpless little mother image with her folded fan. 'Mrs Abercrombie indeed. Why do ye not call me Jessica like ye used to do?' Then she added mischievously, 'Well? Aren't ye going to *examine* me?' She lay back against the cushions and made to undo her bodice. Andrew reached for the bell.

'I hardly think it necessary,' he said coolly, 'in a simple case of milk fever, and possibly not even that, but if you wish it I had best call your maid.'

'Oh dinna' be such a *prig*,' snapped Jessica, at the same time sulky and frustrated. She stood up and moved towards him. 'And there's nae use ringing for Mairi for I tellt her to take the bairns to their Nana Abercrombie as soon as ye'd finished wi' them.' She lowered her voice before adding archly, 'so we could have a bitty peace together.'

She laid a soft hand on his arm, opened her dark eyes ingenuously wide and looked up at him with simulated innocence and trust. 'I didna' mean to annoy you, Doctor Andrew. Come and sit by me, here on the sofa, and show I'm forgiven?'

Instead Andrew took a step backwards, shook off her hand and said firmly, 'No, thank you Jessica. My consultation is over for the day. You may tell Fenton the vaccinations have been entirely successful.' Andrew had called only to check the progress of the smallpox vaccinations administered the previous week.

'Dinna' be so pompous, ye great neep,' jeered Jessica. 'I mind when ye were plain Booky Noble so there's nae call to act the high and mighty physician mannie wi' me.' Then, as he ignored her, she added, 'I'll bet ye arena' sac standoffish wi' yon bidey-in o' yours. And there's nae call to look outraged, for the whole town knows it and why not when my Mairi had it frae yer ain washerwoman and she ought to know, seeing as how yon quinie took her bed – except that it's your bed she's taken now and you still in it. She was telling half the town at the well the ither day. Jealousy, Mairi says. The auld wifie likely fancied you hersel', you being a fine unmarried doctor-mannie, but ye maybe dinna' go for older women? Young widows is more your line. Young and peely-wally, like yersel'.'

'I have not the least idea what you are speaking about,' said Andrew when he could get a word in, but in spite of himself his cheeks were burning.

'Course ye have, ye randy devil. A quiet wee thing, yon washerwifie tellt Mairi, but a fine bed-warmer nae doot. Wi' a child, too, the wifie said, so she's fine and healthy. Ye'd best tak' care she doesna' give ye a child o' yer ain afore the year's out.'

But Andrew had heard enough. 'I will send in my bill in the morning, Mrs Abercrombie.' He took up his bag and made for the door, but Jess darted round him to reach it first and spread her arms to block his passage.

'But ye canna', Andrew! Fenton'll make me have McKinnon and I canna' abide him. I didna' mean what I said, honest I didn't. It's just gossip, that's all. Ye ken how wifies blether among themselves.'

'Excuse me,' said Andrew with cold courtesy. 'I have an appointment to keep.'

'Aye!' cried Jessica, 'wi yer *bidey-in*!' She flung wide the door in fury and, when he pushed past her without a word, called after him, 'I hope she gives ye the clap!'

Outside in the gusty freshness of Union Terrace, Andrew was appalled. He had been naive, foolish, ridiculously blinkered against public opinion. What had possessed him? How could he have exposed Isla to such calumny? Poor, innocent Isla. He had meant to go to the hospital after his visit to Fenton's children, but now he could not face anyone till he had put his thoughts in order. Over the parapet of the bridge he glimpsed the drying green where women were spreading linen and Jessica's words came back to him with added spite. '*Mairi had it frae yer ain washerwoman . . . she was tellin' half the toon.*' Could it be true? *Was* he the talk of the town? Even to think such a thing brought the blood burning to his cheeks. How could he look anyone in the face again? He had meant only to be kind and instead had been *stupid*. Uncomfortably, he remembered Louise and that awkward meal at the Forbes's house. He had wondered at the time what he had done to offend. Suppose Mairi had told the Forbes's servants and they had told their mistress? Certainly Andrew had not been invited to the Forbes's house again. He had thought it the pressure of the summer season, but perhaps it was more than that?

Oh God, how could he have been so naive? For himself he did not care – or told himself he did not. Let them think what they chose. He was innocent of all blame and need not be ashamed. But what of Isla? She was not as robust as he. She was vulnerable and weak and, because of his stupidity, her reputation would be nothing now. How would she find any sort of decent job? He had thought the Medical Society might have been persuaded to put her into their new hall as housekeeper, but now if he suggested such a thing people would only think . . . he shuddered. He had meant only to help, and instead he had hurt her when that was the last thing he wanted to do.

At the thought, Andrew Noble, dedicated scholar and healer, had the first inkling of what might be going on in his heart – that part of his anatomy which, as long as it functioned according to anatomical necessity, had been of no interest to him. But it was only an inkling and one he resolutely suppressed. He had no time for personal involvement: his life was his *work*.

105

He found that he had walked, without noticing it, along Union Street to the Castlegate, past the Aberdeen Hotel and the splendid new building of the Union Chambers, past Baillie Galen's house, almost finished now and into the familiar bustle around the market cross. In his black coat and black hat he was indistinguishable from a dozen other city gentlemen going about their business, but he felt as conspicuous as if he had been dressed like a Hottentot, or an Apache Indian brave. He was sure every egg-seller, every washerwoman, every housewife, fish-wife, vegetable-seller or quack looked at him with com-plicity. Every smile was a knowing one, every greeting – and there were many for Dr Noble was well-known and well-liked – held a double meaning. Quickening his steps he swung into the Shiprow and made for the harbour and the Fittiegait. There was only one person he could talk to about the situation: only one person who might help him.

'I am so glad you came, Miss Forbes,' said Rachel, wiping her floured hands on her apron before untying it and laying it aside. She had been baking bread, for the *Steadfast* was in at the moment, and with George and William home their needs would more than double. Maitland, as usual, was in the planning loft, working: the new ship's keel had been laid the day after the *Bonnie Annie*'s launching and the cutting of scale models for the next was well in hand. Maitland had the plans drawn for another, too, and was increasingly restless for more space. He had already consulted Rachel and when James returned he intended to call a family conference and discuss expansion. Meanwhile, he had brought much of the paper work to the cottage so that Rachel need not be forever walking to and fro between North Square and Pocra, a short distance which she gladly undertook but which, with her advancing pregnancy, was becoming burdensome. Maitland, in James's absence, felt responsibility weigh heavy, especially as, with the shortening days and the frostier nights indicating the onset of autumn, there was no more news of the *Bonnie Annie*. Uneasiness stirred at the back of his mind: the *Hibernian* of Aberdeen had made Riga in a record time of seven and a half days. That had been in July with an experienced captain on a familiar route: but James was experienced too. Of course, James would have to establish contacts in Riga, choose an agent to guard their interests, discharge the cargo and reload, and if there had been difficulties with hull or rigging there could be repair work to attend to. Yet even with a slow passage either way that ought not to add up to more than two months and James had been gone two months and a day.

It was not as if the Riga route was closed by adverse weather, either. Farquharson's ships still plied regularly, exchanging herring for hemp or grain, and the only mishap reported was of an Aberdeen brig going aground off Dundee – and she had been speedily refloated and no harm done. But casual inquiries among the sailors in the quayside taverns had brought no results. The *Bonnie Annie* had been sighted in the Sound and again somewhere off Gotland, but after that nothing, and Maitland did not press the matter. He had no wish to stir up anxiety unnecessarily. It was bad for trade, and worse for Rachel whose face was growing drawn about the cheeks and whose clear eyes were too often troubled.

Now, however, she smiled with genuine welcome to greet her visitor. In the past, when Annie Christie had been failing in her last illness, Louise had often called to sit with the old woman and give Rachel an hour's release. But since old Mrs Christie's death their paths had rarely crossed and that usually through Andrew. In fact, realized Rachel, she had not seen Louise since the wedding.

'I called,' explained Louise, with her customary honesty, 'because Andrew said you had not been well lately. Oh I know I should have come before, but you know how it is. The fever hospital has taken up so much of my time I have had little left for friends or pleasure.'

'Andrew told me how hard you have been working,' said Rachel, offering her visitor tea. Tea was a recent luxury, a present from James before he left – 'and I dinna' want to see one leaf of it left when I return,' he had warned her, teasing, 'for I'll be bringing you back another ton o' the stuff, so ye can rest wi' yer feet on a cushion like a lady and nurse my bairn in comfort.' Rachel's face clouded at the memory, for, like Maitland, she was counting every hour till the *Bonnie Annie*'s return.

'What is it, Rachel?' asked Louise, quick as always to sense another's trouble. 'Is it the child?'

'Oh no.' Rachel laid a protective hand on her swollen waist and managed a smile. 'I am very well, as you can see, and Andrew should not have alarmed you. Not that I am not glad to see you,' she added hastily, afraid she might have given offence. 'But ever since that day on the Quay when I fainted for no reason worse than the heat he has been over-anxious for my welfare. It is no doubt because James is away.' There was a brittle edge to her cheerfulness and Louise said, with new concern, 'Is there news of the *Bonnie Annie*?'

Rachel shook her head, then said bravely, 'But what can I expect? After all, Riga is a new port to them and there will be so many things to arrange. Besides, I believe it is a fascinating town. There is a church spire 440 feet high and a castle and *two* cathedrals. Canals, too, connecting with other rivers for trading, though in midwinter they have to use ice-breakers because of the cold. And James did say that should he hear of good trading

108

prospects he might go on to St Petersburg. That too is a fascinating place, I believe.'

'Then I expect James and Alex are busy exploring,' agreed Louise, though she could not imagine James, for one, spending time on anything but business. 'They will come home loaded to the gunwales with souvenirs for you and the infant. How soon do you expect them?'

'I do not know.' At the stark misery behind the simple words Louise hastened to change the subject.

'But I was forgetting, Rachel! You have started building another ship since I last saw you. Soon you will have a yard as big as Hall's. Tell me, will the sign over the main gate be "Christie Brothers", or "Christie and Son" or perhaps "Christie Brothers *and* Son"? Or will you call it something quite different, like "Christie's Dream"?'

To Louise's relief, Rachel laughed. 'That shows confidence, anyway! Though I suppose it is one better than "Christie's Folly" which I sometimes think it is.' She glanced upwards to the rafters where fishing nets and creels were carefully stowed away, against an uncertain future. 'The herring catches were excellent this season. Perhaps it might have been better to stick to the fishing?'

'Nonsense,' said Louise briskly. 'You did quite right to venture into new ground. There'd never be progress otherwise. Look at Andrew, for instance, always working at some new approach to an old problem, and Dr Dyce's midwifery lectures are a revelation. Which reminds me, what arrangements have you made for your own lying-in?'

'None yet,' said Rachel, surprised. 'But I have good neighbours and Andrew said that he . . .' At that moment the door to the cottage opened, after only the briefest of knocks, and Andrew himself stepped inside.

'Rachel, I am in trouble and I need your . . .' He stopped at the sight of Louise and a slow flush spread upwards from collar to brow. 'Excuse me.' He removed his hat and stood awkwardly turning it in his hands, looking from one girl to the other. 'I did not know you had a visitor, Rachel. I am sorry to intrude, Louise. Perhaps I should come back some other time.'

'Nonsense,' said both girls together. Then, 'Come inside and join us,' said Rachel, taking his arm and pulling him towards the fire. 'We were drinking tea and talking of nothing in particular and generally enjoying ourselves. Louise very kindly rescued me from the drudgery of baking, so you must excuse my disarray.'

'There is nothing to excuse, and well you know it.' Andrew kissed her lightly on the cheek. 'But you are looking tired again.' He took her chin in his hand and studied her. 'Is she not a little drawn, Louise? And dark about the eyes?' Without waiting for an answer he went on, 'You are doing too much and sleeping too little, am I not right? And worrying about that absent husband of yours.'

'You said you are in trouble,' interrupted Louise and Rachel gave her a quick smile of gratitude. 'Tell us what it is, Andrew, so that we can help.'

Andrew hesitated, remembering that scene in his own house when Louise had asked why he had not mentioned Isla Duthie. But she had been right. He should have mentioned her from the start, then none of this would have happened. He took a deep breath and began.

'I do not know whether you are aware, Rachel, that some months ago I gave shelter to a homeless widow and her child . . .' Gradually, as he recounted Jessica's accusation and what must be the gossip of the town, he felt his trouble dissipate in relief until, at the end of the tale, he felt cleansed, healed and positively happy. 'So you see, Rachel, what a quandary I am in. Isla Duthie is innocent as I am of any sin. For myself I do not care: those who know me can judge for themselves how false such accusations are, but for poor Isla it is a different matter. She had hoped to find a good situation eventually, and may still do so, with the aid of influential friends.' He looked with new hope at Louise. 'For instance, perhaps your mother might hear of somewhere? Isla is a gentle, dignified creature, Rachel, undeserving of calumny. She has had a hard life, suffered great unhappiness, and borne everything with fortitude and touching courage. In fact, she is wholly admirable, would you not agree, Louise?'

He turned to her eagerly, expecting confirmation, but instead she drained her cup, stood up, and collected shawl and reticule almost in one movement. 'Thank you for the tea, Rachel,' she said, ignoring Andrew. 'I will call again when you are not *encumbered*.' Then she was gone, slamming the cottage door behind her.

'Andrew!' cried Rachel as soon as the door closed. 'How could you be so insensitive and cruel?'

'Cruel? I do not know what you mean, Rachel. What have I done?' He looked so comically hurt and bewildered that Rachel might have laughed, had she not been so angry and so close to tears. Instead, she pulled herself awkwardly to her feet, tied her apron over her spreading waist, and resumed kneading the dough for the evening's bread. 'You have wounded Louise to the heart,' she cried, thumping the dough with unnecessary vigour, 'that is *all!* Don't you realize she cares for you?'

'Louise?' Andrew looked taken aback, but after a moment's thought in which he watched Rachel turn and stretch the dough, then knead it into new shape, he said, with an edge of bluster to his voice, 'Of course. As I care for her. We are old friends and have been so for too long to fall out over a misunderstanding.'

'Andrew, you are denser than I thought, you infuriating man. Louise may be more intelligent than other women, more open and honest, and certainly more guileless, but she is still a woman and I tell you, Andrew, she cares deeply for you. Is it any wonder you hurt her by praising some pretty little widow to her face?' Rachel bent awkwardly to one knee to open the bread oven and test its heat.

'Isla is not "some pretty little widow",' retorted Andrew, avoiding the question, 'as you so dismissively describe her. She is a competent, honest woman whom life has treated badly. Her husband died before her child was born. Ask yourself how you would feel if . . . Rachel, I am sorry!' he cried in alarm, as Rachel swayed suddenly and grasped the table for support. Her face was white as the dough, newly crossed and dusted on the metal tray, but after only a moment she regained composure. 'It is bending and standing again too quickly that makes me feel faint,' she explained, but her heart was pounding fast and her voice trembled. She did not resist when Andrew led her to the chair beside the fire.

'I have an idea,' he said quietly. 'I wonder I did not think of it before and of course it is the perfect solution. Isla must come and live with you until your child is born. She will be company for you and help, too. You need a woman companion at such times, especially with James at sea, and I see no reason why the arrangement should not be ideal until such time as Isla finds permanent employment.'

Rachel saw every reason, especially in the light of Louise's pain, but she was for the moment too weak to say so. Andrew's thoughtless remark had shaken her to the core of her being and she still quivered with mingled anguish and fear. For that unknown widow with her fatherless child could so easily be herself. The fear robbed her of all power to protest and when Andrew said happily,

'I will bring her to see you tomorrow,' Rachel had not the strength to disagree.

But later, in the sleepless darkness of her box bed, conflicting thoughts gave her no rest. Part of her mind worried, as always, about James, questioning over and over *why* was he not home? She ran through every conceivable reason, from dismasting to dysentery and back again. She imagined James in prison, drifting lost and rudderless on a foreign sea, dying in some Russian hospital or, worst of all, rolling eyeless to and fro with the movement of the waters on some fathomless ocean bed. She remembered his promise to come home, swift as the wind and the unspoken fisherman's oath, '*Or may my boat be a bonnet to me.*' She even, in her lowest moments, imagined him carefree and laughing with Wee Alex in the steamy conviviality of a foreign brothel, simply reluctant to come home. She was instantly ashamed of her disloyalty and tears of remorse blurred her eyes as she turned her thoughts determinedly to practical matters. Where, for instance, was she supposed to put Andrew's protégée to sleep?

At the memory, her fighting spirit stirred into life again. Fond as she was of Andrew, he had no right to foist his homeless widow lass on her, just to keep his own conscience clean. She did not want an unknown woman in her house, let alone an unknown woman's child. At the back of her mind stirred a memory of her own childhood when, as an orphan, she had been taken grudgingly into the Noble family. But that was not the same: the Duthie child had a mother, a grown woman old enough to fend for herself, and whereas Rachel was sorry for both of them – who would not be? – she had no wish to house them in her cottage which had residents enough as it was. When both ships were in harbour there would be five menfolk at home and little enough room for extras.

Certainly not for an unknown widow girl. It was not as if they were fishermen any longer, needing their lines baited every day against the next day's fishing, when an extra pair of female hands would have been a blessing. And when James came back, she admitted, she did not want to share him with anyone. Certainly not with Andrew's 'wholly admirable' widow. No, decided Rachel as sleep at last crept over her, when Andrew came in the morning, she would tell him she had no need of help. He must look elsewhere for a solution.

But when Rachel opened the door to Andrew's knocking the next day, all thoughts of hostility fled. There, standing shyly a little behind Andrew, was a tall, slender girl with pale hair, cornflower-blue eyes and a tilt to her head that was somehow familiar. She held a small child by the hand, but it was not the two pairs of inquiring eyes that brought a frown to Rachel's face. It was the effort of recall as somewhere, deep in her being, memory stirred.

'Well?' prompted Andrew, with feigned cheerfulness. 'May we come in?'

Rachel stepped back to hold the door wide, but her puzzled eyes remained fixed on the girl who was loosening her shawl as the heat of the fire reached her. Then the shawl slipped from her shoulders to reveal a beautiful lace collar, with butterflies in the points. As Rachel stared in growing disbelief, the girl looked slowly round her, as if drinking in the very atmosphere, her eyes ranging over table, armchair, creepie-stool and hearth, then beyond the looped-back partition curtain to the bunk beds and the family kists, and finally the dresser. Suddenly she darted to the latter and picked up the mouth-organ. Cradling it lovingly in her hands, she turned to Rachel and murmured, 'Davy's?'

'Of course,' cried Rachel, her face radiant. 'I remember who you are. You are Davy's girl, from Stonehaven. And this,' she added, suddenly sober as she looked down at Pearl. 'This is . . .?'

Silently, eyes moist with emotion, Isla nodded. 'Davy's child,' finished Rachel in a voice of quiet wonder. Then she turned indignantly to Andrew. 'Why did you not tell me, you great *gowk*, that it was *Davy*'s girl you were speaking about?' She remembered James's vow when his father died to provide a home for his brothers and his brothers' children. He would be proud to welcome Davy's little family. 'Of course they must stay with me,' she said, her eyes alight now with pleasure. 'James will be as pleased as I am to welcome them.'

But please God he come home soon, before our own child is born.

The arrival of Isla Duthie and little Pearl was no more than a nine days' wonder in the Square. Andrew judiciously put it about in as many quarters as possible that he had been sheltering Rachel's 'sister-in-law' merely until Rachel herself was strong enough to take her in and eventually all talk of bidey-ins ceased, at least in Andrew's hearing. Even Mrs Forbes consented to unfreeze sufficiently towards him to invite him back to dinner, almost on the old footing.

Almost, for though Mrs Forbes was prepared to forgive and forget – 'How like Andrew to be so naive,' she twittered, 'but then the innocent often are' – Louise found it more difficult. There was a reserve between herself and Andrew that had not been there before. It was not that Louise nursed any resentment against Isla or Andrew. With her usual open, honest outlook she had quickly recognized that no one was to blame if she felt wounded, but herself. Andrew had made her no promises. He was free to befriend whom he chose, male or female, and she would be a poor friend if she could not listen to his enthusiasms, whoever they concerned. So she continued to visit Rachel, as Andrew had suggested, though she knew she must meet Isla when she did so. When, as often as not, she found Andrew there too, she told herself it was only natural that he should keep an eye on Rachel now that her time was drawing close, especially as there was still no news of James, and she did her best to smooth the conversation and avoid awkwardness.

Awkwardness, however, seemed to have entered the house with Isla. Maitland was shy of her and the twins more so. Isla herself had little conversation and on the occasions when Louise visited, Rachel found herself making a conscious effort to include Isla in the talking. But for the most part, the girl was self-contained and reserved, except, noted Rachel, when Andrew visited them. Pearl, however, was a different matter. From the first, she slipped into the ways of the household and by the end of a week had the menfolk eating out of her plump little hands. She would climb on to Maitland's knees when he was working at the table, wheedle the pencil from his fingers and a moment later Rachel would see them both happily absorbed as Maitland guided the child's hand in drawings of ships or birds, or the first letters of the alphabet. When the *Steadfast* docked and William and George appeared, after only a moment's wary scrutiny, Pearl was peeping out at them from behind her mother's skirts and gleefully daring them to 'Catch me!' Then would follow a game of roars and growls on their part and of squeals of delighted terror on hers, till one or other of the twins caught her, tossed her high in the air, or tickled her till her gurgling laugh had all of them joining in. Then they would dandle her on their knees, in turn, with chants of 'Eatle ottle, black bottle' or 'Bye Baby Bunting' till Rachel told them to stop, before the child wet herself with excitement or was sick.

Yet Rachel welcomed Pearl's uncomplicated happiness and generous affection, which she remembered in the child's father, as a buttress against her growing fear. It was two and a half months now since James had left, and Alex with him, with no news of boat nor men since that sighting in the Sound.

'Maitland,' she said one morning, unable to bear the suspense another day, 'I hear the *Flora* is in harbour, with a cargo of Riga hemp. Will you go to her and ask the men if they have any news?'

Maitland did not tell her that he had already done so, and that the universal denial from every member of Farquharson's crew had alarmed him as nothing had before. It was as if there was a conspiracy of concealment which he was powerless to penetrate. He had taken William and George aside and urged them to inquire of every ship in the Port of London when the *Steadfast* sailed south. But he could not tell Rachel so.

'I will ask,' he assured her, 'This very day.' But he had not left the house an hour before the answer came.

Rachel was in the yard on Pocra Quay, checking the newest purchase of yellow pine from St John's, when a footfall made her look up. A familiar figure was coming slowly towards her through the gusty freshness of that late October morning. Sawdust rose up in dancing swirls, a thin wind rattled the roof of the planning shed and a distant door banged to and fro against its frame. Rachel bit her lip to stop its trembling while her nails dug deep into her palms and she could not take her eyes from his face, as, faltering, he stopped, head drooping and ashamed, three feet from where she stood.

'I am sorry, Rachel.' She hardly heard the words as fear rose like a scream inside her head and she could not speak. Beyond the yard and Dixon's patch, the harbour waters were choppy with a thousand cat's paws, seagulls

117

loitered, bickering, on the harbour wall or, fat-chested, rode the swell. Over the water lay Torry and the green hump of the Girdleness, with cows grazing. Further inland, on Waterloo Quay, men were busy loading tubs of salt herring into the hold of a battered brig. Everything is exactly the same, thought Rachel with disbelief. Nothing has changed. Yet before Alex spoke she knew her world had shattered. He had aged in the short time he had been away.

'I am sorry, Rachel. I went ashore in Riga. Don't be late back, James said, or I'll sail without ye. I didna' mean to be late – and I didna' think James meant it, but when I reached the quay, the *Bonnie Annie* had gone. I've searched everywhere, Rachy. That's why I took so long to come home. I've asked from the Kattegat to St Petersburg for any sighting o' the *Bonnie Annie* or of Jamie and I canna' find him . . .' His voice broke and the next moment he was weeping.

'Come, Alex.' Rachel took his hand and led him gently into the planning shed and through into the office. 'You can pour us both a dram, for the shock of seeing you so unexpectedly has fair made my heart race.' Alex brushed the tears from his eyes with his sleeve and set about finding the best glasses and the whisky flask which they kept on a shelf in the office for the easing of negotiations, or the sealing of bargains. When the whisky was poured, they touched glasses, then Rachel said quietly, 'Tell me everything, Alex. It is best so.'

'We went ashore in Riga. It had been a good passage, though not as fast as the *Hibernia*'s best. We saw her in the Sound, and Farquharson's *Flora*, but they docked ahead of us. The *Hibernia* was in ballast and the *Flora* had a cargo o' herrings. It's a fine port, Rachy, wi' such a trade o' shipping, but cold. 'Tis nae wonder they need ice-breakers for the river mouth.'

'And you went ashore?' prompted Rachel.

'Aye. We disposed of our cargo with nae much bother, but wi' the *Flora* ahead of us, James hadna' all the flax he wanted – wi' the cotton crop failed in India prices are rising and competition was fierce. It's nae easy wi'out an agent, neither, nor wi' the language like none ye ever heard, and the mannie James had found upped and left wi' nae reason. We were five days finding another. It seems Farquharson's agent is the big fish there and the others were helpless tiddlers, but nae matter. Anyway, wi' the hold only three-quarters filled, and nae more grain nor flax nor even hemp to be had, James decided we'd sail, so he gave us all shore leave and . . . and . . .' Alex's voice broke for a moment before he went on, 'He tellt me to be back aboard by sundown or he'd sail wi'out me.'

Rachel raised a mental eyebrow, remembering that London visit: James's threat suggested further provocation on Alex's part, but she made no comment.

'Then . . . then . . . I am sorry, Rachy, and I know I shouldna', but we went to this tavern and, well, there were women there, and somehow or other – and I dinna ken how, truly I don't – a fight broke out and the harbour guards came and we were to be locked in the town jail. At least I think that was what they planned or maybe they were a press gang for the Russian navy? I couldna' make out a word o' their jabbering. Anyway, I bribed a guard wi' what money I had left and I ran for it. But I darena' show mysel' in case o' capture, so I hid for a whilie wi' . . . wi' some women I'd met, till the town was quiet again. Then I ran. But by the time I got back to the quay the berth was empty and all I saw was the outline o' the *Bonnie Annie* on the horizon. I didna' think he meant it, Rachy.' There was hurt as well as guilt behind the complaint: he had trusted his brother to wait for him, whatever happened, and to find himself deserted had shaken his trust. But Rachel offered no comfort.

'Which way was she sailing?' she demanded. If she could know for certain that James had gone east, to St Petersburg, it would ease her anxiety a little, but Alex shook his head.

'I couldna' tell. It was dark, Rachy, wi' only a wee bit moon, and the ship far out in the bay. The men must ha' got aboard sharpish and James was aye impatient to sail once the hatches were down.' James had obviously had to wait for young Alex on previous occasions. 'I am sorry, Rachel,' he finished, his face downcast.

Rachel did not answer. Alex had told her what she had dreaded to hear: the *Bonnie Annie* was not, as she had tried to persuade herself, laid up in Riga, but had put to sea weeks ago. Long enough ago to have sailed home and back again, twice over. Unless James had sailed to St Petersburg in search of hemp and been somehow delayed? It was a small enough twig to cling to, but in her desolate state, any hope was welcome.

Then one of their crewmen arrived back in port, Baxter's Davy, and came straight to the Christie yard. The tale he told destroyed any lingering hope that the *Bonnie Annie* would sail home unscathed. He and the other crewmen, he said, after that bar-room brawl, had spent three days in Riga jail. The brawl had been none of their instigating, he insisted. There had been men from the *Flora* there and they had started it: though none of *them* had gone to jail. The other crewmen had found places on other ships, he did not know which, but he had made straight for home, though his passage had been a slow one, via London and Leith.

'But I came straight to tell you, Maitland,' finished Baxter's Davy. 'I reckon there was mischief afoot and ye'd best know it.'

'So,' said Maitland quietly, standing at the outer door, his back to the planning loft, and staring along the quay to the Shiprow and the window of Farquharson's office. 'If Alex was in a brothel and the rest of the crew in jail, who sailed the *Bonnie Annie*? James could not handle her alone and there was only one other man aboard.'

'Boy,' corrected Alex, red-faced at Maitland's choice of words. 'George's Willy from South Square.'

'Do you reckon it was piracy?' asked Maitland. Baxter's Davy shrugged. A stocky, fresh-faced lad of twenty, he was staunchly loyal, but not gifted with original thought. 'She's a good ship,' he said. 'Wi' a good cargo. Too good to send to the bottom of the sea.'

'Unless a squall did it for them.' Only that morning Maitland had read in the *Journal* of a ship lost on Gotland and another on the island of Osel. Either could have been James's ship. 'Or unless you're rich enough to afford vengeance,' he finished, his eyes on that office window on the Quay. Farquharson, they all knew, had vowed to 'get' the Christies one day, for reasons both sides preferred to keep secret. Though Maitland had not been present at that meeting in the Pocra office when Farquharson had been forced to sign the agreement concerning Dixon's patch, and had made that vow of revenge, he had nevertheless heard enough from those involved to know it was no idle threat.

'I still don't see why he sailed wi'out me,' persisted Alex. 'His own brother . . .'

'Unless he had no choice.' Maitland's words hung ominously in the silence as the three men stared at that building in the Shiprow. Sunlight glinted in the glass of an upstairs window and Maitland swore under his breath. 'The bastard's spying on us. Give me my glass.' He snatched up the telescope, trained it on Farquharson's office, and adjusted the eyepiece. 'Blast,' he said after a moment. 'The sun's in my eye.' But they all knew he was right. Farquharson *was* spying on them – and the very fact that he was, confirmed suspicion.

'That bastard Farquharson's at the bottom of it,' growled Abercrombie when Maitland sent for him 'on a matter of urgency'. He drained his whisky glass and held it silently for a refill. 'I'll not deny it is a blow, Maitland lad. I've plans to build new premises in Union Street, but wi' the loss o' the *Bonnie Annie*, I stand to lose a deal o' money, one way and another. There'll be the insurance, likely, but not for a while. She'll need to ha' been missing a deal longer afore she's accepted "lost". I had hoped for a fine profit from this Baltic venture.'

'So had we all,' said Maitland quietly.

'I'm sorry, lad.' Abercrombie put an arm impulsively around Maitland's shoulders. 'Here's me moaning on about money when you've lost something far worse. A fine man, James.' There was a moment's silence before he went on, 'How's Rachel taking it?'

'You know Rachel. She is brave and unshakeable. She has faith and even a little hope.'

'As we should have, lad, till proved otherwise. And by God we will prove *something*. Yon villain's aye been against us.' Abercrombie's eyes narrowed as he looked along the Quay to Farquharson's office. 'Give me that glass o' yours, Maitland.' Abercrombie stood for a long time, staring at that upstairs window before he shipped the telescope and handed it back to Maitland. 'He's our villain. Nae doubt at all. He thinks we dinna' know it. He thinks he's won and we'll nae disabuse him. Yet. We'll need to ask about, quiet like, among his men till we get to the bottom of the mystery. Then we'll get him.'

'William and George are to do the same in London,' said Maitland, 'and I am sending Alex along with them for a while. He knows the *Bonnie Annie* better than the twins do and he's better able to ask about. Suppose she's been re-painted or re-rigged, he'll spot her. And he has his own reasons for tracking her down.' Alex, chastened and ashamed, was eager to do what he could to make amends.

'We'll find the *Bonnie Annie* somehow,' he boasted to Kirsty Guyan, skating over his own shortcomings with a 'while I was ashore'. 'Or what has become of her – and James too.' Though of finding James they had little hope. Maitland, Alex and the twins had come to a silent agreement not to talk of James in front of Rachel, and if they spoke of him among themselves, it was as of someone dead.

Rachel, however, refused to believe James was dead. In spite of that secret nightmare vision of an eyeless body tossing on some distant sea bed, she was sure that somewhere her husband lived: otherwise she would have known it. There would have been an emptiness where her heart was. Instead, she was racked by anxiety and dread and by the tortured imaginings her brain produced in the sleepless small hours before dawn. November was a bad time, she told herself, in the Baltic sea. There would be ice. James might be ice-locked in some Russian river, unable to move till the ice-breakers arrived, or the spring. Meanwhile, he was thinking of her as she was of him. If she lay quiet in the darkness, she could almost hear his voice, murmuring to her; if she closed her eyes she could almost see his face. As for those other, treacherous imaginings, they belonged with the past. Before his marriage James had been as Andrew so quaintly put it 'not unacquainted with the female sex.' That life had ended when he married Rachel. James was her husband. He loved her and the child she carried. One day, as he had promised, he would come home. So she went about her duties with a dogged faith which nothing could shake. Not

123

the arrival of a ship from St Petersburg, with no news of the *Bonnie Annie*, not the finding of ship's debris off the coast near Goteborg, with a portion of bow timber and a painted 'A'. Not even Isla's misplaced comfort of 'At least you will have his child to remember him by.'

But even Rachel's faith was strained towards the end of December when the pains of childbirth struck with relentless torment for the space of two and a half days. She cried on James to help her as pain blurred all thought, and she wanted only to die so that she and her baby and James could walk in peace together in some other world.

'It is all my fault,' wailed Alex, distraught with anxiety and guilt as he and Maitland and the twins paced up and down the office at Pocra, sent there by the womenfolk with orders to 'keep out from under our feet.' Ma Brand, too huge to be of much practical use, except as an encouraging raconteur of her own painless, numerous and easy childbirth experiences, had removed wee Pearl to the noisy squalor of her cottage a few doors away, so that the Christie men had nothing to occupy their thoughts but Rachel and her absent husband, dead somewhere, no doubt, though none would put the thought into words, in a cove of the Baltic sea.

'It is my fault,' repeated Alex over and over. 'I shouldna' have been late. I shouldna' have gone ashore at all. I should have . . .'

'Never mind what ye should have done,' interrupted George and William, needled beyond endurance. 'That's nae help to Rachel now.'

'Ye'd better be thinking, all o' ye,' said Maitland, 'how the family's going to manage wi' a ship lost and James lost and a new bairn to care for.' With James missing, dead like as not, it was up to Maitland as eldest to take over the running of both business and family as best he could.

'But the bairn's nae born yet,' reminded Alex and

124

anxiety once again took over in spite of Kirsty Guyan's offer of broth and bread and cheese, and Abercrombie's present of a bottle of best cognac brandy, 'for the nerves'. He too was anxious, for he was genuinely fond of Rachel and of James. 'Pray God the child is born safe,' he said, on his hasty visit to Pocra when he heard the news of the impending birth. 'And thank God there's Andrew Noble to advise her and that sensible Forbes girl.'

Louise Forbes called frequently and stayed long, and by her quiet confidence and faith did more than anyone to help Rachel in her trouble. 'Do not lose courage, Rachel,' she urged her. 'Or strength to fight for the wee one's life as well as for your own. Fight for James – think of his joy when he sees his child.'

Rachel, sweat-drenched and exhausted, clung to Louise's hand and to the straw of hope she offered, gathered her meagre strength for the next onslaught and managed a momentary smile. Mrs Baxter sent Isla hither and thither to stoke the fire, boil the pot, light candles in auspicious places, hold cups of water to Rachel's parched lips – and mugs of a stronger potion to her own – all the time chattering about the doings of her own numerous brood, including her Davy. Louise soon gave up any attempt to stop the woman recounting the tales her Davy had told her about Riga. '. . . and he reckons yon ship'll never be seen again,' she mouthed in a stage whisper across poor Rachel's pain-racked body. At least the tale held Rachel's interest and anything that did that, Louise told Andrew, was welcome.

Andrew Noble, summoned by the twins as peremptorily as on the previous occasion, had ascertained that the birth was taking a normal course, done what he could to ease Rachel's pain, and left again. There was a difficult case at the hospital which required his attention – a workman loading stones at Waterloo Quay by means of a metal crane had let a cog-wheel accelerate too fast and while trying to stop it, had lost three fingers and half a fourth. 'But ye must send again for me at once, Louise, if I am needed.' Louise, however, had attended midwifery classes and studied all aspects of childbirth both at Dr Dyce's lectures and, with Andrew's help, from his own textbooks.

'I will manage,' she said now and Andrew, looking at her calm, plain face and honest eyes, knew she spoke the truth.

'You would have made a fine doctor,' he said quietly, taking her hand and giving it an impulsive squeeze. 'I leave her gladly in your care.'

Isla Duthie saw the clasped hands, though she could not catch the words, and felt the usual stab of jealousy and dislike. Isla was a little afraid of Louise, who made her feel uncomfortable and ignorant, and though the Forbes woman was not at all attractive by Isla's lights, she seemed to share an intimacy of friendship with Dr Noble which excluded Isla completely. Ever since that time when Miss Forbes had called at the doctor's house and Dr Noble had sent her, Isla, out of the room to fetch tea, she had felt threatened by the woman, and excluded. Now when Andrew turned to leave, Isla followed him to the door and out into the Square.

'Will Rachel be all right, Andrew?' she asked anxiously, her blue eyes wide and trusting.

'I hope so. There is no reason to doubt it. Come,' he went on as Isla looked at him with brimming eyes. 'There is no need for tears, surely? A new life should be a joyful thing.'

'I know, but . . .' Isla bit her lip before finishing, eyes lowered, 'There is still no news of her husband and I cannot help remembering . . .'

'Of course. I am sorry, Isla. Rachel's situation must

certainly revive painful memories, but there is still hope for her, and as for you, you must endeavour to put the past behind you and rebuild on a new foundation.'

'I will try,' said Isla humbly.

'Now run along back and help Rachel all you can. She will be relying on you more than ever now.'

But Louise Forbes, by her air of competent authority, had taken charge and there was little for anyone else to do but carry out her directions. Even Mrs Baxter, recognizing superior learning, bowed to Miss Louise's orders and without rancour.

'Thank you, Louise,' gasped Rachel in a lucid interval and clutched her hand. 'It is . . . kind . . . of you . . . to stay.'

'Not at all,' said Louise briskly. 'Pure selfishness on my part. It is not every day I get the chance to assist at a birth.' In fact, though she did not tell Rachel so, it was her first lying-in. 'I look upon it as an honour.' That was not, she knew, how her mother would regard it, but Mrs Forbes's outrage could wait till another day. 'I shall certainly stay with you, if I may, until the child is born.'

Six hours later, on the last stroke of midnight, Louise held the slippery, dark-haired little miracle in her hands and said, in a voice of awe and wonder, 'It is a boy, Rachel, a fine, healthy boy.'

With a sigh of blissful fulfilment, all pain forgotten, Rachel held out her arms for her child. 'We have a son, James,' she murmured, her lips against the downy softness of the infant's head. 'So come home, my love, soon, to see him.' Then she slipped into the first untroubled sleep she had known since the day James sailed for Riga.

Jessie Abercrombie was one of the first to visit Rachel and her newborn son, driving along the Fittiegait in her London gig with the folding leather top raised against the wind, though not high enough to obscure the grandeur of her plumed poke bonnet and velvet pelisse. To everyone's astonishment, she brought her own daughters with her – Augusta, fat, red-cheeked and black-haired like her mother and, though not yet two years old, dressed in equal if miniature splendour, and Victoria, a pale-haired four-month-old who was swathed in layers of lace-frilled linen, her round face 'for all the world like a puddin' in a cloth' as Kirsty Guyan unkindly whispered, and carried by the maid, Mairi.

It was the first time Jess and Rachel had met since Rachel's wedding, but the room was full of friendly people and Rachel too bemused by the wonder of her son to revive past rivalries. She extended the same welcome of whisky, cheese and fresh bread to her as to the others, with sweetmeats for Augusta, whom Pearl immediately took charge of and removed to a secret corner.

'My, but he's a fine and handsome laddie,' said Jessica, studying Rachel's infant with her head on one side. 'Like his Da. A pity James isna' here to see him, but he'll come home soon enough, dinna' you fret.'

Rachel was grateful for this cheerful comfort, even from Jess, and as a result was unprepared for what followed. Jessica took her infant daughter from Mairi, sat down on the bed beside Rachel and said, confidentially, 'I'd have called Victoria "James" if she'd been a loon. It's a fine name and would ha' been *fittin'* somehow.' She put her head on one side and studied Rachel's child. 'Isn't likeness a strange thing? There's your wee Jamie the spitting image of his Da, yet sometimes I look at my Victoria and I canna see a single bit o' *Fenton* in her. I don't know who she puts me in mind of, except maybe other infants. Queer how they look alike when they're little, isn't it? I know my Victoria's bigger and older, but when ye see the two o' them side by side, they could almost be brother and sister.'

'Ye're off your head,' said Kirsty Guyan who disliked Jess for her own reasons. 'Or blind. Wi' one of them dark-haired and handsome and the other a red-faced puddin' wi' no hair at all that I can see. You'll be comparing yoursel' wi' the Empress Josephine next, just because ye both go about wi' a bare bosom and thrust it under men's noses.'

'Empress who?' demanded Jess belligerently, but though in the ensuing squabble the cause of it was forgotten, the harm was done. Rachel told herself over and over that Jess was a malicious and mischievous woman, never content unless causing discontent. When Augusta knocked baby Victoria's bonnet awry and Rachel saw the down of golden hair, she told herself it was exactly the colour of Fenton's. But some of the Christie men were fair, too – and was there not something odd about the child's eyes? In spite of all determination, that conspiratorial 'brother and sister' gnawed like a worm into her fragile happiness and cast a new shadow over her heart. She remembered the woman's veiled remark at Rachel's wedding and James's anger. Then she remembered James, her husband, when the wedding guests had gone, and she mourned for him with a new intensity of yearning.

1820

At the beginning of the year His Majesty King George III died and was succeeded by the Prince Regent, now George IV. The new King was proclaimed by the Lord Provost on the Plainstanes, in the presence of the Magistrates, Town Council, Deacons and Convener of the various Trades, with the Principals and Professors of both Colleges, and all the eminent Gentlemen of the neighbourhood. Trumpets sounded and the assembled populace duly cheered. But the replacing of one king by another in far distant London was a matter of little import beside the continuing mystery of James Christie's disappearance.

'There's nae news,' snapped Abercrombie, with his usual asperity when matters touched on the missing Christie ship. 'And nay likely to be neither, wi' yon shark silencing every mouth from here to Riga wi' his ill-gotten gold.'

Fenton fidgeted nervously with the tobacco ledger on the desk in front of him before saying, 'I ask only because Jessica was inquiring again this morning. But never mind. She was asking also how the plans for the new Union Street premises were progressing, and I could tell her nothing except that . . .'

'Nothing's all ye should tell her,' interrupted Abercrombie. 'I've the best architect designing it for me and the best builders waiting to build it and that's all ye need to know. I dinna' mind telling you, Fenton, for ye're

131

nae a fool and ye no doubt know it already, but I'm disappointed in yon wife o' yours. I had hopes she'd be a fine worker wi' her coming o' working stock like yer ma and me, but instead she's dafter i' the head than our Clemmy, wi' her talk o' clothes and carriages and yon Assemblies she's aye naggin' at you to attend. Maybe I could stomach that, for she's still a fine looking woman, but what I canna' stomach is the way she blethers to all and sundry o' the family affairs.'

'I am sorry, Father . . .' murmured Fenton, but Abercrombie hardly heard. He had been wanting to get the matter off his chest for months.

'She's aye telling folk at parties how the Christie ships are coming along and I ken fine she does it in a spirit o' boasting, but the town's full of ears to snatch and carry tales. I've even seen her yappin' to yon rat Farquharson! There's nae saying what secrets she gives away wi' her talk of freight and profits, so see ye tell her none yersel'.'

'No, Father.'

'Not that we've secrets to tell wi' the whole town knowing we've lost the *Bonnie Annie* and a fortune with her. Nigh on £3,000 she cost to build and that's wi' the Christie lads working for nought and nae account taken o' the fittings. On top o' that there's the cargo and when we get the insurance money, if we ever do, it'll not make up a half o' what we lost. It's nae so much for ourselves, Fenton lad, that I grieve, for we've other irons in the fire and we'll manage – it's yon lass Rachel I feel for. She's a brave, hard-working lass and she doesna' deserve the ill-fortune o' a ship and a husband lost, especially wi' a fine wee son to think of.'

Fenton was silent. He knew his father longed for a grandson, and though Abercrombie doted on little Augusta, his eldest grand-daughter, and had welcomed the second, Victoria, at first philosophically, then with genuine affection, for the old man loved children, Fenton knew he expected, or rather *required* Jessica's next to be a boy. Unfortunately, as after Augusta's birth, his wife was proving difficult. He could hardly tell his father that his wife barred the door on him night after night, on some pretext or other, or, lately, merely because 'I dinna' want ye'. Though no doubt Mairi would relate the gossip soon enough, at the pump or the washing green, then the whole town would know it. Perhaps they already did? Perhaps they also knew what he chose not to know: whether or not his wife had a liaison with someone else?

'Ye're nae listening to me, lad,' snapped Abercrombie and Fenton realized that his father had been talking for some time. 'I said, we'll need to give the Christies all the help we can. Yon new ship's coming along fine and they've orders for more and nae space to handle them. They've the knowledge now and an abundance o' determination and they plan to expand. It's only the money they lack. I wish I had more to lend them mysel', but wi' the Union Street project to pay for, I canna' see how I can manage more than a couple o' hundred, and that'll have to be at ten per cent. No, dammit,' he exclaimed, thumping his fist on the ledger. 'For them, I'll make it five.'

'We must borrow,' said Rachel firmly. In the brief silence that followed they remembered, with vivid clarity, a scene long ago in this very room when Fiddly Christie and Annie were alive and the family had gathered, as they had done now, for the evening meal and had discussed, as they were doing now, plans for the future. They were fishermen then, and when James and Maitland had talked of building a boat and borrowing the money to do so, their father had forbidden it in words that still rang clear in Rachel's memory. 'We'll have no debts. *Or may my boat be a bonnet to me.*'

Glancing up, she caught Maitland looking at her and knew that he, too, remembered. But they had come a long way since then. James himself had been prepared to borrow, if necessary, to secure the launching of the *Bonnie Annie* and James, she knew, would want her to do the same to ensure the future of the yard and of the family. Rachel remembered James's vow, long ago, to buy a house one day for himself, his brothers and his brothers' children, a house on the Quay with room for them all. James was gone: where she no longer asked, or for how long. James was on a distant journey, that was all. But he expected her in his absence to guard hearth and home. She meant to do more than that. She would build on the foundations he had left, so that when he returned he would find the shipyard of Christie Brothers as flourishing and as prosperous as James himself would have made it, for his son. The aim gave new purpose to her life and, if she felt her spirits fail, as inevitably they sometimes did, she had only to look at James's son to regain strength.

There was Davy's daughter, too. Pearl was as much a part of the family now as Jamie, and adored her little cousin with a fiercely protective love which held no jealousy. Young as Pearl was, Rachel knew she was absolutely reliable where Jamie was concerned. More so than her mother, reflected Rachel, with a gathering of the brow. Isla was too often absent-minded or forgetful. She was biddable and willing, hard-working too when need arose, but she grew no more communicative than on that first meeting. Whereas Pearl had slipped instantly into the family group, finding her own niche and happily so, Isla remained on the periphery, in spite of all persuasion and overtures of friendship. After three months she was still a visitor, with a visitor's politeness and a visitor's reserve. But she was Davy's girl and homeless and James, Rachel knew, would regard it as his duty to give her and Pearl a roof. Now, with Jamie asleep in the wooden cradle which had been a present from the carpenter at the shipyard, and little Pearl curled up, thumb in mouth, in the fireside chair, Rachel looked round the assembled faces and repeated, 'We must borrow. We need more space for Maitland to build his ships and we need more men.'

Maitland leafed through the papers which he had spread out among the debris of the evening meal while Alex fidgeted and the twins continued to push crumbs of bread across the table in an intricate and private game. But all four kept one eye on Rachel, waiting for her to continue. Only Isla seemed unconcerned. She was stitching a garment of fine cambric, with stitches almost too small to see. For the purpose she had positioned a lamp on the table beside her and in its glow her hair gleamed like polished gold. Maitland thought for the hundredth time how ethereally lovely she was – and for the hundredth time forgot her, as Rachel spoke.

'As you all know, the *Bonnie Annie* is now officially "lost".' Her voice faltered for only a moment before she continued, 'There will be compensation of sorts, but not enough to equal what would have come to us from trading profits in the last six months. The *Steadfast* continues to do well, thanks to William and George.' The twins blushed with pleasure and jostled each other playfully. 'And Maitland will tell you of progress in the yard, but it is not enough. That ship is spoken for. We need a ship to replace the *Bonnie Annie* and more. In the Pocra yard there is room for only one slipway. We have the expertise, the experience – and the orders – to justify two.'

'As you all know, we have the lease of the Pocra yard

as long as we want it,' explained Maitland, 'but there is the disadvantage of Dixon's patch.'

'But we have permission to . . .' began Alex, only to be silenced by a frown from Maitland. That piece of paper granting perpetual access to the Quay revived too many painful memories.

'We cannot always be building rolling-platforms,' said Rachel. 'We need direct access to the Quay.'

'Then what we really need,' said Alex, 'is Dixon's patch.'

There was a moment's silence before Rachel said, tentatively, though she already knew the answer, 'I suppose we could not buy it from Farquharson?'

'Nae chance. He'll hang on to it out o' spite. Tho' he's nae using it himself.'

'No, Rachel,' said Maitland. 'We all know Atholl Farquharson. As long as he knows we want that land he'll nae sell it.'

'Then as soon as any other comes up for lease in Pocra,' decided Rachel, 'we will take it, borrowing or no borrowing, and build more ships.' This, she was sure, would have been James's decision. 'There is a steady stream of emigrants now, going over to the Americas, and needing better passages than present ships provide. There's the tea trade and the spice trade. There's the West Indies for sugar and they say South American guano fetches a fine price.'

'And there's the whaling,' said Alex. But Rachel seemed not to hear.

'I remember at the launching,' she went on, 'James drank to "the Christie fleet" and I mean to see we have that fleet, with a ship for every Christie man and every destination.'

'There's the *whaling*,' repeated Alex loudly and this time everyone heard. Alex's face was red with emotion

136

and he half rose to his feet to secure everyone's full attention before continuing, with a mixture of defiance and pleading, 'Remember years ago, when we needed money for the *Steadfast* and James went to the whaling? Well, I reckon I owe it to James to do the same.'

'But you're only sixteen, Alex,' said Maitland. 'You're best here at home wi' me. Ye can help me in the yard. Ye aye had a flare for drawing, remember.'

'Aye, but I'm nae *needed* i' the yard and the twins dinna' need me either.' The unspoken implication was that any further search for the missing ship would be fruitless and that Alex's inquiries in London were no longer of use. 'Any crewman could do my job in the *Steadfast*. I should be at sea in the *Bonnie Annie*, wi' James. I was to be master o' her one day, James said, and now, thanks to me, she's gone and the devil alone knows where and James with her and it's all my fault. Just like Davy . . .'

'Alex!' cried Rachel quickly, reaching out a hand, 'Davy's death was *not* your fault.' There was a gasp from Isla and Rachel went on quickly, 'The fire on the *Steadfast* made little difference. You know his lungs were diseased beyond cure. So *we will have no more talk of that*. As for James,' she continued, more quietly, 'I still have hope, and I pray all of you to hope with me. There is no call for blame.'

'But there *is*!' Angrily Alex shook off her hand. 'You do not know what it is like to remember. To have folk asking "what were ye doing ashore?" and "when did ye last see your wee ship?" and know what they're really asking is "why did ye not stay aboard wi' your brother?", knowing it was a foreign port and a hostile one at that, wi' Farquharson's men ashore. And they're right. I *should* ha' stayed aboard. So dinna' tell me it's nae my fault, Rachel. It *is* and I know it. I lie awake o' nights thinking of it and it's no good pretending to me that it doesna' matter. Do you think I don't see you all looking at me and thinking "if yon stirk hadna gone a-whorin' our Jamie'd be here today"? Do you think I dinna' *care* that I've widowed our Rachy and sent wee Jamie's Da to the bottom of the sea?' Alex was on his feet now, thumping the table with his fist and trembling with emotion. 'You're all of ye aye humouring me and babying me as if . . . as if I were a child like yon,' and he pointed at Pearl who had opened one sleepy eye to stare at him over the comforting stopper of her thumb. 'But I'm nae a child any more. I canna' hope to make it up to you, Rachy,' he said, choking now on his emotion. 'Nothing and nobody could do that. And I canna' hope to take James's place – but I *can* work, for you and for wee Jamie and everyone. So please, Rachy?' He turned to her, with unconscious acknowledgement of her authority. 'Let me go to Greenland?'

'Can you find a place?' asked Rachel quietly. She had not realized the depth of Alex's misery, nor the extent of his guilt, but now that she did, her heart ached for him. He had always worshipped his brother James and now, as well as mourning him, he carried a self-imposed burden of guilt for his brother's death. With a shock, Rachel realized that it was the first time even in her thoughts that she had framed the words, and though she instantly amended them to 'supposed death' the harm was done. The first crack had appeared in the shell of hope which had guarded her heart for so many months against despair.

'Aye, I'll find a place.' Alex squared his shoulders, rubbed his eyes with the back of his sleeve, and vowed, 'This very night.' He pushed back his chair and strode for the door.

'Don't forget the *Steadfast* sails tomorrow,' called Rachel after him.

'I'll nae forget.' The smell of sea mist wafted in from the darkness with the distant boom of the foghorn from Girdleness, then was shut out again as the door closed.

'Where's Uncle Alex gone?' mumbled Pearl sleepily. At two, she took a lively interest in everything that happened in her own house and out of it, and talked as fluently as a child twice her age. 'Why's he awa' in the dark?'

For a moment no one answered. Isla was studying her sewing with exaggerated concentration, the glint of tears on her cheek, and did not seem to hear her daughter's question, while Maitland was watching Rachel's face with new anxiety. The flicker of hopelessness which had momentarily touched her had not escaped him.

'Where?' persisted Pearl, struggling to disentangle the blanket which covered her. 'Where's he gone?'

'Out, my wee lamb,' said George and Willy added kindly, 'Hush, or ye'll wake our Jamie.' Pearl looked quickly at her little cousin, then, seeing he was safely sleeping, decided to trust her uncles. Satisfied, she replaced her thumb and settled back into her cocoon, her eyes already closing.

'It is best,' said Rachel quietly. She looked unseeing at the plate in front of her and at her own hands, for once idle. 'He has a heavy burden to bear.' Then, with a quick shake of the head, as if to rid her thoughts of irritation, she pushed back the bench and stood up. 'We will talk of this tomorrow, Maitland. Tonight, I am a little tired.' She began to gather up the plates and carry them to the shelf under the window where stood basin and pail.

Maitland watched her as she swung the kettle from the fire, took the handle between a protective pad of flannel and tipped hot water into the basin. She refilled the kettle

139

from the water pail, swung it back over the embers and began to wash the dishes, as she had done for as long as Maitland could remember. He watched her hands redden with the heat of the water as they moved deftly in and out of the suds. The twins pushed back the bench with exaggerated care, so as not to disturb Pearl or the baby and, taking an empty pail each to refill before they returned to the *Steadfast*, went out into the Square. Isla still sat at the table, the cambric in her hands a froth of creamy snow in the lamplight and her hair almost as pale. Her hands were white, too, white and slim as they guided the needle along the row of tiny, perfect stitches. Suddenly Maitland's patience broke.

'Why can't you *help* her?' he demanded in a furious whisper.

Isla looked up, startled, her blue eyes innocent and questioning. 'But Rachel always . . .' She faltered to a stop.

'Rachel always *what*?' he prompted in a dangerously soft voice, but Rachel herself interrupted.

'Isla has sewing to do, Maitland. Something special which we may not know about, but which is important to her.' She dried her hands on her apron and took up the brush to sweep the hearth.

'Leave that.' Maitland put a hand on her arm. '*Isla* can do it later. You said you were tired.' He scooped up the sleeping Pearl and laid her gently in the little truckle bed where she slept at night. Then indicated the vacated chair. 'Sit there and let me mix you a soothing drink. I know just the thing.' When she began to protest, he silenced her with the best argument of all. 'It will give you strength, which you will need if you are to feed young Jamie properly.'

So Rachel allowed Maitland to mix her his own version of 'stourum', watched him measure oatmeal and hot water, heat milk over the fire and finally stir in a measure of whisky, and tried not to let despair engulf her. But her eyes were moist as she took the glass from his hand. 'Thank you, Maitland. You are kind to me.'

'Kind?' They were speaking in voices lowered for the sleeping children's sake, but this in no way diminished the vehemence of his protest. 'I wish to God I could do more, Rachel. I tell you, I have been tempted more than once to take ship to Riga and find out for myself what happened.'

'And I. But Alex has looked already and we cannot speak the language. Besides it is winter now and there will be ice. And who would run the shipyard while we were away?'

'We?'

'Surely you would let me come with you, Maitland, to look for my own husband?' The bleak despair behind the quiet words wrung Maitland's heart with an anguish the worse because he knew there was no cure, except James's return.

'If . . .' Maitland took a breath. 'The shipyard is working smoothly and I have a good team o' men. In the summer, if James has not come back, perhaps we will go, you and I, to look for him. Isla can keep house for you here.'

'Do you think we could?' At the light of hope in her eyes Maitland's heart turned with misgiving, but he could give no other answer.

'Yes, if young Jamie is strong enough to stand the journey, and that, my lass, depends on you. So drink up your medicine at once, and go to bed.'

'You must help her, Isla,' said Maitland quietly when Rachel had at last retired to the box bed and closed the doors. 'She is still weak from the child's birth and she

141

suffers much from James's absence. So do what you can for her, won't you?'

Isla's blue eyes were misted with emotion as she looked up from her sewing to nod her assent. 'It is so terrible for her and reminds me so much of my Davy, but I will try.'

'Are you not going to bed yourself?' he asked after a moment's silence in which she bent her head in the lamplight and continued to sew.

'In a while. First I want to finish this seam.'

Some garment for the baby, thought Maitland indulgently. She had known her own sadness and in her way, he supposed, Isla worked as hard as Rachel. Almost.

When at last Maitland himself went to bed, Alex had still not returned.

Rachel spent every morning in the office on Pocra Quay. It was a simple lean-to extension leading off the planning loft, but with its own door so that either office or loft could, if necessary, be open when the other was not. It contained a table, with shelves above it and drawers below, a stool, a chair for visitors, a lamp or two, and little else. One small window gave a view of the Quay and the harbour basin, and, when the inner door was open, she could see the length of the planning loft which was Maitland's domain.

In the office, Maitland had rigged up a makeshift cradle from a drawer in which the baby Jamie slept while Rachel attended to the increasing paperwork of their shipbuilding and trading venture. She could have left the baby at home, with Isla, but she found she could not bear to be parted from him; on the one occasion when she left him sleeping in the house in the Square she had not been in the office five minutes before she was seized with a terrifying fear that Isla had neglected him, that he had choked, suffocated, fallen, or that some spark had flown from the fire and ignited his cradle. She had run out of the office in such terror, leaving drawers open, doors unlocked, that had not one of the apprentices seen her and had the presence of mind to close the office door and lock it, any enemy might have walked in and helped himself to what he pleased. For the Christies had enemies, as everyone knew. James Christie's disappearance proved it.

After that, Rachel took Jamie everywhere, bundled in a plaid at her breast or sometimes, like a nestling bird, in a creel on her back. He was her only link with James and she adored him with an intensity which frightened her, sometimes, by its strength. Whenever she felt loneliness or despair threatening, she would cradle her baby close against her breast and let the warmth of his tiny body warm her own heart again with hope. When he woke, hungry, and she held him to her breast, the gentle tugging as he fed sent pleasurable sensations tingling through her body and filled her with remembrance, poignant and sweet. In those moments she knew, with simple faith, that her man would come home. Jamie replete, she would hold him over her shoulder, gently rubbing his back until his little digestion had settled and he fell asleep. His back was no wider than her hand, his shoulder blades frail as the thinnest mussel shell. Then she would cup the silky head in the palm of her hand and gaze at his sleeping face with a wonder which familiarity in no way diminished. His hair was dark, like James's, his face had a look of James about the eyes and mouth and even in the shape of his tiny feet and toes she saw James in miniature.

'Come back to me soon,' she whispered over and over in her head and, like an eastern mantra, the repetition gave her a kind of peace.

* * *

But that peace was threatened from a different quarter on the day after Alex's declaration. The *Steadfast* was to sail for London on the morning tide, with a load of stone. Rachel had worried much about the loading, lest the blocks of dressed ashlar should shift and scupper the ship, but the consignment was a good one, promising a high return, and the twins were skilled enough at distributing cargo in the hold. There was also, for the first time, to be a passenger – a client of George Abercrombie who required a berth at the last minute and was prepared to bed down wherever space allowed.

'A good fellow, Rachel lass, and knows his wine. Used to be at sea himself once, way back. Like me.' Abercrombie winked. Rachel knew, as they all did, that Abercrombie had made his money from smuggling brandy. 'Though *he* was in His Majesty's navy, so he'll pull his weight if need be. And he'll pay. Just you tell William and George that I've guaranteed Mr Bonnington a five-day passage and I want no hold-ups.'

That in itself was anxiety enough, for with the wind their master who could say when it might prove treacherous or fickle? But Alex being difficult made one more worry.

'Mind and tell them *good*, Rachel. Yon Farquharson crook's talking o' putting a steam-packet on the London run and you know what that'll mean, so see yon daft pair give Bonnington a trip to remember – for the *right* reasons. Who knows? He's a family man and he might need to send a daughter or a son to the capital one o' these days. So feed him well, too.'

Rachel had done the best she could to see that the ship's provisions were of highest quality, but short of sailing herself, she could do no more. Except worry. With the *Bonnie Annie* lost it was more than ever vital that the *Steadfast* made a good profit. At least the return shipment should be no problem – assorted goods of the usual kind, including a shipment of China tea, both Black and Green, for Abercrombie himself, a load of umbrellas for a merchant in Broad Street, and several hogsheads of cider.

Rachel banked the fire, checked the pot, picked up her sleeping infant and stepped out into the Square. She walked through North and South Squares to Coastguard Point and the pier at Pocra, and turned westwards towards the town. The Christie shipyard was the first she came to. On her right as she faced the town, it consisted of a planning loft and piece of open land set a little back from the road, behind the strip of land known as Dixon's patch. The Fittiegait divided Dixon's patch and the water, and from it, at right angles, a small lane led to the Christie yard and the adjoining warehouse – a semi-derelict property used by a city merchant to store a miscellany of goods from parasols to hobby horses, lamp-glasses and ink. Over the entrance in the lane Maitland had erected a sign, 'Christie Brothers, Shipbuilders', and when Rachel pushed open the gate and went in, a fellow appeared out of nowhere to bar her path before she had taken more than two steps; an old man, but light and quick on his feet.

'Oh, 'tis you, Mrs Christie. I am sorry, ma'am.' He doffed his hat and stepped out of her way with a nod of apology.

'That's all right, Watty. I am glad to see you do your job so smartly. We don't want all and sundry walking in here uninvited and unannounced. Is Mr Maitland about?'

'Aye, but there's a mannie wi' him, in the office. He sent for more whisky,' Watty added helpfully.

'Good. They'll likely be sealing a bargain.' The Christies used the old-fashioned method of sealing a contract – hands clasped over a Bible and health drunk in a dram. It would be best if she and Jamie did not interrupt. 'Then I will just look around the yard till he is free.'

Timber was stacked at one side of the yard, neat lengths of yellow pine and best English oak. They were building up quite a little business there, with Canadian teak, Scottish redwood and Scandinavian fir. At the other side of the yard stood the gleaming hull of the current ship, a smack of 150 tons for the coastal trade and almost complete. There was muffled hammering from somewhere deep inside the hull and the rasp of saw on plank.

The sea air was fresh and clean on her face and laced with the familiar smell of sawdust and seasoned wood, oakum and tar. It was a scent full of memories of the years when their enterprise first began – and of James. Rachel moved away till she could see beyond the ship and the boundary of their land, across the open space of Dixon's to the inner basin of the harbour with its calm water and roosting vessels. Beyond, the jagged skyline of Shiprow curved up from Quayside to Castlegate, with the upper window of Farquharson's company near its foot.

'Look, Jamie,' she whispered, though her child still slept. 'That's the man we have to watch.' And, she thought with a sinking of the heart, who will be watching us.

But it was good to have a constant reminder so close, lest they grow careless and forget. Rachel looked the other way, to the east, towards Pocra pier and the *Steadfast* at her moorings. Reassured by the controlled activity aboard, she turned her attention once more to the Christie building behind her. One day, she thought, we'll have a real office for the shipping company, with a fine oak desk and panelled walls, a fireplace with an overmantel, leather chairs and maybe a globe of the world on a stand. Large vessels still had to unload at Pocra before they could negotiate the inner basin. One day the harbour would be deepened, widened, made more accommodating for the increase of shipping which was sure to come with the end of war and with developing trade. Already a long chunk of the new jetty had been trimmed to make access easier for sailing traffic. There were capstans too, to haul in ships in a west wind. But the Pocra site would remain a good one however the harbour basin developed. And an even better one if they could expand.

Rachel studied their premises with a calculating eye. There was room for expansion, as James had said. One day, perhaps, they could buy the ground on either side of them and that stretch between them and the Quay. Dixon's . . . Rachel found her eyes drawn to the buildings which lined the Quay between Pocra and the town. There were warehouses, offices, Weighhouse and Sugarhouse and, at the inner end, close to the foot of Shiprow, tall, narrow, three-storeyed buildings which she knew were merchants' houses and similar. Trinity Quay was still a fashionable part of town, though not perhaps for much longer. She remembered when she had first arrived in Aberdeen, a shivering, half-drowned waif, and had told Andrew she would live in one of those houses one day. It had been only a day-dream then, but now . . . One of those houses, in a year or two, with the ground floor as offices and the rooms above for the family? A house on the Quay?

'Maybe we *will* live there one day, Jamie,' she whispered, 'when your Da comes home.' Meanwhile, they must make the best use of the land they did have. The days when the Christie men had done all the building work themselves had passed. They now had some half-dozen men working for them, including journeymen, apprentice, sawyer and blacksmith, and Maitland talked of hiring more as soon as they found more space. During the months James had been away Maitland, with Rachel's help, had established a tolerant and kindly dictatorship over his little workforce. He expected them to work with dedication and enthusiasm and, when orders required it, at full stretch, into the night if necessary, till the job was finished. In return he paid them well, had the brewery deliver a cask of ale to the yard in hot weather, gave them whisky and water with his own hand if the hours were unduly long, and allowed their wives or girlfriends to gather wood cuttings for their fires when they brought the men's midday 'piece' to the yard. Each man, from the oldest joiner to the youngest apprentice was regarded as one of the Christie family and expected to give loyalty in return.

So far, reflected Rachel, they had been fortunate in their choice. She knew, when she came here with her baby, that she came among friends who sympathized with her, worried with her, and hoped with her for James's return. They called her baby 'the wee master' and though they had long given up asking if there was news of his father, she knew they would tell her the slightest scrap of information they gleaned and expected her to tell them the same. Now she inquired kindly after Watty's family and moved on. Surely Maitland would not be long?

But Maitland had sealed whatever bargain had been in train and was ushering out his visitor. Rachel waited quietly in the shadow of the hull until the visitor had gone and Maitland turned back to the office, then she stepped forward and called to him.

'Rachel! How long have you been here?' He took her arm and steered her up the two steps to the office doorway, stepping aside to let her enter. 'If you had come five minutes earlier you would have been in time to seal an excellent bargain for the upholstery and painter-work of the new smack. It was not the lowest of the tenders but it was, I think, the most reliable.'

'Have you seen Alex?' asked Rachel, hardly glancing at the papers.

'Not since last night. He's likely at the *Steadfast*. But let me show you the leatherwork speci . . .'

'He is not. I have asked. And you know this voyage is an important one. They cannot sail a man short.'

'He'll not let us down,' soothed Maitland, and added, destroying any confidence he might have built up, 'and if he does, we'll easy find someone in the Square.' But at that moment the door behind them burst open and, panting and flushed with haste, Alex himself erupted into the room.

'I've run all the way frae the Whaling company,' he managed, collapsing into Maitland's chair and spreading his legs wide. 'To tell ye I've found a place. On the *Bon Accord*, with Captain Parker, sailing end o' March. They'd pay me from tomorrow if I work aboard on the fitting out – ye've no idea, Rachy, of the work to be done afore a whaler can put to sea, what wi' strengthening the hull and the guns and whaleboats and a', but I tellt Cap'n Parker I was bound to you for one more trip in the *Steadfast* and he said loyalty and honour was what he liked to see in any man he took on.' Alex's face was happier than for many months. 'I'm to go straight to him when the *Steadfast* returns. Fifteen days, I said,' he finished ingenuously, with a questioning look from Rachel to Maitland and back.

'Good,' said Rachel briskly. 'Then ye'll be able to see that the *Steadfast* makes London in the five days Mr Abercrombie has promised.'

She refused to think beyond that time to when Alex left them for Captain Parker's whaler. 'Ye may not have heard, but ye've a passenger with an appointment to keep in London. So, see he keeps his and ye'll maybe keep your own as well.'

149

'You are not angry, Rachel?' asked Alex, suddenly anxious. 'I would not want to hurt you in any way. Or wee Jamie,' he added as the infant stirred in Rachel's arms and began to whimper.

'No, I am not angry. Not now you have reappeared.'

'We did not know where you were,' explained Maitland mildly, his mind still more than half on the question of cabin upholstery, 'and the *Steadfast* sails in an hour.'

'But I know that,' protested Alex indignantly. 'Did ye think I would forget and miss the . . . tide.' He faltered to a halt as he realized the implication of his night's absence. 'I was asking about, like I said! I tellt ye I'd find a place before morning and I did. It took longer than I thought, that's all. Well, don't *look* at me like that,' he cried as neither of them spoke. 'I wasna' *whoring* if that's what ye're thinking!'

'There's nae call to shout, Alex,' said Maitland. 'Ye're upsetting the baby. And naebody's accusing ye of anything, so there's nae call to bluster neither.'

'I am sorry if I doubted you,' said Rachel, rocking her baby gently to and fro and managing a smile, though the memories Alex's outburst had aroused were painfully sharp. 'And I am glad you've found a place for the Greenland season. I had best start knitting, for you'll be needing thick stockings and vests to venture that far north.'

'Thank you, Rachel.' Impulsively, Alex put his arm round her and kissed her. 'And I am sorry if ye were worried on my account. But there's nae need. I let ye down once, I know, but I'll not do it again. I promise ye.'

'Alex . . .' Rachel's voice was at the same time hesitant and urgent. 'Remember the spring's coming. The ice will be melting soon in St Petersburg and in Riga Gulf. Ye will ask about for any news in London, won't you?'

For answer, Alex kissed her again, with comforting

affection, then straightened, squaring his shoulders like the man he aspired to be. 'Of course, Rachel. I will do all I can and bring you word.'

'Is there any news o' the Christie ship?' asked Jessie Abercrombie in a voice she thought carefully off-hand, but which made her husband raise an eyebrow in surprise. He laid down his fork, and looked at her across the table before saying carefully, 'The *Bonnie Annie*? None that I know of. Or did you mean the *Steadfast*?'

'Ye ken fine what I mean,' retorted Jess, 'so dinna' play the high-and-mighty wi' me. Ye've tellt me nowt for weeks now and I'm fair bustin' wi' curiosity, so out wi' it. What's the latest news?'

'Nothing at all, my dear.' Ever since his father's warning, and, if the truth were told, for several months before that, Fenton had kept what he thought of as business matters strictly to himself. Not only the business of Abercromble and Son, but of the Christies too. There had been too many rumours regarding Farquharson's villainy for him to ignore the fact that Jess was a friend of the man, and though they could not altogether avoid Farquharson's company, his son being married to Fenton's sister Clementina, Fenton could make sure that when they did meet his wife had nothing to gossip to him about. It had not been easy and had led to several unpleasant scenes, another of which seemed to be threatening now.

'What do ye mean, *nothing*?' demanded Jessica with a dangerous look in her fine eyes. Then, as Fenton, without replying, picked up his fork to resume the attack on Mairi's boiled beef, she changed her tactics to disarming feminity. It was a trick she had always had and one which, though he saw through it instantly, Fenton still had no power to resist.

151

'I am sorry, Fenton,' she said sweetly, reaching across the table to lay a warm, soft hand on his. 'I shouldna' nag ye, when ye need all yer strength to tackle yon piece o' leather Mairi's sent up. I dinna ken how she manages to ruin good butcher meat like she does, but I'll see to yer dinner mysel' tomorrow, I promise ye. Have some more wine instead. It's best claret from yer own Da's cellar, so I ken fine it's good.' She refilled his glass and topped up her own. 'Here's to us,' she said, 'and the wee ones.' Fenton, she knew, adored his little daughters, especially Augusta. 'And,' she added, looking over the rim of her glass with a deliberately provocative air, 'to the next?'

In spite of his resolve to remain unmoved, Fenton felt the stirring of an excitement which he knew she deliberately schemed for and would as cold-bloodedly deny, if she chose. It was a trick she had always been skilled at and meant, as he had learned too late, that she wanted something from him.

'Wi' Rachel Christie producing a fine son and showing him off like he was heir to the King o' Scotland I reckon it's time we did the same. Though we'll have a fine business to give *our* wee son, what wi' your father's new shop and all. I doubt the Christies will have owt but their fishing nets left by the time yon wee loon's a man.'

'Why do you say that?' asked Fenton carefully. Jess refilled his glass and her own, lowered her voice confidentially and said, 'Because they've lost yon new ship o' theirs, haven't they, and their cargo and custom with it. Word gets around. Folk don't like losers and they dinna' choose an unreliable ship when they can choose a better. Stands to reason. One more slip up, wi' yon London brig o' theirs, for instance, and they'll have no custom left, like as not. Especially wi' the steam-packets being so handy.'

'Did Farquharson tell you that?'

'Na, na,' said Jess airily, lapsing into the dialect of her childhood. 'Ony loon'll tell ye the same. But they'll maybe be planning to build more wi' our money?'

'Of course. They'll not let one setback put them . . .' Too late he realized the trap he had fallen into. But Jess rang the bell for Mairi at that moment and when she came, suspiciously quickly considering she should have been in the kitchen and not outside the door, her mistress said sweetly, 'I'll not be needin' you again tonight, Mairi. When ye've dealt wi' the dishes, ye can awa' to yer bed and have an early night.'

When the door had closed behind Mairi and her laden tray, Jess took her husband's arm and led him to the sofa in what she called the 'withdrawin' room'.

'I thought you could undo my stays for me tonight, Fen,' she murmured, drawing him down beside her and leaning against him. 'Later, when we've had a wee news together and maybe a brandy, to settle the stomach. Yon meat was awful tough. But you were telling me about yer Da's plans for the new Christie ship.'

'He hasn't any really,' began Fenton uncomfortably, then, as Jess began to caress the nape of his neck with a soft hand, all resistance broke. They were, after all, man and wife. They should have no secrets. Also, there was little enough to tell.

'They're planning to borrow, find more space and build ships faster than ever,' reported Jess with satisfaction. She and Fenton had been invited to dinner at the Farquharson house, or more specifically, the separate wing in which Robert Farquharson lived with his wife Clementina. The Farquharson parents were also there, with various other pillars of City society but, the dinner over, when the party reassembled in the drawing-room with its spacious proportions, long windows, beautifully corniced ceiling and elegant Adam fireplace, Farquharson senior had taken the first opportunity to steer Jess into the window recess out of hearing of the others and to ask about the Christies. '*And*,' she finished, 'they're taking passengers on the London run.'

Farquharson smiled without mirth. 'Are they, by Jove. I feared as much. Who's lending them the money?'

'Fenton's Da, of course. But ye needn't worry. Afore ye ask, he's nae planning a steam-boat, not yet awhile.'

'You are most accommodating, my dear,' said Farquharson with almost his old smoothness, 'and so well informed. I believe the days are growing longer,' he went on, raising his voice slightly. From the corner of his eye he had seen his wife edging window-wards, but a second, surreptitious glance told him she had been cornered by the Forbes woman, under the chandelier, and he relaxed again. 'The tenders for the new Public Rooms are going splendidly, by the way. The opening ball, in a year or so, will be the highlight of the Season and tickets difficult, if not impossible, to acquire. You must let me know, nearer the time, if you would like me to procure one for you.' He half turned away, then, as if by an afterthought, said lightly, 'No news of *James* Christie, I suppose?' Jessica hesitated. Farquharson knew a thing or two about Jess that she would not want broadcast across the town, but she also knew the same about him, and whereas she would give her eye-teeth for a ticket to that opening ball, she was going to go as an equal with anyone there, not as some sort of extra, in the crowd. She had seen Atholl Farquharson in less than flattering circumstances and he'd best not forget it.

'Yes and no,' she said airily. 'Ye know yon Christies are hard to keep down. I remember a time when everyone thought they'd never launch yon ship o' theirs, but they managed it. In fact, you let 'em use your land, though no

154

one in town could imagine why, you being a rival o' theirs.' She smiled innocently at him. 'Very kind of you, folks said. If only they knew . . .'

'Folks say a deal too much,' snapped Farquharson, made uncomfortable by the memory her words had aroused. 'But you'd best watch your husband doesn't get word o' *your* part in the proceedings.'

'He wouldna' believe it if he did,' retorted Jessica, though with hollow conviction. She was not at all sure that Fenton's jealousy, once aroused, might not be violent and implacable. Jessica liked being Mrs Fenton Abercrombie, with all the social status that conveyed, and had no intention of losing her position, especially not through the ill-will of that weaselly villain Farquharson with his yellow face and yellower belly.

'What is it ye want to know?' she asked, off-hand, and turned her back to look out of the window, apparently at the vista of Cairn o' Mount which was no more than a dark outline against the evening sky, but really at the reflection in the glass. She could see the room behind her, the crystal chandelier, the firelight, the elegant white walls and gilt-framed paintings, the rich colours of the women's dresses and the darker shapes of the men. But in front of them all she saw herself and unconsciously preened, reassured. Her figure was still good, in spite of two pregnancies and, she thought resignedly, no doubt a third. She fingered the emeralds at her throat and said aloud, 'I wonder if I'd suit amethysts?' Farquharson moved closer.

'We will have to see. A present from Clemmy and my son, perhaps? On the birth of your daughter? It would be a sisterly gesture, and with them having no children of their own to spend their money on. But you were saying . . . the Christies have given up all hope of James Christie's return?'

'No. I said they hadna'. They're sending again to

London, now the ice of the Neva's breaking, in case he's been frozen up somewhere in Russia.'

'Surely not?' Farquharson's voice was as light as his touch on her arm, but his naturally sallow face had paled. 'A foolish hope. From what I heard, both boat and man are at the bottom of the sea and have been these six months past.'

From what I heard. 'It's true then?' pounced Jess. 'You *were* involved.' One look at his face was enough. 'Why you evil, scheming . . .' then as voices sounded behind her, she broke off with a tinkling laugh like breaking china. 'La, sir, you *are* a caution. Isn't your husband a wag, Euphemia?' she added, deliberately familiar, and exulted in the look of helpless fury which Mrs Farquharson directed at her. But even that triumph was not enough to still the agitation which, most disconcertingly, troubled her thoughts.

Jessica was not used to thought, except on the simplest level. She liked or disliked, wanted or discarded, was entertained or bored. She had little acquaintance with the subtler shades of emotion, with the torment of divided loyalties or conflicting beliefs, and when they assailed her as they did now, she was at a loss to deal with the situation. She had always coveted James Christie, even after her marriage to Fenton, but when he rejected her for Rachel, her own childhood friend, Jessica's self-esteem had taken a buffeting. She had withdrawn to the bastion of her superior wealth and social position and ignored the Christies – or treated them with scorn. Now, however, she found herself sympathizing with Rachel in her trouble and suspiciously moist-eyed when she thought of James Christie dead, and by that rat-faced, chicken-legged Farquharson's doing. James was worth ten of him any day, amethysts or no. Forgetting James's rejection of her and his scorn, she remembered only the brief time when she and James had been together and could almost have wept. Almost, for she was not given to tears. When Farquharson kissed her hand at the end of the evening and murmured 'Amethysts?' she was tempted to clout him: instead, she gave him her coolest, most scornful smile.

The *Steadfast*, as promised, made London and back in record time. But it was a record with a price. One of the hogsheads of Jersey cider was opened by the customs men, making an unexpected and apparently random check, and was found to contain not cider but French brandy. The Christies were heavily fined. George Abercrombie was furious when he heard the news and hurried to the Pocra shipyard for a hastily summoned Company meeting. He found the Christies already gathered, including Rachel with wee Jamie asleep in her arms. Abercrombie scarcely noticed the child in his fury. 'Naebody will believe it wasna' me!' he shouted, crashing his fist down on to the table so that Maitland's plans and drawing implements scattered in confusion and the baby woke with a wail of fear. 'They'll say I was behind it. They'll say "There's Abercrombie up to his tricks again, smuggling brandy just like the old days." Why did ye not take more care, ye clumsy, stupid *gowks*?'

No one answered. What, after all, could they say? William, George and Alex had done no less than usual. Besides, the shipper was reputable, the porters known to them.

'Hush,' soothed Rachel to her son, then added loyally, 'They did their best in the time available, Mr Abercrombie.'

'Would ye have had us sample each cask?' asked Alex.

'And drink ourselves senseless afore we put to sea?'

157

said William and George. 'A cod to a kipper we'd ha' scuppered the ship.'

'Or taken so long sobering up we'd nae have been home yet.'

'Aye, aye, fair enough,' agreed Abercrombie. 'But remember all the same and keep yer wits about ye. Ye'd best not slacken vigilance even in distant ports, for yon villain's fingers reach far.' He glared through the window towards the inner basin and that building on the Shiprow. 'And wherever his ships go, his venom goes wi' them. There's aye men who'll do anything, even murder, for gold. Just remember, lads, he's out to ruin us, one way or another. He never could abide competition.'

But it was more than competition that drove Farquharson, as Rachel and the Christies knew: it was revenge, remembered mortification, and pure hate. Abercrombie, however, was aware of no more than business competition. 'Competition means he's to look to his standards, and his prices,' he said, 'and he's aye kept the lowest o' one and the highest o' the other.'

'I believe his emigrant ships are no better than cattle boats,' said Maitland quietly. 'He crams so many below decks that it is a wonder there is air to breathe. The conditions must be appalling.'

'But the money's good,' said Abercrombie grimly. 'What's it matter to him if half his "cargo" dies on the way across? He's got his profits and he's an empty ship to fill wi' timber on the return trip.' He glared morosely through the window, his brow furrowed with thought. 'Yon fine's going to set ye back a fair bit, Maitland.'

'Yes.'

'Had ye thought of the emigrant run yourselves? There's money there and as long as yon landowners are clearing out their crofters to make room for sheep, there'll be folk needing a crossing.'

'We have no suitable ship,' began Maitland, but Abercrombie interrupted impatiently, '*Suitable*? Any ship as floats is suitable. Ye're over-particular, lad.'

'Maitland is right,' said Rachel firmly. 'We have no ship fit for the transport of families in large numbers and until we have, and can offer both comfort and safety at a fair price, we'll stick to the coastal trade.'

'It's worth considering, though, one day,' said Maitland, a dreamy look in his eye. 'We could maybe buy up a brig and refit her. It would be quicker than building from scratch and we've a good team o' men.'

'We have no space and no money,' pointed out Rachel, 'and will have less than none when the fine is paid. We cannot borrow more. We have debts enough as it is.'

'Dinna' you worry, Rachel,' said Alex. 'You'll have money enough soon. Did they tell you, Mr Abercrombie, that I'm away to Greenland wi' the *Bon Accord*?'

Abercrombie looked from Alex to Rachel and back, then, with instant understanding, slapped him heartily on the back. 'Well done, lad. I see ye'll make the Christie fortune yet. Well Maitland, what are ye waiting for? Bring out the whisky and we'll drink to Wee Alex here – and confusion to our enemies!'

Maitland fetched glasses and the whisky jar and, glasses filled, all five drank to 'Wee Alex'. Alex blushed with pleasure and embarrassment, raised his own glass in a mumbled 'Thank you' and looked away out of the window. Then he stiffened. 'I do believe the old devil's watching us. Give me your telescope, Maitland.' He trained the glass briefly on the Shiprow window. 'Yes, by God, he *is* He's got that spyglass of his trained on our office.'

'Well?' said Abercrombie, grinning broadly. 'Ye know what to do.' With one accord all turned to the window, raised their glasses and cried, 'Confusion!' This was too much for the infant James who added his voice to theirs with all the vigour of his healthy, three-month-old lungs. In the laughter that followed, the fine was momentarily forgotten. 'It is all right, Jamie,' soothed Rachel, still smiling. 'It is only your uncles, celebrating. 'Tis nothing to be afraid of.'

'You're a grand wee mother, Rachel lass,' said Abercrombie kindly. He put an affectionate arm around her shoulders. 'And dinna' give up all hope. One day, God willing, yon man o' yours might come back, if only to see his wee son is behaving as he should be, eh lad?' He gave the baby a playful poke in the chest and the child, affronted, howled louder than ever.

'My, but he's a fine pair o' lungs,' said Abercrombie, in no way offended, 'but ye'd best give him his sup, lass, afore he deafens us all.'

Rachel had not asked if there was news from Riga. The brothers' silence on the subject was answer enough.

The day after the *Steadfast*'s return from London, the weather turned hostile with gusting rain and a high wind which rapidly became a hard, north-easterly gale. The brig *Perfect* was driven on to the rocky shore south of the old breakwater. The lifeboat was quickly launched but it, too, was driven on to the rocks by the tremendous breakers and the pull of the powerful flood tide. The crew saved their own lives, but the boat was badly damaged and unfit for further rescue work. As always, the wreck of a ship had a sobering effect on the seafaring community. Rachel saw in the wreck of the *Perfect* the wreck of their own *Bonnie Annie*, and all her secret terrors came crowding upwards to blacken any remaining hope and fill her dreams with nightmare.

Maitland, however, had other thoughts. 'We'll build up a repair shop one day,' he said. 'When we've the space.

Then we could salvage and rebuild as well as serve our own ships.'

'Aye,' put in Alex enthusiastically. 'We could maybe refit a brig for Greenland and send our own whaler?' He was to sail in the whaler *Bon Accord* the first fair wind, and the persistent gales made him impatient. 'I'd like fine to be in charge o' my own whaling ship one day.'

'Ye'd best wait till ye've seen a whale,' teased George. 'Ye might not like what ye see.'

'And neither might the whale.'

'They're nae all willing to be catched, lad, and if they choose they can lead ye a merry dance.'

'Cod to a kipper he doesna' catch a single fish.'

'And a pin to a scrimshaw I do,' retorted Alex, in the familiar childhood pattern of taunt and retort.

While her fingers flashed over the wool of Alex's stockings, Rachel could not help remembering the time when her James had gone whaling and the anxieties of his absence, anxieties which were as nothing to the raw ache in her heart over the past six months. Alex would be safe enough. Captain Parker was renowned throughout the whaling fraternity and she had no fears on that score.

Nevertheless, when the *Bon Accord* put to sea at the end of March she, with the rest of interested Aberdeen, followed the progress of the city's whalers with anxious attention. Only Isla seemed unconcerned. To be sure she expressed anxiety till news came that the Aberdeen whaling fleet had reached Lerwick safely and relief when it did, but she did so with a detachment which, thought Rachel, was almost absent-minded in its calm. Isla had merged into the household tolerably well and was useful in her way, taking over various tasks which freed Rachel to spend more time at the shipping office, but she was no more intimate now with Rachel or any of the Christies than she had been on arrival. She mourned still for Davy,

161

Rachel told herself in the girl's excuse. She is lonely and burdened with the responsibility of a child, alone.

Pearl was certainly developing into a child of ability with, said Louise in an unguarded moment, twice the spirit of her mother and ten times the character. For Louise and Pearl had formed a relationship close and mutually satisfying. The child was full of questions which Louise delighted to answer, and she was already teaching Pearl her letters and simple addition sums with pebbles from the beach. 'That child has brains,' Louise told Rachel, 'and should be allowed to use them. She must go to school as soon as she is old enough and be encouraged to study hard. I see a great future for her one day.'

'You'll have her a doctor before she's ten,' teased Rachel. 'I saw you drawing her a picture of a skeleton with all the bones named.'

'And why not? One day there will be female doctors, though sadly not in my time.'

'I do not see how you can talk of such a thing,' ventured Isla who had been sewing quietly in a corner and taking no part in the conversation. 'Illness and pain are so frightening.'

'All the more reason for learning how to cure them,' said Louise briskly and Isla, deflated, returned to her stitching. Afterwards Louise was ashamed. She had resolved to tolerate the Duthie girl for Rachel's sake, and to be as pleasant to her as she could, but in spite of her resolve she continued to find the presence of Isla an irritant and on the occasion when Andrew's visits coincided with hers, a source of awkwardness and even reproach. For try as she might, she could find nothing to say to the Duthie woman and Isla certainly had nothing to say to her. But when Andrew Noble visited Rachel, as he did regularly since baby Jamie's birth, to keep a brotherly eye, he said, on both mother and son, Isla

Duthie sparkled into an animation which needled Louise even more than did the girl's usual lack of conversation. What made it more galling was that Andrew apparently enjoyed it, and after such encounters Louise invariably spent the rest of the day struggling to subdue a jealousy which she felt was not only unworthy of her, but presumptuous too. For Andrew was free to befriend whom he chose without seeking *her* permission.

But Louise continued to call on Rachel nevertheless, to cheer and support her as the weeks passed and to bring her news of the whaling fleet. It was Louise who told them of the bankruptcy of a city trader and the impending roup of his effects 'Including his warehouse,' she finished, 'which is adjacent to your yard.'

The warehouse itself was in a state of near collapse, the land area small, but it was, as Louise said, next to their own and, as theirs was, divided from the Quay by Dixon's patch.

'We could demolish the warehouse,'
'Sell the wood for timber,'
'Clear the land,'
'Lay the keel of a second ship,'
'And we've still the paper, granting launching permission.'

The family discussion was swift, excited, and unanimous. They would borrow, buy the land, clear it, and lay down the keel of a new ship as soon as work could begin. Fearing double-dealing, they found an agent to bid for them – successfully. The following day Maitland directed the entire work force to erect a new boundary fence, enclosing the old land with the new, and at the end of the day, the Christies gathered to drink to the new land and to the future.

'We've done it, Rachy,' said Maitland, his eyes bright with excitement and hope. 'We can build two ships

163

together now, take on more men, speed up production
. . . I see such a future for us.' Rachel was silent, but her
eyes as she looked over the new land with that semi-
derelict building and weed-pitted turf, were as bright as
Maitland's. The successful purchase seemed a good omen
to her, not only for the future of the yard, but for her
private hope.

'I will write the usual letter to Farquharson tomorrow,'
Maitland was saying. 'We'll aim to launch by the end of
next week. Then, God willing, we'll put all hands to
clearing the new land so we can lay the keel of that 300-
tonner Abercrombie wants, for the Baltic trade.'

But though by now the ice had melted in even the
remotest estuaries of the Baltic, there was no news from
Riga of Rachel's husband or of that other, missing,
Christie ship.

April 1820

He opened his eyes to the sound of seabirds and the low
muttering of the old woman's prayers. Slowly, he looked
upwards, past the wooden crucifix on the timbered wall,
to the roof beams and the darkness beyond, a darkness
speckled here and there by paler points where gaps in the
thatch let in early light. Puzzled, he stared at those specks.
They had not been there yesterday. Usually the layer of
snow which had lain like a sparkling slab on the roof top
throughout the winter months insulated those inside from
light, as it did from the worst of the cold. He lay quietly,
as he had learnt to do, waiting for thoughts or memory to
visit him. Instead, he heard a slow drip from somewhere
beyond the wall at his head, then the tinkling of a hundred
others, pitter-pattering in broken rhythm from fir branch
and eave with, now and again, from deeper in the forest,
a dull thud as a pat of snow slid from its winter perch to
the ground. Was it imagination or was the air on his cheek
of a different quality? Had the grip of winter loosened at
last, so that he would be free to go? But to go where?
Like a great, trapped bird the question beat at his brains
as it had done now for weeks, ever since he had regained
full consciousness after his long illness and had realized
the emptiness of his mind.

Between the rafters and the rooftop were bulked shapes
and the sprawled darkness of nets. Fishing nets. Staring
at them, he tried, as he tried every day, to remember, but
the empty basin of his mind remained blank and clean as

new scrubbed wood. Every morning, staring at those fishing nets, he knew they were familiar, and the cry of the seabirds brought an echoing cry from somewhere beyond the edge of memory. As always, he strained into that darkness, willing it to clear, willing a crack, however small, to appear in the vast, blank veil which screened his mind. Sometimes when the old man sat at the fire in the lamplight, carving a little wooden animal or a boat, he almost remembered, or when the old woman bent over the fire. Almost. But always the memory slipped away, eluding, teasing him, dancing out of reach like a mischievous child. He raised himself on one elbow to survey the room which was also in many ways familiar: yet whether with the familiarity of his six-month sojourn there or with something deeper, he did not know. The floor was sanded earth, the hearth an open fire on iron fire-dogs, with a cooking pot suspended from a hook. The walls were of timber with a shelf for wooden bowls and platters. Dried herbs and strips of dried meat hung from the low beams and there was a wooden tub of flour in one corner. In another, tied to a peg in the wall, was the family goat. Soon the old man would lead it out to the edge of the trees and tether it to a stake, to root out food as best it could. The old woman herself was bundled up in shawls and an assortment of black woollen garments and the old man, though not in the room, would be wearing the fur hat, fur coat and leather breeches he always wore. They were called Friida and Priit, that he knew, and they called him 'Jan' because the initials on his shirt were 'J. C.' but whether Jan was his name or not, he could not tell. He furrowed his brow with the effort of memory and felt the flesh pull. It had become a habit with him in such moments to finger the jagged scar across his forehead, feeling the ridged span of new skin in the hope that he might remember who or what had disfigured him. He had

166

a scar on one hand, too, but that was an old scar, he could tell, belonging to that other life.

Carefully he listened to the familiar sounds of morning, hoping as always that something would trigger the latch and open the door of memory: in the distance, the sea breathing gently against the headland; seabirds mewing and mourning somewhere high overhead – out to sea, perhaps, following a shoal of herring? The herring, too, were familiar, salted and packed into a barrel at one end of the cottage, though the barrel, at the end of winter, was almost empty. From the far corner of the room came the gentle, rhythmic grinding of the goat's jaws, chewing endlessly at the bundle of dried furze the old woman had given it, and, from closer at hand, the low mumble of the old woman herself and the click of her beads. It was a soothing sound, at the same time peaceful and reassuring and he found himself repeating with her, under his breath, 'Sanctus, sanctus, sanctus Dominus Deus Sabaoth . . .' She knelt under the crucifix fixed by a nail to the wall above the simple *prie-dieu*, her head bent, her gnarled fingers moving over the polished beads. Then she made the sign of the cross and pulled herself creaking to her feet. Her joints were swollen and knotted, her back bent, but the face she turned on him, though furrowed, was sweet-tempered and serene. She smiled and nodded to him, said something in her own language which he understood to be a greeting. He swung his legs carefully to the floor and as carefully stood up. His leg no longer pained him as it had done and with exercise was growing straighter and stronger, though he would always walk with a limp. But Friida was beckoning, urging him to sit at the table on the carved wooden chair which Vanya Priit himself had made. She ladled a basin of warm goat's milk from the pot beside the fire and set it carefully in front of him. Then she broke off a chunk of black bread from the loaf on the table and handed it to him with smiles and encouragements to him to eat. She stood watching him until he had dunked and eaten the last of the bread and had drained the basin of milk, then she smiled with pure joy.

'*Deo gratias.*' She made the sign of the cross and repeated the words, urging the stranger to do the same. Carefully, haltingly, he pronounced '*Deo gratias.*' The old woman beamed delightedly, took his hand and guided it to forehead and breast, then from left to right. '*In nomine patris, et filii et spiritus sanctus.*' Then she stood waiting, her lined old face eager as a child's. Slowly he repeated, '*In nomine patris et filii et spiritus sanctus,*' and made the sign of the cross. Friida's face lit up with a sunburst of joy and she clasped him to her breast, kissing him first on one cheek, then the other. Then, chattering excitedly, she took his hand, drew him to the door and opened it on to a changed world.

Where until yesterday had been a snow-laden, ice-locked daguerreotype of black and white, with silver grey from the sea beyond the headland, there now was a speckled landscape of sparkling blues and yellows, greens and browns. In the stream bed the ice had split apart and green water frothed up through the cracks.

In the forest, green spines of fir and larch and the delicate buds of aspen shook free from their snowy covering and sprang upwards in all the glory of pale new leaf. Underfoot, the trodden snow of the yard beside the little wooden cabin was a shimmering sludge of brown earth and yellow strands of straw and the depleted wood-stack against the north wall of the house, though still capped with shrinking dabs of snow, sparkled and danced in the sunlight with every shade of cream and gold and rich dark brown. Seeing that fresh, clean wood, stacked so neatly, his brow furrowed in habitual puzzlement.

Lately, since his leg had grown strong enough to bear his weight, he had helped Priit to cut and stack the logs, going once into the edge of the forest to fell a small tree. Together they had sawn it into manageable lengths, together they had stacked the pieces on to a kind of sleigh and drawn them home to the yard, where he had sawn them into shorter lengths, and finally split the largest with a wedge and a mallet till they were of a size to stack against the wall. He had enjoyed the work, but the smell of the sap and the sawdust had disturbed his memory as the gull's cries did, and as the fishing nets and Priit's carvings did. Now, seeing the logs sparkling fresh in the warmth of morning, he crossed to the pile, took up a log and studied it, noting the grain of the wood, the slightly spongy layer between bark and core. He peeled off the crust of bark and stroked the wood beneath. It was smooth as satin, both straight and strong. Fine for shipbuilding.

But Friida was tugging his arm. 'Come.' The tiny, one-roomed cabin stood on the edge of the woodland, facing eastward to the sea. Between hut and sea was flat marshy land, ending in a cliff, in some places twenty feet high, in others, ten. To both north and south stretched the coast-line in a curve so wide it was almost straight, but though today was a clear day, he could see no sign of town, village, nor even homestead and not a single ship on the sea. He knew that sea was the Gulf of Riga, choked with pack-ice throughout the winter months, knew that Riga itself was somewhere to the south-east, though how far away he could not tell. To the right of the cabin, beyond the privy and the vegetable patch, the land dipped into the shallow valley of a stream, hitherto ice-locked and festooned with icicles, but now gurgling and bustling into life.

'Spring is here,' said the old woman in her own language. 'Come.' She set off down the path which followed the line of the stream bed till it widened into a river and met the sea. He followed. In the months he had lived with the old couple, he had ventured only once to the sea, with Priit, but they had gone no further than the estuary of the river where it widened into a natural pool, before narrowing again at the outlet to the sea. Here Priit's boat lay upended in the sheltered cove above high water mark. Priit had inspected his boat, pointing out various parts of it to the younger man, asking him questions, but his brain had not been able to sort out the strange language enough to understand what the old man wanted, and though the sight of the boat had nudged gently against the closed door of his mind, the tremor had faded again and the old man, disappointed, had led him home. They had not gone again.

Now, however, when Friida led him round the last curve of the sandy path, which was piebald with melting snow and tangled with sea-plants and the sharp spines of marram, they saw Priit had righted the little boat somehow and was inside it, greasing the rowlocks with a lump of animal fat. A pair of oars was propped against the cliff and the young man recognised them as those from the rafters of the cottage. The old man saw them approaching, called a greeting, and when they drew close enough, indicated that he was to help to launch the little craft.

Friida stood watching, smiling and nodding encouragement, her shawl drawn tight over her head and shoulders to keep out the breeze which, though milder than the winter winds, was still sharp enough to penetrate old bones and set them aching. Priit gestured and chattered to his companion in the pattern they had evolved between them over the months, sometimes repeating one word

170

several times, with accompanying signs, sometimes lapsing into a flood of explanation till his uncomprehending stare or puzzled frown brought him up short again and he resumed the single words. Now, however, the young man needed no instruction. He moved to help Priit as if he had always done so, manhandling the boat to the water's edge with natural skill, then pushing it into the calm waters of the pool, at the same time boarding the craft and slipping the oars into position in the rowlocks. The old woman, seeing his expertise, clapped her hands with pleasure and called aloud, 'Bravo, Jan!' He manoeuvred the boat and held it steady while her husband climbed aboard, then the old man took the rudder and with a wave of farewell to his wife, told him to row.

Friida watched the tiny craft slip into the tossing current at the mouth of the river, ride the billows successfully and move on into the deeper troughs of the sea, then, raising a hand in blessing, she turned to make her slow way home.

He watched her, frowning. The figure waving was somehow familiar, yet not familiar. The small, stooped peasant woman, hobbling back up the sandy path, was dear to him for her kindness and loving care, but he knew she was alien, as the windswept stretch of the headland was alien, with the crowded trees of the forest and the tiny cabin, the potato and barley porridge and black bread, and the sulphorous, alien beer. He shook his head impatiently to dislodge the shrouding mist, but it merely shifted position and settled again. He gave up the effort and concentrated on rowing.

The old man was steering them northwards, following the line of the coast and near in to the shore which, on closer acquaintance, yielded clefts and fissures in its seemingly unbroken curve. In one of these fissures, some ten minutes' rowing time from the cottage, they came upon what Priit was seeking. With a swing of the rudder, the old man directed the boat shorewards and he, glancing over his shoulder to judge depth and draught, saw the frosted outline of a timber skeleton, black against the sandstone cliff.

Minutes later, he and the old man were standing in the lee of the wreck which had been driven hard against the cliff edge and pounded repeatedly by winter seas, had been split, de-masted, disembowelled, and finally silted up with stony sand. The inlet seemed to be a trap for flotsam and debris of all kinds and together, as by unspoken agreement, the old man and the young began to pick over the tangle of seaweed and splintered wood which choked the rocks at high water mark. He knew by a combination of sign language and scratched pictures with charcoal and wood, that Priit had found him unconscious on the shore, had conveyed him somehow by means of the sleigh and his wife's help to their hut, had given him the harsh white spirit they called vodka, with gruel and black bread, and had nursed him back to health. Now, standing beside that broken skeleton of a ship, he supposed the ship must have been his, but he felt no affinity with the sea-sodden, hoar-frosted bones which were all that remained. The prow had gone, snapped off by the rocks or the grinding waves, and the stern was barely recognizable. Nowhere was there any trace of a name. He kicked the sand from a broken spar and turned it over with his foot. Then he dropped to his haunches, wincing briefly at the pain in his injured leg, to study it closer. Priit came hurrying up to investigate as he stood up again, the wooden spar in his hand.

'Look,' he said, holding it out to Priit. There in the wood was a round hole, perhaps three inches across, smooth on the inside, but burst into splinters on the outside, as if an iron stake had been hammered through it. The old man nodded his head as if he knew all about such things and pointed to the hull, saying something incomprehensible.

'There are more of them?'

'Ya. Ya.' Together they inspected what broken spars and planking of the hull remained and the old man was right. There were holes in several places, not, as one would have expected from the vessel's pounding against jagged rock, penetrating from the outside inwards, but in every case the opposite, and too neat to have been made by accident. There were also broken sections where whole areas had been splintered inwards, as was usual when a ship was driven, helpless, against a cliff, but it was those treacherous, man-made holes which intrigued both men. Old Priit looked at his companion hopefully, one eyebrow raised. 'Jan remember?'

Slowly he shook his head. 'No. *Niet*. Nothing.' The old man shrugged, raised his eyes to heaven and spread his hands wide, then turned away to renew his search along the tide line. After a moment he followed, working his way in the opposite direction. He found a nail, a broken link of chain, a section of panelling with a carved leaf motif, and finally, a piece of varnished plank, with painted letters on it: 'NIE   AN'. He was staring at the disconnected letters, his brow painfully furrowed, when he heard an excited shout from behind him. He turned and saw the old man waving his arms about in agitation. 'Come, Jan, come!' he shouted and pointed to something in the sand at his feet. The younger man dropped his plank beside his pile of treasures and ran across the short stretch of shingle which separated them, past their own small craft, over rocks slippery with seaweed and past swirling pools of seawater which eddied and sucked with every wave, to where Priit stood looking down at a painted wooden mass, half buried in the sand. He saw the glint of gold leaf, the glow of scarlet and the shimmer of ebony, then he dropped to his knees in the sand and began digging like someone demented, to unearth their treasure.

It was a figurehead in the shape of a mermaid with golden tail-scales and flowing golden hair. Her lips were scarlet, her eyes almonds of black, her bare breasts round as melons. Some of her paint was chipped, she had lost a tail fin, one wooden nipple and the tip of her nose, but apart from that she was miraculously whole.

He stretched out a hand and touched her, tracing the line of hair and tail and for the first time the curtain lifted long enough to show him a shipyard with men working and himself in charge. Carefully, he turned away from the recollection, lest too close examination scatter the pieces. Later, in the darkness of his bed at night, he would examine that scrap of memory closer, but for the moment he was content to let the curtain gently fall.

'We will take it home,' he said to the old man and together they manhandled the heavy, sea-sodden object to their boat and heaved it over the gunwales. He fetched his other treasures, the nail and panel-piece and holed plank, and they pushed away from the shore, dipping in the waves which were growing livelier as the breeze freshened.

The sky was pale with scudding cloud, the sea an ice-green expanse flecked with foam and as he dipped the oars and raised them, sunlight glinted in a string of water-pearls. Looking at the pale gold sandstone of the head-land, with the bent-grass singing in the wind, then at the sea behind him and beyond, he felt his shoulders straighten and his heart quicken with excitement. He was in his true element. He was a seaman, born and bred. The figurehead at his feet was his, with that skeleton of salted timbers buried in sand and sea. Into his brain washed a confusion of pictures, a ship's deck, flapping canvas, sea spray and men's voices, and somewhere, in the hazy distance, a softer voice, loving and gentle – a woman's voice. Overhead the gulls wheeled and cried into the spray, echoing that other cry inside his memory. He shook his head, with impatience, trying to shake the scattered fragments into some sort of picture. Instead, they blurred into one opaque mass and dispersed. No matter. His heart was quickened, his new faith strong. Now that spring had come and unlocked the ice-bound land, he would come again to where his ship lay and search for the rest of his ship's name. He would piece together what scraps he could find and surely then, with patience and the sun's healing, he would remember?

The following day he was woken by the noise of the stream in spate. Its water boiled white and green and high against its banks and from all over the forest came the steady patter of thawing ice. That afternoon Vanya Priit took him north along the headland again, but this time on land. They came to a patch of grass in a natural dip of the dunes, with clumps of sea-pinks here and there and a sort of flowering bush. There were several simple wooden crosses, each with a date. Old Priit indicated the newest and he read, 'Sept. 1819'.

'A man from your ship,' the old man said, in his own language. 'You too were like one dead, then you groaned and I fetched my wife.' He beamed at the younger man. '*Deo gratias*,' he said and made the sign of the cross.

'*Deo gratias*,' he echoed and did the same. When they returned to the hut, Friida had made thick potato soup and fresh bread and there was a new pat of goat's cheese. Flowers sprang up on the headland and in the soft grass under the forest trees. The birds' chorus in the mornings was deafening. He went every day now to search for wreckage, sometimes on foot along the shore, sometimes

175

with Vanya Priit, in the boat. He went fishing too, with Priit, and at those times he felt so much at ease he could have sung aloud, and in the evenings when the old folk sat at their fireside, she with her lacework – a complicated tangle of bobbins and thread – and he with his woodcarvings, he too would whittle at a stick or mend holes in the old man's fishing net, and sooner or later either Friida or Priit would hum a tune gently or break into song. 'All roses I would offer to you,' they sang, 'and with garlands adorn your head.'

The goat was taken out to pasture and tethered on the headland and he grew strong on her milk and the cheeses Friida made. He and Priit caught fish, and set traps in the woods for hare and rabbit. So the spring days passed till the trees were in full leaf, the air warm and the turf lush underfoot.

His collection of flotsam yielded him no jolts of memory, but he persisted in his search until, on a day in mid-May, his search was rewarded. He and Priit had risen early and been shooed out of the house by Friida who had embarked on a frenzy of house-cleaning. They had felled another tree and now that the heavier work was done, he had left the old man splitting logs and gone, as usual, along the shore, head down, eyes alert and searching. He did not take the boat alone: the old man was afraid for him and did not wish it and besides, on foot he could search a greater stretch of shore. He found it half a mile north of the wreck, a piece of lettered wood bearing the sea-scoured letters 'BON . . .' He had no need to fit it against the other to know the inscription.

'The *Bonnie Ann*,' he breathed in wonder, then, 'No. Wait. The *Bonnie Annie*.' Slowly, almost fearfully, he waited, motionless, as the memories crowded in, disjointed scraps, tumbling and jostling for precedence – a harbour, a shipyard, a group of men. But the edges were still in shadow, the details blurred. Who was he? Where was he from? Perhaps, when he fitted the two pieces of wood together those other jigsaw pieces would also connect? He turned and made fast for home.

But when he rounded the headland and the brow of the dunes, something about the cabin was different. Vanya Priit was not in the yard, nor in the little vegetable plot, and Friida was nowhere in sight. Usually on a fine day she would be pottering about the yard, spreading linen to dry, or helping Priit, but today there was a smart, scoured look about the little homestead, as if it had been put on its best behaviour. And there were strange hoofprints in the yard. His steps slowed as he reached the door and finally stopped. He stood a moment, listening, propped his new find against the wall and hesitantly pushed open the door.

'Jan!' cried Friida, hurrying towards him and seizing his arm. 'Come! Here is Anya, our daughter,' she chattered on excitedly in her own tongue. 'Anya speaks English.'

He saw a red-cheeked, dark-eyed and smiling girl in a black and red striped skirt, black waistcoat and white blouse. On her head she wore a little pyramid of decorated lace, with ribbons and embroidery and was obviously dressed in her best. He noticed there were little cakes on the table, tea with butter in it, fresh bread and honeycomb and on the fire a pot of something bubbling which smelt aromatic and delicious.

'Embrace, embrace!' cried Friida, laughing, and thrust them together till they were kissing on both cheeks, he as red-faced now as she.

'Now the ice has melted,' chattered Friida happily, while Anya smilingly translated, 'my Anya has come to visit me. She has brought us a fine hen for the pot, with herbs and eggs and honey from her bees. Is she not a fine daughter to her old mother and father? Her husband,

177

too, is a good son, though he could not wait. He needs the horses for the ploughing. But he will fetch her tomorrow and you will meet.' Anya and her husband Toomas lived inland, it seemed, on a small tenant-farm.

'We have told Anya all about you, Jan, our new son whom God sent to us and who had no family of his own. Pour vodka, Priit,' urged the old woman, beaming, 'so we can drink the health of our family – Jan and Anya and Vanya Toomas who is not here, and little Toomas who is.'

For the first time he noticed the bundle on the bed. Cocooned in layers of spotless flannel and wedged from rolling by a cloth bundle which he took to be Anya's clothes, lay a fat-cheeked and sleeping infant with a fringe of light brown hair protruding from his embroidered bonnet.

'Show Uncle Jan his nephew Toomas,' ordered Friida, beaming with pride and love.

Shyly Anya picked up the infant and held him out to the stranger, her dark eyes soft and timid, but with a hint of laughter in her full red lips. 'See,' she said. 'Take him.'

Awkwardly he held out his arms and took the child, but his hands were shaking. The infant stirred, opened his eyes, looked up at the strange, bearded face so close to his own – and howled. Friida, Priit, and Anya laughed in unison, but he did not laugh. Instead he stared down at the tiny creased face, the flaying, helpless fists and the toothless mouth, while the cries rose in a piteous crescendo of appeal.

'Here, let me take you, little one,' crooned Friida, scooping Toomas deftly from his hands. 'You will give Uncle Jan a headache. Mamma will feed you very soon. There, there, there, there . . .' she soothed while Anya seated herself at the fire and held out her arms for her son. Then, with one shy glance at the stranger, she

178

unbuttoned her bodice and put her child to the breast. Abruptly the cries ceased and as abruptly his knees gave way. He slumped on to the bench at the table and held his head in his hands. From somewhere beyond the turmoil he was aware of Friida speaking, then of Priit. Someone touched his shoulder, put a glass in his hand and obediently he drank, while his brain filled with a tumble of memories so thick and colourful and urgent that he thought his head would burst. For the infant's cry had shattered the fragile door which had shut out memory and at last he knew who and what he was. A huge tide of rage swept him to his feet and he cried, 'I must go!'

'Hush, hush,' soothed Friida, anxious now. Even little Toomas's eyes opened above the full dome of his mother's breast and studied him with brief curiosity before closing again in blissful concentration. 'Anger is not good.'

'Tell us, my son,' said Priit quietly, a hand on his shoulder, 'In your own language. Anya will explain.'

Obediently he sat down at the table, but the face he turned on them was harrowed with pain, anxiety, anguish and anger.

'I am James Christie,' he said, though his voice trembled with the power of his anger. 'I sailed my ship to Riga from Aberdeen in Scotland. My brother was with me, and other crew. I do not remember yet what happened to the others,' for that part of his memory was still blurred, 'or how my ship was wrecked, but there were evil men and treachery.'

There was the hiss of indrawn breath and both Friida and Priit, standing anxiously on either side of him, crossed themselves swiftly with a muttered prayer.

'By God,' swore James, striking the table with his clenched fist. 'I will avenge the wrong done to me and my brother.' He remembered that headland grave with its simple wooden cross. Suppose . . .? *I swear it.*

179

'No,' cried Friida. 'You must not. Tell him, Priit. Tell him, Anya.'

'My mother is right,' said Anya in her halting English. 'To seek revenge is bad. *Vengeance is mine, saith the Lord*. You must not presume to do the work of God.'

'Does he understand?' asked Friida anxiously.

'I understand,' said James, 'but . . .'

'No "but".' Friida put her arms around him and clasped his head against her breast. 'Promise old Friida that you will not seek revenge. Promise Friida who loves you as a son. Promise.'

But the word 'son' had brought back other memories. James pushed back his chair and rose to his feet. 'I have a wife,' he said, with wonder in his voice. He took Friida's old hands in his. 'And, God willing, a *child*. So you see,' he finished simply, 'I must go home.'

'Toomas will take you to Riga,' said Priit. All talk of revenge was forgotten in this new urgency.

'Tomorrow,' added Friida, the tears standing already in her eyes. 'Your poor wife will be so unhappy. You must hurry home to her.'

'But promise to come back and see us,' she pleaded the following day when he prepared to leave. All that was left of the *Bonnie Annie*, except the figurehead which he left in their keeping, was in a bundle with a change of shirt and the bread and cheese Friida had pressed upon him. Priit had given him silver, which he had refused, but Friida had pleaded so tearfully that he had had to give in at last and accept.

'You are not yet well,' she insisted. 'You will need food and lodging until you find a passage home. Take it.'

'Thank you,' he said. 'I will repay you one day. I will not forget.'

'And you will not give way to anger and to violence?'

'I will try not to, Friida, for your sake.' James would

not promise, for though he wished to please her he felt the rage of revenge seething hot and violent like a constant pain now, inside him. James did not know whether he could continue to curb it or whether one day such emotion might not erupt and sweep him, helpless, on a course of action beyond his control.

Friida seemed to understand. She sighed with sadness, and said only, 'You will come back again to see us?'

This time James felt no hesitation. 'I promise.'

Anya's husband Toomas was to take him to Riga in his wagon and return again for Anya and his son. 'It is nothing,' he insisted when James protested he could travel on foot. 'You are my brother. I will take you.'

Now first Priit, then Friida hugged him in a tearful embrace, but it was Friida's final words that brought the tears to James's eyes, too.

'Promise me, Jan,' she said, 'that you will say your prayers as I have taught you, for my sake?' Wordless, he nodded. She reached up and slipped a chain with a simple wooden cross over his head. '*Pax domini vobiscum*,' she whispered. 'God keep you safe, my dear, dear son.'

On a day in June, Louise found Rachel sitting in the doorway of the cottage, a piece of sewing in her hands and Jamie asleep in a cradle at her side. Behind her, the cottage door was open to let in the late afternoon sunlight and inside the house Isla was pressing a garment with a flat-iron on the table. Maitland had taken Pearl with him to the shipyard, where she liked to play with the ship models and with the building blocks of polished wood which one of the carpenters had made for her from off-cuts. The *Steadfast* was expected hourly, but the hen was already simmering over the fire, the bread made and nothing more to be done but wait.

It was a tranquil afternoon, the shadows clear-cut and

181

lengthening into evening. Gulls drifted lazily at the harbour mouth, or stood in idle crowds along the shore, knee-deep in the shallows, enjoying the lingering warmth of sand and sun. In the Square whole families sat outside their doors, some knitting, some mending nets or lines, some merely smoking or sleeping or idly passing the time of day with a neighbour. The air was scented with lilac blossom from a distant garden and with woodsmoke. Rachel fetched a chair for her friend, but they had hardly settled down together when Andrew arrived to join them.

'It promised to be such a pleasant evening that I thought I would stroll over and see how you are faring, Rachel,' he began. A movement in the doorway caught his eye and he added, 'But where is Isla? Surely not inside on a day as fine as this?' He made to enter the cottage, but Isla cried, 'No, you must not come in! It is a secret,' and obediently Andrew retreated, with a questioning look at Rachel and an expressive shrug.

'It is some garment she is ironing,' explained Rachel, 'which we must not see. She will not be long.'

'What news of the medical hall?' asked Louise. 'It is some time since I saw you. Is the library safely set up again?'

'Yes, indeed, and the whole hall practically finished,' began Andrew eagerly. 'But we still need funds to furnish the building and we continue to rely heavily on the generosity of the public. As you know, we had to borrow to pay the builders' bills. The loan must be repaid and then there are the great hall and the committee room to furnish, as well as the museum. We hope to install two fine black marble chimneypieces in the large room, which will be an imposing lecture theatre when complete.'

'When is it that you deliver your own lecture?' asked Rachel. She knew the members took it in turns to read learned papers to the company, with a fine of half a guinea for any member absent when it was his turn.

'Next week,' said Andrew, 'though I still have much work to do upon it to bring it up to standard, and many notes to collate.'

'If I can help you, I would be glad to . . .' began Louise, but was interrupted by the emergence of Isla, blushing slightly and with a folded garment in her hands.

'This is for you, Andrew,' she said, smiling shyly at him and holding out her offering. 'It is a shirt and neckcloth for you to wear when you give your special lecture and to thank you . . .' She lowered her eyes. 'For all your kindness to me. I hope it will fit,' she finished humbly. 'I took the size from . . . from . . .'

'I am sure it will,' he interrupted, blushing in spite of himself. 'I am touched by your thoughtfulness, Isla. Is it not a beautiful piece of work, Rachel?'

Rachel, who had assumed the piece of fine cambric to be a robe for Jamie and had averted her eyes accordingly whenever she saw Isla at work on her 'secret', was momentarily chastened and taken aback. Not so Louise, who, with natural forthrightness, said, 'But I thought you were sewing something for Rachel's baby!'

'It is certainly fine enough cotton to clothe the most cherished infant,' agreed Andrew, unaware of any tension, 'and see how neat the stitches are. I am honoured.'

'And will you wear it for your lecture?' asked Isla, her cheeks becomingly pink and her blue eyes bright.

But before Andrew could answer there was the sound of a commotion from the far corner of the Square which led to Pocra Quay and the Fittiegait. A ripple of interest ran round the Square and what had been a murmur of casual conversation became charged with curiosity. The group at the Christie doorway paused, with the others, to see what was amiss, and as they watched a knot of men emerged into the Square on a bow wave of boisterous urchins and cheering lads.

Rachel's heart stopped, gave a thud, then raced with such a mixture of terror and hope that first her hands trembled, then her whole frame shook. For at the centre of the group there were four tall men: first the twins, William and George, with Pearl swinging and skipping between them, then Maitland in the familiar faded blue shirt, his fair hair glinting in the evening sun. But beside him, Maitland's arm protectively around his shoulders, limped a dark-haired, weatherbeaten stranger in unfamiliar clothes.

Rachel did not hear the excited speculation turn to a roar of certainty, did not notice the cheers of welcome. She had eyes only for that stranger, with the scar on his forehead and the uneven gait, and ears only for his voice which, when it came, was choked with emotion. 'Rachel. I am come home.' Then his arms were around her and holding her so tight she thought her ribs would crack, his tears were on her cheek and her own brimmed so thick she could not see.

'Hush, hush,' he murmured in her ear. 'Surely you are not so sorry to see me home? And there were William and George telling me what a brave wee wifie ye'd been while I was away. Come, dry your eyes and show me my son!'

The next hours passed in a confusion of joy and disbelief. A constant stream of neighbours poured in to welcome James home, to congratulate him on his return and to hear yet again the story of his escape, a story which William and George were happy to relay to anyone who could not get close enough to James to hear it from his own lips. For James had found passage first to London and inquired for the *Steadfast*.

'I did not want to startle you too much, Rachy, by

184

arriving out of nowhere,' he explained, 'and besides, I was sick with worry for Alex. I did not know if he was alive or dead.' He told her of the grave of an unknown boy on the cliff top near Riga, and of his anxiety when he could not remember the details of the attack on his ship. 'But I will one day,' he said. 'I know it. Already my mind is filling fast with memory. And when I do remember . . .' His face set in an expression of such implacable revenge that Rachel's heart raced with sudden terror.

'Please, James.' She clutched at his hand, pleading. 'Do nothing rash, I beg of you. I could not bear it if you . . .' but he did not seem to hear her.

'He has done me great injury,' he said quietly, his eyes turning westward towards the inner harbour. 'It must be avenged.'

'No, James! Please. It is enough for me to have you safe again at home.'

'We canna' let it rest, Rachel,' said Maitland at James's side. 'Such violence must be answered.'

'But not *with* violence! Please, James?'

James looked into her clear grey eyes, misted now with standing tears, and remembered Friida and Priit. They, too, had begged him.

'Perhaps not with violence,' he admitted, though reluctantly. 'But he must be visited just the same, and soon.'

'Tomorrow will be soon enough,' urged Rachel, 'or the next day. Not tonight, please?'

'Not tonight,' he agreed, his voice suddenly soft and his eyes holding hers with an intensity of private promise that brought a blush to her cheeks. Flustered, she began to talk again of Alex. 'He will be so glad to know you are safe, James. He has suffered greatly from remorse and shame. He went to the Greenland fisheries only to make amends, as best he could. When he comes home, do not be harsh with him, for my sake?'

185

'How could I be harsh with any of you, least of all Wee Alex? I feared he was dead, Rachy. I was frightened for you, too, and for myself. Had you died in childbed, I do not think I could have borne it. So I was a coward. Instead of sailing straight to Aberdeen to find out for myself what fortune Fate had sent me, I preferred to ask first of the twins, in London. Do you forgive me?'

Rachel could have forgiven him anything, even the threat of tomorrow's vengeance. Just to have him back was blessing enough: to see his joy in his son, his pleasure in Pearl and his welcome for Isla were added blessings, and to have the whole Square rejoicing with her filled her heart to overflowing. Somehow George Abercrombie got word of James's return and arrived himself to welcome him, to clap him over and over on the back with protestations that he knew all along he was too good a lad to be kept down by any villain in Christendom, to drink James's health and Rachel's and their baby son's over and over and finally to announce to the room that it was time everyone went home.

'Awa' to yer beds, all o' ye,' he said. 'Ye've all homes to go to, so leave James and Rachel to theirs. I reckon they've things to talk about, eh lass?' and he gave Rachel a knowing wink.

'Mr Abercrombie is right,' said James. 'You are all my dear friends and welcome, but for tonight I wish to be alone with my wife.'

'Come on lads,' ordered Maitland, steering the twins outside. 'We'll sleep aboard tonight.'

Louise Forbes took her leave, with Mr Abercrombie, and in twos and threes the company dispersed till only Isla, Pearl and Andrew Noble remained.

'I will bid you goodnight,' said Isla with embarrassment, taking Pearl by the hand and leading her towards the bunk beds beyond the partition. 'We will not disturb you.'

186

'I think it would be best,' said Andrew, to break the awkwardness which had suddenly descended on the room, 'if Isla and Pearl came home with me tonight. You need not worry,' he added hastily as Isla blushed and mumbled something incoherent. 'Mrs Mutch sleeps in the house now so you will be chaperoned.'

'A splendid idea,' beamed James, his arm round Rachel's waist. 'Not that you are not welcome, Isla,' he added seriously. 'It is a joy to me to welcome my brother's widow into my house, and to give a home to my own wee niece. But you will understand . . .' He looked into Rachel's eyes and the current between them burnt with such open intensity that Isla turned away in distress. 'Rachel and I need a little time to get to know each other again, alone.'

'Thank you,' said Isla when the door of the cottage had closed behind them and they stood in the night darkness of the Square. 'I did not wish to intrude upon their happiness, but,' she finished bleakly, 'I did not know how to avoid it. I have no home but theirs.'

'You have mine,' said Andrew cheerfully, scooping the child Pearl up on to his shoulders. 'For tonight anyway. So banish those tears and smile. It is an evening for rejoicing.'

But Isla, hurrying along at his side as they made their way along the darkened quayside towards the town, could think only of the contrast between Rachel's happiness and her own lonely state. How could she bear to see them every day, engrossed in each other's love, smiling their secret understandings, murmuring intimacies behind the closed doors of their bed? How could she bear to see them united, with their little son a loved and loving bond between them? How could she bear to be reminded daily of what Rachel had found and what Isla had never had?

'How can I go back there?' she asked Andrew the next morning when she and Pearl had spent a short and, on her part, sleepless night in the kitchen, with old Mrs Mutch, who snored. 'They will not want me. I am not even family, not really. And when I look at their happiness it only reminds me of . . .' Her blue eyes blurred and she finished, helplessly, 'Sometimes I feel so lonely.'

Instead of reminding her briskly of the dangers of envy and of her own good fortune in having friends and Pearl, as he might once have done, Andrew took a handkerchief from his pocket and gently dried her eyes. 'There is no need to feel lonely,' he said quietly. 'I am here. I have missed you,' he went on, wondering at his own weakness. 'Now that you are back, the house seems warmer and more friendly. Perhaps you should give them longer together and stay another day or two?'

'On one condition,' said Isla, smiling through her tears. 'That you try on the shirt I made you, now this minute, so that I may alter it if need be.'

'But I will be late for the hospital,' protested Andrew, consulting the fob watch in his pocket.

'Then Pearl and I will go,' pouted Isla, turning her back in mock dudgeon. 'I will tell her you are too busy to have time for us and she must leave Mrs Mutch to make her bread alone.'

Andrew laughed. 'You have the most expressive and delightful back, Isla, and I suspect you know it. So you may keep it turned while I put on the shirt in question.'

Two minutes later, Isla found it necessary to help Andrew with the buttons. 'I fear I made the buttonholes a little too tight.' And to adjust the lie of the collar and to smooth the set of the shoulders with her soft, pale hands. This brought her very close to him. He could smell the lemon scent of her hair and the lavender scent of her clothes and, when she kept her hands lightly on his shoulders and looked up at him with those innocent, questioning eyes which were as blue as cornflowers this morning, murmuring 'Are you pleased with it?' there was only one answer he could give.

'Ma!' Pearl's high, indignant voice broke into their privacy. 'Stop kissing Dr Andrew!' She tugged at Isla's skirt. 'I want ye to see my wee loafie!' Laughing, Isla pulled away from Andrew's arms and, with a teasing look over her shoulder, followed Pearl into the kitchen.

Andrew, however, was not laughing. What had he done? Pearl had shouted loud enough for Mrs Mutch and half the neighbours to hear. The news would be all round the washing green by noon and who knew who would hear it after that. Memories of Jessica's jibes about his 'bidey-in' brought a flush of shame to his cheeks. But Isla was no common servant to be used at his pleasure. She was a sweet, gentle and affectionate girl whom life had treated harshly and who needed his protection.

He had not thought to marry for many years, if at all. He was of an ascetic and scholarly nature. His work was his life. Yet now he knew there could be no going back. He could not hurt her. Could not bring back the bruised look to her eyes. She was too vulnerable. She needed a man to care for her. Not a brother-in-law, though James, he knew, was a good man who would treat her fairly and accept her child as one of his. She needed more than that. Seeing Rachel and James together had opened her old wound and left her heart raw and lonely. That wound only a husband could heal.

Soberly, he put on coat and hat, took up his medical bag and left the house without a goodbye. He had much to think of and much to do. But there was no need for goodbyes. They both knew Isla would still be there when he returned.

* * *

'Christie's back!' The words raced round the harbour with the speed of summer lightning and stopped Atholl Farquharson in his tracks as he mounted the stair to his office the morning after James's return. He clutched the stair rail for support while the blood left his face and fear clamped a steel band around his chest.

'*What?*'

'James Christie's back, sir,' amended the clerk from the open doorway of his office at the head of the stair. 'Arrived last night, by the *Steadfast*, with his brothers. What tales he'll have to tell,' the man finished in all innocence and unwittingly tightened the screw.

'No. Impossible!' Farquharson's heart was beating painfully hard and he felt hot and cold together. 'He cannot be.' But there was a window at the turn of the stair. It was small but clean, and through it he could see the Shiprow and a stretch of Quay. Even as he stared with fearful eyes at that empty stretch a group of men appeared, tall men, walking close together and with purpose. Farquharson had a sudden vivid memory of that evening of November mist when Christie men had visited him, had marched him along that Quay, had threatened and humiliated him and finally made him sign a paper attesting his own guilt. That guilt had been nothing compared to this. He licked dry lips and croaked, in a terrified whisper, 'Bar the door.'

But it was already too late. There was the sound of voices below, someone said, ineffectually, 'You cannot . . .' then James Christie himself was mounting the stair, his swarthy face implacable, a vivid scar like a brand across his brow, his brothers at his heels. With a strangled gasp, Farquharson's knees gave way and he slumped on to the steps, his face ashen, his mouth moving soundlessly, his hand clutching at nothing.

'He'd ha' fallen the length o' the stair if they Christies

hadna' caught him,' the clerk relayed over and over to anyone who would listen, when Farquharson himself had been carried, speechless, into his office, laid out upon the couch with a makeshift pillow under his head, and a doctor summoned. Mrs Farquharson was also sent for and arrived with her son and daughter-in-law in a state of uncommon agitation, an agitation in no way soothed by the presence of the Christie men in the outer office, or by Dr McKinnon's pronouncement.

'A seizure, but so far not a fatal one. Impossible to tell as yet what the damage will be. Rest and care, Madam, rest and care are the best medicines.' A sedan chair was sent for and Farquharson carried carefully home, to lie immobile in the curtained quiet of his dressing-room, his speech apparently gone and much of his wits with it. His wife and daughter-in-law accompanied him, leaving Robert to face the Christies who, 'with not an ounce of propriety or feeling,' as Euphemia Farquharson reported indignantly to city society, refused to leave the premises until they had spoken to Robert.

Robert Farquharson knew something of his father's rivalry with the Christies, knew that he had been involved somehow in the *Bonnie Annie*'s misfortune, but Atholl Farquharson's opinion of his son was not high and he had kept his own council on that as on many things. So, though he regarded the confrontation with disquiet and some distress – for his father's collapse had shaken him to the core – Robert had no real reason to deny entry to James and his brothers. He assumed the matter would be a trivial one, of poached custom perhaps, or undercutting rates. But his voice was not entirely steady as he said, 'Good morning, gentlemen. I must thank you for your timely help in my father's illness. We are grateful to you. But you will understand, I am sure, that this is not an opportune moment for any business transaction.'

'My business was with your father,' said James Christie quietly. 'I came to seek vengeance for the great wrong he had done me, but *"Vengeance is mine, saith the Lord"* and God's retribution has been swifter than ours.' There was a note of wonder in James's voice, even of awe.

'Retribution?' Robert Farquharson licked his lips nervously. 'I do not . . .'

'Come,' said James impatiently. 'You cannot pretend ignorance of something the whole harbour knows. Your father has schemed against me and mine for years. He caused the fire in the *Steadfast* which brought about my brother's death. He did his best to block the launch of the *Bonnie Annie* and, when he failed, he instigated the attack which lost me my ship and almost my life with it. I came seeking vengeance, but God has struck my blow for me and with far greater force. I cannot pretend grief at your father's seizure. You may tell him, however, if it is any comfort to him and if he has wits enough left to hear, that I am content to forget his past wickedness and to accept the Lord's vengeance as mine. But tell him also, and hear it well yourself, that if he, or you, or any of your blood, make any further attempt to hamper me and mine or to harm us in the smallest way, *I vow to be avenged not only for that crime but for all the others too*. Do you hear me?'

Robert Farquharson heard, but could find no words to speak. For the power of the Christies' anger was like a steel wall bearing inexorably in upon him to crush and destroy. The man's face was scarred and twisted, his weird, mismatched eyes unnaturally bright and his voice unnaturally quiet. Robert found his hands were trembling and he clasped the table edge to retrieve what supremacy he could. 'Have you finished?' he managed with what he hoped was icy calm.

'No.' It was the fair-haired Christie who spoke. His

voice was almost conversationally mild, but as inflexible in its way as his brother's. 'Tell your father that we intend to recoup our shipyard's fortunes, to build and expand till we have a better ship than he on every run, to whatever ends of the earth they may sail.'

'Tell him he'd best watch his trousers,' said a twin and the other, winking, added, 'If he wants to keep 'em on.'

'Tell him,' finished James Christie, 'and take good note yourself, that we intend to beat him in every field and to do so honestly. Tell him *God is on our side.*'

'God!' gasped Robert when the Christie men had left, though the word was less repetition than oath. He crossed to the cabinet in the corner of the room and poured himself a large brandy, though it was barely nine o'clock in the morning. But his teeth chattered against the glass and he found it necessary to pour a second and to mop his brow repeatedly with a handkerchief. By the third brandy he was beginning to feel better, his confidence, never his strong point, almost restored. There was no need to mention the matter to his father. No need, in fact, to mention it to anyone. God on their side, indeed. God *damn* them. The Christies could go to the Devil, the whole pack of them, and the sooner the better.

'I thought I'd call round, soon as I heard, to congratulate you,' said Jessica, stepping graciously over the threshold without being invited. 'It isna' every man who comes back from the dead, almost as good as new. Ye'll be right glad to have yer man home safe, Rachy,' she went on, sitting in the best chair and carefully arranging her skirts. She looked appraisingly round the tiny cottage. 'My, but ye've got the place awful neat. Neat and cosy like, but then wi' such a wee bit space ye have to be careful or ye'd be aye fallin' over each other. Nay like Union Terrace.' She smiled complacently. 'Ye've a rare red scar there, James.

193

Who gave ye that? Nae wonder Atholl Farquharson took one look at ye and dropped dead – or as near dead as makes no matter. Ye're a rare sight and no mistake, isn't he, Rachy?'

But James had recovered control. He had risen from the table where he had been working on some business figures on Jessica's arrival, and now he moved to stand at Rachel's side. 'Thank you for calling so promptly, Mrs Abercrombie,' he said, with cold politeness. 'My wife and I appreciate your concern. But you will excuse us if we do not offer refreshment. As you can see, we have work to do.'

'Aye, right enough. Ye were aye a one for *work*, James Christie, o' one kind or another. But I like a man wi' a bit o' go about him, don't you, Rachel?' She stood up and moved to the cradle where the baby lay asleep. 'What a fine wee lad your Jamie's growing to be. And there'll be more where he came from, eh James?' She gave him a coquettish look and an open wink. 'If ye havena' made a bairn or two already, ye sly devil, since ye came home – or before. But then ye'd nay "remember" that, would ye? Convenient thing, memory . . .' She waited for laughter but none came. James, she saw, held Rachel's hand in the folds of her skirt where they reckoned she couldn't see. Devilment stirred.

'Ye havena' seen my Victoria yet, have ye?' she said archly, looking directly at James. 'A bonny wee bairn, fair ye ken, nae like Augusta, but then families are aye different. Look at your Maitland and you. And I still canna' decide what colour her eyes are. They're aye different somehow till I think . . .'

'Mrs Abercrombie,' interrupted James. 'Unlike you, my wife and I do not have unlimited leisure to spend in idle blether.'

'Hark at him!' jeered Jessica, losing patience. 'Idle

194

blether indeed. Ye great stuffed pillock! And here's me come out o' kindness to welcome ye back and I get an earful o' *unlimited leisure* and *may waif and ay*. What did yon Riga fellows do ter ye? Cut em off?'

'You will leave my house,' said James quietly. He held open the door. 'Do not come here again.'

'Goodbye, Jessica.' They were the first words Rachel had spoken, but her voice was quite calm. 'Please give my regards to Fenton.'

Jessica looked from one to the other in astonishment, then as the realization dawned that she was actually being put out, she flushed with fury. 'That's the last time I go out o' my way for a Christie, God rot the lot o' ye in hell,' and she slammed out of the house with a toss of her splendid head.

'I am sorry,' said James when she had gone. He drew Rachel close and kissed her. 'Forget her. The past is *past*, my love.'

But Rachel knew Jessica Abercrombie could not so easily be wiped out of their lives. She had seen the expression on the girl's face as she left. 'She is mischievous, James. She will not forget.'

'You worry too much, Rachel. She is a silly woman, that is all. She cannot come between us. Believe me, *nothing* can, now God has brought us together again, and blessed us.'

But something Jess had said lodged in Rachel's mind, like a minute splinter, tiny but irritating when accidentally touched. '. . . but then ye'd nay remember'. Suppose things had happened when James had not known who he was, things he had 'forgotten' now, conveniently or otherwise? There was almost a year of his life she knew nothing about and all she could do was trust.

* * *

195

James made no idle boast when he claimed God's patronage. He spoke only what he believed to be the truth. With his own eyes he had seen Farquharson struck down by an unseen hand, and had not Friida urged him to leave vengeance to the Lord? Friida had been proved right, and if right in that instance, why not in others too? The sight of Farquharson's collapse had humbled him and made him thoughtful in a way that was new to him. Though James had sailed to Riga with the same offhand attitude to the church as the rest of them – lip service paid when required, and in return consolation and comfort in times of anxiety, sickness or death – he was now an altered man. There was a seriousness that had not been there before and a tenderness and all-embracing calm, a strength of purpose and humility of spirit which together might have been maturity, but which Rachel knew was more than that.

Some hint of the reason came when, waking in the warm half-light of dawn the next morning and turning towards her sleeping husband to reassure herself yet again that he was no mere dream, she saw something glinting on James's bare chest, and saw that he wore an unfamiliar wooden cross on a chain about his neck. She reached out a gentle hand to finger it and James moved sleepily to draw her closer into the warmth of his arms. In answer to her murmured questioning, he told her of Friida and Priit, of their kindness to him and of Friida's gift. 'I promised her that I would not forget her teaching and I promised myself that if her God did go with me, as she asked, and keep me safe, if He did unite me once more with all I love, then ever after I would pay Him my proper respects. I had almost forgotten that promise in the joy of seeing you again, but Farquharson's fate reminded me of it and of the cross which, to my shame, I had hidden away. I shall wear it now, always, to remind me.'

Rachel was silent, thinking of the suffering James had undergone, of that unknown couple's kindness to him, and of her own prayers in James's absence, prayers which had been so blissfully answered. 'We have so much to give thanks for,' she agreed, and kissed him.

It was Jamie bellowing indignantly for his morning feed that finally brought them from bed, and James watched in wonder as his wife suckled his little son, till his heart almost burst with gratitude and love. Afterwards, while Rachel rubbed the child's back for wind and soothed him into sleep, James told her the morning ritual of the Riga household and repeated, without embarrassment, Friida's morning prayers.

'Are they not papist?' asked Rachel anxiously, wondering what their minister would say should he hear of it.

'They are Christians, as we are,' said James firmly, 'and good people. I see no difference except of language and of circumstance. From this day onwards I shall do as I promised Friida, and, if you love me, so will you. We will say prayers every morning and we will build another Bonnie Annie so I may return to Riga one day and pay my debts. I see Abercrombie thought the same and that you have already laid the keel. You have done well while I was away, Rachel. The new yard is splendid. But now that I am back, I mean to build us up a shipyard to be proud of,' he told her, 'with that fleet o' ships I promised you for our fleet of sons. We'll maybe even have a whaler for Wee Alex, one day, if he likes the life – there's money in whaling – and we will trade to the ends of the Seven Seas.'

Rachel had heard those plans before, but whereas then they had been little more than daydreams, now she recognized them as resolution.

* * *

197

Andrew Noble, his decision made, decided to act on it without delay. Isla had been three days with him now and he had no doubt of her answer, nor of the happiness it would bring her; his doubts were reserved for Rachel and, he admitted uneasily, for Louise. It would be best to declare his intentions at once, before they heard rumours from some other quarter. Consequently, instead of going home when his work at the hospital was finished for the day, he called at the house in the Square where he found Rachel radiant, bathing her baby in a wooden tub before the fire. She made the opening for him.

'Hello, Andrew. Have you brought Isla back?'

'No, I . . .' but Rachel interrupted. 'Come away in and shut the door, lest there's a draught. See what a fine wee laddie my Jamie's growing to be.' She lifted him, dripping, from the tub and swathed him in a towel before turning again to Andrew. 'Well? Where is she? What have you done with her?'

'She is at home.' He paused uncomfortably. He had not thought it would be so difficult. 'I . . . she . . . I have decided,' he finished in a rush, 'to ask her to marry me.'

All the joy left Rachel's face and she stared at Andrew in disbelief.

'I know what you will say,' he hurried on. 'That she is untaught and dependent. That she understands nothing of my work. But she needs me, Rachel, and I,' he gulped before finishing, with embarrassment, 'I believe she also loves me, as I . . . love . . . her.'

'And what of Louise?'

'What of Louise?' countered Andrew, but his tone of blustering defence betrayed his guilt. 'She and I are friends, and will, I hope, remain so. There has been no other understanding between us, ever. She will be happy for me, as I had expected you to be.'

Rachel was silent, struggling with her anger and her

pain on Louise's behalf. Andrew was wrong on one point: Louise would be desolate. But he was right on the other. He had made his choice in good faith and Rachel, as his half-sister, ought to rejoice with him.

'I am sorry, Andrew,' she said, managing a smile. 'It is just that you took me so much by surprise. I had not expected you to marry, let alone to marry Isla. But now that you have made your decision, I wish you joy. James,' she cried as the door opened and her husband stepped inside. 'You are just in time to congratulate Andrew. He is to marry Davy's Isla.'

In the back-slapping congratulations that followed, and were repeated when first Maitland, then the twins arrived, Andrew almost forgot the unease of his arrival. But watching Rachel and her James together, seeing the unspoken strength of love between them and the absolute understanding, he wondered, with misgiving, whether he and Isla would be the same.

'We will miss wee Pearl and that's a fact,' said the twins over and over and Maitland agreed. No one, Andrew noticed, said they would miss Isla though perhaps that was politeness on their part, not wanting to make him feel guilty for removing Rachel's helper? But it was obvious to him now that he was doing the right thing. Isla had been out of her depth and overwhelmed in the crowded vigour of the Christie home: in the quiet protection of his house, she would blossom into confidence and thrive.

'Isla and Pearl will call often to see you all,' he assured them, 'and to give Rachel a helping hand. It will really be little different from before.'

But when he had gone, Rachel turned to James with a face of anguish. 'Poor Louise. Whatever will she do?' It seemed the more terrible to Rachel that her own happiness in James's return should have contributed, if inadvertently, to her friend's despair. If Isla had not gone with Andrew . . . How would Louise survive the pain of it?

Louise, after the first shock and the desolation which followed, responded with courage and a generous-hearted forgiveness which almost brought the tears to Rachel's eyes.

'I should have expected it,' admitted Louise. 'After all, she is an appealing girl, feminine and pretty, which even my best friends must agree that I am not. She is dependent, too, and obviously in need of a man's protection, which again I am not. But I can tell you, Rachel, in the confidence of friendship, that the news has saddened me. I am . . . fond . . . of Andrew, and then my mother . . .' She stopped, remembering Mrs Forbes's wails of 'I told you to make more of yourself. I told you some prettier girl would catch him if you did not put yourself forward more. I told you . . .'

'My mother tells me over and over that it is my own fault, which perhaps it is,' she finished ruefully, 'though if the fault be only to be myself, then I can do little about it.'

'Nor should you,' cried Rachel with protective affection. 'You are generous-hearted and loyal, intelligent and brave, and if other people cannot see that such things are worth a dozen pairs of blue eyes then . . . then . . .'

'Then I had better make the best of it,' finished Louise, 'for there is nothing else to be done. And I would not want to be denied Pearl's company for anyone. Soon I hope to teach her simple lessons in science and arithmetic. Perhaps after all I am better suited to be useful on the sidelines, like everyone's maiden aunt, than to be the centre of the home? I am not domestic,' she finished with a touch of sadness. But Rachel knew her heart to be as warm and as needful of love as any prettier woman's and her mind to be twice as intelligent as most. When Louise added, 'I hope at least that Andrew and I can continue to be friends,' Rachel said with truth, 'I am certain of it.'

For Andrew needed someone sympathetic with whom to discuss his work and Rachel doubted very much that Isla would offer either interest or understanding beyond a wifely 'yes' or 'no'.

Dr Andrew Noble and Isla Duthie were married three weeks later. It was a small affair, with only the Christies and two of Andrew's doctor friends present and there was no dancing. They had their first disagreement before the honeymoon month was past.

'I hear there is a new consignment of broadcloth in Mackies in the Broadgait,' said Isla at breakfast. 'I will speak a length for you so that you may have jacket and trousers made up. A black would look very well, or perhaps a blue . . .'

'I do not need new clothes,' said Andrew, without looking up from the sheet of notes at his side. His lecture had been postponed, on account of his unexpected wedding, and was to take place the following week.

'But if you are to give a public lecture, you must at least look smart, dear,' urged Isla, laying a gentle hand on his arm. 'You look so very fine in the shirt and neckcloth I made you that it would be a crime not to set it off to best advantage. What about new nankeen breeches with a cut-away jacket? Wide lapels would . . .'

'No.' Andrew shook off her hand with exasperation. 'Your shirt is well enough,' he began, then at the tears which welled instantly to her eyes he continued, more gently, 'Your shirt is *beautiful* and all I need. Truly, my love, my colleagues are not interested in the garments I stand up in, merely in the words I speak. In *these*,' he repeated, tapping the notes with an impatient finger. 'So please be good enough to let me study them. I have little enough time as it is.'

'But you were studying all night, Andrew, till I thought . . .'

'*Not* all night. Merely till midnight, but certainly I only stopped because you called me so repeatedly.' It was proving increasingly difficult for Andrew to find time alone since his marriage. At the hospital his work involved him utterly, and at home his young wife made constant demands upon his time, craving his reassurance on the quality of the dinner or of her appearance, asking his advice on trivial details of household management or on matters of childish discipline concerning Pearl. To be sure, she left him alone when, exasperated, he requested it, but her silent hurt was an almost tangible reproach and he found he could not concentrate until he had asked forgiveness and made her smile again. And if, in desperation, he tried to work late at night, as he had been accustomed to, she would appear at intervals in the doorway, her hair about her shoulders in beguiling disarray, her eyes anxious, and ask, 'Will you be very long, dear? The bed is so cold without you,' till he found his normally equable temper sorely strained. Pearl, in contrast, was no trouble at all. She had a seemingly endless store of inner resources which kept her happily occupied whether alone or in company and Andrew never found her presence a hindrance to concentration.

'I am sorry,' said Isla humbly, looking down at her hands in a position of penitence which both touched and irritated her husband. 'I only want to be a loving wife to you and it is not good for you to be overtired.'

'Study never tires me. Except when I am prevented from completing it. As I am now.' Pointedly, he picked up the sheaf of papers and, pencil in hand, began to make corrections. For a full minute there was silence, then Isla ventured, 'It is only fourteen shillings the yard.'

'Out of the question,' said Andrew without looking up. 'Besides, I have promised £10 to the Medical Society.'

'Ten pounds!' cried Isla, aghast. 'But that is almost a month's salary! Where is the money to come from for the household expenses if your Society takes it all? Can they not take it from Dr Dyce or Dr Ewing who have money enough surely and can spare it?'

'Every member of the first class of the Medical Society is contracted to loan £10, without interest, to pay off the Society's debts. Would you have me refuse to do what the rest do? Or would you have me resign?'

'No, of course not, my love, I only meant . . .'

'The £10 is to pay off *past* debts,' said Andrew sternly. 'There will be more expense in the future. We intend to purchase a complete male skeleton,' here Isla gave a little scream, '*and* a complete female one as soon as possible. The study of anatomy is of increasing importance to all medical research and until we have a proper anatomy school here in Aberdeen, which I pray we will have one day, we must make the best use we can of present resources, both official and unofficial,' he finished under his breath, for any mention of dissection or of the 'resurrectionists' who obtained 'subjects' for those dissections was guaranteed to alarm his wife almost to hysteria. But that trade, private and secret as it still had to be, was also a drain on his limited purse. 'So you will please me, my dear,' he finished more kindly, 'by limiting all unnecessary household expenses.'

'Yes, Andrew,' said Isla humbly, but his warning did not prevent her buying a particularly succulent looking piece of mutton for his dinner that evening, and a bowl of fresh strawberries at two shillings the pint.

In that same month of August, news came from the Davis Straits in the form of a letter from Captain Parker, printed in the *Aberdeen Journal*, which Louise brought instantly to show to Rachel. She found her nursing her baby, with James at her side, a mug of ale in his hand.

'I know you have been worrying for news of Alex,' she explained, flushed with heat and haste, 'so I came directly. I hope you do not mind?' she finished, looking from James to Rachel and back. 'It is early, I know, for a social call.'

'It is never too early to see you,' said James cheerfully, his eyes bright with good humour. 'I can see what you are thinking – that I'm awful late going to my work, but before ye disapprove I'll tell ye I've spent three hours in the shipyard already and am newly back for my morning piece, a kiss from my wife and a wee keek at my fine son. I tell James I'll be taking him to the yard wi' me any day now. Tis never too early to teach a lad a trade and he'd best get the feel o' the place, the sooner the better.'

Louise laughed. 'At least he will enjoy playing with the wood chips. I know Pearl has built architectural wonders with her blocks. But I did not come for idle chatter. I brought you this.'

She spread the newspaper on the table. 'Give me wee Jamie for a while,' she said to Rachel, 'so you can study it together. He will be quite safe with me, won't you, my wee lamb?'

'Read it aloud, Rachel,' said James, with a wink at Louise. 'She was aye a quick reader and I'd rather look at my wife while she reads to me than at a page o' print.' James was in good humour that morning. The work at the yard was going well, the *Steadfast* continued to prosper, with no repetition of the contraband incident, and Maitland had just secured an order to build a coastal brig, a mere 180 tons and well within their means and capacity. Added to that, though he had not the heart to say so to Louise, he had already heard news of the *Bon Accord* at the yard that morning and relayed as much to Rachel. But Rachel, he knew, would be doubly reassured to see it for herself, and in the *Aberdeen Journal*. Rachel had already found the place.

'"On board ship *Bon Accord*,"' she read excitedly. '"Davis Strait latitude 74°N 4 July 1820" – why that is a full month ago, James. Why does news take so painfully long to reach us? But listen. "We have at present nine fish, equal I suppose to 110 tons of oil." It is a letter from Captain Parker himself, though he makes no mention of Alex,' she finished, a little disappointed.

'And why should he?' teased James. 'He canna' be mentioning every member of the ship's company by name or he'd have no space for news o' the fish! But if he had nine in early July, he will likely have a fine catch come September.'

'Do you think Alex knows you are home?' asked Rachel.

James shrugged. 'There's messages been sent to Lerwick when any vessel's bound that way, but whether they reached the fisheries or not, I canna' say. No matter. He will find out soon enough when he gets back – and do not frown so, Rachel.' Then, to Louise, 'Rachel is convinced I will beat the boy and clap him into irons for desertion. I wonder she has not sent him a message herself, with a warning to flee the country.'

'There is only one reason he might want to do that,' said Rachel, 'and that is a determined young woman called Kirsty Guyan.'

'Oh? You told me nothing of that.' James was instantly alert, the responsible elder brother and prepared to play the part.

'Because there is nothing to tell,' countered Rachel and added archly, 'Yet.'

'And there'd best not be, neither. He's too young still

205

and feckless to take on such a responsibility.' Mention of Alex and the memories called up by his past behaviour reminded James of a different responsibility of his own, one which sobered him when, as now, it thrust to the forefront of his mind. But, looking at the sweet contentment of her face, he knew he could not remind her, could not shatter the happiness of their newfound marriage so soon, for his own sake as well as for hers: it would be time enough to tell her when all his plans were made.

'Well, ladies,' he said, draining his mug. 'I must leave you to your own company. I'm away to the yard to keep Maitland up to scratch.' He kissed Rachel, nodded to Louise and strode out of the house. Watching him, Rachel saw that the limp which had so distressed her on his return was mending fast. Soon it would be no more than a seaman's roll. The scar on his forehead was fading too, and could the memory of her long anxiety for him and of the events which had caused it fade with equal speed, Rachel would have been entirely happy. For in spite of James's public avowal to seek no further revenge than God had sent, on his behalf, to strike Atholl Farquharson and in spite of his dutiful private prayers, she feared that the craving for revenge had not entirely left his heart. At present James sought that vengeance through his shipyard; please God, prayed Rachel, may it remain so.

'How is Atholl Farquharson?' she asked now of Louise. Louise's father was the Farquharson lawyer.

'Much as before,' said Louise. 'It really was an extraordinary coincidence that he should be taken with a seizure when he was.'

'Yes.' Rachel was not sure how much Louise had heard of the affair and had no wish to speak ill of the dying, if Farquharson *was* dying. Even were he not, Maitland and James both had warned her of the dangers of slander. 'Remember, he has a tame lawyer ready to swear black is white if it suits him – and anyone who matters knows the rights and wrongs of the affair anyway. Best not to give them a stick to beat us with.' Louise, however, had heard more than Rachel gave her credit for.

'It looks almost like retribution, though do not say I said so to anyone or I will be in the dock in the shake of a cat's tail. He has had to leave the running of the business to his son, the very thought of which is guaranteed to make him worse. They even say Mrs Farquharson herself has decided to lend a guiding hand.'

'I am sorry for them,' admitted Rachel, busying herself with making her baby son comfortable prior to taking him with her to Pocra. 'It is hard enough to lose a husband's companionship, but to lose a husband's senses must be ten times worse.'

Mrs Farquharson, however, rose majestically to the occasion. She paid frequent visits to the shipping office, directed her son on every aspect of the business (about which she knew practically nothing) and, said Maitland cheerfully, 'is fair set to ruin the Farquharsons quicker than any competition of ours could do.' She instructed the captains of their two emigrant ships to cram in as many 'heads' as the ship would hold without actually sinking to the harbour bottom before setting sail. She upped the freight rates, overloaded where she could in the face of the shipmasters' opposition, and generally interfered. Only in one area did she allow pride precedence over purse, and that was in the matter of steam. She was determined, for prestige, that the Farquharson shipping company should be the first to have a regular steam-packet on the London run, refused to listen to any arguments regarding cost or efficiency, and insisted that research go ahead on the project and plans be drawn up, whatever the cost. To her husband, she said nothing, refusing to let business matters be mentioned in his sickroom, and though he mouthed and twitched in an agony of effort to make his wishes known to her, she blandly refused to comprehend. She was enjoying her new power too much to relinquish even an invalid scrap of it – and as for Robert, he was so in awe of his father that he dared only say, 'All is well, Papa. The Baltic run and the London run proceed as you would wish them to do. There continues to be a demand by emigrants for passage to New Brunswick, and the whaling shares promise good returns this year.'

When his father attempted any reply, Robert averted his face from the incoherent contortions and talked quickly about something else – the progress of the new public rooms in Union Street, or the medical hall – until he could decently bid adieu and scurry out of the room. Had the Christies sought revenge for the misfortune of the *Bonnie Annie*'s loss, they could not have found a better, albeit administered by Farquharson's own wife and son.

But James, in spite of Rachel's fears, sought no revenge – except through success. All his energies were now channelled into the rebuilding of the Christie fortunes so that his brothers and his children – for when Jamie was weaned Rachel surely would conceive again – might prosper. 'And one day, Rachy, we'll have that house on the Quay.' But first there was that other, private promise to be honoured. James's face sobered whenever he remembered, but his resolution did not waver. When the time came, he would go. Meanwhile, there was no need to worry Rachel: she had worries enough with Jamie's teething, her sorrow for Louise and her anxiety for Alex. There had been a particularly harrowing account in the latest *Journal* of a whaler trapped in the ice and only freed after five days of work with the ice saws, two days of hard pumping, and finally patching the holed hull with a bandage of sails. The ship was not the *Bon Accord*, yet Rachel worried lest Alex's ship, too, had been ice-trapped and holed. But at last the whalers began to drift home, bringing news of those left behind. In mid-September the *Bon Accord* was reported as having fourteen fish.

'Fourteen is good enough,' said Maitland and James added his reassurance, but in both men's voices Rachel detected a note of disappointment. When a week later the *Bon Accord* herself sailed triumphantly home with nineteen fish equal to some 240 tons of oil, it was the largest catch ever brought into port.

'I'll get a fine share of the profits,' beamed Wee Alex, radiant with pride and relief and the joy of James's return. The money would go a fair way towards restoring the Christie business on a more secure footing. Although they were still working on borrowed money, the shipyard was in full production now, with two ships on the stocks. 'Wi' my money,' said Alex proudly, 'we'll be able to pay off some o' the family debts. That is, if ye'll take it, James?'

'Aye, lad, and gladly. But first, there's things I want to discuss with you, in private.'

Alex and James had taken a long walk together and when they returned, Alex was suspiciously red-eyed, but all tension had gone. Later, in the privacy of their bed, James told Rachel everything that had passed between them. 'He is young, foolish and too susceptible to a determined woman's wiles, though I think he will not stray so easily in the future. But he told me what I wanted to know, Rachel. It *was* Farquharson's men at the back of it all – they engineered the brawl and the arrests, they boarded the *Bonnie Annie* and, as far as I can piece things together, for I cannot recall the details even yet, they overpowered me somehow, holed my ship, and left her to sink in the waters of Riga Bay.'

Rachel shuddered at the reminder but James slipped an arm round her and said, 'There is no need to be afraid. Our knowledge in itself is a weapon and though we may have no definite proof, I have evidence enough – and Farquharson's own conscience has done the rest.'

After three months, Farquharson's condition had not changed and rumour had it that he would be paralysed for life. '*Vengeance is mine, saith the Lord*,' murmured Rachel and her words reminded James of that other commitment: that, however, must wait till the spring.

1821

At the end of March Alex sailed again for the Greenland fisheries. 'Whaling is in my blood now,' he explained and Rachel recalled that, years ago, on the one occasion when James had sought a fortune in the whaling, Bonnie Annie had said, 'When the danger and the adventure get you and the thrill of the chase, you'll be trapped for life.' James had not succumbed, but Alex was younger and of a different temperament. Already James was talking of building or refitting a whaler of their own. For though he might not have caught the enthusiasm for whaling himself, his ambition burned stronger than ever. He aimed, as he told everyone openly, to build Christie Brothers into the biggest and most successful shipping company in Aberdeen. 'For us and for our children.'

In April the Christies sent the usual letter to the Farquharson company, stating their intention to cross Dixon's patch, 'In accordance with permission graciously granted,' for the purpose of launching their newest ship.

Robert Farquharson read the letter with mild surprise, then remembered his father had given permission for the Christies' last ship to be launched in a similar fashion and assumed he had agreed at the same time to allow this one. He thought no more about it. Mrs Euphemia Farquharson however also saw the letter, on one of her erratic and interfering raids on the family shipping office, and frowned.

'Effrontery,' she snapped. 'And it's time you did something with that land, Robert. What your father was thinking of buying a piece of scrubland practically in the sea I cannot think. You must build a warehouse on it or a boat shed or something. Or sell it. We cannot have all and sundry wandering over our property whenever they feel like it. Next time those Christies finish a ship, they must find some other way to get it into the water – or turn their hands to building furniture instead.'

The Christies, however, were unaware of her plans and the launch duly went ahead. Everyone had long known how the ship would be named. The new *Bonnie Annie* was a symbol of survival, recovery, defiance and determination, and while the second ship under construction, a schooner for the coastal trade, progressed steadily enough, all the yard's best efforts had gone into completing the *Bonnie Annie*'s replacement with all possible speed. James, lest any one of them forget, had mounted on the wall of Maitland's planning loft the pieces of broken timber salvaged from the wreckage of the lost *Bonnie Annie* and the second ship had been built as nearly similar as they could fashion her, while at the same time modifying the hull for the better shipment of timber. 'There are good timber markets in the Baltic,' James had reported, 'and I mean to import for our own use as well as for sale.'

Rachel, watching the launch, felt a sinking of the heart, though she tried as best she could to echo James's triumph. For the new ship was destined, as the old one had been, for the Baltic run. First, however, the final fittings must be completed and, after the usual 'play' day in celebration of a successful launch, the yard was busy as ever. Work resumed on the schooner and the keel of another brig was laid.

In May Rachel began to hope she might be pregnant and Isla Duthie gave birth to Andrew's son.

In June, James told Rachel what she had dreaded to hear. 'I must go back to Riga.'

'No!' she cried with involuntary terror. She could not hear Riga mentioned without remembering the long horror of James's absence. 'Please, James, not yet.' But she knew as she spoke that it was futile.

'I must, Rachy. I have business in St Petersburg as well as in Riga. There is something, too, that I intend to bring back – and I do not mean that tea I promised you long ago and never brought you.'

'I want nothing, James, but you. You know that. Do not leave me again so soon.'

'I am sorry, my love, but I must. If I go now, I can be back again long before winter is even thought of.'

'Then take me with you. Like you took me to London? I can help you as I helped you then. Take me and Jamie, please?'

'No. Can you not see you would be a worry to me? How could I concentrate on my ship with my two most precious possessions to claim all my attention? Besides, there is business to do which I can best do alone. There may also be danger, Rachel, I will not deny it, and I would not want to expose you or little Jamie to any unnecessary hazard. They say there is fighting in Latvia and parts of Poland. Revolutions. Uprisings. I am not sure of the details, I only know you are best here at home. Besides, I *need* you to stay here and guard our interests.' His brow gathered in the now familiar frown and Rachel knew he was thinking of Farquharson. Although Atholl was still ill, his business ventures flourished, if erratically, and enmity between the two companies was by no means dead. 'I trust you, Rachel, to watch while I am away for any hint of devious dealing. You understand me?' Bleakly she nodded. 'Besides,' he went on, smiling now, 'I want to think of you here, at my own fireside, safe. You and my little son.'

Rachel knew James was right, knew her place was at home in the Square and the shipping office, knew she was of more use here than on board ship in a foreign port, but all the fear and loneliness of that last separation washed over her with overpowering memory and with it came that persistent prickle of doubt. Her voice trembled only a little, however, as she said, 'Promise you will not delay? Promise that this time you will come home "swift as the wind"?'

'I promise or may my boat be . . .'

'Don't say it,' cried Rachel in agitation. The fisherman's oath never failed to set her heart thudding with fear.

'I am sorry if I frightened you,' said James, looking at her with concern. It was not like Rachel to give way to such imaginings. 'Come, you are a mother now,' he said gently, 'with responsibilities. What will Jamie think if he sees his Ma with tears in her eyes? Especially when she ought to be choosing the best salt port and cheeses to send to Friida and a bottle o' best whisky for Priit. That spirit they drink there is *terrible*.'

With an effort, Rachel pushed back her fears and managed a smile. When, a week later, the *Bonnie Annie* sailed for Riga and the Baltic ports, Rachel was on the headland, wee Jamie in her arms, to wave a brave farewell.

The bells for the King's Coronation began to ring at an early hour and continued at intervals throughout the day. The Christie yard, like everywhere else, had a holiday and Christies, Baxters, Brands, together with all the Square, closed their doors and went up into the town to celebrate with the rest. But not before Rachel had

214

checked that the *Steadfast*, like all the shipping in the harbour that day, was spick and span and decked with every scrap of bunting they could produce, the Christie pennant fluttering triumphantly from the mainmast. She took Jamie to watch the Militiamen march to the Links and he marched proudly along behind them until his little legs grew tired and he scrambled up into her arms. She held him up to watch the trades' procession march down Union Street, the young men smart in their Sunday best, their flags and emblems gleaming bright against the shimmering granite of the new buildings, while he kept time with his fists in the air. Maitland and the twins were never far away, with Kirsty Guyan and the Brand girls, and they seemed to move in a pool of laughter. They met Isla and Dr Andrew in the Castlegate, Louise and her mother near the new Aberdeen Hotel, even glimpsed the straight-backed disapproval of Euphemia Farquharson in a gig near Golden Square. It seemed the whole of Aberdeen was in the streets that day. The guns fired a royal salute at noon from the heights above Devanha brewery and were emulated by a party of musketry on Torry Hill and echoed up and down the city for hours after by a peppering of pistols and firearms of every kind. Even the mail coaches paraded the streets, strung about with flags and branches of laurel – 'like a trundling great bush,' commented Jessica Abercrombie sourly, as Fenton drew their own neat, leather-topped gig out of the way of one of these City splendours. 'It'll be full o' beetles and slaters and forky-tails for weeks after.'

Jessica was not enjoying the day. There were too many reminders of what others had and she had not. 'If old Farquharson hadn't as good as snuffed it,' she had complained that morning as they prepared to set out, 'We'd have had tickets for the Coronation banquet. They've completed the banqueting hall in the new Public Rooms specially.'

Fenton knew better than to point out that the banquet was a gentlemen's affair and the only person who would have gone would have been himself. Instead he said merely, 'The bonfire tonight should be splendid and there are sure to be fireworks and singing. I have promised the children they might see it for a while, if they are good.'

Jessica had not bothered to reply. What was a public bonfire compared to a private banquet, even if there were to be hogsheads of free porter provided by the magistrates in a dozen streets?

Now, as the children squealed and giggled at the various antics of the crowd, she caught a glimpse of the Farquharson gig in the distance and frowned with dissatisfaction. The truth was, Jessica was restless. The news of Atholl Farquharson's stroke had brought an initial 'Serve him right, the crafty old devil.' But once the satisfaction of knowing that he had received his just rewards for plotting against James Christie had worn off, she felt a touch of genuine regret, especially as James Christie himself had come back from Riga a pious, toffee-nosed prig who thought himself too good to speak to his old friends. Atholl had been useful to her. Until that affair in the Christie shipyard, which she preferred to forget, he had treated her like a lady, introducing her into city society and seeing she got invitations to all the right occasions, theatres and dinners and the like. Even since that affair he had continued to be her protector. He had to be, or she might have told his precious city folk a thing or two, but for months now she had had no one to get invitations for her, or to give her presents: except Fenton and that wasn't the same. There was Robert Farquharson, of course, but he was a spineless puppet, jumping every which way whenever his Ma pulled the strings. He'd be no use to her and as for his Ma, Euphemia had never liked her and with every reason. Jessica grinned briefly at the memory of their various encounters, most of which Jess had won. But Euphemia would no more get her a ticket to a society ball than walk barefoot to Timbuctoo. It was a pity Atholl got struck when he did, and before she'd got her amethysts, too. Remembering the occasion when the amethysts had been suggested, Jessica remembered something else, less pleasing. 'Watch your husband does not get wind of your part in the proceedings,' Farquharson had threatened. She glanced speculatively at Fenton from lowered lids. He was talking happily with Augusta, pointing out some landmark and she wondered, with a stab of apprehension, how his face would change if he did hear. Well, Atholl could tell nobody anything now, by all accounts. At the thought, Jessica felt more cheerful. She might have lost her protector, but she'd also lost her threat. Now only the Christies knew and they would never tell. She remembered that last encounter with James Christie with resentment and lingering annoyance. What right had he had to shove her out of his house as if she were nobody? He'd been glad enough to have her once, before he married and went pious, the randy hypocrite. He'd been a fine, lively fellow then, full of vigour and energy, a man any lass would be proud to catch. Mind you, he still had energy . . .

At the thought of the Christies a speculative look came into her eyes. Folk said they were prospering since James Christie came back and found God. They were always hardworking, but now, so folks said, James Christie worked twenty-five hours a day and they were certainly building ships faster than most folk, and good ships too. None of your cockleshell makeshift nonsense, but real, solid, oak-built vessels and each one personally designed. 'They're getting a name for quality,' her father-in-law had boasted when that last brig was launched. The *Bonnie Annie* again . . . as if they hadn't had enough trouble with the first and no wonder when they named the ship for a mad woman. But at least it was better than George Abercrombie's suggestion for the next ship, which they had started already. The *Rachel Christie* indeed! Why should a peely-wally quinie like yon Cove lass have a ship called for her?

If she can have a ship, why can't I? thought Jessica with returning resentment. She was aye giving herself airs and here's me wi' a house in Union Terrace and a man wi' a fine city job and more clothes to my back than she's had hot dinners, and nae ship named after *me*! And it's Fenton's Da's money they're doing it with, after all. Brooding over the use her father-in-law's spare money was put to, Jessica suddenly saw her way clear. The Christies were not the only ones who were prospering. The Abercrombies were doing all right, too, and Kirsty Abercrombie she knew for a fact had her eye on the next rung up the social ladder. Agitating to get her man into the Country Club, folks said, though George himself wasna' keen. Maybe Jessica had been too offhand with her mother-in-law in the past? Maybe it was time for a bit more family unity? Kirsty was no doubt as anxious as Jessica to go to the Opening Ball and what more natural than that she should want her own family to go with her? Especially if that Farquharson cow was going. Yes, Jessica decided. She had lost one patron and had better find herself another, and who better than her own father-in-law? And if the Cove lass could ingratiate herself merely by a bit o' work, then so could Jess.

There and then she vowed that the very next ship the Christies built should be named not for Rachel but for *her*. She had the sense to know it would not be easy. James Christie was not exactly a friend and since that day when he had put her out of his house he had not spoken a word to her, though they had passed each other on at least two occasions in the street. No, the move would have to come from Abercrombie. But George Abercrombie had a soft spot for the Christies and had been less than friendly to Jessica the last time they'd met. He used to be so amiable towards her, too. Now he was aye grumbling that she spent too much on clothes and didna' take an interest in the shop. True enough Jess hadn't much time for the shop in the Guestrow, with its dark little rooms and the barrels and jars heaped everywhere and stinking so strong of soap and camphor that ye couldna' smell the nice things, like cinnamon and sugar plums. The new shop in Union Street would be different though, and hadn't old Abercrombie said it was nearly finished?

Jessica sat so long in thought that Fenton had to speak to her twice before she heard him and even then she did not seem to understand. 'I said, would you like to go home now, dear? The children are tired.'

'No. I'd like to visit your Da's new shoppie, in Union Street.'

'But it is closed. Today is a holiday, as you well know, and the workmen . . .'

'Well I can *look* can't I? Ye're aye going on at me to take more interest in your Da's business and when I do, ye make difficulties. I'm thinking,' she went on as Fenton obediently touched whip to flank and steered their gig out of the press and into a more open stretch of Union Street. 'I reckon it's time I helped in your father's shop. Augusta and Victoria dinna' need me all day and I'd like fine to get out of the house now and then. Well, don't just sit there wi' yer mouth open like a stranded cod! Anyone'd think I'd suggested going on the streets. It's nae so astonishing to want to lend a hand wi' the family business, is it?'

219

'No, but . . .'

'I was aye a dab hand at selling,' she went on, with a rare reference to her life before her marriage when she and Rachel had sold fish together, door-to-door, in the town. 'Yer Da'll be glad of my help.'

Fenton was too astounded to answer. The idea of Jessica working at anything was such a novel one that he still could not take it in. She had been rude enough about his work when he had hesitated about today's celebrations. Now she was even scorning these, apparently.

'I've had enough o' these junketings for today, Fenton. Idle folk strutting and showing off and making spectacles o' themselves and such a clattering and banging o' guns everywhere fit to burst a body's eardrums. I've better things to do wi' my time. I want to tell yer Da mysel' what I've decided. When we've seen the new shoppie, we'll call in and ask the pair o' them to dine wi' us tomorrow.'

'But he'll not . . .'

'Not what? I ken fine he's nae expecting us if that's what ye mean. If he's out, we'll leave a message, or wait. It'll be a rare surprise for him. Yer Da and I always got on well,' she finished, folding her hands complacently in her lap and conveniently forgetting the years of disagreement. 'He'll be glad to see us. We'll ask him and yer Ma to dine tomorrow and I'll see to the meal mysel' so Mairi canna' spoil it like she did the last time. Let's see, we'd best have a good bit of butcher meat. Yer Da's a man wi' a fair appetite. Maybe a gigot o' best lamb and I know it isna' the season really but he was aye partial to a cloutie dumpling, yer Da, though I'd best get in something simpler for yer Ma. Maybe strawberries or a nice fresh pineapple.'

Fenton listened in amazement, but he had long ago abandoned all attempt to understand the devious workings of Jess's mind. She was up to something, that he knew, but what it was he had no idea.

George Abercrombie, too, was dumbfounded and said so, but after the initial shock he accepted the idea with less suspicion than his son.

'I'm right pleased ye've seen sense at last, lass,' he said the following day, 'and that was a rare piece o' lamb you served me. Haven't had a better since I canna' mind when. And there was I thinking you were as stuck in yer silly ways as our Clemmy. It's no game, though,' he warned, 'so if ye've a mind to play shops for a while in a frilly apron, say so now and forget it.'

'I ken fine it's no game,' said Jessica meekly. 'How could your fine new shop be a game? It's an *emporium* and ye'll have all the gentry o' the neighbourhood flocking to yer door afore ye know it, and I'll see they buy plenty afore they leave again,' she added archly, with a roll of her fine eyes in Abercrombie's direction. 'Or have ye forgotten I started life as a fisher lass? I sold fish to yer own wife *and* I overcharged her, though dinna' tell her I said so.' Boldly she gave him a wink and Abercrombie laughed.

'Aye, we could maybe find a place for ye, Jess, but I reckon ye'll sell more to the menfolk than the women. What do you say, Fenton?'

'I say,' said Fenton crossly, 'that Jessica has enough to do at home.'

'But I wouldna' work *all* the time, Fenton dear,' said Jessica sweetly. 'Say three mornings a week? I'll need to learn the trade, of course, Mr Abercrombie. I'm only an ignorant fisher lass, after all.' She gave him her most winning look from under lowered lashes. 'But I do want it to be a real *family* business, like the Christies' business is, and Rachel works, though I'll maybe not be able to work as hard as she does. But then I have *two* wee ones to think of and maybe I'll not be able to manage even three mornings for very long.' She tucked a hand into

Fenton's and snuggled closer. 'But when the baby's born
. . .' She lowered her eyes and waited for the congratulations which she knew would come – premature, though
they didn't know it. But after all she *might* be pregnant
for all they knew and she'd make sure she was before the
month was out. George Abercrombie's reaction exceeded
even her expectations.

'Another, by Jove! That's the best news yet, lass. No
wonder ye're taking a proper interest at last, wi' a son
coming along to take over the business. Congratulations,
Fenton lad. I reckon this calls for a double celebration.'

Even Kirsty Abercrombie who had so far remained
frostily impervious to all Jess's overtures managed a thin
smile when her husband raised a glass to 'Abercrombie,
Son and *Grandson* – and to the future.'

Jessica was well pleased with the day's work and when
she produced the family heir, as she supposed she would
have to do now, she was sure she'd have no difficulty
getting old Abercrombie to name a ship for her. But it
wouldn't be just any old brig like that *Bonnie Annie*. No,
she'd have an East Indiaman, 500 tons at least, wi' gold
paint all over her and a fine figurehead. The new *Bonnie
Annie* had been picked out in ordinary red and black
paint and had had no figurehead at all.

'Mer-may! Mer-may!' chanted Jamie delightedly, bouncing up and down on Rachel's hip as she hurried along the
quayside towards the sparkling hull of the *Steadfast*
moored in her usual berth below Pocra. She had been in
harbour for the past two days, unloading and refurbishing
ready for the return trip to London. Her decks were
newly holystoned, her canvas neatly furled, her yards
varnished and gleaming, and on this particular morning
one of the apprentices sat in a rope sling under her bow
touching up the paintwork on the mermaid figurehead. It

was this last sight which had filled little Jamie with such glee. The mermaid fascinated him and invariably sent him into squeals of delight while he reached out eager arms in an attempt to clutch the splendid object and explore it closer. 'Mer-may! Mer-may!' he squealed as they approached and Rachel laughed.

'It is only the *Steadfast*, Jamie, your uncles' ship. See, there's Uncle Willy waving to you and Uncle George too. No, you cannot have the mermaid,' she said as he lunged sideways in an attempt to reach the glittering object so that Rachel almost missed her footing. 'The mermaid lives on the ship. She shows your uncles the way to go and brings them safe home again.'

The *Bonnie Annie* had had a mermaid figurehead too, remembered Rachel, but that mermaid had led her ship to disaster against a cliff in Riga bay. The new *Bonnie Annie*, by all accounts, was on a safer course. News had come via the Sound list that their ship had reached the Baltic in almost as good time as the *Hibernia*'s best. Rachel had scoured the list over and over for mention of any Farquharson ship on the same route, and when she found none, had allowed her anxiety to relax, though not entirely. There were natural hazards as well as man-made ones on any voyage and her worries would not be over until the new ship sailed safely home. But the weather was good and the world a cheerful place. The new King's Coronation had lightened everyone's spirits and national pride had been boosted and reassured by news of Napoleon Bonaparte's death in exile on the island of St Helena. A spirit of optimism prevailed and was reflected in their own shipyard where work went ahead with even greater speed. After the launch of the *Bonnie Annie II*, Maitland had lost no time in laying the keel of the next and when the schooner was launched, in another month or so, they would have another company ship. Their timber yard was prospering, too: at the first timber roup of the season, Maitland had been able to secure a good batch of yellow pine *and* on credit. One day, James promised, they would send their own ships to Canada. Meanwhile, trade was booming with more inquiries coming in than they could handle, mostly for small ships of no more than 150 tons for local owners to use in the coastal trade, but Maitland's own ships, as he thought of them, were to be larger vessels, 300 tons or more, the design of which he was constantly improving. He meant one day to send a ship to the China Seas, but when he did it was to be a white bird of grace and beauty, of swooping speed and effortless passage. 'One day I will do it, Rachel,' he told her, tearing up yet another discarded plan and starting afresh. 'And when I do, she will make the Christie name in the shipbuilding world.'

'Do you ever think of steam?' asked Rachel hesitantly. It was common knowledge now that Euphemia Farquharson had placed an order for a steam-packet which was intended for the London run. The *Velocity* and *Tourist* steam-yachts of the Aberdeen and Leith Company operated daily now between those harbours, with a licence to carry parcels and packages under three or four barrel bulk as well as passengers, and they intended to add another, larger steam-yacht soon to go as far as Inverness.

'Think of it?' Maitland paused. His blue-grey eyes were thoughtful as he looked out of the window towards the Farquharson office. 'Of course I do. Steam is the future, Rachel. Once man has discovered something, he does not discard it. Progress is a beast that must be fed. But not by me. Steam will come, but to the other shipyards. I hope it does not come like a ravening beast to devour us all before I have made my white bird. Wind and sail are my element, Rachel. I know it and as long as there are men who think as I do, I will build ships for them. Afterwards

. . .' He shrugged with a touch of sadness. 'I hope that will be after I am gone. Young Jamie will have to deal with the steam. And I reckon he will take it all in his stride, coal, noise, smell and all. He's a fine wee lad, and full of spirit.'

'Full of curiosity, too,' laughed Rachel, 'and a bit too much of it at times.'

'Curiosity is the stuff of invention,' said Maitland seriously. 'Do not discourage it. One day Jamie will be head of Christie and Sons and at the helm of one of your steam-ships, no doubt.'

Meanwhile, there were the bread-and-butter schooners to be built and the mundane business of repairs and refits, an increasingly profitable sideline which Maitland had established on a spare corner of the new land, as well as the operation of the *Steadfast* on the London run. It was the success of the *Steadfast* which had brought Rachel hurrying to the quayside on that balmy midsummer morning, little Jamie bouncing excitedly on her hip. He loved the bustle of the quayside, the squawking, squabbling herring-gulls, the mewing cry of the dapper little oyster-catchers with their black and white elegance and their brilliant orange bills, the racing water and flapping sails, the coiled ropes and clean-scrubbed timber, the smell of tar and holystone and varnish. At twenty-one months Rachel still took him everywhere with her, though he was increasingly cumbersome to carry and when walking, as he much preferred to do, unwilling to be fettered by the rope harness his father had devised for him. He wanted to explore, to touch, to taste. At home he climbed on to a three-legged stool which tipped over on top of him and blacked his eye. At the yard he put wood shavings into his mouth before Rachel could stop him and almost choked. At the office he tore up and ate several pages from Rachel's orders book when her concentration was engaged in balancing a column of the men's wages. But through all adversity he bounced and laughed and put such loving little arms around her neck to hug and kiss her that Rachel could not be angry with him, and could not hand him over to the care of another.

Now, aboard the *Steadfast*, she put him down on the deck, tethered him to a stanchion and with a stern, 'Be a *good* boy, Jamie,' cast her eye swiftly around her. 'Mr Bonnington wants passage again to London,' she said as William's head appeared in the open hatch. He swung himself up on to the deck, followed instantly by George.

'Five days again? Pound to a penny he's important business as can wait for no man.'

'Not exactly,' smiled Rachel. 'He's taking his daughter to London where she is to catch the stage coach to Bath, to school.'

'There's an awful long way to go to find a school.'

'Will the Aberdeen schools no' have her?'

'She's maybe such a hoyden naebody in Scotland will have her.'

'So she's having to be sent among the English.'

'Where naebody'll notice!' and they slapped each other on the back in mutual glee.

'She is nothing of the kind,' said Rachel sternly, 'so see you make no such remarks during the voyage. She is a well-behaved young lady going away to a school for gentlewomen, to learn society manners. Her Ma and Da go with her.'

'*Three* o' them? But we've nae the space.'

'Mr Bonnington knows what the ship can offer and I have promised to do as best I can for them. They've heard tales of the *Dora* which they dinna' like. Rats and dirt and splitting timbers.'

'All ships have rats,' said Willy doubtfully. He and

226

George often trapped them, to race on deck in the idle hours of the dog watch.

'Maybe,' said Rachel briskly, 'but not feeding off a man's plate at dinner! Nor nesting in a lady's boot.' It was this last tale which had so frightened Bonnington's daughter. A passenger on the *Dora* had stamped and stamped to get her foot into her little kid boot one morning only to find it full of rat. 'And I reckon ye'd have heard her screams from Tilbury to Inverness,' her informant had finished gleefully. Remembering other aspects of the gossip, Rachel added sternly, 'And I want no cockroach races across the dinner table, do you hear?' William and George looked sheepish. 'Racer and Pacer must keep out of sight on this voyage or I swear I will confiscate them and personally drown them.'

'Rachy, you *wouldn't*?' they cried in unison. The pair of tame cockroaches had been with them for many voyages and though James accused them of replacing either or both whenever one died and no one the wiser, the twins vehemently maintained that Racer and Pacer were original and unique. Rachel could not have thought of a better threat.

'I would and I will,' she said, 'if you do not offer the high standard of cleanliness and efficiency I have promised the Bonnington family. I could not promise them comfort, but I will one day.' She and Maitland had plans for a luxury passenger ship to operate between Aberdeen and London and, if James agreed, they planned to lay down the keel in the very next slipway that was free. 'Meanwhile,' she went on briskly, 'I want you to make sure there is clean canvas for an awning on deck, should they wish to use it, and ye'll see the "heads" are spotless.' The 'heads' were the ship's toilets. 'I will see the steward myself about provisions, though I expect the Bonningtons to bring a hamper and their own linen. Then there are the lamps to check, and I noticed a chip in the cabin ewer. I have bespoken a new copper basin and jug from the chandler and they will send them round, back of two today.' She moved towards the companionway, unhooking Jamie and tucking him on to her hip as she went. 'Come along, Jamie, we're going below to see the wee cabin.'

At the foot of the companionway was the tiny chart room with its maps and nautical instruments and, immediately adjoining, a little panelled cabin with a pair of bunk beds ingeniously slotted into the curve of the hull, with guardrails and parapets, and drawers built under the bunks, a table top with cut-out holes to take basin and ewer and a chamberpot beneath. Through the porthole Rachel could see a stretch of quay, a bollard and hawser, with the Weighhouse in the distance and the usual bustle of quayside traffic. She put Jamie down on the floor and began to check the cabin for dust, mice, mould, old tobacco, and any other unpleasantness the twins might have overlooked. Satisfied, she moved on to the galley, Jamie at her heels.

She lifted the lid of the meal tub, dipped in a hand and let the oatmeal sift slowly through her fingers, looking for signs of maggots or weevils. Mr Abercrombie had promised her the best, but it was wise to check, just the same. She was inspecting the supplies of eggs and cheese when she became aware of a sudden emptiness like a chill draught at her back and her heart stopped with a thud of fear. 'Jamie?'

Instantly she remembered the companionway, the open hatch, the water . . . '*Jamie!*' He was not in the galley, the cabin, the chart room. She almost fell up the steps to the deck. '*Jamie!*' At that moment she heard the splash and simultaneously came a child's shriek from the quayside. 'Uncle Willy! Jamie's in the water! Uncle *George!*'

228

Afterwards Rachel went over and over the slow detail of that endless moment, over and over till her mind was saturated with the horror of it, yet at the same time could not have enough. She saw herself, paralysed, one foot on deck, one still on the companion ladder, her hand clutching the rail; saw little Pearl, valiantly struggling to escape Louise's grip and jump into the water after her beloved cousin; saw William poise briefly on the gunwale then curve like a scimitar blade over the brim, followed instantly by George. Ridiculously, inside her head, she heard the inane, reproving voice say over and over, 'It is too cold for swimming,' while terror shook her and the harsh talons of loss already tore at her heart, wrenching and twisting.

People were shouting from the quayside, someone threw a life belt, another a rope, then hands were outstretched to grasp and heave. She saw George emerge like a sea-prince, streaming seawater from hair and beard and every inch of him, his broken nose gleaming in the sunlight like a ludicrous warning lamp, William beside him, his gap-toothed mouth spitting seawater, a sodden bundle of blue cotton in one arm.

She saw them grouped, like that picture Andrew had once shown her of an anatomy lesson, in one of his books, all staring at the bundle on the quayside while the water spread in a dark stain like blood across the cassies to flood her brain. Then a woman moved, knelt in the spreading pool and began to pummel the bundle, kneading and turning it like dough till a thin wail of protest came from somewhere far away – and snapped the band which had held Rachel paralysed. She fell, scrambled to her feet again, tumbled, ran, threw herself somehow ashore screaming 'Jamie!' 'Loud enough to terrify the fiercest bogle in hell,' as William and George said afterwards. 'Tis nae wonder the sea kelpies fled and didna' tak' wee Jamie after all.'

But it was Louise Forbes's ministrations that saved the child, emptying the seawater from his lungs, making him breath again so that he finally vented all his fear, outrage and anger in a full-blooded howl. The anxious bystanders smiled in murmuring relief. As Louise sat back on her heels, triumphant, Rachel snatched up her dripping son and clutched him to her breast with a final cry, where he clung, sobbing, his little arms tight around her and his face buried in her neck.

'Jamie 'wim, Ma,' he sobbed, over and over. 'Nasty 'wim.'

'He saw me, Auntie Rachel,' explained Pearl, 'through the little window. Auntie Louise was bringing me to see the *Steadfast* and I waved. I didn't mean him to run away from you, Auntie Rachel,' she finished tearfully, 'I didn't mean him to swim.'

'Call that swimming?' jeered William, blustering with relief. 'A *dog* would be ashamed o' yon paddling about.'

'Tell you what,' added George, 'we'll teach the pair o' ye to swim one day.'

'Aye, like fishes in the sea.'

'I think that would be an excellent idea,' said Louise Forbes, dusting off her skirts and straightening her bonnet. 'Especially if young Jamie here plans to fall in the water often.'

'Oh Louise, look at your clothes,' cried Rachel. 'And it is your new dress, your pretty lavender one, ruined.'

Louise at last, in spite of her mother's comments about horses and stable doors, had bought new clothes, feminine, more becoming ones in softer shades which suited her. Now she merely shrugged. 'No matter. What is a dress after all?'

'But you will catch pneumonia, Louise, and all on my

account. I am so grateful to you.' She looked at her friend with brimming eyes. 'I can never thank you enough – or you, William and George – or you, Pearl, for warning us as you did – or any of you,' she finished helplessly, looking round the kindly, beaming faces. 'My heart is so full . . .'

'Nonsense,' said Louise briskly. 'Stop blethering, woman, and take your infant home. Can you not see he's soaked to the skin? And so would you be if you'd taken the dunking he has. As for you two,' she went on, turning on the twins, 'You should have more sense, grown men that you are, than to stand around dripping wet. Away home and change your clothes this instant.'

'Come home with us, Louise,' urged Rachel. 'Please?'

'You can dry your skirt before the fire, Aunty Louise,' urged Pearl. 'Uncle Willy will not look, will you Uncle, nor Uncle George, and you must not look at them while they undress because they are very shy.' Through the laughter which followed Pearl announced loudly, 'It is not *funny*,' then added, in her quaintly elderly manner, 'If you stop laughing at me, I will make you all a glass of hot toddy – and I *do* know how.'

That night, Rachel miscarried.

'It is not surprising,' comforted Louise. 'You suffered a shock which could make anyone miscarry.' But Rachel thought it more than that. She had thanked God over and over, from her own heart, for Jamie's deliverance and again, as she knew James would wish her to do, in the words of his Riga prayer, yet when she felt the twisting, draining pains begin, it seemed only inevitable payment, a life for a life. Jamie had been given back to her, but she must pay for her heedless neglect. And it was neglect, whatever they told her. She had been inattentive, had taken her eyes from her darling son to search for *weevils*. Was it any wonder God had punished her? Yet when, in

231

her wretchedness, she voiced something of her thoughts, Louise said firmly, 'Nonsense. It was an accident that could have happened to anyone. He is a lively lad with an independent and inquiring mind. It would take anyone all her time to keep him out of mischief, let alone a woman with three other jobs to do as well, and no real harm has come of it. Jamie is well and you will have more children. Nevertheless, as I have told you for a long time now, you should hire a nursemaid.'

'And so have I told her,' added Maitland, his face grave. As always when James was away at sea he felt responsibility heavy upon him and the story of his little nephew's near-drowning had shaken him more than he cared to show. 'Rachel does too much and will not share the burden.'

'It is no burden,' cried Rachel. How could she explain to them that now, more than ever, she wanted Jamie to herself? In the loss of that other, unknown little life it was only her son who could give her comfort and she clung to him with a possessive passion which frightened her. If she lost Jamie how could she bear to live?

'Nevertheless,' warned Louise, 'if you hope to have more children you had best give the matter thought. Remember the trouble you had when Jamie was born? If you do not let your body settle in rest and quietness is it any wonder you miscarry at the slightest shock?' She went on, deliberately brutal, 'And you will do so again if you do not alter your ways. Andrew himself says so.'

'I will talk it over with James,' temporized Rachel, 'When he comes home.'

'No,' persisted Louise and Maitland echoed her. 'It is your decision and you must take it now. It is a pity that Pearl is not older. She will be a great help to you one day.'

But she had been a help already. With her mixture of

232

childish naivety and elderly common sense, she had done much to cheer her stricken aunt. When told why Dr Andrew had been summoned to the house in the Square and why Rachel was spending a day in bed, resting, she said, 'You must grow another baby, Auntie Rachel, for Uncle James. Like my Ma grew one for Dr Andrew. But you must take care not to work too hard and pop him out before he is ready. My Ma rested a *lot*.'

'She is lucky to have you to help her.'

'Oh, she does not need me very much. She says I worry her and make a noise and she does not let me hold the baby in case I drop him. I told her I never drop Jamie, but she did not listen. She has Dr Andrew to look after her now,' she added with a stoic acceptance which troubled Rachel's heart, 'and there is Mrs Mutch. They do not notice me and I would much rather help you. Can I stay and help you today, and spend the night, and the next night too? I will see to Jamie if he cries and watch him for you, all the time.'

Pearl spent more time nowadays in the Christie household than she did in her own, often spending several nights together under Rachel's roof, during which time, Rachel suspected, her mother hardly noticed her absence, absorbed as she was in her new little family.

At the Christie house her uncles indulged her shamelessly and as shamelessly taught her all the lore of their fisher ancestors. They taught her how to bait the hooks for the whitefishing, how to coil a line in a skull without tangling the tippens, how to search out and collect the mussels from the 'scarp' on the shore. 'For who is to say she willna' marry a fisherman?' pointed out William and, 'A haddy to a herrin' ye'll nae find a handier wee quinie in a' the Square,' added George. 'See here and I'll show you how to knot a tear in a net so the wee fishes canna' escape through the holes.' For though they rarely went fishing nowadays, they had lost none of their fishing skills and when ashore often helped the Brands or the Baxters or any other of the Square's fishermen who needed an extra pair of hands.

Maitland, too, indulged wee Pearl. He took her into the planning loft, let her help him measure up for the scale models or hold the ruler while he drew a straight line, and carved her her own ship-in-a-bottle which she treasured more than any rag doll.

Louise Forbes was a regular visitor now at the Christie home, preferring to meet Pearl here rather than in the awkwardness of the doctor's house, and she continued to instruct the child in letters and simple sums.

'Ye'd best not teach her too much,' James had teased, 'Or she'll nae be welcome at the school. Yon teachers dinna' like their pupils to know more than they know themselves.'

James Christie was unfailingly indulgent towards Davy's daughter and as for Pearl, she regarded the Christie house as hers. But though Pearl was precocious, she was not yet four and too young by far to have sole charge of Jamie, much as she loved him.

'You will have to hire a nursemaid, Rachel,' insisted Louise, 'until Pearl is older. Or a clerk.'

'A *clerk*?' Maitland and Rachel spoke together and with equal horror. The idea of a stranger having access to the most secret documents of the Christie business was out of the question. Louise, watching the effect of her remark, kept her face carefully expressionless though her eyes twinkled. 'The Farquharsons have two,' she said innocently, 'though I did hear one of them might be leaving shortly. Something about a discrepancy in the petty cash though that may, of course, be merely rumour.'

'Folk who leave their business affairs to others deserve

to be swindled,' said Maitland, but he sounded preoccupied.

Rachel made no answer at all.

'I will watch Jamie for you,' said Pearl stoutly. 'I will watch him *every single minute*.'

'I know you will, pet,' said Rachel, smiling for the first time since Jamie's accident and holding out her arms to the child. 'Did you not watch him for me on the *Steadfast* when I was too busy to see what he was up to? I will ask your Ma if you can stay here for a while to help me. And,' she explained, turning to Maitland for approval, 'I will ask Kirsty Guyan to watch the pair of them for me – but only for an hour or two,' she added hastily, for the truth was she could not bear to share her precious Jamie with anyone for long. Yet at the same time she knew they were right and that her husband would say the same. She could not go on as she had been doing. There was too much work to be done and she could not afford the smallest mistake. The incident with Jamie had been a warning to her and one she had best heed if she wanted to keep her husband's son and his shipyard safe as he had trusted her to do. Only then, with a gasp of horror, did she remember the *Steadfast*. She scrambled to her feet with a cry. 'The Bonningtons! I must check the cabin and order fresh eggs.'

'Too late,' said Maitland. 'She sailed this morning – with a coop o' hens on deck and a crate o' fresh oranges.'

'What about the new copper basin? Was it delivered promptly and did you check it for dents?'

'Yes it was, and no I did not,' said Maitland with exaggerated patience. 'And if you think the Bonningtons are going to remove their trade in dudgeon for a dented wash bowl, then we are well rid of them. Personally, I think they are people of more sense and understanding. The daughter was particularly anxious to know that Jamie

235

was quite safe and they all sent you their sympathy and understanding, together with warmest wishes for your recovery.'

'Which will be achieved all the sooner,' added Louise, 'if you do as you are told and rest. Pearl and I will fetch Kirsty Guyan directly, if she is free.'

But Rachel, lying back on her pillow with a long sigh of relief, for her head had begun to spin alarmingly with the aftermath of shock and her own loss of blood, had no doubts on that score. Kirsty Guyan was a lively, spirited and affectionate girl with plenty of friends, but Rachel knew she would leave all of them at the wink of an eye for the chance of a job in Alex Christie's home.

Alex had sailed for Greenland on 29 March and first news from the fisheries had not been good. One ship had been stove in the bows early in the season and had to return home; another had been lost in the ice though the crew were saved. Another, the *Invincible*, with seven fish aboard, had been stove and considerably damaged by ice and had to turn early for home, bringing reports of an unfavourable season and few fish to be seen. North winds were driving the ships further southwards than they had planned and few had more than one or two fish so far. In mid-July a large whale, newly harpooned, struck one of the whale boats of the *Jean*, killing three of the crew, and ice conditions were treacherous. But more recent reports had suggested that things were improving and at least the *Bon Accord* and Wee Alex were still safe.

Remembering Alex and the reason he was in the Greenland fisheries instead of on the *Bonnie Annie*, with James, Rachel thought of that other time when James had been away and wondered again if she would ever know, for all his telling, the half of what his life had been in those long, lost months.

* * *

236

'Must you go?' pleaded Isla, her blue eyes suspiciously moist. 'It is so very late, Andrew.'

'Nonsense. It will not be dark for an hour at the least.' Andrew Noble sounded more brusque than he meant to do, for these occasions invariably made him nervous.

'But they do not need you at the hospital, surely? No one has sent for you and it is not your day.'

'I have other calls on my time than the hospital,' he said, turning his back and bending over the desk where he kept his papers, lest she see the evasion in his face. It hurt him to have to deceive her, yet it would hurt her far more were she to guess the truth. Not for the first time, he wished he had someone with whom he could have shared the burden of responsibility and guilt. Louise would have understood, encouraged him, even helped, but understandably he saw little now of Louise. Mentally, he went over the arrangements yet again: protective smocks, lanterns, sacking and ropes, shovels. He had told them to procure short-handled wooden ones to muffle sound, and to have everything ready for him at the meeting place. But he had promised the whisky himself. He took up the flask which he had prepared earlier and slipped it into his great-coat pocket.

'Why do you need to take whisky with you?' asked Isla, puzzled. 'Is it to be a party?'

'No, my love. But you know when someone delivers a lecture it is customary to applaud and tonight we have a new member coming among us. You would not have the Medical Society fall short on hospitality, surely?'

'Why did you not *say* it was a Society meeting?' cried Isla, relieved. 'But you should be wearing your best shirt and stock. Hurry and change, dear. I ironed it specially and you know you always wear it for your Society meetings.'

'Tonight is different,' blustered Andrew, surreptitiously

237

consulting his watch. It was almost time. He was not good at lying at the best of times and she was making it impossible with her large, trusting eyes and soft hand on his arm. 'Informal,' he improvised, 'in deference to our guest who is notoriously ill-clad. I am afraid it will be a long session,' he hurried on before she could answer, 'so do not trouble to wait up for me.'

'Of course I will wait,' said Isla with her touching, exasperating devotion. 'You know I cannot sleep till you are home.'

'Then tonight you must *try* to do so,' said Andrew, with an edge of impatience in his voice. He was nervous enough as it was without the added burden of knowing Isla was pacing the floor, her pale hair loose about her shoulders, her eyes increasingly anxious, and counting the minutes till he came home. 'If only for our son's sake. Do you want to make your milk run dry?'

'I am sorry, Andrew. It is just that I . . . that you . . . I worry when you are away,' she finished with a bleak simplicity which touched his heart. Impulsively he hugged her to his chest, kissing first her forehead, then her lips. 'Do not worry,' he said more kindly. 'There is nothing for you to worry about.' And after tonight, he added, under his breath, it will not be my turn again for months.

In fact, had it not been for the excessive nervousness of the students whose turn it was, Andrew would have had no need to take part at all. It was his place to pay, theirs to deliver. If they expected the education of watching a subject being anatomized, then they ought to be prepared to provide that subject, in the appointed manner. But Robert Liston of Edinburgh, reputedly one of the foremost surgeons in Europe and Andrew's idol, was renowned for leading his own students in their necessary quests and Andrew, in deference to his master, could do no less. Nevertheless he was relieved to see, on closing the door of the cottage behind him, that a sea mist had crept in with the evening, shrouding the town in a veil of grey. St Fittick's churchyard on the brae above Nigg Bay would be well hidden.

The haar was not welcome to James Christie, riding in the roads to the east of Aberdeen. He would dare no approach to the harbour till the mist had lifted on any occasion, and especially not now. For one thing, his cargo was too precious to risk; for another, he wanted the whole town to see the homecoming of the new *Bonnie Annie* in all her splendour. Yet at the same time the unexpected delay gave him time to collect and arrange his thoughts and to prepare what he would say. For whereas there was no doubt in his own mind that he had done the right and only thing possible, and no doubt that, once she knew the whole of it, his wife would agree, he had to admit that there might be malicious tongues in the town – he could think of one in particular – which would say otherwise. The thought of what they might say brought a flush to his cheeks and a pugnacious set to his jaw: let them say what they chose. He, James Christie, was his own master and would act as he saw fit. He took out the little silver box he had bought in St Petersburg and laid it on the polished oak table, in the pool of light cast by the hanging lamp which swayed only a little with the gentle rise and fall of the swell. The mist-shrouded water was smooth as silk, the cry of a distant oyster-catcher strangely muted. Regularly through the muffling mist came the melancholy boom of the foghorn.

To the west, somewhere behind that weightless curtain of haar, lay the bay of Nigg with the cliffs of the Girdleness at their back. In that bay his father had been drowned. It was eight years now since he and his brothers had carried their father's body home in a canvas sling, dripping seawater and tears. In those eight years much had happened that neither James nor his father could have foreseen. He had promised to care for them all, in his father's place. 'I have kept my promise, Da, as best I could,' he murmured.

He opened the lid of the little silver box with its pattern of intricate trellis-work and took out the ring between finger and thumb. In the palm of his hand it lay like a single pebble on an expanse of sand. A slim gold hoop with a twisted love knot and in its centre, a diamond. A small diamond, to be sure, but beautiful, as the delicate workmanship of the setting was beautiful. He had known, the instant he saw it in the cluttered, incense-smelling darkness of the St Petersburg shop, that it was Rachel's ring. Looking at it, he felt a glow of anticipated pleasure as he thought of her face when she opened the box. Then his smile faded as he remembered that other 'present'. But she would welcome that, too, with joy. She was loving, compassionate, honest and true. How could she think otherwise than he did?

Nevertheless, when the mist lifted with the strengthening of the sun, the anchor chain rattled and the first sails unfurled to capture the light September breeze in its flapping canvas, James felt a nervousness new to him. But with the helm in his hand, the familiar tip of the deck under his feet and the winds of home in his face, he forgot all apprehension in the unfailing joy of homecoming.

'Mer-may! Mer-may!' shrieked Jamie, skipping excitedly along the Quay between Rachel and Pearl, with Kirsty Guyan close behind them.

'No, pet,' began Rachel. 'It is not the *Steadfast* this time, but the . . .' then she stopped in wonder, for the child was right. There was a mermaid figurehead on the prow of the second *Bonnie Annie* exactly where the old figurehead had been, on the first. And there was James, waving to her from the deck with triumph in every line of his body. If he did not fire a cannonade or dip his sails in defiance towards the Farquharson office in the Shiprow, he might just as well have done so, for everyone on the quayside instantly recognized that battered mermaid and raised a spontaneous cheer.

In the laughter and bustle of docking, furling sail, giving orders for this and that, there was time for no more than a swift embrace for Rachel, a swing in the air and a hug for Jamie, another for Pearl and a cheery nod for Kirsty, and no time at all for privacy. But when the first rush was over and the unloading under way James drew Rachel towards the companionway to the captain's quarters. 'Come, my love. I have something to show you. No, leave Jamie here with Pearl. You will keep an eye on them, won't you, Kirsty?'

'Kirsty does already,' began Rachel. 'She . . .' Then the strain of the weeks since Jamie's accident overwhelmed her and she buried her head in his chest while her whole frame shook with silent weeping.

'Hush, hush,' soothed James, his face anxious. He raised a questioning eyebrow in Kirsty's direction, but she, competent lass that she was, took Pearl and Jamie each by the hand and with a firm, 'Come along and we'll watch the wee parcels come flying up from the ship's middle,' led them away towards the gangplank and the shore.

'I lost our baby,' sobbed Rachel, when James had bundled her down the short ladder and into the cabin, a replica of the one where they had once voyaged together to London. 'Jamie nearly drowned.'

'He is not lost,' soothed James, puzzled and increasingly anxious. 'He is fine and strong and skipping about the quayside even now, leading Kirsty a rare dance.'

'He fell in the harbour,' she insisted. 'It was my fault.' She poured out the whole, horrifying tale while James held her and comforted her and finally kissed her with tenderness and concern.

'Thank God he is safe,' he said quietly. 'You have suffered and I was not here to help you, but you must blame yourself no longer. All is well again and I am home.'

'No, you do not understand. I lost our baby. I miscarried.' The misery of her loss washed over her with undiminished pain and her eyes were bleak as she looked into his. 'I am sorry, James.'

After the first shock, James's face lit up with sudden joy. 'Then it is as I thought, and as Friida said. It is *God's will*.'

'What can you mean?' Rachel brushed the tears from her eyes and tucked back a stray strand of hair. She had expected a sorrow from him to match her own, not this secret excitement.

'Never mind, never mind. You will see very soon. First, hold out your hands and close your eyes.' He placed the silver filigree-decorated box on her outspread palm. 'Now open them.'

'James, it is *beautiful*,' she breathed and when she lifted the lid and took out the ring, which slipped so easily on to her finger it could have been measured for her, she could only reach up and kiss him. 'Thank you. And thank you for coming home safe and soon.'

'How could I stay away,' he murmured, his lips against her hair, 'with such a loving welcome awaiting me at home? Besides . . .' He held her at arm's length and looked deep into her eyes, his own alive now with pleasure and excitement. 'The ring and the box were not the real present. I have something far more wonderful. I confess I had a moment's doubt, but now I know it is

God's true will. Come.' He took her hand and led her out of the cabin, through the saloon with its polished table and guardrails, its mahogany sideboard and tiny grate, past the galley, and on to the crew's quarters and a fresh-faced, cheerful apprentice lad who shot to attention at the sight of James and repeated, 'Broze at mid-day sir, bedded down, and all's well.'

'See,' murmured James, bending over the humped blankets of the boy's bunk. He peeled back a corner to reveal a thin, sallow face in a grubby bonnet, tied awry over a tangle of colourless hair, one minute hand clutching the edge of what had once been a beautiful crocheted blanket, the other clenched round a little carved bear.

'This is Toomas,' said James proudly. 'Isn't he a fine wee lad?'

Rachel was speechless as shock obliterated all thought and feeling.

'When you told me you had miscarried, I saw at once the workings of God's ways. We have lost one child and found another.' He bent over the bunk and carefully lifted the sleeping boy. Then, turning to her, he held out the bundle with a face of pride and love. 'This is Toomas. Take him, Rachel, and love him as I do. He is a heaven-sent brother for Jamie and our new, wee precious son.'

But Rachel, reaching out obedient arms for the alien child, felt a wave of revulsion so strong it almost overwhelmed her.

'I knew it would be a shock to you,' said James happily, his arm around her shoulder, 'and will not Jamie be surprised?'

Jamie welcomed his new brother with instant, unquestioning affection and Pearl bustled busily between the two of them, happily ordering them about and mothering them in her generous-hearted way. Kirsty Guyan, after the first

243

raised eyebrow, accepted him too. 'The poor wee mite, orphaned in a foreign country, wi' only his dottled old grandparents to care for him. 'Tis nae wonder he's an under-grown wee runt, but he'll soon fill out wi' good food and sea air.' The fact that Latvia was not a foreign country to the child himself, but his own home, did not occur to her and would have made no difference if it had. And her evidence that the grandparents were 'dottled' was based solely and erroneously on the fact that the infant's crocheted garments were of a strange and decidedly grubby nature. 'Best thrown on the fire,' was Kirsty's first comment and Rachel, handling the unfamiliar garments with distaste, agreed with her. James, however, thought differently.

'His Ma made them herself and I wouldna' want them burnt. They'll be fine when ye've given them a good scrub and an airing. We did our best on board, but ye canna' expect a shipload of seamen to care for a baby as a woman would. I fed him carefully though, Rachel,' he went on, seeking approval in her face which was strangely expressionless and closed. 'I did all I've seen you do wi' our Jamie. I spoon-fed him myself, poor wee fellow, and gave him a fine mutton bone to chew on, for his teeth, though he prefers yon carved dancing bear his Grandda made for him.'

As always when he spoke of Friida and Priit his face saddened. 'They will miss the wee mite, and that's a fact, but they'll be right glad to hear he's safely settled with a new family of his own, poor orphaned laddie.' James was to sail again to Riga within the month. 'It is a pity there is no time to have his portrait done, with Jamie, before I sail. Yon Edinburgh mannie does a fine job, I'm told. Abercrombie had his wife's likeness done only last month and is fine pleased with it. But enough o' this blether. Let

244

the womenfolk see to the bairns, Maitland, and tell me what's been happening while I've been away.'

'Well,' said Maitland slowly, gathering his thoughts, though his eyes followed Rachel with puzzled concern. It was a common practice among fisherfolk for a man to take in a neighbour's orphaned child – Rachel herself had been so adopted – and the Christies needed sons. You would have thought she would be glad.

'Well?' prompted James. 'Are ye so taken wi' Toomas that ye've lost your tongue?'

'I fear he has lost his,' said Maitland, grinning, 'and will learn a queer kind o' talk from Pearl and Jamie.'

'And they, no doubt, from him. He's a fine wee bletherer in his own language. Which is more than I can say for you, man.'

'I am sorry, James. Let me see . . . The King's crowned, the Queen's dead and buried, the captain of the *Jane* and the steersman too were murdered and thrown overboard off Gibraltar, and the crew made away wi' the cargo of gold to Lewis.'

'But they lost their way and sailed right into the Custom mannie's hands,' put in Kirsty from the fireside where she was soaping the new arrival vigorously in a wooden tub. 'More fools them. They'll be hangit for murder. It'll nae be in Aberdeen though, more's the pity. I like a good hanging.'

'Kirsty!' cried Rachel in horror, but Kirsty only laughed. 'Where's the harm? They dinna' hang good folk, do they? Only the villains, and the University gets the bodies for yon Anatomy classes Pearl's Da attends, so ye ought to be pleased.'

'How is Andrew?' asked James. 'We must have him look at wee Toomas and maybe vaccinate him against the smallpox. We dinna' want him catching anything, do we, little fellow?' and he took the newly washed child from

Kirsty and perched him on his knee. 'This is your new family, Toomas,' he said solemnly, 'Here's your Ma, and your Uncle Maitland, and your wee Cousin Pearl. Your Uncles Willy and George are away, and your Uncle Alex, but they'll nae be long and when they come home, they'll play some rare games with you, Toomas, and ye'll hear fine tales . . .'

Rachel, watching from the shadows, struggled against the outrage which threatened to choke her. That child was not *her* child. What right had James to thrust him upon her unasked, when all she wanted was to mourn her own lost baby and to cling to Jamie? What right had James to share his love with a stranger when she and Jamie saw him so little and needed him so much?

If the child *was* a stranger. Her mind blurred and blackened momentarily with the memory of Jess's insinuation that James had fathered other children and conveniently 'forgotten' them, and what did she know of Riga but what James had told her? What did she know of the child? The splinter which Jess had planted long ago in her mind pricked and burned as she prepared bread and milk for the children, drew ale for the men. The child is a stranger, she said over and over inside her head. He has no place here.

She heard James's voice explaining to Maitland and the others. 'The husband was killed in the rioting, some territorial dispute which I could not understand, and the mother died in childbed soon after. Friida and Priit took the child in. There was no one else. But they are old and frail and poor. You are our son, they said. We have waited for you to come to us. You have a wife and a home. Take him and care for him as your own kith and kin. So what else could I do?' he appealed to the company. 'I owe them my life.'

'You did right,' said Maitland quietly. Kirsty whisked

Toomas from James's knee and took him into a corner to feed him from a little wooden bowl while Pearl hovered anxiously, ready to help at the slightest opportunity, and Jamie, exhausted by the day's excitements, slept. Neighbours came and left again. Others stayed, to join the group – crewmen and friends. It was a warm, convivial, happy evening, fitting for a sailor's homecoming. Only Rachel stood apart. She thought no one noticed as the talk moved on to tales of Customs men and smugglers, tubs of Geneva found in the sand at Belhelvie, hundreds more found in a Dutch lugger in Aberdeen harbour itself.

'Put in for caulking, but wi' ankers o' Geneva and tubs o' tobacco worth a fortune.'

'And hidden all over the ship in places ye never thought possible.'

'The *Brilliant* steams regularly now to Inverness, *and* wi' cargo space.'

'A coach to meet the steam-yacht at the new pier.'

'A coppered brig.'

'Montego Bay.'

Rachel hardly listened as the talk flowed around her, talk as always of ships and destinations, of cargoes, ship's design, ambition. When appealed to she made appropriate comment, filled glasses, fetched cheese and salt beef, drank . . .

But at last the company dispersed to their homes and their various beds and the children slept. Then James took his wife to bed and closed the panelled doors.

'I saw your face, Rachel,' he said quietly. 'I know what you think, but it is not true. I swear to you, as God is my witness, that Toomas is Anya's and her Toomas's son, and no son of mine – until Friida gave him into my care and I promised to be a father to him. Did you think me capable of so little faith?'

'I am sorry, James. It was the shock. I did not mean

. . .' But she would rather he thought that, than knew the truth.

'Why, when I saw him first, the little rascal took one look at me and bellowed! It was his cry that first split my memory, Rachel, and brought me back to you. So you see we have a lot to thank him for and he is an appealing wee chap, as you will find for yourself. You do believe me?' he finished as she made no answer.

'Oh yes.' But the belief gave her no comfort.

'Then there is no more need to be sad,' he murmured, drawing her close and kissing her eyelids. 'I am home, Rachel. Our children are safe and sleeping – and it is a long time till morning.'

Who first called him Riga Tom was never known, but within a week it was his name throughout the fishing community and he was accepted as one of them. The sea was a greedy master and they were used to orphans.

William and George were delighted with their new nephew, declared happily, 'One more for the Christie fleet,' and immediately set about teaching him 'proper talk' instead of 'yon foreign blether'. They made him toys out of wood-ends and cork and, when Rachel was safely at the office in Pocra, with Jamie and Tom together set up a race track on the trestle table and gave Pacer and Racer a cockroach steeplechase or placed bets on a ten-penny Stakes. They taught the lads sea-shanties and, when Rachel protested at the words of some of them, redressed the balance with 'God save the King'. When summer came again, they vowed to teach the pair of them to swim, 'So ye can both fall in and out o' the sea as much as ye like without upsetting Rachel.'

Rachel, however, remained strangely remote with an unnatural composure which baffled Maitland, the only member of the family who noticed. For James sailed again to the Baltic on what was to be a regular run, the twins continued to operate the *Steadfast* on the London route and Alex was not yet home from the Greenland fisheries, though as the weeks passed and the whalers drifted home both Kirsty and Rachel looked increasingly anxious and dark about the eyes.

In mid-September a whaler, the *Don*, sailed into the bay with a bumper catch of twenty-one fish and reported she had passed the *Bon Accord* with a similar, but beset in the ice. Two weeks of anxious waiting passed before the *Bon Accord* herself arrived, the last whaler of Aberdeen to come home, but with a catch to beat her own best record.

'Twenty-six fish, Rachy!' cried Alex, bursting through the door of the cottage with a yell of exuberant triumph and swinging her up in his arms. Then he saw Kirsty, feeding an unknown child, and his face was a picture of shock, incredulity and outrage.

'Dinna' tell me, Kirsty, that ye've been and had a child behind my back! I've been away seven months I know, but . . .'

'And why not?' countered Kirsty with a toss of her pert head. 'I can have a child if I've a mind to, without asking *your* permission. But it isna' mine,' she relented, 'ye great *gowk*. How could it be, and Tom nigh on two years old? He's Jamie's new wee brother, all the way from Riga. Say hello to your uncle, Tom.'

'Well I reckon I've more to celebrate than my fish,' beamed Alex, 'It isna' every day I come home and find a new wee nephew. When's the next to be, Rachel?'

But Rachel turned quickly away to clear the papers she had been working on from the table – estimates for the final fittings for the new schooner which they planned to launch as soon as James returned – and busied herself at the fire. She longed for a child of her own whenever she looked at Tom, but so far she had not conceived again.

'I came to see the wonder child,' announced Jessica Abercrombie, presenting herself on the Christie doorstep the next day. She knew it would be open house at the Christies: Wee Alex would have tales to tell the stay-at-homes which would while away the winter evenings for weeks to come. Tales and taller tales to feed the whole Square's curiosity. But it was a different curiosity which had brought Jessica.

'I'm expecting again,' she announced complacently, seating herself in the best chair, 'so I'll sit here if ye dinna' mind. Ye'd best hurry and make another yersel', Rachel, before your man fills the house wi' *orphans*. But he's nae a bad wee tike, for a Russky. I thought he'd be hairier, wi' tiny eyes, square shoulders and no neck.'

'Ye're thinking of a Russian bear,' said Kirsty scornfully. 'Some folk canna help their ignorance,' she added in a murmur pitched just loud enough for Jessica to hear. For once Jessica ignored the taunt. She had decided to be gracious to the Christies, in the interests of business, and gracious she would be, if it choked her.

For what Jess had begun in a spirit of self-seeking had unexpectedly become a pleasure. She found she enjoyed working in the Abercrombie 'emporium', enjoyed the power it gave her to offer or withhold, the bargaining, the social contact, the gossip. But it was a remark of Mrs Abercrombie's which had prompted Jess's present visit, and the knowledge that James Christie was safely at sea.

'A fine wee boy by all accounts,' Mrs Abercrombie had said, 'though it isna' everyone as would take a strange child into the family. Ye canna' tell what might be bred into them. Mind and remember, Jessie, that even if your next's a daughter, ye're to try again and dinna' scour the

250

streets for a spare laddie.' Kirsty Abercrombie, after weeks of Jess's efforts, had consented to unbend enough to gossip to her daughter-in-law once in a while, usually when no other audience offered and she had a particularly succulent gobbet of news to share. 'Mind you,' she had finished, 'in the circumstances James Christie had no choice but to take the lad and they say he treats him no different from his own son.'

'*In the circumstances.*' What had the old girl meant? Her curiosity intolerably tickled, Jess had armed herself in her best pelisse, chosen her moment, swallowed her pride and called at Rachel's door. But the lad they called Riga Tom was disappointing – small, sallow-faced, with colourless hair and queer, yellowish eyes. 'The colour o' pale treacle,' she said, studying Tom.

'Amber,' retorted Kirsty Guyan, but then the girl would hear no criticism of a Christie, old or young.

'I wouldna' know about amber,' said Jess airily. 'I wear diamonds myself. How old is he, Rachel?'

'I am not sure,' said Rachel carefully. 'A month or two younger than Jamie, perhaps.' She could see, as through a window, the calculations in Jess's mind. 'Or older. He has more teeth than Jamie,' she fabricated, knowing that Kirsty would back her in all she said, 'and is always dry at night.' Before her unwelcome guest could make further comment, Rachel turned her back. James had put Jess out on the occasion of her last visit and had the circumstances been different, Rachel would have done the same now. As it was, she sought refuge with the menfolk, filling their glasses and plying them with oatcakes and cheese, while they talked of whaling and the dangers of the arctic seas. Two boys from Alex's ship had been drowned and many vessels were reported lost, though most of the crews, by some means or other, had been saved.

'The ice was the thickest ever seen,' recounted Alex, in

full flow now and enjoying his audience. 'Great white mountains of it, towering on every side of us, wi' huge slabs crushing and crunching and blocking our passage till we were ploughing through a sea like a field o' broken granite, wi' the wind howling and the air so cold on a man's face that his beard and eyebrows froze.'

Jamie's face, Rachel noticed, was rapt, his mouth open, as he stood at his uncle's knee, Alex's arm carelessly around his little shoulders. After a while the little Riga boy plucked up courage to ease nearer till he stood at Alex's other side, his face as absorbed as Jamie's, his strange eyes puzzling to understand the words. With hardly a pause in the narrative, Alex scooped him up and sat him astride his knee with an 'Up ye come, Tom lad, afore ye get trampled underfoot. Now I was telling ye about one ship that was beset by ice. Giant blades of it slicing from all sides and the ship helpless, till the ice bit through the hull, carried away the mainmast and split the ship in two – like the two halves of a walnut shell.'

'Were you frightened, Uncle Alex?' asked Pearl, her eyes huge and anxious.

'Na, na,' boasted Alex. ''Tis only ice after all, and the sea's the same, wherever ye be. Besides, we had our fish, didn't we? Twenty-six of them.'

'I can see we're to have nothing but boasting from yon stirk if we sit here all night,' announced Jessica, rising majestically to her feet. 'He's discovered Greenland and thinks he invented it. I havena' heard such a clattering since the King's Coronation, and my ears canna' stand the strain.' She sauntered to the door and opened it. 'I canna' be all day blethering. I have my business and my family to attend to. I think it was right generous of you and James to take in yon Russky loon,' she added in a conspiratorial whisper. '*In the circumstances.*' She stepped out into the darkening Square leaving a cold draught behind her.

Among the whalers lost in the ice that season were two in which the Farquharsons had a major share. Their losses were considerable. Further loss occurred when one of their emigrant ships was driven ashore in a gale off the west coast of Scotland and wrecked. The captain of the *Flora* was found to be selling short measure on a cargo of wheat and heavily fined, and one of their older coastal vessels, carrying an ill-loaded cargo of lime, caught fire and burnt to the water line. It was a run of bad luck which, opinion said, the Farquharsons had brought upon themselves by their cheese-paring attitude to maintenance and their greed for profit, but it was one which they could ill afford, especially as Mrs Farquharson still insisted on pouring money into her steam-ship project, so far with little to show for it.

'Something must be done,' she announced, sailing uninvited into the shipping office one morning in early October. Through the office window the Quay was clearly visible, with its bristle of masts and its bustle of deckhands and shore porters. A crane was unloading a series of tea chests from the nearest vessel and outside the Weighhouse was a pile of bales waiting to be collected. Shore porters trundled barrels and packing cases to and fro on wooden barrows and a clean wind whisked and swirled around the harbour basin, snatching up and tossing straw ends and assorted debris into the air. A handful of herring gulls molested a fishing boat, newly arrived with a full catch, and the sky was busy with cotton wool clouds.

But the air of brisk prosperity only increased Mrs Farquharson's annoyance. 'We must call in our monies.'

'But Mamma,' pointed out Robert. 'We have no monies owing to us. On the contrary we . . .'

'Nonsense,' she interrupted with a grand gesture of her heavily-ringed hand. 'In your father's day people always owed us money. I remember him complaining about it. The Council in particular were most dilatory.'

'The Council bonds, Mamma, were redeemed long ago. For that property in Ferryhill.'

'Then sell it, Robert. Do I need to tell you *everything*?' she finished in exasperation. Atholl had been particularly trying that morning, mouthing and gurgling in a nonsensical manner which had driven her beyond all patience.

'We *have* sold it, Mamma,' sighed Robert, whose own patience was wearing thin. It was hard enough running the business as it was without his mother continually interfering, countermanding his orders and putting her totally unskilled oar in whenever she felt like it. 'In May.'

'Robert, you are being *tiresomely* unhelpful. I cannot believe we have *no* resources to draw upon. You forget the fine for that ridiculous affair at the Weighhouse will have to be paid and I promised Mr Macready another £50 towards development costs.' Mr Macready was the engineer employed in designing her steam-yacht.

'Really Mamma!' It was Robert's turn to be outraged. 'Must you pour good money after bad? Need you send to Glasgow for your precious steam-yacht design when you could just as easily have it built here, at Hall's or the Duthie yard? I expect the Christies will be moving into steam before long, too, and they would give you a far better bargain.'

'The *Christies*? You know how your father felt about . . .' But at that moment there was a nervous knocking at the door, and the clerk's head appeared in the crack. 'This letter just arrived Mr Farquharson sir. Mr Christie said to hand it to you in person. Mr Maitland Christie.'

'A good ship's designer, by all accounts,' said Robert, breaking the seal. 'You could do a lot worse than . . .' his

254

eyes scanned the short paragraph. 'Again? It's barely six months since the last launch. Those Christies are producing ships faster than ever, it seems.'

'What is it?' Without waiting for an answer, Mrs Farquharson snatched the letter from her son's hands and perused it. '". . . intention to cross Dixon's land for the purposes of launching . . . Permission graciously granted . . ." *Did* you grant permission, Robert?'

'No, Mamma, but I believe . . .'

'Then the answer is "No". How dare they run all over our property without so much as a by-your-leave? Churning up the ground. Reducing the market value. Which reminds me, I told you months ago to sell that land, or build on it. What have you done about it?'

'Nothing, Mamma, I . . .'

'Then I shall see Mr Forbes about it immediately. I *knew* we had some sort of redeemable asset,' she said triumphantly. 'You will send a reply at once to that impertinent note, refusing absolutely to allow access.'

'Well?' said Maitland, looking round the assembled company. 'What do we do?' The Farquharson reply had come as a shock and, in James's absence, Maitland had hastily summoned all available Christies to the cottage in North Square, to confer. Now they sat round the trestle table in what had become the traditional manner, with cheese and fresh bread on wooden platters, and a large earthenware jug of ale. But their faces were as worried as Maitland's. For if access was denied them to Dixon's patch, there was no other way they could possibly move their ship to the water – unless they dismantled it again and moved it piece by piece.

'Obviously Robert Farquharson is unaware of the circumstances,' said Rachel with an anxious face, pouring Maitland more ale. 'I am sure when he realizes . . .'

'He must be *made* to realize,' interrupted Alex, and the twins said, 'We'll sort him out for ye, Rachel, like we sorted his Da.'

'No,' said Rachel firmly. 'This time we have documents to fight our battles for us.'

'And if they fail?' demanded Alex, impatient for action.

'We will decide that when the time comes. Meanwhile I think we should visit Robert Farquharson in his office and show him the paper his father signed.'

'We ought to wait for James,' said Maitland doubtfully, remembering their last encounter with Robert Farquharson on the day of Atholl's stroke and James's threats. 'He would want to be there, I know, and he is due home daily.'

'Write a letter,' suggested Alex. 'Tell Farquharson we have a legal right to cross his land and intend to go ahead. See what he says. That'll give James time to get home. Then, if there is still trouble, we'll *all* go round.'

Robert Farquharson was worried. He had a niggling suspicion that there was more to this launching business of the Christies than appeared on the surface. His father had hated them, he knew for a fact, but there had certainly been occasions when he had allowed them to cross his land in spite of that. Also, he had an uncomfortable memory of the Christie men's last visit to his office and the threats James Christie had made. He remembered the man's face, with that ragged scar across the forehead, and those weird, mismatched eyes, and a small worm of fear ate into his confidence. Suppose his mother was wrong and the Christies were entitled to access? But he had scoured the office files and found no trace of any agreement. Perhaps, after all, the Christie letter was no more than empty bluster?

'Legal right?' he puzzled. 'What legal right?' Their lawyer Forbes knew nothing of it certainly, or he would have said when Mrs Farquharson told him of her intention regarding the land in question.

'I do not understand,' he complained to Fenton Abercrombie when they met at the house of Abercrombie senior, at an evening party which Kirsty Abercrombie, with her daughter-in-law's encouragement, had arranged in order to 'make the right connections' for the season. Abercrombie himself, after the initial outburst, had shrugged, turned his back with an, 'As long as ye dinna' expect me to dance attendance on all your grand lady-folk,' and left her to it, his only stipulation being that his particular friends among the neighbouring tradesmen also be invited. It was an odd mixture but, after an hour of Abercrombie's generous hospitality the edges had blurred and the party was, as Kirsty said, in a pleased aside, 'Going very well.' Only Robert Farquharson seemed out of sorts, but then it was common knowledge the Farquharsons had business worries.

'Father made no mention of a legal right,' he said now, 'and there is no trace of any agreement in the files.' He drank deep of the brandy in his glass and continued, more bravely, 'I think I shall ignore the reference, forbid them to trespass, and point out that the land is to be sold for development.'

'I wouldna' do that if I were you,' said Jessica lazily, coming up behind them in the corner of the drawing room, to which they had retreated for privacy. Splendid in turquoise silks, her dark curls heaped high and topped with a curling ostrich plume, her bosom sparkling with diamonds, she was enjoying her reinstatement as favoured daughter-in-law. But as well as enjoyable, Mrs Abercrombie's party was numerous, noisy and inquisitive, with eager ears strained everywhere to catch the slightest snatch of gossip.

'Why not?' asked Fenton and Robert together.

257

'It's in the agreement, that's why not.'

'What agreement?' demanded Robert, his normally sallow face flushing with annoyance. All this talk of things he knew nothing about was draining his confidence.

'Why the one your Da has with the Christies of course. "From this day forward and for all time."'

'How do you know?' asked Fenton and the quietness of his voice should have warned her, but Jess was too set on impressing Robert with her superior knowledge to notice. Illiteracy had given her an excellent memory and now, exhilarated by several glasses of her father-in-law's best Rhine wine she rushed on, '". . . at any time of day or night for the purpose of launching any ship, of . . . any . . . kind . . ."' She faltered to a stop as she saw the expression on her husband's face and finished belligerently, 'Ask Atholl yourself if ye dinna' believe me.' With that she turned her back and flounced across the room to the safety of the ladies, leaving Robert and Fenton staring thoughtfully after her.

'Whatever can she mean?' said Robert at last. Fenton did not answer. Somewhere at the back of his mind memory stirred: a misty November evening, his wife's unexplained absence and late arrival home, some tale of the Christie yard . . . What did she know about the business, and how?

'I cannot ask Father, of course,' Robert was saying. 'At least, I could, but I doubt I would make much of any answer. No. I shall reply as I had intended,' he decided, draining his brandy glass and looking round hopefully for more. 'It will be up to them to prove it, if they have a right. Which I doubt,' he finished happily, seeing his father-in-law approaching with the decanter. 'Yes sir, I *will* have a refill. Most excellent cognac. Splendid bouquet.'

* * *

The following day the *Bonnie Annie* sailed into port. A mere hour after she docked, Robert Farquharson's clerk opened his office door to announce the arrival of James Christie 'on urgent business'. The clerk omitted to say that Maitland and Alex were also with him and the sight of the phalanx of Christie men bearing down on him drained the blood from Robert's face.

'Yes, gentlemen?' he managed, through dry lips, wishing he had not gone to bed quite so late nor drunk quite so liberally of Abercrombie's brandy. 'What is your business?'

'This,' said James, throwing Farquharson's latest letter down like a gauntlet on the desk. The man's face was more fearsome even than Robert remembered it, black as it was now with anger. 'And before you make any answer, Mr Farquharson, I would remind you of my last visit to this office and of the promise I made you then, should you be so foolhardy as to interfere with me and mine.'

'It is hardly interfering to develop my own land,' stuttered Robert, 'and to wish to do so without "interference" as you put it, from others.'

James glanced at Maitland and nodded. Maitland reached inside his coat, withdrew a folded paper, unfolded it and held it out to Robert Farquharson. 'I would advise you to read this, Mr Farquharson,' he said mildly, 'before you say anything further.'

Robert took the proffered paper gingerly and studied it, at first with suspicion, then with close attention. It seemed to be an agreement between his father and these Christie men, signed by his father and witnessed by, of all people, *Jessica Abercrombie*, and, as they claimed, giving them perpetual access to Dixon's land. He was reading it through for the second time, trying to gather his thoughts into some sort of order when the door burst open and his mother erupted into the room, breathing fire and fury.

'Kindly instruct your clerk, Robert,' she stormed, 'to allow me access at all times to your office, whether or not you are "in conference".' She paused to gather breath, took up her lorgnette and studied the Christie men with frowning annoyance. 'As for you,' she said, 'No doubt you have come about your launch. Before you start whining and pleading, I tell you here and now that you trespass on my land *at your peril*.'

'Mamma,' said Robert unhappily, 'they seem to have some sort of an agreement.' He held out the paper Maitland had given him. She snatched it from his hand, brought the twin barrels of her lorgnette to bear upon it and read it in a silence punctuated by 'humphs' and snorts of derision. When she had finished, she looked at the three men in turn, said clearly, 'So much for your agreement,' and tore it systematically into little pieces which she tossed into the grate behind her. Then, dusting her hands together with satisfaction, she said, '*I* made no agreement with you. *My son* made no agreement with you. If my husband did, we have only your word for it. *We* know nothing of it and he can no longer tell us. If you continue to say he did, we will deny it, and you have no proof. The matter, therefore, is *closed*. Good day.'

'Madam,' said James Christie with dangerous quietness, 'surely you did not think us simple enough to risk the original document here? That which you so foolishly destroyed was merely a copy. The original is already lodged with my solicitors who have been instructed to put it to good use, as and when it might prove necessary.' As mother and son stared, momentarily taken aback by this new turn of events, James continued, 'You will have noticed the opening sentence of the document, confessing responsibility for the firing of our ship four years ago, following which my brother Davy died? I had assumed you would prefer to keep that matter private between us.

260

However, if you persist in disregarding what I am sure is a legally binding agreement, we will have no choice but to . . .'

'Blackmail!' cried Mrs Farquharson in fury. 'Barefaced blackmail. You should be horse-whipped, the lot of you. You will be my witness, Robert, that this, this . . . *fellow* has uttered menaces. As for you,' she turned on James himself with a contemptuous sneer, 'you will hear from my solicitor.' With that she swept from the room, pausing in the doorway only to say, 'I will send up your men, Robert, to see these *fellows* out.'

But when the men in question scrambled hastily up the stairs, as they thought to rescue their threatened master, they found Robert Farquharson seated safely enough at his desk, his visitors also seated and apparently in quiet conversation. 'We would of course purchase the land at valuation,' the eldest Christie was saying and their master, instead of crying for help, merely waved them impatiently away.

'The land is sold and you have your money, Mamma,' explained Robert, skimming over the unpleasantness and the straightforward threat of the Christie proposition. 'They are pleased and so am I. We need have no more truck with them. It was the simplest solution, Mamma.'

'It was the simplest solution, dear,' repeated Euphemia Farquharson to her bedridden husband. She had, as she had threatened, consulted her solicitors, but Mr Forbes's reply had not been encouraging and, as Robert said, they did have the money. 'And the land never was any use to us. I cannot imagine why you bought it in the first place.'

No one knew what thoughts went through Atholl Farquharson's head as his wife talked on, but from that day forward he went into a steady decline, and three weeks later he died.

The Christies, on the other hand, prospered. 'God has blessed our enterprise,' said James with awe, when the documents transferring Dixon's patch to the Christies were safely signed, sealed and delivered into his hand. He went home directly to tell Rachel. Little Toomas came running to meet him as he approached across the Square and James tossed him up into the air and caught him again with a laugh of triumph. 'You have brought us good luck, little lad.' Taking Jamie by one hand, Tom by the other, he looked over his shoulder to where Rachel stood quietly in the doorway and said, 'Come, lass. Let us inspect our new property.'

December 1821

A bitter December wind knifed down Broadgait, buffeted
the Castlegate and rattled the windows of the Reading
room in the Athenaeum as Louise Forbes folded her
reading glasses, replaced them in her reticule and prepared to leave the warmth of the fire for the cold walk
home. There had been violent storms all around the coast
and the shipping had suffered badly. (The Farquharsons
had lost two ships and a third was missing.) Louise would
like to have stayed on to read more of the journals and
illustrated papers provided for the reading public, on
annual subscription, but she knew her mother would be
impatiently waiting in her warm-panelled upstairs
drawing-room, with a bright fire and a simmering kettle
and all the paraphernalia of the tea-making ceremony laid
out ready on a polished mahogany tray.

Nevertheless, she stayed an extra five minutes to read a
particular item which caught her eye. On Friday last, on
the Old Town Links, a group of Preservation officers had
come upon three young men, with a look of medical
students about them, and carrying a dead body. In their
haste to escape capture, they had abandoned their spoils
and the corpse had since been claimed to be that of a
young man gone missing in the Spital that very night – a
claim not yet substantiated and, thought Louise, probably
untrue.

Mentally, she went through the neighbouring grave-
yards – St Machar's, Belhelvie, Potterton, Newhills. It

was barely two weeks since George Thom had been hanged and his body given legitimately for dissection. But if students are to wait only for hanged men, thought Louise wryly, scholarship must look for a long and slow advance to knowledge. She hoped the lads escaped detection. But she had delayed too long. In consequence she stepped out into the Castlegate at the exact moment that Dr Andrew Noble stepped in and they collided violently on the step.

'My dear Louise,' cried Andrew, clasping her against him in an inadvertent embrace. 'I almost sent you tumbling to the ground. I am abjectly sorry.'

'Please do not apologize,' said Louise though her cheeks were unaccountably pink and it took her a full ten seconds to regain composure. 'It was entirely my fault. I was, as usual, thinking of other things. But you must excuse me, Mamma will be . . .'

'No, Louise.' Andrew detained her with a hand on her arm. 'Do not run away, please. Come inside out of the wind for a moment and talk. We have not met for far too long. Besides, I believe it is offering to snow and you had far better wait till the flurry is past.'

'Perhaps you are right,' agreed Louise with a smile. 'Mamma can wait another quarter-hour without undue harm.'

Andrew held open the door for her to re-enter the building and followed after, limping slightly as he did so. 'Oh, Andrew, I have hurt you! I am so sorry.'

'No, no, it was not you. A slight fall a few days ago, that is all. A strained ligament, nothing worse. Shall we sit here?' He indicated a pair of chairs near the generous fire and they sat down. Other chairs were placed strategically about the room, high-backed, leather chairs designed for privacy and the encouragement of serious reading. The dark red patterned Turkey carpet deadened

264

sound and encouraged the 'Silence' enjoined by an ornately executed sign above the mantel. Two long windows gave a view of the Castlegate, obscured now by falling snow and the gloom of a mid-December afternoon. Lamps had been lit on either side of the fireplace and in sconces between the windows and the general effect was of a warmly civilized haven in a chilly world. Louise drew off her gloves and laid them aside.

After a moment's awkwardness, she asked in a suitably low voice, 'How are your anatomy lectures progressing?'

'Slowly,' sighed Andrew. 'How I wish we had an anatomy theatre here, in the city, instead of having to make do with what poor rooms we can find. I vow we will have it one day, when enough enlightened people band together to fund and build one. A fine, airy hall with tables, spaced on either side, for students to carry out dissections of their own. I can see it now, Louise. High windows like these, for light, though not on to the streets for decency's sake, and perhaps an overhead cupola for more light, so every student can see clearly the demonstrations of the surgeon. There will be cleanliness and air and every antiseptic precaution to avoid unpleasantness – and such an advance of medical science as men have not dreamed of.'

'It sounds an unattainable ideal, Andrew. You know the general attitude here to you and your students. You had best look to London for such forward-thinking luxuries.'

'I have looked,' said Andrew with an edge of envy to his voice. 'And I have found a course of lectures to be given by Joshua Brookes, FRS, with dissections. If I had ten guineas and the cost of a passage I could attend. My job and my obligations to the University could be arranged for and I would return with knowledge I would gladly share, but Isla will not hear of it. You know how

265

she feels about my work at the best of times.' He sighed with a rueful smile. 'I dare not mention anatomy or dissection for fear she might faint. I talk of limbs and she immediately imagines they are separated from their trunk. As for "stomach" . . . No, it is best that I say nothing of my work at home. Or any aspect of it. But it is a strain sometimes.'

Louise listened with sympathy and understanding as he went on to talk in a low but eager voice about the lectures he planned and his research. As she listened, surreptitiously studying his ankles, outstretched now to the fire, his left hand which rested on the chair arm and whose knuckles bore the scabs of old abrasions, and his earnest, mobile face, a mischievous idea took root in her mind and, as he talked on, grew to certainty.

'Andrew,' she interrupted in a teasing whisper, 'where were you last Friday night?'

He stopped in mid-sentence, stared at her, then, as the twinkle grew in her eyes, his mouth twitched at the corners and suddenly both were snorting and gurgling in a gale of suppressed laughter.

'Sh!' came a warning voice from across the room and, still smiling, Andrew bundled Louise to the door.

'I do not need to ask you to keep my secret, Louise,' he said, his hand on her arm. 'I know I can trust your discretion.'

'Completely.' She drew on her gloves, adjusted her pelisse and stood a moment on the step, reluctant to leave. The Castlegate was almost deserted, peopled only by a handful of hurrying grey figures, heads bowed to the wind. Underfoot, the Plainstanes glimmered in the light shed by the open doorway. The snow had eased, but what had already fallen was snatched up and tossed by the icy wind in mournful flurries at empty street corners. The oil lamp by the Mercat cross glowed ineffectually weak in the gathering darkness and the lights in the Broadgait shops were being dowsed, one by one. Her mother would be growing petulant. 'Goodbye, Andrew, and promise me you will take care?'

'Of course.' She had moved only a few steps away when he called her name. She turned eagerly back to see him still standing in the open doorway, watching her with a puzzled expression. He had forgotten how animation lit up her face, and surely that violet-coloured thing she was wearing was new?

'Yes, Andrew? What is it?'

'Nothing. Merely that I have enjoyed our talk. I hope we meet again.'

'And I.' She turned away into the twilight to battle her solitary way home.

1822

At Auld Yell James Christie brought two mysterious packages home late at night and hid them in the rafters. The little boys unwrapped them in rapturous excitement the following morning to find two identical hobby horses, shining with varnish and new paint. There was feasting and laughter and a great to-ing and fro-ing of neighbours and friends. Andrew brought Isla and his small family to visit: the Abercrombies called, and Louise Forbes, with presents for everyone. A silver scent box for Rachel, a bead purse for Pearl, tortoiseshell combs for Kirsty and a host of puzzles and coloured books for the children. There was tobacco for the menfolk, with brandy and a huge box of sugar plums.

'Louise, you shouldn't!' cried Rachel, hugging her friend with open affection. 'But I am glad you did. And I have a present for you. James brought it specially from St Petersburg.' She held out a small packet which contained a silver buckle, beautifully ornamented with scrollwork and leaves. 'It will set off the waist of your new skirt to perfection.'

They laughed and sang and drank, played games with the children and danced and Rachel was almost happy. Later into the night, when it was close to morning, Louise, talking quietly in a corner with Andrew about something quite unrelated, said suddenly, 'I am worried about Rachel. It seems to me that since the summer she has lost her tranquillity. With the new yard established and her little family she should be happy but . . . I wish you would find the time to talk to her.'

Lazily, Andrew followed her gaze to where Rachel was cutting slices of fresh bread for the children who crowded round her, jostling and pushing and determined not to flag till the night was over. He watched her butter a slab for James and another for Tom, cut cheese for Pearl. Take up a damp cloth and wipe first James's face, where he had dribbled butter, then Tom's. Pour milk for them. Smile. He noted the same slim figure, the same quiet self-possession, the same dignity and he remembered Rachel's longing, years ago when they were children, for a home of her own, with no cold corners and a family to fill it. She had all that now *and* a flourishing shipyard. Yet perhaps Louise was right? There was a tenseness about Rachel which had not been there before. A strain about the eyes, though surely anyone would feel a strain in a small room full of people, all demanding attention?

The partition had been looped back to give as much space as possible, but even so the room was packed, the air stifling, the noise deafening and the heat enough to melt the clothes from a man's back. In one corner of the room the twins led a boisterous group in a singing contest which seemed to consist of no more than two lines of any song and a great deal of laughter. The words, suspected Andrew, would be unrepeatable in polite company. A gaggle of womenfolk chattered at one end of the table, Maitland drew solemn plans of ships' elevations with knives and spoons at the other while the more sober menfolk of the party gave advice, and at the end of the room, furthest from the fire, James was laughing with his children, their bread already eaten or forgotten, in some noisy game which seemed to consist of squeals and tickles and little else. As Andrew watched, James snatched up the two boys, one under each arm, and growled while

Pearl danced round him, beating futile fists against his legs and squealing, 'Put them down, Uncle James.' Contented, Andrew relaxed.

'Rachel is happy enough, Louise. This is what she always wanted – a family of her own in her own wee house, and a man to love her. If she has any troubles, it will be only the wish for another child.'

His own son Andrew was asleep in spite of the noise, tucked neatly into a corner of Rachel's bed and wedged with pillows, while Isla sat beside him on a low chair, sewing – though how she could see the stitches with the room so full of people and the shadows leaping he could not imagine. She looked up, caught him looking at her and before she mouthed the words he knew what she would say. 'We must go home.' It was always the same when he found congenial company. Tonight, however, he shook his head. Why should they leave? Their house was barred and bolted, with the watchmen on regular patrol. Mrs Mutch was away and their son here with them, safe in Rachel's house, tucked up in the blanket Kirsty Guyan had produced. Kirsty herself was nowhere to be seen. Nor Wee Alex. He had wanted to ask the lad if he had seen any cases of frostbite in the Greenland waters or the skin sores known as futtlie-bealins. Instead he turned to Louise. 'She will be wanting a daughter next, to help her, though I sometimes think,' he added ruefully, 'that Pearl is more a daughter to Rachel than she is to us.' Louise began to talk of Pearl and of her reading lessons until Andrew, glancing up, saw Isla watching him with a fixed and familiar expression. With an inward sigh, knowing the reproachful scene that would inevitably follow once they were alone together at home, Andrew rose unwillingly to his feet. But Maitland was explaining the design of the new ship he was building and Andrew lingered to listen, then to join in the discussion and the questions. A shipyard in Dundee was building a 'mixed' ship, part wood, part iron. It was much cheaper to fit iron 'knees' and straps than wooden ones, apparently, but the argument as to whether the result would be effective occupied them happily for another hour.

It was morning before the party dispersed, Louise escorted home by the twins, a little unsteady and decidedly boisterous so that it was not entirely clear who was escorting whom, the rest in twos and threes to their various homes. By this time Isla Duthie Noble was not speaking to her husband. Dr Andrew, however, was too happy to notice and, if he had done, too full of whisky to care.

In March, Alex went again to the whaling, and in April Rachel asked Kirsty Guyan outright if she was pregnant. At first James Christie was furious. 'He'll marry ye the moment he sets foot ashore,' he vowed. 'If he wasna' in Greenland I'd fetch him back myself this very day to see ye right. As it is, there'll be trouble enough wi' the minister. Ye know the kirk's line on fornication.'

Kirstie Guyan, however, was a lass of spirit. 'Who says I want to marry Alex?' she challenged. 'Who wants a man who's half the time at the other side o' the ocean?' She could have bitten out her tongue the moment she spoke, for James Christie spent more time away from home, on one voyage or another, than he did at his own fireside and when he was not sailing the *Bonnie Annie* to the Baltic he was working eighteen hours a day, like as not, at the yard.

'Of course you do,' said Rachel quietly. 'No girl sleeps with a man she does not love. That is for whores. Besides, you carry Alex's child.'

'But he hasna' asked me, Rachel,' Kirsty confessed

later, in private. 'I'd have liked him to speak of it himself. Not to feel I'd trapped him.'

Impulsively Rachel put her arms around the girl. 'I know, Kirsty. But think what the Square will say of you if you don't marry him. They'll likely say the child is not his. Besides,' she added kindly, 'he will ask you the moment he sees you and be glad.'

'He'd best hurry back,' warned James when he returned from a long and serious session with the minister. 'If it wasna' that the minister knows we're a God-fearing family . . .'

'And needs our money,' put in Maitland with a wink at Rachel.

'. . . there'd be more trouble than there is. I promised I'd see the young stirk marries the lass as soon as his ship comes home and I hope to God he's nae ice-bound or the wee mite'll be born a bastard.' But James Christie's anger was soon spent. 'It will be fine to have another wee Christie bairn,' he confessed to Rachel later. 'And soon, maybe, we'll have another of our own.'

'Please talk to Rachel,' urged Louise when she and Andrew met some weeks later by chance, as they seemed increasingly to do, at the Reading Rooms. 'Something is troubling her and she will not tell me what, but she might confide in you.'

Andrew made a pretext to call at the house in the Square the very next day and found Rachel preparing to leave for the Pocra office. 'No matter,' said Andrew. 'I merely looked in to tell you there is measles in the town and to warn you to take care. I will walk with you, if I may.'

'Of course. I am waiting only for Kirsty to arrive. See the boys behave, Pearl, while I am out. No playing near the fire, remember.'

'I will watch them, Auntie Rachel, like I always do. I'm teaching them to count today.'

Pearl was sitting at the table with Tom and Jamie on either side of her, playing a game with a pile of mother-of-pearl counters her uncles had given her at Auld Yell. There were ovals, discs and oblongs, shimmering green and pink when the light caught them, but the best of all were the fishes. 'One fish for Tom. One fish for Jamie,' she counted, sharing them equally and giving herself the plain ones. 'How many fishes have you, Jamie?' She slipped off the bench to greet Dr Andrew, then scrambled hastily back again as Jamie cried, 'Three fishes!' while Tom, snatching one from the centre pile, squealed 'I've catched four!'

Andrew laughed. 'They will catch better fish than that one day, won't you, lads?' He ruffled their hair with affection. 'You have a fine pair of sons, Rachel.' At that moment Kirsty Guyan arrived and Rachel dropped a quick kiss on each boy's head, hugged Pearl, took up her leather-bound ledger and stepped into the Square, trailing a chorus of 'Bye, Ma' as she went.

The sky was patterned with cloud, the wind fresh, with a tang of salt air from the sea. The first spring ships for Quebec had sailed a month ago.

'Let us walk the long way round,' he said, taking her arm and steering her round the gable end towards the shore. 'And give me that cumbersome book of yours so you can take my arm. I have not walked on the shore since I don't know when. You are not in any hurry, are you?'

'No more than any day. But should you not be at the University?'

'The session ended last week. Or had you forgotten?'

Rachel sighed. 'Yes, I confess that I had. It seems so many years since you set out to the University for the first time and I counted every week until the vacation when you would come home again.'

There was a sadness in her voice which made him study her with new concern. 'Are you not happy, Rachel?' She stood on the headland where she had always stood to wave the Christie ships on their way, her eyes on the huge sea, calm today and pale so that it was hard to tell where sea met sky. The fishing boats had put to sea hours before, at first light, and there was only a heavy-bottomed schooner in the near roads and an unknown lugger, far out to sea. Soon the *Velocity* would spew chugging from the harbour mouth in a trail of black smoke, *en route* for Leith. Those steam-yachts ran regularly now, every lawful day, with a guaranteed passage of 12 hours and no need to whistle for a wind. The *Steadfast* was in London, the *Bonnie Annie* somewhere beyond the horizon buying timber to bring home and use to build more ships to sail the seas. When they reached the North Pier and turned inland towards the harbour, they would see it full of shipping, huddled like sheep in a fold – or flotsam driven into a cleft in a cliff. She wondered if James was in Riga now, living that other life of his in which she had no part, or visiting Friida and Priit?

'Sometimes,' she said slowly, not looking at Andrew and moving away along the shore, 'it seems as if a knot was tied inside me when . . . when *he* arrived.' She even had difficulty speaking Tom's name. 'I have understood and forgiven your mother a hundred times since then.'

Andrew stood still in shock. Then, as the full implication of her words came home he said in horror, 'Surely you do not . . .?'

'Oh no. I could beat no child, not even . . .' She shook her head, impatient of her own impediment. 'No, I do not strike Tom. I treat him exactly as I treat Jamie: gently, kindly, with infinite patience and care. I hold his hand, I

275

kiss him goodnight. I even take him on my knee. But I give him *nothing*. A place at my hearth, that is all. Every day I try to love him, till I ache with trying, but something stops the love at source. And I find I cannot show my love for Jamie as I used to do, lest Tom see the difference and be hurt. I would not hurt him, Andrew – but *I cannot find it in me to love him*. I do not know why. He is, as you say, a fine wee boy. But when James gave him to me, with such pleasure and such pride, I felt only distaste. I sometimes think that were he James's love-child, as I thought for a brief, disloyal moment that he was, I might be able to love him more. But he is a stranger's child from a different, foreign land . . . Do you think I could be jealous, Andrew? My husband loves him and so does Jamie. Because of that they have a closeness which I cannot share. I feel excluded and alone, at my own fireside.' Still he made no answer and she turned to look at him. 'Are you shocked, Andrew?'

'No,' he said slowly. 'At least . . . I must be truthful, Rachel, as we have always been together, and admit I was shocked at first. I had thought you happy with your little twins, happy with James and . . .'

'You will not tell him?' cried Rachel in agitation. 'He does not know. He treats Jamie and Tom with equal love, as the others do. It is only I who fail – I who should love him the most – and I am punished for it. I wish I could bear another child . . .' she finished, with a longing which pierced Andrew's heart.

'You will one day, I am sure of it,' he comforted, his arm around her shoulder. 'You and James are both healthy and young. And as for Tom, you do not need me to tell you he is a bright, affectionate and lively child. He loves you, I know, as one day I am sure you will grow to love him.'

'Do you really think so?' Rachel smiled for the first

time since their meeting. 'If only I could. But you must promise to tell no one what I have told you?'

'I promise.' He tucked her hand under his arm and led her across the last scrubby patch of sand and bent grass, round the Coastguard's point and on to the North Pier. 'See what a fine view of the harbour we have from here and there is the Christie yard, clear as clear. How proud you must be to have a flourishing shipyard of your own at last. But I can see the door of your own office waiting for you. I must not keep you longer.'

'Thank you for listening to me, Andrew.' Rachel felt happier than she had felt for months. 'You and I could always confide in each other. Now that I have told you I feel as if a window had opened in my prison and let in the sunlight.' She looked up at him with the clear-eyed trust he remembered from their childhood and suddenly he too felt the need to share a private burden.

'I must confide in you too, Rachy, before I leave you. If your office can wait another minute or two? Isla is unhappy, I am sure of it. Without cause she is jealous of all I do – of my work, of you, of Louise. She heard I had been seen talking to Louise on one or two occasions in the public Reading Rooms. She said . . .' But in all loyalty there were some things he could not tell even Rachel: that Isla had said Louise was scheming to steal her children from her and to steal him, too, out of envy. 'That interfering masculine cow,' she had called Louise with a contradiction that would have made him laugh, had it not been so painful. 'I fear she is afraid of losing me, as she lost Davy. Poor Isla, she has so little faith in herself and what she has is easily shattered. I feel sometimes as if I am walking on precious eggs. I wish you could help her, Rachel. Make her realize she *is* of value, and is dear to me.'

'I will try.' And Louise, thought Rachel, how dear is

she? But they had reached the door of the Pocra office. Andrew handed back the ledger and took his leave.

'Thank you,' smiled Rachel, reaching up and kissing his cheek. 'You have done me good.'

'I am glad of it. And do not worry, Rachel. All will be well again one day. You will see.'

In May, Jessica Abercrombie gave birth to a third daughter. After his initial disappointment, George Abercrombie shrugged philosophically and said only, 'Next time, lass.' Jessica had done well in the new shop. She had a knack of selling folk more things than they intended to buy and could shift a load of surplus stock quicker than anyone, with her persuasive tongue and her fine eyes. These she exercised mainly on the menfolk: for their wives she had a line in deferential persistence and an apparently guileless wish to save them money which would have deceived the most cynical. She refused to touch any book work, but Abercrombie had others to do that and Jess was more help to him in the shop. It was a tribute to Jessica's ingenuity that Abercrombie had yet to discover that she could neither read nor write. She had early familiarized herself with the shapes and colours of various jars and bottles, the pattern of this and the scents of that and if ever baffled, would turn on the nearest apprentice and say, 'You heard what the customer said, Archy. Fetch a pound of Lexia raisins,' then she would while away the interval with questions of the customer's family or comments on any current scandal or gobbet of local news. It was out of this jumble of names of groceries, spiceries and other commodities that she had plucked the name for her third daughter, India.

'A daft name,' pronounced her father-in-law. 'What's wrong wi' Kirsty?' but his wife, surprisingly, disagreed.

'India Abercrombie,' she repeated thoughtfully. 'It has

a distinguished ring to it, like County folk. Or gentry.'
She had still, in spite of all persuasion, failed to interest
her husband in the Country Club, but with Jessica's help
she hoped at least to persuade him to an Ordinary in the
County rooms next season. 'Yes, I reckon India will do,
Jessica.' She already saw the announcement in some
distant newspaper '. . . *the marriage of India Abercrombie
with* . . .' She could not decide between the handful of
County names, but it would certainly be someone distinguished, for by that time the Abercrombies would have
made their name in the City and a fortune with it.

A fortune was to be made in the whaling, too, though it
would not last much longer, warned the shrewder fishermen. Too many ships had flocked to the Arctic fisheries
after the once plentiful right whale, and now those same
whalers were forced to sail further north and dangerously
close to the ice floes to find their complement of fish. Gas
lamps were beginning to replace oil lamps, rape seed oil
was cheaper than whale oil, and the number of whalers
and the size of their catches had begun to dwindle. But
the best whaling captains continued to make a fortune for
themselves and for their crew.

Wee Alex came home with a bulging purse and a new
beaver hat, to find James waiting for him, with the
minister and Kirsty Guyan. A mere three weeks later the
Christie fleet was increased by a daughter, Kirsty's Annie.
Space was found for them, too, in the house in the
Square. With Alex away at the whaling half the year and
James absent equally often, there was room enough, one
way or another, though Maitland took to sleeping more
and more often at the Pocra yard.

'We'll buy a house on the Quay one day,' promised
James. 'But first we must establish the Christie business
on a sure foundation.'

1827

In the years since they had acquired Dixon's land, with its valuable water frontage, to add to their own, the Christies had built up a flourishing and prosperous shipbuilding business, with a workforce of some thirty men, including journeymen, apprentices, sawyers and blacksmiths. From the two slipways they had launched a succession of excellent vessels, the smallest a 90-ton schooner, the largest a ship of some 400 tons, and the repair side of the enterprise had no shortage of orders. Last year the Christies had put a second ship, the *Anya*, on the London run with George as Captain, and the twins sailed to and fro like twin halves of a weather-clock, passing each other at regular intervals, when they would dip their pennants in private salute. The year before, with Abercrombie's help, the Christies had sent the *Rachel Christie* to Canada: the occasion had been marked by one of the few disputes the Christie family knew. For Alex, against all expectation, had refused to captain the ship and had insisted on going instead to the Greenland fisheries. James had been furious: his declared policy was to captain Christie ships with Christie men. 'I'll captain her for you, Da,' young Jamie had offered, amid laughter, and James had promised, 'So you shall lad, one day.' Meanwhile, he had been forced to hire a captain in the harbour and though Mr Morgan was competent and honest and, moreover, a second cousin, it went against the grain to have a 'stranger' in charge.

'That young stirk'll toe the line one day, Rachel,' vowed James later, in the privacy of their bed. 'And be glad to. Yon whaling boom willna' last for ever.'

Meanwhile Mr Morgan sailed the *Rachel Christie* regularly to Canada, taking emigrants on the outward passage and returning with the timber essential for their shipbuilding. Next, they planned a sturdy, copper-bottomed vessel for the West Indies guano trade, but all work had been suspended on this particular day, mid-week though it was, to enable the workforce, with the rest of Aberdeen, to attend the launching of the first steam-vessel to be built in the port. Built on a timber frame, it was the length of a 36-gun frigate, with a spar deck and poop and two splendid cabins separate from the sleeping compartments. These were ranged along each side of the ship, with entrance from the main deck, and moving stanchions which, if necessary, could allow her to carry 15 guns on each side. She had two engines of 75 horsepower each and could carry, besides her machinery and the fuel necessary to feed it, some 300 tons.

'An impressive sight,' said Maitland, turning up the collar of his greatcoat and shaking the water from his hat. The rain had fallen incessantly since daybreak, but had been no deterrent to the huge crowd assembled to see the wonder vessel take to the water. And possibly sink – for with all those bits of iron machinery inside her, who could tell? The band of the Aberdeenshire Militia had entertained the waiting crowd with stirring music until, at precisely 1.15, the *Queen of Scotland* glided majestically into her future element amid cheers from the multitude and a spirited rendering of 'God Save the King' from the waterlogged band.

'They plan a trial trip for August,' said James thoughtfully, 'with over a hundred mechanics on board. If successful, they talk of using her regularly on the Aberdeen-London run.'

Both were silent, thinking of the implications for their own little London ships, the *Anya* and the *Steadfast*. Apart from an incident last summer, when the *Anya* had been becalmed for so long that she had almost been given up for lost and had finally completed the run in twice the normal time, they had established a smooth-running, efficient and well-patronized service which brought them a steady profit. Since the death of Atholl Farquharson, his company had gone progressively downhill and competition on the London run at least had ceased from that quarter. Though it was rumoured that old Mrs Farquharson was only awaiting the outcome of this particular launching to put her own plans into action for a steamship to ply regularly to London. If she could find the money . . .

'I like the *Bonnie Annie* best,' announced Jamie stoutly. Riga Tom at his side said loyally, 'So do I – but I'd like fine to go aboard yon ship and see how the engines work.' He and Jamie, both eight years old now, spent every hour when not at school in the shipyard or on board whichever of the Christie ships might be in port. They had long decided that as soon as they were old enough they would be apprenticed to the sea: the only point they could not agree on was whether to sail to South America or to the China seas.

'But first, I will go to Riga,' Tom always ended up, 'To see my grandparents.' Friida and Priit were still alive, but increasingly frail. James Christie visited them whenever he could, to bring them gifts and news of little Toomas, and one day, he promised, when the lads were older, he would take both James and Tom to Riga with him. 'But not till ye've done your schooling and are fit to be taken as apprentices and earn your passage.' For his own part, he would have taken them now – the grandparents after all were old and might not last another winter – but

283

Rachel, he knew, did not wish it. 'Wait till they are older, *please*,' she had pleaded on the one occasion he had suggested it, with such urgency in her voice and such anguish that he had not asked again. He had no wish to make her unhappy: she had enough grief as it was, for in spite of all longing, there had been no more children. Andrew and Isla Noble had a daughter, Amelia. Alex and Kirsty Guyan had twin sons and another child on the way. Even Jessica Abercrombie was expecting again. Only Rachel, to her increasing sorrow, remained barren. So James had promised her the boys should not go to sea until they were twelve.

'At least twelve,' she had amended, her anxious eyes on Jamie, but even Rachel knew she could not keep her son beside her for ever. Now, standing beside James in her best blue dress and protective plaid, she said, 'Will we be allowed aboard? I would dearly like to see the cabins and whether they are one whit better than our own, on the *Anya*.'

'I will see what I can do,' said James indulgently. The men of the Duffus yard whose ship it was were known to him and, whereas they had already set up barriers 'to repel boarders' and deter the bulk of the inquisitive crowds, later, when the crowds had dispersed, there would be time for genuine visitors to see over the wonder ship.

'Tomorrow, perhaps,' James said now. 'I will see if I can fix up something at dinner.'

James and Maitland, as fellow shipbuilders, had been invited to the celebratory banquet in the new Assembly Rooms with other prominent men in the shipping world. They had congregated in the supper room, a square room with domed ceiling leading off the spacious central promenade and itself connecting with the card salon. This magnificent rotunda with Corinthian columns and pilasters and a splendid painted ceiling, was clearly visible through the connecting doors which had been thrown open for the purpose, and the spacious recesses between the columns were furnished with invitingly comfortable sofas which more than one gentleman in the company noted and filed away for private investigation later in the evening.

The tables were sparkling with fresh linen, gleaming silver and an abundance of crystal which was rapidly filled with suitable liquids for the succession of succulent dishes and increasingly imaginative toasts. Conversation grew lively and loud.

Maitland entered into a heated defence of sail against steam with his opposite neighbour, James pursued an intricate and highly technical discussion of the merits of various different timbers for different sections of a ship, someone else told a succession of stories involving the outwitting of the Revenue officers and there was general laughter when one of the company solemnly rose to his feet and offered to corroborate the tale, himself being the Revenue officer concerned. Altogether it was a most genial occasion and even Robert Farquharson, who was also of the company, managed to forget his business worries and relax. He was talking amiably with his father-in-law, George Abercrombie, between one rambling after-dinner speech and what would surely be a worse, when a messenger intruded on the festivities to hand George Abercrombie a folded note on a silver tray.

'A *son*, by God!' he cried, striking the table with a delighted fist. 'She's done it at last. Three quinies one after the other till I was beginning to think she'd got into the habit, and now at last, a wee loon! I give ye a toast, gentlemen. To my new grandson. God bless him.'

When the congratulations had subsided after several

more toasts to infant, father, grandfather and infant again, Abercrombie looked around him, beaming with unquenchable glee.

'A grand day, a grand day,' he repeated over and over. 'And I'm thinking,' he went on with sudden inspiration, 'that I should mark the occasion with a new investment.' He looked around the table, seeking out James Christie's face. 'Ah, James lad. Ye've seen the fine steam-vessel our hosts have produced and a credit she is to them – I've a fancy to invest in steam myself. How about it? Can you and Maitland build me a steam-yacht? For my wee grandson's future?'

Maitland shook his head. 'One day, perhaps, when we've an engineer in the family. For the moment I'll stick to what I know best, and that's sail.'

'Aye,' said James, with a sober expression, 'Maitland's right. If steam is the future, as may well be the case, then we'll need to adapt to it one day. But not until we've the knowledge and the resources to produce a vessel as good as or better than the *Queen of Scotland*,' he finished, remembering his hosts and raising his glass in salute to the head of the Duffus Company. 'Young Tom is a clever lad, wi' an interest in things mechanical. He'll maybe develop a steam-engine for us one day. But until that day, we'll stick to Maitland's "white birds".'

'I'm sorry to hear it,' said Abercrombie, momentarily deflated, 'for I've set my heart on a steam-ship for my new grandson. I'd have liked fine to have you build her for me, for you're good lads, both of ye, and fine shipbuilders. But if ye willna' do it, I'll have to look elsewhere.'

'Perhaps I can help, sir?' said Robert Farquharson from across the table. Since the sale of Dixon's land, he had had little contact with the Christies. Five years of truce had brought no closer relationship, but no further enmity

286

either and they could eat at the same table without acrimony. Similarly, the death of Atholl had removed George Abercrombie's old enemy and with him the barrier between father and son-in-law. Though George Abercrombie had no higher opinion of Robert now than he had ever had, he tolerated him and even, on occasions, steered a little business his way. Now he looked at Robert with interest tinged only slightly with suspicion and demanded, 'How?'

'You will remember that my mother has long had it in mind to invest in a steam-driven vessel? She has employed a Glasgow engineer to design one such for her. The plans are now complete to the last specification and are, I think, excellent ones. All that has prevented us going ahead with the idea has been the lack of immediate finances. But were we to have a partner in the enterprise . . .' He paused, surprised at his own daring, drank deep from the brandy glass in his hand and continued rashly, 'Come in with us, sir, and you can have the naming of the vessel. For your grandson, maybe.'

'Or for his Ma.' Jessica had been nagging him systematically for years now to have a ship named after her, but it hadn't seemed right to ask the Christies. Abercrombie had enough sensitivity to realize that whatever friendship there had once been between Christies and Jessica existed no longer. What she had squabbled with them about he had no idea, but he knew better than to ask James to name a ship for her. The Farquharsons were another matter. It would be one in the eye for Euphemia Farquharson if her precious ship was named the *Jessica* – as it would have to be if he, Abercrombie, put up the money for it. Thinking of Euphemia's furious face at the naming ceremony, his own broke into a broad smile. Mischief bubbled up inside him with the happiness of his grandson's birth and the wellbeing induced by excellent food and unstinted drink. 'Aye, lad. Give me the naming o' the vessel and I'll do it. I'll come in wi' ye, equal partners. There's my hand on it.' He reached across the table and took Robert's limp hand in his own strong fist. 'Now, to seal the contract, raise your glass, Robert. To us!'

James Christie, witnessing the bargain, felt a moment's regret that the Christie yard could not have given Abercrombie what he wanted. But Maitland was right. Until they had the expertise, they must leave such developments to others. One day, perhaps, when the boys were bigger . . . Jamie was a sailor, pure and simple; he would follow his father into the tall ships, square-rigged brigantines or schooners. He had the same communion with wind and canvas, wave and wood. He would sail to the China seas one day and race back again, with every inch of canvas spread, to land the first tea cargo of the season. But Tom was different. He was interested in the mechanics of things, in the cranes on the quayside, the pulleys and weights, in the whys and wherefores of power. Already he could explain the new steam-engine to his betters and draw diagrams. One day, perhaps, Tom would be the engineer they needed. But Abercrombie was speaking to him.

'I am sorry, James lad. I'd have given you the custom gladly. But ye see how it is. I must have the newest kind o' ship for my wee grandson. It's only fitting.'

Fenton Abercrombie paced up and down his study in an agony of excited expectation. He had a son at last. A blessed, precious son. He could not wait to see the child, to hold him in his arms, to search his little, new-born face for family likenesses, to kiss him. Fenton's heart was overflowing with tenderness for his wife and adoration for his little unseen son and still they would not let him in. Since the midwife had put her head round the door to tell him, 'It's a boy' an age seemed to have rolled by. He had dispatched a note to his father at the celebratory dinner, knowing he would welcome the news as Fenton did, with rapturous relief. He had sent another to his mother, offered Dr McKinnon brandy (the least he could do, remembering Jessica's noisy and uninhibited abuse of the old man), had run upstairs to the nursery to give the happy news to his little daughters, who should have been asleep, and finally taken to pacing up and down the floor, trying the sound of various names on his tongue. Fenton George Abercrombie. George Fenton Abercrombie. Yet still his wife's door remained closed to him and still he waited, kept out by women's work, as he thought of it, and fuss. Piles of dirty linen had been carried out of the room, piles of fresh linen carried in. Jugs of hot water, basins and pails had been hurried to and fro with fire buckets and fresh logs and finally a small tray with brandy and water and ratafia biscuits.

When Fenton noticed that last, he knew the moment could not be far away, surely, when he would be admitted?

'You can come in now, Mr Abercrombie sir, for five minutes.' Mairi's cheerful face appeared round the door of the study and Fenton almost knocked her down in his hurry to reach the bedroom. Jessica lay, triumphant, in the connubial bed, her hair newly brushed into love-curls, her bedlinen spotless, the neck of her lace-trimmed night-gown flatteringly low, all trace of her recent sweat-drenched and noisy labour obliterated. The damask bed-curtains were neatly looped back, the folding wooden shutters closed to shut out the darkness and the April rain which still streamed relentlessly against the window pane. There were flowers on a low table, sweet-scented narcissi and early tulips, the wood fire crackled busily in a wreath of aromatic fumes and the eau-de-Cologne which Jess had daubed liberally about her person drowned any lingering odours of doctor's lotions and disinfectants.

Between the bed and the fire, in the wooden cradle that had housed his three sisters, one by one, lay the infant Abercrombie, swathed in white frilly linen and a minuscule lace cap. His eyes were tight shut, as were his tiny fists and there was nothing particularly notable in the sleeping face, yet Fenton, gazing down at him in awe and wonder, had never seen an infant more miraculously perfect.

'Thank you, Jessica,' he murmured, his voice choked with emotion and his eyes moist. 'Thank you. This is the happiest day of my life. A son, at last . . .'

Jessica lay back on the pillow with a satisfied smile. Old Abercrombie ought to be pleased with her now. Maybe she'd get that ship named for her at last? A good big ship, bigger than the *Rachel Christie* anyway. Though she'd been angry at the time, it really wasna' much to have a copper-bottomed brig named for you. Yon ordinary, old-fashioned ships were ten a penny. She'd have something a deal better than that. Maybe even a steam-ship?

'What are you thinking of, my love?' murmured Fenton, sitting down on the edge of her bed and taking her plump hand in his.

'Ouch!' she said loudly and swore. 'Dinna' *bounce* the bed, Fenton. I'm sore, remember.'

'I am sorry, my love.' Fenton scrambled hastily to his feet. 'What can I do for you? What can I give you to mark this splendid day? My son's birthday!'

'Well . . .' Into Jessica's eyes came a calculating look as she went rapidly through her wardrobe and jewel box. 'I've a fancy for amethysts. I reckon I'd suit purple, don't you?'

'Then amethysts it shall be, Jessica. I will visit the jewellers myself tomorrow.'

'I'll need a new gown to set them off, o' course,' she went on, 'and maybe a cape wi' a wee bit fur?'

'Anything, my love. Anything you say.' At that moment Fenton in his happiness would have promised her the moon and all the stars with it, strung on a chain to wear round her neck. But Jessica, for the moment, was satisfied. The lack of those amethysts Atholl Farquharson had promised her had long rankled. And if old Abercrombie could be persuaded about that ship . . .

'At least yer Da will be pleased,' she said. 'Maybe he'll stop going on at me, now he's got his blessed grandson.'

'His *first* grandson,' corrected Fenton. 'There's no reason why we should not have more.'

'Oh yes there is,' declared Jess. 'I'm nae going through all that bother again, blowing up like one o' they air balloons for months so none o' my clothes fit, and feeling sick and all. Not to mention the bother o' getting the little sod out into the world. It's all right for you. All you have to do is . . .'

'Yes, yes, dear,' interrupted Fenton hastily. 'I am sorry if I seemed unfeeling. It is just that . . . a *son*,' he finished, incoherent with happiness. 'Our son.' He tiptoed over to the cradle and gazed down at the sleeping bundle, with open adoration. 'How shall we name him, my dear? "George" first, of course, then . . .'

'*George*? I'm nay callin him anything sae common. Half the men o' the town are called George. I've a fancy for something wi' more style, like Randolph maybe, or Ferdinand.'

'It will have to be George, dear,' said Fenton mildly. 'For my father. He expects it. But the baby's second name could be . . .'

'I dinna' care what it is,' snapped Jessie, suddenly tired. She turned her back and pulled the bedcovers up to her chin. 'Suit yourself. You always do.'

This last was particularly untrue, but Fenton, in the circumstances, could not contradict. His wife was emotionally and physically exhausted. She needed rest to recuperate from her ordeal. Though how she could regard it as anything but a triumph he could not imagine when she had at last produced a *son*.

'I am sorry, my dear. You are exhausted. I should not have mentioned it at such a time. We will talk of it tomorrow, when you are recovered.'

Jess pulled the blankets higher with a gesture of dismissal and made no reply. Nevertheless Fenton bent gingerly over the bed, kissed her on the ear, it being the only piece of her left accessible, and whispered, 'God bless you, my dear.' Then he tiptoed from the room.

He dined alone, hardly noticing what he ate, thinking only of his son, imagining his first steps, his first words, his success at school. He saw him capped at the University, maybe taking the Latin prize or the Greek, or both. Saw him an eminent judge in a full-bottomed wig. Or perhaps a distinguished surgeon, like Andrew Noble would one day be. Or a Professor – Principal – Vice Chancellor. If he gave distinguished service, as he would naturally do, he might even be created a peer of the realm. Lord Abercrombie. Sir George. No, George, as Jessica said, was not in itself a distinguished name. The lad would have to be George, naturally, but he could also have a name of his own, a name of flair and style, a name to remember . . .

'What do you think we should call the young master, Mairi?' he asked when the maid came in to remove the cover. 'Have you and the mistress spoken of it perhaps?'

'Well, it's not for me to say, sir, but he's a fine dark-haired wee loon, wi' all his wits about him and I reckon "James" is as good a name as any.'

'James?' Fenton was startled. 'Why James?'

292

'Well that was what Mrs Abercrombie was plannin' to name Victoria only she couldna' because she was a quinie. It'd be only fittin', she tellt that Rachel Christie, and then she put our 'Toria next to yon Christie baby and whatever that bitch Kirsty Guyan says I reckon our 'Toria was the best o' the two. Then they took to comparin' and they was like brother and sister, the dear wee mites, just like the mistress said. There's nae likeness at all, ye silly cow, yon Kirsty tellt me. But I sorted her, I can tell ye; and now to look at our 'Toria you'd think she was Miss Clemmy all over again. It's amazing . . .'

Mairi clattered the plates and glasses on to the tray, balanced it precariously on one hand while she opened the door with the other, kicked the door wider with her foot and held it there. 'Yes, sir. I reckon James is a fine name, and the mistess'd be right pleased.' Then she withdrew her foot and scuttled through the door before it slammed behind her.

Fenton sat immobile, the brandy glass in which yet again he had been going to toast his son's arrival suspended half way between table and mouth. *James . . . Only fitting . . . Brother and sister*. Scraps of Mairi's guileless gossip whirled like a snowstorm in his head and as suddenly settled: but the pattern they formed drew the blood from his face and the happiness from his heart. His whole body trembled. Viciously, he drained the glass, refilled it, drained it again.

James Christie. He remembered that November occasion of his wife's absence, her unexplained knowledge of the Christie-Farquharson agreement. He had thought she was in collusion with Atholl but perhaps after all it had been James Christie she was visiting. That would explain why Rachel had not asked them to her wedding, why the friendship between the girls had ceased. It would explain so many hints and nuances . . . but *Victoria*? What had

Mairi said? It would be only fitting to name her James? Feverishly now Fenton tried to remember the child's birthday and that November night. Or was it December? He added weeks on his fingers. Months. The implications were appalling. Then what of India, his third daughter? *What of his little son?*

He crashed back in his chair and rose unsteadily to his feet. He would have it out with the lying bitch now, this minute, whether she slept or not.

The bedroom was in darkness, except for the lingering glow from the fire, and heavy with sleep. Fenton struck a light, lit a candle and set it beside the bed. The child he had adored not two hours before lay sleeping in his wooden cradle, but Fenton ignored him.

'Jessica!' He shook her roughly by the shoulder.

'What . . .? What is it? Oh, it's you, Fenton. Go away, will ye. Ye're nae getting into my bed tonight.'

'Jessica!' This time Jess's eyes jerked wide and she looked at her husband in growing alarm. His face was white, his whole body quivering, and his eyes like nothing she had seen before. Nervously, she clutched at the bed linen, searching out of the corner of her eye for the bell pull.

'Whatever is the matter, Fenton? What are ye looking at me like that for?'

'What is James Christie to you?'

'Nothing, Fenton. Why should he be?'

'Why did you plan to call Victoria "James" and say it was "only fitting"?'

'Oh God,' breathed Jessica. That fool of a Mairi must have been talking. 'It was a tease, Fenton,' she improvised. 'You know how high and mighty Rachel Christie gets. She was lying there preening herself wi' her new wee son as if naebody else's children mattered. So I said it to annoy her. That's all, Fenton. Honest.'

But Fenton had seen the momentary fear in Jess's face and read her guilt.

'Do not lie to me, woman. *What is James Christie to you?*'

'*Nothing*, Fenton.' But what was the use of denying it? He obviously was not going to believe her and she had not the energy to put up a fight. '*Now*.' she added, trying a different tack. 'Oh I dinna' deny I fancied him once, but that was before I met you, Fenton.' She stretched out a hand with an appealing expression. 'Come here, my love, and dinna' frown so. Surely ye canna' be jealous of something that happened years back, before we were married?'

'Then why plan to name Victoria "James"?' His implacable voice was beginning to unnerve her.

'But I *didna*'. I tellt ye it was a *joke*. I only said it to tease Rachel. I . . .'

'That was cruel of you, Jessica. But then you are a selfish, heartless woman. You taunted that poor girl with her husband's past indiscretion. Am I not right?'

'I don't know what you're on about, Fenton. I'm tired. I havena' slept long and the wee loon'll be waking soon for his sup – if ye dinna' wake him long before wi' your din.'

'Jessica!' Fenton seized her forearm and gripped it so tight she gasped aloud. 'I will have the truth, do you understand me? What has there been between you and James Christie?' His fingers dug hard into her flesh.

'Let me go, Fenton. You're hurting me.'

'Not until you tell me the truth.' His face was that of a stranger, a violent stranger, and suddenly Jess's nerve snapped.

'All right, Fenton. I'll tell ye. But it's nothing, honest. Nothing at all. I was in the Christie office, doing your Da's business for him, seeing about the shipping and all,

295

and, well, James kissed me. There was naebody else there, see, and I couldna' stop him.' She opened her eyes wider in feigned innocence. 'But then Atholl Farquharson and the others came in so it was all right and no harm done. They all signed yon agreement about Dixon's land and that was why I knew about it. I was helping, see.'

For a long moment, Fenton did not answer. He stood staring down at his wife, his hands limp at his sides, and seeing her, for the first time, for what she was. An undeniably attractive, but stupid woman, selfish, devious, dishonest, shallow. She would be blowsy one day, if she didn't take care. Blowsy and vulgar. He recognized the element of truth in her fabrication and saw, as clearly as if he had been there, what had happened. His wife had sought out James, when she knew she would find him alone; had made advances, and Fenton knew how adept she was at getting her way. The only doubt was how long had elapsed before they were interrupted: Fenton was inclined to think it had been long enough for more than the simple kiss she admitted to. Much more.

'It was nothing, Fenton,' she was pleading now, with genuine fear. She could not read his face. Could not tell what he was thinking or what he would do. Her usually mild and malleable husband had become an implacable monster of retribution and she was growing frightened. Suppose he struck her, turned her out of the house, sent her packing? 'Honest, it was *nothing*. And it was no harm to Rachel. All right, maybe I shouldna' have, wi' Rachel and me being friends; but James wasna' married then.'

'*But you were!*'

'I know, Fenton,' she gabbled, wondering if she dare snatch at the bell rope and ring for Mairi. 'Surely ye didna' think I'd forget it? I've been a loyal wife to you, honest I have. I've borne your children. I've given you

296

your own wee son,' she finished, playing what she thought was her trump card. 'A fine, strong laddie who . . .'

'How do I know he is *mine*?' Fenton's voice was scarcely above a whisper, but the passion in his words sent shivers of fear down her spine. She licked dry lips and opened her mouth to speak, but before she could utter a word of self-justification, Fenton had turned on his heel and left the room.

He paced his study long into the night, fighting his lonely battle before finally, exhausted, he came to his decision. He would not turn Jessica out, as had been his first violent inclination. Instead, he would continue to do his duty as a husband and father. He would name the child George Finlay Abercrombie and accept him as his. He would continue to give a home to his wife and her three daughters and to present the picture of a united family to the world. But he would not share Jessica's bed again. That way, at least, were she to bear more children he would know them to be bastards. As it was, all joy in his new-born son was spent.

His decision reached, Fenton held his head in his hands and wept.

The Abercrombie christening was a grand affair, though several people noticed that Jessica Abercrombie was more subdued than usual. 'A difficult labour', 'time to recover', 'not as young as she used to be' – sympathetic tongues found ready explanations and the envious merely noted that 'she's learning her place at last'. But where the mother was subdued, the grandfather was bursting with pride and vigour. Orders for the steam-ship had gone ahead and Abercrombie already planned a journey to Glasgow in the autumn to see for himself how the work was progressing. He could tie it in with a bit of business, too.

'I've a fancy to open a branch in Glasgow one day,' he confided to Fenton when the naming ceremony was over and the hospitality flowing. 'Ye'll maybe come with me, lad, and we'll look the place over. With young Finlay coming into the business we'll need to expand and consolidate. There'll be the girl's wedding settlements, too.' He beamed at his three granddaughters, decked in muslin and ribbons for the occasion. 'They're a fine set o' lassies, wi' Augusta the image of her Ma, Victoria as like our Clemmy as two peas in a pod, and wee India a pretty wee lass wi' a style all her own.'

Fenton made no reply. He had loved his daughters dearly, and still did, but now that love was tainted inevitably with suspicion. Even nine-year-old Augusta, with her dark-eyed, dimpled beauty and her bouncing ringlets whom he believed, deep in his heart, could only be his, was not above secret scrutiny. Five-year-old India, as her grandfather had realized, was nobody's child, her quicksilver vitality and freckled, bright-eyed laughter being all her own. Nobody's? Or anybody's? As for Victoria, supposedly his sister's double, surely her pale hair and fair complexion could just as easily stem from Christie blood as from Abercrombie? Look at Maitland Christie and Alex. They were fair where their brothers were dark, blue-eyed to their brown. And likenesses lay in more than colouring. In the line of the nose, for instance, or the chin. Fenton found his eyes drawn yet again to James Christie's face, searching for similarities.

For the Christies had, inevitably, been invited. As business colleagues of George Abercrombie, Fenton could not prevent their coming. Lawyer Forbes and his wife were also there, with their daughter Louise. Robert Farquharson too, and his mother – though that lady spent most of the afternoon in a corner, gossiping with Mrs Abercrombie and privately comparing every item in

298

Fenton Abercrombie's drawing-room disparagingly with her own. It had cost Euphemia Farquharson a deal of pride to accept the invitation, but she was shrewd enough to recognize that without George Abercrombie's money the Farquharson company would be doomed, if not to actual bankruptcy, then certainly to failure. Dr Andrew Noble, Fenton's old college friend, with his wife Isla, and everybody's children were there, squealing and chattering, spilling things, eating too much, and generally enjoying themselves.

India, Fenton noticed, had spent the entire afternoon with Jamie Christie and that lad they called Riga Tom, while Augusta and Victoria had been taken in hand by Andrew's stepdaughter, Pearl, a good-natured, capable lass of ten, who seemed to keep the whole tribe of them in order.

'They're a grand sight, Fenton,' beamed Abercrombie, clapping his son on the back, 'and when young Finlay's a man, he'll be the best o' the bunch. Raise your glasses all o' ye, to my wee grandson, George Finlay Abercrombie. Well, cheer up, Fenton lad. This is a christening, nae a funeral! What's got into ye the day? Or is it the responsibility o' being a father that's weighing ye down? If there's anyone in this room today wi' a reason for depression, it's nae you, Fenton. So smile, lad, and see your guests' glasses are nae left empty. There's James Christie needing a fill-up, for one. Come over here, James, and tell me how that latest ship o' yours is faring.'

Mumbling something incoherent, Fenton filled James Christie's glass and fled 'Well, James,' said Abercrombie looking after his son with mild surprise. 'I'm right sorry we couldna' steer our custom your way. But you do see how it is, with me needing a steam-yacht and you not having the wherewithal to build me one?'

'Certainly,' said James, though the removal of the

Abercrombie patronage had been disquieting. For once he had put money into steam, who was to say he would return again to sail? Another Aberdeen yard was building steam, too. Alexander Halls were to launch a steam-tug any day now, a vessel with a 40 horsepower engine and designed to tow other vessels in and out of harbour in the place of the labourers on the pier who were used to hauling the ships by rope to the harbour entrance. When the tug was in use, that would put a good few men out of work for a start. And if the drive for steam continued, it would not only be the pier labourers who were out of work. At the moment the Christies' order book was full, but who could say what would happen in the future?

'Dinna' look so glum, James lad,' said Abercrombie, clapping him on the shoulder. 'I don't know what's got into folk today. There's Fenton wi' a face more fit for a wake than a christening, and Jess wi' hardly a word to say for hersel' these days, and now you. Tell ye what, lad.' He winked with gleeful mischief. 'I'll place an order wi' ye now, for a fine, iron-bound coffin from yon blacksmith o' yours. I hear he makes a fine job of it, so none o' Dr Noble's Resurrectionists has a chance wi' *his* work. Isn't that right, Andrew?'

Andrew Noble laughed. 'You are obviously far better informed about such things than I am, sir. I bow to your superior knowledge.'

'Nonsense,' said Louise Forbes, joining the group. 'I am sure Andrew can tell us exactly how these Resurrectionists go about their business.' She looked at him straight-faced though her eyes were twinkling. 'There was an article in the *Lancet* on the subject only the other day. Apparently, it is necessary to sink a mine, some twenty feet away from the head of the grave and dig a slanting tunnel of some five yards long so as to strike the coffin head . . .'

'Rubbish,' interrupted Andrew rashly. 'That's not at all the way it is done. First you must take good note of . . .' He stopped, too late, suddenly aware of Isla's horrified eyes upon him.

'Go on,' urged his listeners. 'What's next?'

'Take good note,' resumed Andrew uncomfortably, 'of any markings on the grave's surface.' But it was time Isla knew. She could not spend her life with her head in the clouds and she was, after all, his wife. 'You will understand, Miss Forbes,' he went on solemnly, looking at Louise without expression, 'that I speak not from personal experience, but from the reports of colleagues, who, until the government make such things legal, are regrettably forced to rely on such a clandestine supply of "subjects". So, you clear the grave carefully, preserving every marking twig or straw, then dig down to the head and shoulders . . .'

Isla, listening, felt the familiar panic and the familiar dread. She hated Andrew's work, hated the hospital, the illness, the pain. Hated the smell of his medicine chest, the glint of his scalpel and scissors, the snake-like rubber tubing of his stethoscope. Hated his black hat, his overcoat, even his shirts which once she had stitched so lovingly for him and which now always smelt to her of carbolic and death. As for the anatomy lectures, she had closed her mind to those, she had thought successfully, but now, listening to her husband describe how to extract a naked body from its resting place – 'but not the shroud, or one lays oneself open to a charge of theft if caught' – she saw with nauseating clarity a long room, rapt faces, and Andrew, knife in hand, 'opening' as he called it, the body. And among the rapt faces, watching her Andrew with fascinated interest, was that of Louise Forbes. Auntie Louise, as Isla's children called her. Auntie Louise who played with them, brought them presents, taught

301

them to read and count, took them for picnics. Auntie Louise whom they loved – and whom Isla hated, with a jealous, unreasoning hatred that shrivelled her heart. She hated Louise's intelligent, homely face, hated her plain hair and angular figure, hated her lavender-coloured gown, her spectacles and her books, hated her lively talk, her sympathy, her laughter. Hated everything about her, but most of all she hated the easy conversations Louise had with Andrew and their shared interest in things medical. Isla knew they met often. She had taxed Andrew with it more than once and been told not to be ridiculous. Could a man not discuss his work with a friend without being accused of infidelity? But for all his protestations of innocence, Isla knew Louise possessed a part of her husband which Isla had never possessed and never could; that they shared a world she could never share, and because of that she felt excluded and betrayed. Andrew would never leave her, she knew that, but he would not renounce his friendship with that woman either. 'But Louise is one of my dearest friends,' he had said in astonishment when she dared to suggest Louise should not come to the house so often.

Now, listening to that gruesome talk of body-snatching, she saw Louise's eager participation in everything Andrew was saying as if they were talking alone together in a room of strangers. Jealousy rose like bile in her throat. She clapped a hand over her mouth and fled from the room.

Andrew, in full flow now, hardly noticed. 'There is an outstanding student at the University here, Andrew Moir, who claims, and I entirely agree with him, that anatomy can only be learned by dissection and until such a fact is recognized and legally encouraged we will see no further advance in medical knowledge. We need an anatomy school, here in the city, and when we have money enough, by God, we'll *build* one!'

'Well said, lad,' said Abercrombie. 'And if it will cheer ye up, I'll pledge ye a hundred pounds here and now for your blessed building – on condition ye dinna' whip me into it for one o' your "subjects". Ye'd best make that coffin a double-bound one, James, wi' a padlock and chain. But where's that wee wife o' yours? Ye'd best get her to write it in her order book afore ye forget.'

'She is with the children, I believe.' The room was packed with people, the noise level deafening, the heat from the fire almost overpowering. The generosity of the Abercrombie hospitality was beginning to tell. The minister was asleep on the sofa, his mouth open and his feet extended to show an unsuitable expanse of ankle. Mrs Abercrombie was similarly dozing, though in an upright and more decorous position. Euphemia Farquharson, her headpiece awry, was talking animatedly if incoherently to anyone who would listen. Robert Farquharson was being led through the steps of some intricate dance by the Abercrombie girls, with much giggling and pushing, and it was some moments before James picked out the still figure of Rachel. When he did, his heart twisted momentarily with the familiar pain.

She was standing by the cradle which had been set in a corner to the left of the fireplace, well out of the draught, and was looking down at the sleeping infant with an expression of such hopeless yearning on her face that James closed his eyes in pain and turned away. 'Is there any medical reason?' he had asked Andrew long ago, 'why Rachel should not conceive?'

'None at all,' Andrew had told him. 'We can only wait and hope.'

'And pray.' But even James's prayers had not brought Rachel the child she longed for.

'Jamie,' he said now, catching his son by the arm as he darted past in pursuit of one or other of the children. 'Tell your Ma it's time we went home. We've stayed long enough.'

Two years later, the steam-yacht *Jessica* was successfully launched in the Clyde and eventually arrived, amid the usual fanfares and cheering multitudes, in Aberdeen harbour to be welcomed proudly by her new owners.

Abercrombie was celebrating the event in his house in the Guestrow with selected friends, when an unusual rumpus impinged on his joviality: the noise of shattering glass and splintering furniture, the ominous sound of a mob on the rampage made him double-bar his door and put up the shutters a full two hours early. Only a month before, William Burke, the notorious grave-robber and murderer, had been hanged in Edinburgh and a distrust of doctors and medical students had flared up again and could be sparked to violence by a mere chance. In the Guestrow it was Dr Andrew Moir, Andrew Noble's friend and colleague, who drew the crowd's attention when rumour spread that he was dissecting a body in his own rooms. The riot was quelled, Dr Moir resumed his lectures, and peace, on the surface, was restored. But the crowd remained suspicious and uneasy, nervous of letting their children play in the streets lest they be snatched by the 'Burkers' and sold to the villainous doctors to be cut into pieces; convinced, were any guest overdue or any man late coming home, that the 'Burkers' had got him.

Meanwhile, in London a select committee was set up to investigate the manner of procuring 'subjects' for anatomy schools, and in Aberdeen Dr Moir's friends continued to collect subscriptions towards the building of a special anatomy theatre. George Abercrombie, in spite of the unwelcome disruption to his launching party – or perhaps because of it – pledged his support, as he had promised Andrew Noble he would do. 'If only to keep yon vandals out o' my street,' and even the Christies gave money, as Rachel said, 'To help Andrew in his work.' Besides, they could afford it.

The Christie yard was doing well. After a slack year or two when everyone seemed to be watching how the steam-vessels progressed and holding back their orders accordingly, trade had picked up again. The steam-yacht service to London did well enough, but not all folk liked – or trusted – those smoke-belching, grumbling engines, or could tolerate the noise and the vibration. It made some folk ill, others plain nervous. The new steam-paddle tug in the harbour did conspicuously valiant work, but it ate up coal and it was not everyone who could handle yon engines. Folk said they could blow up in your face, no warning, and at least a man knew where he was with sail. Soon Maitland had two large vessels on the stocks and a full order book again. A wreck off Belhelvie, and another in the Bay of Nigg, gave them valuable salvage. The repair shop, too, flourished.

The new church of St Clements was completed at Footdee and given the status of a parish church. James Christie was enrolled as one of the Elders, and with the rest of the shipmasters paid his levy to the Beadle in the Beadle Box on the stairs. The Christie family went regularly to the church, but no amount of prayers had sent them another child.

The sons they did have, however, continued to thrive, as did Alex's children and Andrew Noble's. Alex still spent six months of the year at the whale fisheries and when not in Greenland was, as like as not, on one or other of the Christie ships, in the Baltic or the Mediterranean. Kirsty did not mind those voyages: it was the whaling she abhorred, but no amount of persuasion on her part could make him give it up.

'We need the money,' he told her, 'so James can buy us a house on the Quay one day.'

That house was still a dream, though a dream that grew closer with every year that passed. The yard's debts grew steadily less, profits crept higher, and at the end of each whaling season Alex brought home a bulging purse, the bulk of which he handed to Rachel 'for the Christie business', and the rest to Kirsty. Then, the year King George IV died and his brother William took the throne, there was a disastrous year for whaling. Nineteen British whaling ships were lost in the ice, including four from Aberdeen, and Alex's donation to the family purse was non-existent.

'Come home,' urged James. 'We need you in the fleet. We're driven to hiring strangers, lad, when it ought to be Christie men only on our decks, and we've money enough now. Ye've paid your debt long ago.'

But Alex would not be persuaded. At first he had gone to the whaling as restitution for the loss of the first *Bonnie Annie* and what he saw as his part in James's disappearance. Then, after he had come home to find Kirsty Guyan, a full eight months pregnant, waiting for him with the minister, he had fled to Greenland as an escape from a responsibility he had neither looked for nor expected. He was young still and craved his freedom. He was used to the life now, and though he had yet to have his own whaler, he had a mate's ticket on a good ship.

'I'll go after the fish a while longer,' he told James. 'Till we've bought yon house you promised Rachy.' But the pace of shipbuilding was speeding up, and with the demand for emigrant vessels to the United States, as well as the normal trade routes, James Christie's hands were full enough without diverting energy and money towards a house of their own, with all the extra responsibilities involved. Besides, the house in the Square was good enough for the moment. Other houses had two or even three families in them: the Christies were no different, and with so many menfolk away so much of the time, they managed well enough. Had there been more children, of course, it might have been different. But with only two of their own, Alex's four fitted in easily enough and now that Pearl was a grown lass and her schooling finished, she was back at her mother's house above the Denburn – when she was not helping Rachel in the Pocra office.

For Pearl had turned out to be a great help with the book-keeping and the order books, writing a clear, neat hand and with a ready head for figures. She was a willing lass too, happy-natured and loving. She'd make a man a fine wife one day.

Rachel's great friend Louise Forbes, Auntie Louise as the children called her, remained unmarried, to Rachel's secret sorrow, and Louise's cheerful acceptance, at least on the surface.

'Who'd want to marry me? A middle-aged spinster with nothing to recommend her but a house in the West End? If any man comes after me, it will be solely for my money,' she would finish, laughing, 'and I am hanging on to that myself.'

She had parted with a considerable amount of it, however, to fund the building of the anatomy theatre which, in the early months of 1831, at last went ahead on a site called Hospital Row, beside a bleaching green at the west end of St Andrew Street – and in full view of Isla Duthie Noble's windows.

'It is *horrible*, Andrew,' she complained, shuddering and pulling the curtain across the window. They were pretty curtains, of a yellow and white checked gingham, but in

Andrew's private opinion unnecessary. Why shut out a perfectly good view? And the sight of the anatomy theatre at last taking shape was a continuing joy. To anyone but a doctor, it was a forbidding building, with three high but false windows on to the street, to discourage prying eyes, and other functional windows out of sight and reach, at the back. Why should they build a structure no one could spy into unless it was to conceal wickedness? Warily, the population watched as the building took shape, warily the women gave it a wide berth as they fetched water from the Denburn pump, or spread linen on the drying green. Warily, they warned their children not to play near the area where the 'Burkin' Hoose' was being built. Isla caught the general unease and no amount of patient explanation on her husband's part could change her opinion. 'It's horrible,' she repeated, trembling now with agitation. 'I cannot bear you to have anything to do with such things, Andrew.'

'But I must,' sighed Andrew, for the hundredth time. 'Dissection is essential to my work. I know you do not like to hear me speak of it, but really, my dear, it is time you made a little effort to understand the profession to which I have dedicated my life. Anatomy can only be learned by dissection, and the advancement of medical science depends on . . .'

'But I do not *want* you to dedicate your life to such things,' she cried in agitation. 'What of your children? What of me? Could you not . . . Could you not work in a nice consulting room, like those doctors in the Nether-kirkgate, and give medicines for coughs and stomach pains? We could take a house in the West End and . . .'

'No. I can see there is no point in trying to explain to you, as you refuse, wilfully, to understand. I am a specialist and a teacher. If I hope, as I do, to become a better one, then I need to learn as well as teach.'

'But, Andrew, all that anatomy is so horrible and so frightening. I have nightmares whenever I think of it and I am sure that one day the people will turn on you, as they did on Dr Moir. They will follow you home, Andrew, and break our windows and our furniture. I know they will. It is all very well for you. You are brave and do not mind, but I am frightened.' Her eyes filled with tears and she turned away.

Andrew's compassion was stirred as it had been all those years ago when Isla had arrived at his hospital destitute and helpless, her baby as pitifully uncared-for as herself. Pearl was a fine, healthy young woman of fourteen now, and better able to cope with life than her mother would ever be. He pushed back his chair, stood up and would have put his arms about her, to reassure and comfort her, had she not said, 'I am sure your plain, rich lady-friend is *never* frightened.' All compassion died in Andrew's heart and he said coldly, 'I would prefer you not to speak of Louise in such disparaging tones. She has been a good friend *to us both* for many years and deserves better from your tongue than cheap sneers. Good-bye.'

He strode out of the house on a wave of indignation which carried him as far as the Hospital. Only then, when he saw the first of his pitiful patients, did his anger drain and he thought of Isla with renewed compassion and an exasperated tenderness. She was so helpless, so incapable of coping with life alone; he should not expect from her the same independence and strength he looked for in others. She needed him and, in spite of all irritation, he still loved her. He would tell her so, at the end of his day. He might even take her a posy of flowers, if he could find any.

Nevertheless, he wished she would not complain about the anatomy theatre. It was the principal pleasure of his life now, to look from his study window and see the walls growing higher, till finally, in the smoky splendour of autumn when the trees glowed russet and golden and the grass on the drying green withered to pale straw, the cupola on the roof was set in place and all was ready for the new anatomy theatre to receive its lecturers, its pupils, and its 'subjects'.

'Tom,' said Rachel one dark December morning when he and Jamie came in from the seamen's school which they attended regularly, if with increasing unwillingness as they grew older. 'I wish you would go over to Dr Noble's house for me and ask if Isla can spare Pearl? I have a deal of paperwork to get through and I would welcome her help. Say,' she added, 'that Pearl may bring wee Andrew and Amelia with her, if it would help, for Kirsty will mind them, I am sure. Oh, and you had better say too that Aunt Isla is very welcome to come herself if she would like a change of scene and a wee news with Kirsty over a fly cup, till Pearl and I are through.'

'Can I go too, Ma?' asked Jamie, reaching out for a wedge of fresh bread and consuming it in two mouthfuls. Jamie was tall for his twelve years, sturdily built, with thick dark hair and a baby's fresh complexion. His blue eyes were usually dancing with mischief or plain merriment and his one and all-consuming love was the sea and the tall ships that sailed her. His father had promised to take him on himself, as an official apprentice, and Jamie could hardly contain his impatience till he reached the magic age of thirteen when James Christie had promised to sign his papers.

Tom, on the other hand, was still small and undergrown, with pale brown hair and unusual, tawny eyes. 'A late developer,' his father told him kindly, rumpling his hair, but his energy was inexhaustible, his quick wits and lively mind the bane of his teacher and the delight of his friends. His aptitude for things mechanical was prodigious and it was his delight to beg a lift in the harbour tug boat, the *Paul Jones*, or to explore the engine room of the *Jessica* whenever she was in port. For George Abercrombie, part owner of the vessel, had a soft spot for Riga Tom and had even suggested to James Christie that Tom be apprenticed on the *Jessica* where he could learn about steam-engines as well as sail. Tom himself was torn between loyalty to James Christie whom he both loved and hero-worshipped with a fierce, unquestioning devotion, and his yearning for a knowledge beyond the straightforward partnership of wind and sail. Had the Christies owned a steam-ship, there would have been no conflict: as it was, Tom's brain whirled round and round with arguments as the time grew closer to the day when he and Jamie would be apprenticed and both sign away their lives for seven years.

But on this particular December day the question was a simple one, and easily answered. Riga Tom worshipped his Ma with a secret yearning love he knew, in his heart, she did not feel for him, and looked on any task she asked of him as a privilege and a blessing.

'No, you can't,' said Rachel now, addressing Jamie. 'Your Da and your Uncle Maitland need you in the yard. And you too, Tom,' she added with the scrupulous fairness Tom had noted long ago but which had never, even in infancy, deceived him. The hurt, however, if there had ever been one, had long been assimilated into the daily bustle and interest of the Christie household. 'But you can go on down, Tom, after you've been to Aunt Isla's. You'll run faster than Jamie,' she added in unnecessary explanation, 'and you'll not dawdle on the way, or get diverted by any sideshow or rumpus that you might see.'

That, at least, was true. For when Rachel sent him on

a message, as she had learned long ago, Tom was swift and competent, and absolutely reliable. Jamie, her beloved Jamie, on the other hand was liable to wander home two hours later with some diverting tale of a pedlar with a performing monkey or a fight outside the Lemon Tree Tavern, and it was only when Rachel went in search of the butter or the eggs she had sent him for that Jamie remembered he had forgotten them on the cassies in the Green. Jamie would be abject and remorseful, Rachel would forgive him instantly, and they would hug each other in reconciliation.

When Tom, on the other hand, executed his messages perfectly, she would smile, say 'Thank you, Tom,' and kiss him lightly on the forehead so that he felt vaguely rebuked, as if what he had done had not been quite good enough.

Now he said swiftly, 'Yes, Ma. Of course I will go.' He took the bread and cheese she offered him and set off across the Square, munching it as he went and impervious to the thin drizzle which had gathered in the grey December air. At the corner he turned, as they all did, to wave to the slim figure in the doorway. She called after him, 'Take care, Tom.'

'I will.' He squared his shoulders with the responsibility of his errand and turned the corner into the long, grey mist of the Fittiegait. He was not afraid of the winter gloom of short days and nights that began as soon as midday was past; nor of the shadowed closes and murky wynds lit only by an occasional gas-light or a single candle in an unshuttered window. He did not mind the echoing footsteps in an empty alley, or even the tales of the 'Burkers' waiting at some lonely corner to pounce on the unsuspecting. Or, if he did mind, he pushed the thought firmly away: for was he not a Christie, with a name to maintain? He would not give his parents any cause to

312

regret taking him and loving him as their son – and even were he quaking like a jelly pudding inside, no one would ever know. But today, though clouds had long obscured the winter sun, it was not yet quite dark and as his eyes grew used to the trailing mist which clung to the harbour water, he saw that the Quay was cheerful with lamplight from shipyards and warehouses, ship's chandlers and taverns. A ship, the *Jessica*, was unloading at Pocra in a scattered pool of light and there was an air of cheerful bustle which challenged the dour December day to do its worst. A herring gull swooped hopefully as Tom passed, then lifted up again with a bad tempered squawk to seek its food elsewhere. Tom grinned. He liked the herring gulls. They were such noisy, greedy and persistent company on the long shore line of the bay, ranged in hopeful rows along the north pier, waiting for the fishing fleet, or merely squabbling as they were now, over the harbour garbage. But he had no time to dawdle as he would have liked to do beside the *Jessica*, no time to chat with the engineer or beg a visit to the engine room. He had a message to deliver and resolutely kept his eyes on the Quay ahead.

Riga Tom liked visiting the Nobles' house. If he was lucky and Dr Andrew was in, he might let Tom look through his microscope at the slides he had of human hairs and bits of skin. And if the doctor was out, then at least he could be sure of a slab of Aunt Isla's gingerbread or one of her shortbread biscuits, and a chance to see Amelia. Seven-year-old Amelia with her golden ringlets and her round pink cheeks was the most beautiful girl Tom had ever seen and he had loved her for years with a secret fervour he confessed to no one, not even Jamie. Now, he felt in his pocket for the few pennies he had saved from this and that and resolved to buy Amelia a

313

ribbon or a sugar plum on the way. At the thought of her face when she saw his present, his spirits lifted.

He whistled jauntily as he continued along the Fittiegait, past the splendid entrance to the Christie yard and on towards the town. He could have gone the back way, up Castle Hill, but he preferred to follow the Quay, noting the ships in dock, the cargoes, and filling his lungs with the familiar scent of fish, seaweed, whale oil from the boil sheds, and smoke. There was coal smoke from the steamtug, chugging away towards the harbour mouth, wood smoke and peat smoke, smoke from the chimneys of the town, and the particularly pungent reek from the long, low sheds where haddock or salmon were strung in regiments and smoked to golden yellow or a deep, aromatic pink.

The Green was bustling with assorted life as he emerged from the Shiprow and pushed his way through the press, stopping only to buy a pink sugar mouse from a pedlar and a length of blue ribbon. Then he hurried on along the old path which led under the bridge and up again, following the meanders of the Denburn towards the bleaching green and the hospital. It was dark under the bridge and Tom quickened his steps. There, to his right, was the new building which Dr Andrew was so proud of and which Aunt Isla hated. A dim light glowed from the cupola roof, like a ghostly halo against the lowering sky and there was an odd smell in the air – a combination perhaps of the reek from the neighbouring tannery and the assorted debris left by the recent building operations and now, apparently, become a general rubbish tip. A group of small boys rooted inquisitively among the debris, a mongrel dog yapping and bounding at their heels, while a handful of women with folded linen in their arms, or baskets, stood gossiping on the corner of St Andrew Street. A whistle sounded from the tannery: they must be

314

finishing work early. Tom looked briefly towards that newly completed building, wondered whether Dr Andrew would be there or at home, and went on his way, past the anatomy theatre and on up the hill.

He was almost at the door of the Nobles' house when he became aware of a commotion behind him: shouts from the direction of St Andrew Street and running feet. 'A corpse!' a child shrieked, and someone else, 'In pieces!' For a brief moment Tom saw the mongrel dog worrying something in the rubbish and barking in frenzied excitement, then the street beyond the tip filled suddenly with shouting men as the tannery doors opened and the workmen spilled out. Others appeared miraculously from tenement and close, women shrieked, children yelled and squealed, dogs barked and as Tom stood transfixed and as fascinated as Jamie ever was by any sideshow, the cries swelled to a concerted roar of hatred. He heard the sudden battering of many fists against barred doors and at that moment a frightened voice behind him cried, 'What is it? What is happening?'

Tom remembered his errand and his responsibility and hurried the last few yards to Mrs Noble's spruce little garden and open front door.

'I am not sure, Aunt Isla,' he said, 'but I think it would be best if we went inside and barred the door. I came with a message,' he explained when Isla had let him in and done as he suggested, shooting the heavy iron bolt nervously into its socket. 'From my mother. She asked if Pearl could come to help her, and bring all of you with her, for a visit, but . . .' he finished doubtfully, glancing towards the window, 'it might be best to see first.' He stopped, expecting Mrs Noble, as his mother would have done, to take over, but instead she collapsed into a chair, her face ashen, her hands trembling, and her eyes huge with terror. Amelia, running into the room from the

315

kitchen to see who had come, saw her mother's face and promptly began to cry.

'Whatever is the matter?' demanded Pearl, emerging from the kitchen, her hands white with flour and wearing an apron much too big for her. Mrs Mutch had the afternoon off to visit a sick relative and Pearl had the kitchen, happily, to herself. Her light brown hair was tied up in a kerchief and she had flour on one cheek and more on her skirt. 'Amelia, what are you crying for, pet? I promised you could make a wee gingerbread mannie, remember?'

'There's some sort of disturbance in the town,' said Tom worriedly. 'Is Dr Andrew here?'

'No. He's at the new anatomy theatre. There's only Booky.' Ten-year-old Andrew was known, as his father had once been, by the tee-name of Booky, for reasons which two minutes in his company made obvious. It was already accepted that he would go for the Bursary Competition as soon as he was fourteen. Meanwhile, he spent every working hour in the company of the printed word, in whatever form he could find it. At school, he took every prize there was. At home, he retired to the corner of his father's study, which he had long ago established as his own, and read.

Now, as the external commotion and internal consternation impinged upon his reverie, he emerged blinking from the pages of Homer's *Iliad* and said mildly, 'What? Did someone call me?'

'Yes,' said Pearl with brisk efficiency. 'Get up and look out of the window for us. Tell us what is happening. And if ye canna' see from there, the two of ye go down the lane a wee bittie. But mind and take care. It's all right, Ma,' she soothed, 'We'll look after you. There's nae reason to be feart. Tom and Booky'll just have a wee lookie and see what's afoot. They'll nae be long.'

316

'Not Andrew!' cried Isla, distraught. 'He is not to go outside. Do you hear me?' She clutched her son's hand and clung to it. 'I forbid it, Andy. I need you here.'

Tom had long known that Aunt Isla loved her son with a passion equal to his own mother's love for Jamie. Sometimes it made him lonely, but today he felt only compassion.

'You stay with your mother, Booky,' said Tom, 'and look after her. I will go. I'll not be long. Don't cry, Amelia,' he added gently. 'See, I brought you a wee mousie.' He left her studying the sugar mouse with tearful delight and slipped quickly through the door into the suddenly threatening afternoon.

'Dinna' go far,' warned Pearl, for the noise which rose from the direction of St Andrew Street had grown to tumultuous proportions. Through the gathering gloom of the afternoon it looked as if the bleach green was a sea of people and the neighbouring streets were filling fast. Anxiously she watched his small but valiant figure diminish down the path and disappear. He was a good lad.

Tom had not been out of sight two minutes before a great roar penetrated even the barred door of the cottage and through the window Pearl saw a sudden flame leap high into the early darkness. A moment later, when she opened the door to his knocking, Tom almost fell into the room, his face white and anxious.

'The town's gone mad!' he gasped. 'There's hundreds of folk in the streets and *they're burning the anatomy hall!'*

Isla Noble screamed.

Andrew Noble surveyed the empty classroom with satisfaction. On wooden trestles under the window lay three 'subjects', stretched out ready for dissection and demonstration. Indeed, one of the subjects had already been 'opened' and a lecture given on the frontal lobe of the cerebrum. The instruments were laid out ready on a steel tray, the long canvas aprons folded neatly waiting to be donned by the student anatomists. The first three students were even now arriving at the door with Dr Moir himself. Andrew Noble reached for an apron and was tying the string at his waist when he became aware of a hammering from the back of the building, then a crash of splintering wood and the thunder of many feet on the stairs.

'What on earth . . .?' began someone, but the door of the classroom burst open and the room was suddenly full of men, roaring 'Kill the Burkers!', wielding lengths of timber, kicking, punching, swearing.

'Quick!' cried Dr Moir. 'This way.' He ducked and ran, Andrew Noble and the three students close at his heels, towards a connecting door to a smaller room. Once through the door, they slammed it behind them and pushed a heavy table against it, but the battering ram they had expected did not immediately fall. The mob had found the 'subjects', blatant proof of the doctors' villainy, and their rage, for the moment, had been diverted as they set about lifting the bodies on to makeshift stretchers amid cries of 'To the Drum aisle!' These stretchers were bundled down the stairs and carried out into the crowd and when the first, uncovered corpse appeared a concerted gasp of horror rose from the assembled populace, followed instantaneously by a roar of 'Burn the house down! Burn the Burkin' Shop!'

'This way,' urged Dr Moir, bounding down a short back stairway. 'There is a side door. It is our only hope. Good luck, my friends, and God go with you.'

He opened the door and one by one doctor and students slipped through into the gloom of the side alley.

'There he goes!' cried a sharp-eyed tanner and in an instant the pack was baying after Dr Moir while another spied Andrew Noble, distinctive in the canvas apron he

318

had not yet managed to take off. But when, with whoops and shouts of exultation, half-a-dozen men assaulted him, the apron was ripped away in an instant and Andrew fell to the ground. At that moment the timber that had been hastily piled against the wall of the anatomy hall burst into flame with a roar that sent everyone leaping back out of range of the heat and sparks. In the confusion Andrew rolled over twice, scrambled to his feet, ducked, dodged, and ran. But he had been seen. 'After him!' roared his pursuers and the river of rioters swirled, gathered strength and poured in a torrent of venomous fury close on Andrew's heels.

Abercrombie was counting the stock in his wine cellar, a favourite occupation of his and one he savoured with particular enjoyment, when an ominous rumble interrupted his tranquillity. The ground shook under his feet, the window rattled, and there was a roar as of an approaching tidal wave or buffalo stampede. Surprised, he put down the glass of claret he had been sampling and went to the door. The wine cellar led off what had been part of the shop, until the opening of the new premises in Union Street, and was now a store room for various selected stock. The window, however, looked on to the street and what Abercrombie saw through its unshuttered panes made him leap across the flagstoned floor and shoot home the bolt on the outside door. Then he slammed the shutters closed, barred them, and called up the stairs, 'Kirsty? Kirsty! Close the shutters. The world's gone mad.' Then he made at the run for the back regions and the door into the garden. No riotous mob was going to steal his claret without a fight.

Kirsty Abercrombie was taking tea with Euphemia Farquharson and Louise Forbes in the upstairs drawing room and did not at first hear. The occasion was not entirely social – if it had been, Louise's mother would also have been there, but committees, she declared, always made her sleepy and this particular afternoon involved the hospital blanket sub-committee. Business was not yet over: the question of a collection and distribution rota was proving difficult, especially in view of the latest cholera scare. Euphemia, thought Kirsty Abercrombie, was proving particularly awkward. It might be a good move to get her daughter-in-law Jessica elected on to the committee, for moral support. Since young Finlay's birth Jessica had mellowed into quite an agreeable girl, one way and another. Quieter than she used to be, more willing to please. Musing on her daughter-in-law's maturing character, Mrs Abercrombie absent-mindedly filled up her own tea-cup. 'Oh, I am so sorry, Louise dear. May I pour you some more?' At that moment a particularly violent shout from the street penetrated even her fire-lit cocoon and she put down the teapot and hurried to the window, followed closely by her guests.

'Whatever is going on?'

'It's a riot!'

'A ravening mob with staves and cudgels.'

'Close the shutters before the windows are broken.'

'No, wait.' Euphemia held the shutters closed but for a careful crack, and peered into the lamplit street below. 'They're making for Dr Moir's house. They're surrounding it. They're throwing stones.'

'They're after his blood again, the poor devil,' said George Abercrombie grimly from the doorway. 'I told you to shut that, woman, and bar it. Do ye want to invite a boulder through your window? I've locked the wine cellar, barred every shutter in the place but these, and pushed the table against the door for good measure, but I hope to God they spend their lust for mischief before they move down the street to us.'

'But what is the cause of the rioting?' demanded Louise Forbes, her face paler than usual, her ears alert. 'Did I hear something about "Burking"?'

'Aye, ye did lass. They're baying for the doctor's blood. And if they canna' get his, I reckon any doctor's will do. Or any student's, come to that. There must be ten thousand folk out there in the streets chanting and shouting. Just listen to them.'

For a moment there was silence in the room; only the soft purr of the gas lamp and the crackle of the fire. Then from outside, apparently from all over town, came the rumbling roar of a mob on the rampage, punctuated by the noise of splintering windows, snapping timbers, and the intermittent crash of falling masonry, while from their own street came a tangled cacophony of shouting and breaking glass.

Then suddenly, through that chink of shutter which Euphemia's curiosity refused to close, the sky to the west flared a brilliant scarlet under a billowing curtain of black cloud. Wood ash danced on the wind with the acrid smell of burning tar. 'They're burning the new anatomy hall!' gasped Abercrombie. 'The *fools*!' But the crowd below had also seen the glow in the sky, a glow which illuminated for one brief moment the figure of Dr Moir escaping from a back window. 'After him!' came the concerted cry and the mob whirled with one accord and set off at a gallop for the Gallowgate and the labyrinth of streets beyond. In another minute the Guestrow had drained of rioters like a sink with the plug removed and all that remained on the cassies was a scattering of broken glass and missiles and a single, scavenging dog.

'Poor devil,' breathed Abercrombie. 'He did that to draw the crowd away from honest folk. We owe him thanks.'

'I pray to God he escapes,' said Louise. Mrs Abercrombie, too agitated to speak, had collapsed into a chair and was making ineffectual attempts to open her phial of sal volatile.

'Where are the magistrates? That's what I want to know,' demanded Euphemia. 'Why isn't the town guard on the streets? Or the militia? It is a disgrace! I don't know why we elect such people if they make no effort to protect our interests. No effort whatsoever.'

'I must go home,' said Louise, her face white and anxious.

'You will do no such thing,' declared Mrs Farquharson. 'You will be murdered in the street!'

'You must both stay here,' gasped Mrs Abercrombie, the phial successfully opened and being passed to and fro beneath her nose. 'Until the city is quiet again. I will order another kettle for tea and perhaps, George dear, a little brandy? For the nerves?'

'I *must* go,' insisted Louise, collecting cloak and gloves. 'I am sorry. Please let me out, Mr Abercrombie.'

'At least let one of the servants go with you,' called Mrs Abercrombie after her, but Louise did not hear. All she heard was the roar of that distant crowd, with the different roar of the flames which were consuming Andrew's new anatomy hall. And wasn't Andrew himself teaching there this very afternoon? As soon as Mr Abercrombie had the latch off the door, Louise slipped through the crack with hardly a goodbye, bunched up her skirts in her hands, and ran.

'What shall we do?' said Pearl worriedly. She glanced at her mother who, after that first scream, had broken into hysterical laughter, more frightening even than the scream. Pearl had managed to calm her, sponged her face with cool water laced with eau-de-Cologne, and tucked a rug over her knees. Since then, Isla, though still deathly white, had not spoken a word. 'We can't stay here.'

'Why not?' asked Amelia and it was Tom who told her kindly that Auntie Rachel had asked them all to tea and would be worried if they did not come.

'If they are burning the anatomy hall,' whispered Pearl anxiously, drawing Tom aside, 'they may be hostile to the doctors too, and the doctors' houses.'

'We'd best go to Footdee,' decided Tom, 'and quickly, while the Hall's still burning and before they turn to other mischief. Get your plaid, Pearl, and be sure Amelia has her wee fur mittens. There's a nip in the air today and I fear it's offering to snow.'

'Here's your pelisse, Ma,' said Pearl, attempting to wrap the woollen garment round her shoulders. 'We are all going to Auntie Rachel's.' But Isla only said, in a toneless voice, 'No.'

'Come on, Ma,' urged Booky, 'It'll be quieter in the Square and Auntie Rachel will give us tea.'

'No. You go, dear. Though don't be too long. You know I don't like you to be out late.'

'You *can't* stay. It isna' safe, Ma. You *must* come.' Pearl tugged at her arm to no avail.

'I will wait here for your father. Then I will follow.' She seemed to have forgotten her anxiety for Booky, her fear, everything, and was strangely calm. Almost smiling. It gave Pearl an uncomfortable feeling. 'Your father will be sure to come for me, and what will he say if we are gone?'

'I will leave a note, Ma,' said Pearl. 'See.' She scribbled something quickly on a scrap of paper and weighted it with an inkwell 'There. Now *come.*'

'Please come, Aunt Isla,' said Tom. 'I will be worried to leave you and I cannot let the others go alone.' Still she refused.

'Mrs Mutch will be here directly, Tom. I will be fine.'

323

Through the window, the sky was red above St Andrew Street and he thought of Pearl's words: *'They'll seek the doctors next.'* 'What shall we do, Booky?' he whispered.

'Do as Ma says, of course. It's best.' Booky seemed unconcerned, but then everything was of academic interest to Booky, not really *real*, and besides, the children had learned long ago not to 'upset' Isla. Amelia began to cry again and Tom made up his mind. He would take the children to Footdee as Aunt Isla said. He had been long enough as it was: his mother would be waiting for Pearl's help and his father was expecting him at the Christie yard. But he was not happy. He wished his Ma was here to tell him what was the right thing to do. He wanted only that she should be proud of him – and love him. 'Come on, Pearl,' he whispered. 'We'd best hurry.'

Five minutes later the four children were dodging through the shadows beyond the Denburn, Pearl clutching Booky's hand, Tom holding Amelia's, and all of them running.

As soon as they were safely gone, Isla Noble smiled with the glee she had not dared to show her children and the laughter spread inside her, blotting out all else, as the red stain spread across the sky. They were burning the anatomy hall! She had always hated it and now it would be gone. Andrew would no longer go there to do dreadful things in secret. No longer go out at night when he thought she did not know, with wooden spades and sacks. No longer snip and probe and extract with the twin points of his forceps the slippery threads of someone's spent life. She felt jubilation gather inside her until she laughed aloud: they were burning the anatomy hall and at last she would be free! Andrew would be hers, with no time for anything or anyone except his own house and his own family. With the anatomy hall destroyed he'd have no more need to talk of limbs and muscles with that Forbes woman, no more need of those terrifying diagrams and pages of meticulous notes. No need of anyone but her . . .

Slowly she stood up, crossed to the mirror above the dresser and lifted pale hands to re-adjust pale hair. Pearl had really had no need to fuss and fluster. Sometimes anyone would think Pearl was the mother and she, Isla, the daughter. At the thought Isla smiled and a dimple appeared in one cheek, as it used to do, years ago. She was still young, still pretty. When Andrew came home it would be like those early, happier days, before the children, before the anatomy hall, before Louise. He would find her here, waiting for him, with no one else to demand his attention. She dabbed eau-de-Cologne behind her ears, turned sideways to admire her profile, smoothed the folds of her soft woollen dress. Then an idea struck her. She hurried across the narrow hall and into the bedroom, opened the clothes' kist and felt among the lavender-scented folds. Triumphant, she straightened, closed the lid and went back into the parlour. There she set the lace collar carefully over the neck of her gown and adjusted the butterfly points to fall exactly so. Davy had given her the collar, years ago before Pearl was born. Dear, dead Davy . . . But she had been wearing the collar when Andrew, her husband, had first met her, taken her in, cared for her. When he saw her wearing it again, he would remember and there would be no one in the world but the two of them, together.

She stared into the mirror in tender reverie, oblivious of everything but her dream. Until slowly she became aware that in the depths of the mirror her own window was reflected and the night sky beyond, which should have been black and instead was garish red. Pearl's words when Tom asked for Dr Andrew drifted into her thoughts with cruel intrusion and suddenly she realized.

325

'They are burning the anatomy hall – *and Andrew with it!*'

With a high scream of anguish she ran bonnetless, cloakless out of the house and down the lane towards the town, leaving the door standing open behind her and the lamp still lit.

Andrew Noble ran as he had never run in his life before, dodging down side alleys, scrambling over walls, weaving this way and that till he had lost all direction and his pursuers had dwindled to a half-hearted handful. He crouched, panting, in the lee of a hencoop, to find his bearings and to wipe the blood from his eyes. Someone had thrown a stone which had struck him above the left eyebrow and the blood flowed irritatingly fast. His once-white neck-stock had come undone long ago and he used an end of it to staunch the blood while he waited, heart pounding painfully fast, ears straining for sounds of pursuit. Later, in the blessed silence, he studied the skyline with his good eye and tried to work out where he was. If the glow above his burning hall was to his right, then the spires of St Nicholas should be somewhere south . . .

It would be madness to try to go home past the anatomy hall and the bleaching green, while the fire still burnt and the crowd still roared for blood. It would be best to lie low for a while, till the mob found some other diversion, or were dispersed. At least Isla and the children were safe at home. He held the pad of linen against his brow and felt the cloth moisten with seeping warmth. Isla would faint if she saw him in this state – blood-stained, his clothes in shreds. What a ridiculous, stupid business the whole thing was. Thinking of the new anatomy hall that was to have ushered in a golden age of medical knowledge and which was now a heap of smouldering ashes,

Andrew could have wept had his anger not choked the grief in his throat. He hoped Dr Moir had escaped safely to his house in the Guestrow. He would have dodged up Schoolhill, through St Nicholas's churchyard perhaps, into Correction Wynd and the Netherkirkgate. Thinking of Correction Wynd, Andrew remembered one place where his appearance would cause no fainting hysteria, except perhaps in the mother, and knew, with relief, what he would do.

Louise Forbes did not go straight home. Instead she went to the top of Schoolhill from where, together with a posse of similarly interested citizens, she had an excellent view of the burning anatomy hall. One of them told her the hall was already gutted, its walls toppled and its timbers tossed on to the flames. 'Was anyone inside?' she asked, dreading the answer.

'Aye, but they escaped, more's the pity. Took to the streets. Folk are hunting them now, the murderous Burkers.'

Louise had heard all she needed to know. There was nothing she could do to help Andrew except go home, and wait.

By the time Tom reached the corner of the North Square with the lighted window of his own home clearly visible, he knew what he must do. 'Tell Ma,' he urged Pearl, 'that I've gone to fetch Aunt Isla. I'm nae happy about leaving her there alone and if she willna' come, I'll stay with her till Dr Andrew comes home.' Before Pearl could dissuade him, he had gone, weaving in and out of the shadows in the direction of the town. Night had fallen early on that winter afternoon and the deserted Castlegate was already in a darkness spattered by fitful gas lamps and a watchman's lantern. But even as Tom emerged into the square, there came the sound of drums and marching feet and soldiers of the 79th Regiment the Cameron Highlanders swung down from Castlehill, on their way to the scene of the riot.

Already Lord Provost John Hadden had arrived, with his magistrates and a special Day Patrol, and had tried to make a conciliatory and soothing speech, but the crowd had drowned most of his words in cheers as yet another section of the hall collapsed in a sheet of flame. He tried to read the Riot Act but with no greater success. As by now well over ten thousand people thronged the city streets, in various states of disorder, there was nothing anyone could do but stand aside and watch as Dr Moir's precious hall was systematically destroyed. When the fire brigade arrived they were told outright to leave the fire alone. Havoc ruled. But the old streets round the Green were comparatively quiet as Tom ran, weaving nimbly under the bridge and up the old road, skirting the main mass of the rioting populace who had been drawn like moths to a candle by the inferno in St Andrew Street. When he reached the lane to Dr Andrew's house beyond the Denburn, he saw the lamplit window from the foot of the little hill and slowed his steps with relief . . . only to break into an anxious run when he realized that the wedge of light came not from a window but from the open door.

'Aunt Isla?' He stepped inside, into empty parlour, empty kitchen, empty scullery and finally, empty bedroom. Aunt Isla had gone. Baffled, Tom stood in the open doorway pondering. Something was wrong. Had she gone into the town in search of Dr Andrew? Should he wait till she came back? Anxiously he wondered what his Ma would want him to do. She had told him to fetch Aunt Isla too, if she wanted to come. But Aunt Isla had not wanted. Aunt Isla had said she would wait for her husband and now she had gone. Perhaps Dr Andrew had come back to fetch her and they had both gone to his Ma's house in the Square? But why had they not shut the door? That open door worried him. He saw Pearl's note, in hasty copperplate, still on the table where she had left it. *'Gone to Aunt Rachel's.'* That at least was plain enough. But why was it still there if Dr Andrew had come back again? Or had Aunt Isla changed her mind as soon as Tom and the others had left and come running after them? That seemed the most likely explanation. But then where was Dr Andrew? Tom could make nothing of it and the more he puzzled the more possible explanations whirled in his head to confuse him. *What ought he to do?* What would his father expect him to do? And his Ma? At last the boy made up his mind. First, he would go down into the town to see what was happening – Aunt Isla might have gone to the anatomy hall to look for Dr Andrew. Then he would go back to Dr Andrew's house, and if it was still empty, he would go home to the Square. As like as not he would find Aunt Isla there before him, with Dr Andrew and the rest of them, all eating and drinking at the table, an empty place waiting for him and his Ma frowning and a little worried because he was late. But if he went straight home, without even looking, he would be ashamed. Carefully he turned down the lamp, closed the door and set off at a run down the lane.

The December night was clammy with the familiar chill that always crept in with the haar – a bone-piercing, muscle-aching chill which penetrated the wool of his handknitted jersey and the finer wool of his vest and set him shivering till, as he approached St Andrew Street, a waft of hot air brushed his face with a cloud of flying wood ash. The scene before him was like nothing he had ever seen: at the centre a fireball of twisted timbers and, spreading all around it in wave after surging wave, hundreds and hundreds of people, the faces of the nearest tinged red by the leaping flames, and the rest a heaving, grumbling, constantly shifting mass. Then someone levered a girder under the one remaining wall of the building and it fell with a roar of leaping flame and a crackle of sparks which shot into the air to fall haphazard on the upturned faces of the crowd. In the sudden wave of heat which buffeted Tom's face, he realized what had troubled him about that empty cottage. Aunt Isla's pelisse had lain where Pearl had left it, over a chair beside the fire. He was standing irresolute, puzzling over the implications, trying to reason why she should do such a thing, when suddenly a cry rang out from the edge of the crowd. 'Here's one o' the Burkin' rascals! Let's get him next!' The crowd split, swirled and flowed in a column of whooping frenzy after a single, black-clad, terrified figure who sped round the corner of Crooked Lane and out of sight.

With a thud of alarm, Tom realized that that black-clad fugitive was a medical student, or a doctor. Perhaps even Dr Andrew? Suddenly the city where he had spent most of his young life was a huge and alien place, full of violence and evil. He shuddered and shrank back into the shadows, trembling now with fear as much as cold. He wanted only to be safe at home, with his Ma at the fireside and his family all around him. He wanted Jamie for company. He wanted anything but this shivering, frightening darkness. But what would his Ma think if she asked him, 'Where is Aunt Isla?' and he said 'I don't know'?

'*Pater noster, qui es in coelis* . . .' he prayed, 'Tell me what I should do.'

Isla Duthie Noble pushed and fought her way like a mad thing into the centre of the crowd at the anatomy hall. No one heeded her, thinking, if they thought at all, that her frenzy was directed as theirs was against the Burkers. But

330

even Isla realized, when she saw the blazing pyramid of tangled timbers, that no one could remain alive inside it. 'Where are they?' she screamed at her nearest neighbour. 'Where are the doctors?'

'Fled,' came the gleeful answer. 'Awa' through the toon like foxes wi' all the hounds o' hell at their heels.'

Isla turned and was pushing her way back out of the crowd when the medical student was spotted. 'There's one o' them!' yelled a voice at her back. A hundred heads turned and for a moment Isla saw clearly the solitary, black-clad figure who broke out of the crowd and ran. '*Andrew!*' she shrieked. She was not to know it was an unknown medical student, drawn by fateful curiosity. '*Andrew!*'

But before she knew what was happening, she was being swept along in the torrent, while her communicative neighbour yelled, 'Down wi' the bloody rascal! Kill the Burker!'

'No,' she screamed, running and stumbling beside him. 'Don't touch him!' She clutched wildly at the fellow's arm but he, like everyone, was jostling and shoving in trampling pursuit and her fingers slipped. 'No!' she screamed again, clutching at his clothes and hanging on while her feet stumbled on the uneven ground and she struggled to keep her balance. But he merely lashed behind him to dislodge whatever dragged at his back and with an oath ran on. 'Kill the Burker!' he bellowed. 'After him!' Isla sobbed and stumbled and struggled to keep up with him till her grip slipped, she staggered, lost her footing, grabbed wildly at the nearest man, fell, was dragged several yards before her fingers lost their grip, then fell again, to be trampled underfoot and finally abandoned, one more insignificant scrap of debris in the trail of havoc that swept the town that night.

* * *

Tom found her two hours later in an alley off Crooked Lane where she had dragged herself, moaning. It was the moan that had attracted his attention as he crept nervously along the lane. He had had some idea of going to Louise Forbes's house, but while the crowd milled and thrashed in the streets, burning things and swearing and chasing anyone remotely resembling a medical student, the boy had been too frightened to move very far. From his position at the foot of the lane to Dr Andrew's house, he could see if anyone went to the house and he could also see the smouldering remains of the anatomy hall. Between the two, he reasoned, Aunt Isla would surely appear sometime if she was, as he had decided, searching for Dr Andrew. Dr Andrew himself would be hiding somewhere or . . . But the boy turned hastily away from that sombre possibility. So he had crouched, shivering and miserable, in his protective doorway and waited for the rumpus to die down. By the time the crowd had thinned to isolated, marauding bands of twos and threes it was long past curfew and Tom was cold to the marrow of his young bones. At least his Ma would not be worrying. Pearl would have given her his message, word for word, and she would think he was at Aunt Isla's house. But no one had gone there, he was certain. It was then that he thought of visiting Aunt Louise and asking her advice. She was always so sensible and understanding. She would help him. He had slipped through the shadows of St Andrew Street, scurrying past any dubious shape or particularly dense patch of darkness, to the corner of Crooked Lane which led to Schoolhill, St Nicholas's church and, beyond, Correction Wynd. The lane was narrow, twisting between high walls which clipped the sky to a mere moonless strip. A single, failing, gas lamp glimmered over the cassies which were slippery with moisture from the insidious haar which crept everywhere now, shrouding the rooftops in murky mist.

He thought at first that the moan came from some kitten, locked out or lost, or a hungry dog perhaps, whimpering in the cold. Then through the gloom cast by that mist-shrouded gas lamp, he made out a scrap of white, and what looked like a woman's face, then the huddled shape of her against the wall. He hesitated, thinking her a vagrant, or a drunk. Then she moaned again and at the same instant he saw that the scrap of white which had first caught his eye was a lace collar. 'Aunt Isla?' Tom dropped to his knees beside her, anxiously peering into her strange, blotched face. 'Aunt Isla? Are you all right?' She made no answer and he saw that she had been crying. She had a lump on her forehead and her leg was twisted under her in a strange position. Her hand was cold when he touched it and her clothes damp and torn. 'Come home,' he urged, tugging at her hand. 'I will take you. You will be safe with me.'

This time she spoke, but he could not make out the words. Something about Andrew. But when he tried again to make her move, she screamed.

'What is it, Aunty? Where are you hurt?' the boy asked anxiously, but she had slumped sideways and he saw that her eyes were shut.

'*Kyrie eleison, Kyrie eleison, Kyrie eleison,*' he gabbled, 'What shall I do?' He could call for help – but then supposing vandals heard, or thieves? He could leave Aunt Isla and go on to Aunt Louise's house, but suppose a real Burker came and took her away while he was gone? Isla moaned, opened her eyes suddenly and saw him. 'Tom! Don't leave me!' She clutched his hand with surprising strength and he could not draw it away. 'Stay with me. I'm so afraid. So cold . . .'

'I will stay, Aunt Isla. Of course I'll stay.' There was

nothing else he could do. 'And when the watchman comes this way, I will ask him to help us.' But the watchman did not come. Too much had happened in Aberdeen that night and there was other work to attend to. The hours slipped by, the night shivered into silence and still Aunt Isla gripped his hand with terrified strength. Once she spoke: something about Dr Andrew, and again, more clearly, 'Davy.' But when Tom tried to talk to her she only mumbled incoherently or said nothing at all. But eventually her grip loosened, her hand fell back and Tom was able to withdraw his own cramped hand and massage it, rubbing and kneading to restore the circulation and finally clamping it, ice-cold, under his own armpit. But if his hand was so cold, what of Aunt Isla's? Anxiously he felt her hands, then her sleeping brow and found that her flesh was like frozen stone to his touch. 'Aunt Isla?' he peered into her face by what little light there was but she seemed calm enough and sleeping. 'Someone will come soon,' he murmured, comforting. Then, as the only thing he could think of to do, he peeled off his jersey, wrapped it awkwardly about her shoulders, and resumed his vigil.

Andrew Noble, his eyebrow neatly patched by Louise, his clothes sponged and dried and the worst of the rents mended, slipped out of the house in Correction Wynd and into the silent darkness.

'Are you sure you will be safe?' whispered Louise. 'You had far better stay the night with us.'

'No, I must go. But thank you, Louise, for all you have done.' He took both her hands in his and for a moment she thought he might kiss her. But he turned away with a brisk, 'Goodnight. Isla will be waiting. She can never sleep until I am home.' But when he reached his own house some fifteen wary minutes later, it was to find it empty, the fire dead, and a note in Pearl's handwriting saying, 'Gone to Aunt Rachel's.' Relief flooded through him. There would be no hysteria, no tearful reproaches. His family was safe in the Square and at last he could sleep.

A hammering at the door woke him an hour before dawn. He stumbled painfully from bed, for he found he was more bruised than he had realized, and called warily, 'Who is it?'

'It's me, James Christie. Is Tom with you?' Quickly Andrew drew back the bolt and opened the door. James and Maitland stood in the half-darkness with Alex behind them, carrying a storm lantern.

'Come in,' said Andrew. 'Wait till I light a lamp.' As the lamp sputtered into life, James saw Andrew's face.

'Good God, man, what have they done to you?'

'I'm fine, fine. But what's this about wee Tom?'

'Is he not with you?' There was anxiety in James's voice now and a hint of fear. 'Pearl said he was come back here, to stay with Isla till you came home.'

'But . . .' Andrew's face blanched of all remaining colour. 'But is Isla not with *you*, in the Square?'

'Oh God!' Realization struck all four together. 'Wait!' cried Andrew, scrambling for his clothes. 'There's another lantern in the scullery.'

The Christies, apparently, had grown increasingly uneasy as the night advanced and no word came from Tom. It was not like him to stay away without sending a message, whether he was at the Noble house or no, and Rachel had not been able to sleep for worrying. Finally James had wakened Maitland and Alex, left a message that the twins were to be alerted in the harbour and sent after them if they were not home within the hour, and had set out to find the lad.

Now, with Andrew hurrying and limping beside them, the Christie men began to scour the town.

It was dawn before they found them, huddled together in an alley off Crooked Lane. Tom, in his woollen vest and homespun breeches, frozen to the marrow, and Isla dead.

Andrew Noble was distraught. The sight of his helpless, timid wife, her leg broken in two places and her sweet face battered and bruised, lying dead in the common street filled him with choking anguish – but when he unwrapped that pitiful woollen jersey from her shoulders and saw the lace collar, her particular little vanity which he had often teased her about, he broke down completely and wept.

James Christie took charge. Tom was bundled into Alex's greatcoat, scooped up in Alex's arms and packed, shivering, back to the Square. 'At the double, Alex,' warned James. 'He's frozen to the bone.' James himself carried Isla gently and reverently home to her neat little house on the hill above the anatomy hall, while Maitland supported Andrew, stumbling and weeping behind them. Women were sent for, arrangements made, and the yellow gingham curtains finally drawn.

'I am sorry, Ma,' whispered Tom when Rachel met them at the cottage door, but Rachel, after the first tearful hug of relief, whisked him into bed, laid hot stones at his feet and knees, and thrust a mug of hot gruel into his hands.

'Drink this, Tom. It'll warm ye. We'll talk after.' Alex, in a quick aside, had told her of Isla's death. 'The little lad had given her his *jersey*,' he added, and Rachel bit her lip as something hard inside her snapped and an overwhelming rush of tenderness welled up to blind her eyes with tears.

'Go on, Tom,' she urged gently. 'Drink it, pet. For me.' But Tom shook his head.

'I canna', Ma. I'm nae hungry.' He was remembering Aunt Isla's dead face and Dr Andrew's tears.

'Later, perhaps,' said Rachel, taking the mug from his hands and tenderly tucking the blankets round his thin little, shivering body. 'When you have had a good, long sleep.'

But Tom's sleep turned into fever and his fever to delirium. When on the third day Jamie, distracted with anxiety for his beloved brother, cried, 'Is Tom going to die?' no one answered.

Rachel moved as in some fearful nightmare, sponging, soothing, holding water to cracked lips, watching Tom shrink and burn away, seeing his chest grow hollow, his eyes grow huge and sightless, his tossing limbs shrink to skin and bone; hearing his rasping, tortured breath, his moans and incoherent cries, scraps of his native Latvian, dredged up from some forgotten niche of childhood, snatches of local idiom, disconnected, senseless – and in spite of the aching desperation of her love for him, unable to ease or soothe his torment. She forgot Jamie, forgot Pearl and Kirsty's children, forgot all the others whom she loved, as all the strength of her heart and being were concentrated on that one small, tormented boy. Loyal, faithful, loving Tom who had never given anyone less than his best and had wrapped his dying aunt in all he had to give her, his own small jumper, and had sat shivering beside her till his duty was done. Tom, who had loved Rachel with his whole heart and against whom she had closed hers all those years ago.

She confessed, in her anguish, to James as they sat in the evening shadows at Tom's bedside. 'I have not loved him as I ought. I have wanted only other children of my own.'

'I know,' said James, his face grave. 'Did you think you could hide such a thing from me? But I hoped you would grow to love him one day.'

'I would not let myself,' acknowledged Rachel, burying her face in James's shoulder. 'I thought only of my unborn children, yearning for them and praying to God to let me conceive. Now, if only Tom is spared to me, I want no other. Tom and Jamie are blessing enough. But if he dies . . . oh, James, I do not think I could bear it!' James's own face was pale and drawn. He thought of Priit and Friida, frail and old, kept alive, he suspected, only by the promise of Tom's visit which was to have been this coming summer. How could he face them if their grandson died? How could he face life itself, with Tom gone? Tom whom he had uprooted from his home and family and taken to a strange land and who, uncomplaining always, had loved him as his father? Tom whom James loved as he loved Jamie, his natural son. Quietly he soothed his wife, comforting her as best he could, while his own heart grew chill with fear, and he prayed over and over to God to spare the child, until it was time for him to fill the water pail again and together they would sponge Tom's burning flesh in a vain effort to bring him relief. Then they would watch and sleep and watch again, one or other of them always at Tom's side.

Alex had taken Kirsty and his children to her mother's house in South Square, to avoid infection and to give Tom peace. Maitland slept at the Pocra office, but was hourly at the house to inquire for Tom, young Jamie at his side. Jamie, too, had been banished and a hammock rigged up for him on the *Steadfast*, beside Uncle Willy. The *Anya* too was in port and both twins refused to put to sea again till there was news of Tom's recovery. James's ship, the *Bonnie Annie*, was in dry dock, for careening, but had she been seaworthy he too would have stayed in harbour. For no Christie could think of anything but wee Tom's illness or do anything but hope and pray for his recovery. The men went each day to the yard, but not an hour went by without one or other of them inquiring at the house – a gentle tap on the door, a whispered, 'Any change?' Then they would go again, grave-faced and sombre, to resume whatever work was in hand, but a deadening pall of anxiety lay over the whole Christie enterprise.

George Abercrombie sent grapes and other delicacies from his shop. Louise Forbes came regularly, to sit with Rachel and give her what comfort she could, and occasionally to persuade her to rest, while Louise took her place. But Rachel could not bear to leave Tom's bedside for long, and her face grew as hollow-eyed and gaunt as the boy's. Andrew Noble called every day, though there was little he could do, he confessed, except wait for the infection to take its course. 'He's a wiry wee lad,' he told Rachel, 'with a fine fighting spirit. He may pull through.' But as the days passed with no abatement of the fever, he ceased to give her even that encouragement. The anxiety he felt on Rachel's behalf, however, diverted his attention, if only briefly, from the dragging ache of his own grief and he studied every treatise on every type of fever, working late into the night, in the hope of finding some new approach or treatment he had not tried. And all of them prayed.

Then one morning early, when James was taking his turn to sleep, Rachel smoothed the hair from the boy's brow and felt the skin cold to her touch. Her heart thudded first with fear and then with a sudden, fluttering hope. She felt his hands which were cool, his wrists where the pulse beat faint but slow, touched his brow again and his sunken, sleeping cheek. Then, as she hesitated, wondering if she dare call to James or whether any sudden sound might break the spell, Tom opened his eyes and looked at her with full recognition.

'Ma, I'm thirsty,' he whispered. 'Can I have a drink of water?'

'Of course, my pet.' She put the glass to his lips, then laid her head on his bed and wept with relief and thankfulness and the pent-up, overflowing love of ten long years.

1832

In May, the Christie family moved into No. 3 Trinity Quay. Alex and Kirsty had the top floor of the three-storey house, Rachel and James the middle, and on the ground floor were rooms for Maitland and the twins, should they want them, and a fine, panelled office, with a fireplace, a great oak desk and a brass sign reading, 'Christie's Shipping Office' over the door. At the end of that year, when cholera ravaged both North and South Squares and one in every twenty died, James was to say, with awe, 'God is on our side. For had we stayed in the Square, who knows what might have happened?'

Three months after their move to the new house, Tom and Jamie stood on the Quay beside the *Bonnie Annie*, each with a new knitted jersey, new woollen breeches and a seaman's bundle containing clean linen and several pairs of Rachel's handknitted woollen stockings. In the hold were honey and cheeses, tobacco and snuff, a barrel of best salt herrings, whisky, and a beautiful hand-knitted jersey and shawl, all presents for Friida and Priit.

'Now remember, lads,' warned Alex, cuffing them playfully round the ears. You go as passengers this time so make the most of it. Next time ye'll go as signed apprentices and work for your keep. It'll be the cat o' nine tails and the holystone for you then, lads, and Cap'n Christie's a terrible hard man to work for.' He dodged James's hand just in time and skipped out of reach.

'It'll be the cat for you, too, *Captain* Christie,' growled

James, 'if ye dinna' get back to your ship. Ye've passengers waiting, remember, and a new ship's doctor.'

For Alex, in gratitude for Tom's recovery and following three disastrous years of whaling, had finally agreed to come back into the Christie fleet. He was to sail the *Rachel Christie* to New Brunswick on the afternoon tide, with sixteen cabin passengers and one hundred steerage, all en route for a new life. Andrew Noble was to go as ship's doctor.

'I need time away from everything I know,' he had explained to Rachel. 'From Aberdeen, the hospital, the anatomy theatre, everything. Time to sort out my feelings and my thoughts and to assimilate my grief.' His children were to stay with Rachel during his absence and his house was to be closed. 'Pearl or Mrs Mutch can go in now and then to air it,' he explained to Rachel, 'so that it will be ready for me when I return.' Privately, Rachel doubted whether he would live in it again. Louise Forbes had a house in the West End which was much more suited to be a doctor's house.

'Come on, lads,' said James Christie. 'Say your farewells and get aboard. The pilot's waiting.'

'Goodbye, Ma!' Jamie hugged Rachel and she clung to him, moist-eyed, and kissed his cheek. He was almost as tall as she was now.

'Goodbye, Ma!' Tom reached up to kiss her and Rachel clasped him tight against her breast, cradling his head like a child's before kissing him too. 'Goodbye, Tom, and take care.' He looked up at her, his eyes brimming sudden tears as they exchanged a private greeting and farewell. Tom knew she loved him, as he did her, with a chain no distance could break, and he would have cried as she was crying had he not been twelve years old and almost a man. Instead, he turned away and swaggered to the gangplank as jauntily as any seasoned tar.

'Goodbye, Rachel.' James kissed her deep and tenderly. 'Take care of you both, for me.' Then he was gone, swinging up into the ship, shouting orders, and already lost into that other life of shipboard and foreign ports, with her two sons at his side. But this time she knew she was as much a part of their lives as they were a part of hers.

Louise and Andrew arrived in time to wave as the *Bonnie Annie* slipped out into the channel and away. This time Rachel did not follow to the North Pier. It was a good step away and she had promised James to take it easy. But he need not worry. She was so full of love and happiness that she knew the baby growing in her womb could only thrive.

Louise and Andrew said their private farewells two hours later in Rachel's sitting room. 'Louise,' began Andrew hesitantly. 'I do not know   I may not . . .' then he finished in a rush, 'I need time to think, to readjust. But, will you wait for me?'

Louise laughed, with the spontaneous, open laugh which transformed her face. 'I have waited how many years for you already? What is one more year to me?' He took her hand, drew her close, and kissed her.

Louise and Rachel together waved the *Rachel Christie* on her way. 'One ship to the east, one to the west, and both on the same day,' said Louise. 'You Christies have done well.'

'Yes,' agreed Rachel, though she sounded preoccupied. 'I wonder, would you mind if we called in at the Pocra yard? I heard a rumour this morning that the East India Company may be losing their monopoly to China at last. I want to ask Maitland if he thinks it's time to build that ship for the tea trade he's been planning for so long.'

'You'll be calling your infant India next,' laughed

Louise, 'like Jessie Abercrombie. Or is it to be Lapsang Suchong, or Bohea?'

'If this one is a girl,' said Rachel quietly, 'I shall call her Louise, after my dearest friend.'

'And if the child is a boy?'

'Then I have not the least idea. Unless . . .' A mischievous look came into her eyes as she continued, 'Unless we call him George for Mr Abercrombie? It might be one way of persuading him to put his money back into Christies – and Maitland is going to need all the money we can get for his beautiful white bird.'

Talking happily of the future which would bind them even closer together, they linked arms and strolled eastward along the Quay towards the blue and silver nameboard and the fine, arched doorway of Christie's Yard.

MALCOLM ROSS

**A rich West Country saga
in the bestselling tradition of POLDARK**

On a Far Wild Shore

Young, beautiful and newly widowed, Elizabeth Troy travels to her late husband's Cornish home hoping to find comfort in its fertile hills and valleys. But she is shocked to discover the vast, decaying acreage of Pallas is now solely her responsibility – a legacy as unexpected as it is unwelcome.

Elizabeth's plans for her inheritance provoke the bitter hostility of her sister-in-law, Morwenna, whose word has been law at Pallas for thirty years. To bring the troubled estate back to prosperity Elizabeth must look for help elsewhere. And there are many very willing to be more than a friend to the widow – David Troy, a poor relation whose sober exterior hides some disturbing secrets; Courtenay Rodda, the sensual newspaper proprietor; and James Troy, the rich and worldly wise American cousin who begins a thrilling but dangerous liaison with Elizabeth . . .

'The book is beautifully written, the characters depicted with a passionate realism that held me entranced. I simply loved it!' Patricia Wendorf, bestselling author of *Larksleve*.

FICTION   0-7472-3001-3   £2.95

Headline books are available at your bookshop or newsagent, or can be ordered from the following address:

Headline Book Publishing PLC
Cash Sales Department
PO Box 11
Falmouth
Cornwall
TR10 9EN
England

UK customers please send cheque or postal order (no currency), allowing 60p for postage and packing for the first book, plus 25p for the second book and 15p for each additional book ordered up to a maximum charge of £1.90 in UK.

BFPO customers please allow 60p for postage and packing for the first book, plus 25p for the second book and 15p per copy for the next seven books, thereafter 9p per book.

Overseas and Eire customers please allow £1.25 for postage and packing for the first book, plus 75p for the second book and 28p for each subsequent book.